Volume 6

Secrets

Satisfy your desire for more.

On **Sandy Fraser**'s story: "Ms. Fraser makes your senses reel with her feisty, spirited sex scenes between two equally stubborn people who are thrown together by fate. But no matter how stubborn each can be, there always has to be somebody on top!"

—**Lani Roberts**, *Affaire de Coeur* Magazine

On **MaryJanice Davidson**'s story: "Her sultry sex scenes sizzle with suppressed violence, while combining rough treatment with a gentleness that makes the skin tingle. ... This is erotica at its best."

—**Lani Roberts**, *Affaire de Coeur* Magazine

On **Alice Gaine**'s story: "This story of innocence *deliberately* lost is one long seduction scene created by a mastermind. Alice Gaines shows an insight into the art of seduction and being seduced.... Sex education was never like this in school!"

—**Lani Roberts**, *Affaire de Coeur* Magazine

On **Angela Knight**'s story: "This is one of the sexiest stories I've read in a while and a definite turn-on. This is the stuff that dreams are made of!"

—**Lani Roberts**, *Affaire de Coeur* Magazine

Reviews from Secrets Volume 1

"Four very romantic, very sexy novellas in very different styles and settings. ... The settings are quite diverse taking the reader from Regency England to a remote and mysterious fantasy land, to an Arabian nights type setting, and finally to a contemporary urban setting. All stories are explicit, and Hamre and Landon stories sizzle. ... If you like erotic romance you will love *Secrets*."

— *Romantic Readers* review

"Overall, for a fan of erotica, these are unlike anything you've encountered before. For those romance fans who turn down the pages of the "good parts" for later repeat consumption (and you know who you are) these books are a wonderful way to explore the better side of the erotica market. ... *Secrets* is a worthy exploration for the adventurous reader with the promise for better things yet to come."

— Liz Montgomery

Reviews from Secrets Volume 2
Winner of the
Fallot Literary Award for Fiction

"*Secrets, Volume 2*, a new anthology published by Red Sage Publishing, is hot! I mean *red hot!* ... The sensuality in each story will make you blush—from head to toe and everywhere else in-between. ... The true success behind *Secrets, Volume 2* is the combination of different tastes—both in subgenres of romance and levels of sensuality. *I highly recommend this book*."

— Dawn A. Long, *America Online* review

"I think it is a fine anthology and Red Sage should be applauded for providing an outlet for women who want to write sensual romance."

—Adrienne Benedicks,
Erotic Readers Association review

Reviews from Secrets Volume 3
Winner of the 1997 Under the Cover Readers Favorite Award

"An unabashed celebration of sex. Highly arousing! Highly recommended!"

—Virginia Henley, *New York Times* Best Selling Author

"*Secrets, Volume 3* leaves the reader breathless. Each of these tributes to exotic and erotic fiction offers a world of sensual pleasure and moral rewards. A delicious confection of sensuous treats awaits the reader on each turn of the page. Sexy, funny, thrilling, and luscious, Secrets entertains, enlightens, and fuels the fires of fantasy."

—Kathee Card, *Romancing the Web*

Reviews from Secrets Volume 4

"*Secrets, Volume 4*, has something to satisfy every erotic fantasy...simply sexsational!"

—Virginia Henley, *New York Times* Best Selling Author

"Provocative...seductive...a must read! ★★★★"

—*Romantic Times*

"These are the kind of stories that romance readers that 'want a little more' have been looking for all their lives without crossing over into the adult genre. Keep these stories coming, Red Sage, the world needs them!"

—Lani Roberts, *Affaire de Coeur*

"If you're interested in exploring erotica, or reading farther than the sexual passages of your favorite steamy reads, the *Secret* series is well worth checking out."

—*Writers Club Romance Group* on AOL

Reviews from Secrets Volume 5

"*Secrets, Volume 5*, is a collage of lucious sensuality. Any woman who reads *Secrets* is in for an awakening!"

—Virginia Henley, *New York Times* Best Selling Author

"Hot, hot, hot! Not for the faint-hearted!"

—*Romantic Times*

"As you make your way through the stories, you will find yourself becoming hotter and hotter. *Secrets* just keeps getting better and better."

—*Affaire de Coeur*

Reviews from Secrets Volume 6

"*Secrets, Volume 6* satisfies every female fantasy: the Bodyguard, the Tutor, the Werewolf, and the Vampire. I give it Six Stars!"

—Virginia Henley, *New York Times* Best Selling Author

"*Secrets, Volume 6* is the best of *Secrets* yet. ...four of the most erotic stories in one volume than this reader has yet to see anywhere else. ... These stories are full of erotica at its best and you'll definitely want to keep it handy for lots of re-reading!"

—Affaire de Coeur

Reviews from Secrets Volume 7
Winner of the Venus Book Club
Best Book of the Year

"...sensual, sexy, steamy fun. A perfect read!"

—Virginia Henley, New York Times Best Selling Author

"Intensely provocative and disarmingly romantic, Secrets Volume 7 is a romance reader's paradise that will take you beyond your wildest dreams!"

—Ballston Book House Review

"Erotic romance is at the sensual core of Red Sage's latest collection of short, red hot novels, *Secrets, Volume 7.*"

—Writers Club Romance Group on AOL

Reviews from Secrets Volume 8
Winner of the Venus Book Club
Best Book of the Year

"*Secrets Volume 8* is simply sensational!"

—Virginia Henley, New York Times Best Selling Author

"*Secrets Volume 8* is an amazing compilation of sexy stories discovering a wide range of subjects, all designed to titillate the senses."

—Lani Roberts, *Affaire de Coeur*

"All four tales are well written and fun to read because even the sexiest scenes are not written for shock value, but interwoven smoothly and realistically into the plots. This quartet contains strong storylines and solid lead characters, but then again what else would one expect from the no longer *Secrets* anthologies."

—Harriet Klausner

"Once again, Red Sage Publishing takes you on a journey of sexual delight, teasing and pleasing the reader with a bit of something to appeal to everyone."

—Michelle Houston, *Courtesy Sensual Romance*

"In this sizzling volume, four authors offer short stories in four different sub-genres: contemporary, paranormal, historical, and futuristic. These ladies' assignments are to dazzle, tantalize, amaze, and entice. Your assignment, as the reader, is to sit back and enjoy. Just have a fan and some ice water at your side."

—Amy Cunningham

Reviews from Secrets Volume 9

"Everyone should expect only the most erotic stories in a *Secrets* book. ...if you like your stories full of hot sexual scenes, then this is for you!"

—Donna Doyle, *Romance Reviews*

MaryJanice Davidson

Sandy Fraser

Alice Gaines

Angela Knight

Volume 6

Secrets

Satisfy your desire for more.

SECRETS Volume 6
This is an original publication of Red Sage Publishing and each individual story herein has never before appeared in print. These stories are a collection of fiction and any similarity to actual persons or events is purely coincidental.

Red Sage Publishing, Inc.
P.O. Box 4844
Seminole, FL 33775
727-391-3847
www.redsagepub.com

SECRETS Volume 6
A Red Sage Publising book
All Rights Reserved/December 2000
Second Printing, 2002; Third Printing, 2003; Fourth Printing, 2004
Copyright © 2000–2004 by Red Sage Publishing, Inc.

ISBN 0-9648942-6-2

Published by arrangement with the authors and copyright holders of the individual works as follows:
FLINT'S FUSE
Copyright © 2000 by Sandy Fraser
LOVE'S PRISONER
Copyright © 2000 by MaryJanice Davidson
THE EDUCATION OF MISS FELICITY WELLS
Copyright © 2000 by Alice Gaines
A CANDIDATE FOR THE KISS
Copyright © 2000 by Angela Knight

Photographs: Copyright © 2000 by Greg P. Willis; email: GgnYbr@aol.com

Printed in the U.S.A.

Cover design, layout and book typesetting by:

Quill & Mouse Studios, Inc.
2165 Sunnydale Boulevard, Suite E
Clearwater, FL 33765
www.quillandmouse.com

Contents

This volume of Secrets is dedicated to Sandy Fraser who passed away. She will be sorely missed by her many fans.

Flint's Fuse

by Sandy Fraser

To My Reader:

Change time and place, past to future, city to desert, Earth to the stars. One constant endures: the fiery passion of a man and a woman. Lose yourself in the fantasy.

Chapter One

In the dark of the moon, a phantom shadow masked and dressed in black stalked his target. With cat-like silence he slipped down the hall to her bedroom in the rear wing of the gigantic house. The timing and execution had been perfect. The moonless night, the disabled security system, and access to Madison's estate. He paused, listening to his breathing, preparing to make his move.

Grimly, Flint smiled. Madison had brought him off a big assignment in Australia, given him a detailed floor plan and a picture of his pretty daughter.

"A bitch on wheels," Madison had sighed. "There's not a man alive who can check her. She's a five-star general in the battle of the sexes. The good guys lose. Look, Flint, if I asked her nicely to take a vacation, she'd pry, ask too many questions. But my sources tell me International Investments is not unwilling to threaten family members to up the leverage during a merger." He leaned back in his chair and folded his hands. "Take her to a place I don't know. I'll spread the word she's on safari. Call my lawyer in Lisbon once a week. I'll leave word so you'll know when it's over."

"She'll be scared. How much do I tell her?" Flint thumbed the picture of the leggy blond.

"Anything, but for God's sake, don't tell her *I'm* involved."

The glacial captain of industry had a note of panic in his voice.

"Some simple kidnapping story should suffice. I'll pay the nonexistent ransom, and you'll bring her home."

Flint rose, and Madison got to his feet.

"You've fought your way out of jungles, killed men with your bare hands, taken bullets meant for somebody else. You're not the

kind of man who relies on luck." Madison shook his hand.
"But you'll need all the luck you can get now, you poor bastard."
Flint wrote off the warning as a dose of the tycoon's notorious
gallows' humor. Apparently Madison thought snatching a woman
was a big deal. Real operatives knew it was chump change compared
to the tough jobs.

He turned the knob and eased the door open. Dana Madison was
a motionless slender form under silk sheets in a room scented like
Paradise. Walk in the park, he told himself.

But the instant he touched the bed, Dana sprang up and delivered
a side snap-kick to his jaw. Good placement, he judged, but inef-
fective because the mattress gave her no base for balance, and he
was too fast. Flint grabbed her ankle, toppled her, and covered her,
feeling her lush breasts mash into his chest.

He gripped her thighs with his knees, and to shut off her cry
slapped duct tape over her mouth, bound her flailing wrists and
ankles. "Hush," he whispered. "Be still. I won't hurt you."

She growled behind the tape and tried to wrench out of his grasp.
Easily he lifted her, carried her down the hall, and had to still her
thrashings with a nerve block. He had an image of caressing her,
burying his face in her throat.

Her sudden limpness, sweet false compliance, the softness of her
nestling against him stirred his groin and announced Dana Madison
was trouble. His body signalled he should sneak back to her room
and return her to her four-poster.

"I blew it. So fire me," he could report to Madison the next morning, and ask for another run-of-the-mill assignment, like rescuing
a double-agent from the attentions of an Israeli interrogation team.
Instead, Flint cradled his captive, sneaked out through the French
doors, and arranged her on a mattress in the cargo area of the van.
By using surface streets, he whisked them out of Metro in twenty
minutes, and ramped up the freeway.

When high noon burned the endless stretches of shimmering
desert, Flint slowed the van, stopped at the edge of the highway that
ran and ran until it disappeared into the horizon.

"If you behave yourself, I'll free you, let you use this." He nudged the camping toilet and opened its lid. "And then give you a drink and a sandwich." He waited, impassive. He could out-wait anything, anyone.

Dana Madison closed her eyes and nodded slightly. She was flowing gold hair, and, beneath her filmy nightgown, all tempting curves and nipples that crested under his stare.

"This will sting." Flint knelt beside her and stripped the tape from her ankles and wrists. She simultaneously ripped the tape from her mouth and found her feet. Like a demon, she gouged at his eyes and kicked his shins.

"Ooow," she screamed as her toes connected with massive bone.

Flint let her fall onto the mattress and rock back and forth, nursing her sore foot. "Want a Coke? How about a bologna sandwich, Miss Madison?"

"Bastard." He'd never heard such venom in a voice. What he recognized as the hereditary Madison gaze drilled into him. She spat, "Enjoy yourself for now at my expense, moron. It won't last long. And my father won't give you a cent. He'll hunt you down. He'll put one of his secret squads on your trail."

"Take your panties down."

Dana's lips curled in a sneer. "Can't get it for a burger and a couple of beers, eh? And too proud to pay for it?"

Flint bent, and Dana shrieked while he ripped lace and grabbed her. Despite her fighting, he put her on the porta-potty, handcuffed one wrist and clamped it to an exposed bar in the van.

In a shower of her original curses, Flint fled, slamming the door behind him. He raked both hands through his hair and leaned on the rear bumper. Heat waves rose and distorted the scrub and the dull powdered sand.

Once, in Death Valley, he'd stood unprotected, bare-headed at high noon. He'd been a kid pummelled by unrelenting heat, lost in wondering how a man could tolerate the cruel sun.

But, years later, after Wu Chin had put him on the path of inner serenity and he'd learned the control of the body-mind-heart center, he'd been thrown out of a Jeep to die in the Sahara. On the edge of consciousness, he heard the laughter of his captors when they sped away. He tasted the gritty sand sponging up his blood and last drops of moisture.

In that terrible oven, he'd gotten to his feet, dizzy, sick, and determined. Slowly, he'd centered himself, and hunted a sand shelf where he lay, measuring his breaths in the sizzling shade until night fell and he had walked out to safety.

There was no safety around this woman. His instincts spiked. Where there should have been the soft, yielding, passive coolness of *yin*, the female principle, Dana Madison seemed a wild creature of *yang*, light, heat, action.

The van rocked, she pounded on metal and yelled. Flint sighed. Well, he wasn't paid by Madison to indulge in long meditation sessions. He was being paid to baby-sit a woman whose body and face should've been declared illegal when she was eighteen. Glumly, Flint returned to the van like a man going to the gallows.

Madison's words came back to haunt him, "You'll need all the luck you can get, you poor bastard." Less than a day with this spitfire, and he'd already aged ten years. He refused to think about handling her for a month.

"Clothes," he said gruffly, pointing. "I'm uncuffing you. Get dressed."

Dana jumped up, slammed the lid, and let him apply the key to her wrist restraint. He reached for the clothes, and she caromed off him like an ace billiard shot, leaped out the open van door, and was away and running through the sand.

Flint pursued her, but not at top speed, not even working up a sweat in the heat. Approvingly, he noted she wasted no breath on futile screams. She was saving her strength. He berated himself for his carelessness, thankful that this empty stretch of road carried virtually no traffic, day or night.

He reached out, caught the nightie to jerk her to a stop, but Dana kept running, and he was left following with shredded pink streamers.

He knew all about pursuits, but the sight of her, naked and eluding him, fired an ancient, primitive instinct. His sex grew heavy as excitement pumped hot blood into his arousal. Flint was a man pursuing a woman, a mate.

As he took her around the waist, he tried to be gentle, but her violence and surprising strength demanded more muscle than he cared to use. Unexpectedly, she dropped to the sand, and Flint fell with her. Wrestling in the harsh powder, she panted and he held her down by straddling her. Her eyes were wild, but not with fear. She exuded hate and temper and revenge and something else he couldn't name.

His cock and balls knew, though, and they tensed, ready for Flint to part her thighs and take her here at noon in the burning sand. Her nipples grew erect, and he saw they'd blushed a deep red. He raised her to her feet and twisted one arm behind her back.

"That's right. Hurt me, too, you scar-faced animal."

He kept his voice cold. "The only way you can be hurt by frog-marching is if you try to break away. Now we'll walk slowly together, back to the van."

She muttered curses, and Flint stared into the cascade of tangled golden hair deepened with dark honey. He imagined it swirling around her head, pillowed on black silk, while he sucked those huge nipples, while he wrung groans from her.

Then he looked past her to the van, ordering his tension to disperse, his breathing to regularize, and his focus to narrow on one specific. Getting the job done.

He visualized a calendar, a month, thirty days. Madison's enemies, the bright boys at International Investments, had gravely underestimated Madison's resources. The threats against Dana to force Madison into the merger would fail.

He'd shuck this wild woman as easily as he'd dispose of her torn gown smelling of the unique fragrance that was Dana Madison, a fragrance that made his nostrils flare.

At the van, Dana planted herself, and he had to lift her slick nakedness up in the cargo area. "For the second time, get dressed."

"Not until I have a Coke. *And* a sandwich." She tossed her head and jammed her hands on her hips, daring him to fasten his attention on her golden delta. He read the real message. To Dana Madison out-maneuvering him, distracting him, meant more than modesty.

"Get dressed." Flint leaned over the driver's seat. "Now."

"Is it hard for you to understand? I said no, not until I get what

I want." Her eyes flashed blue fire.

"Listen carefully, Dana. Three times you've been told to dress. Now I have to do it for you." He climbed into the back, and Dana shrieked and grabbed the thin strapped blue top.

"Too late." Flint jerked it away, tossed her to the mattress, and tugged the jeans onto her legs. She clawed and fought when he boosted her hips. Despite her shouts, he trapped her arms under his knees, and completed the job by flattening the unruly curls at the juncture of her thighs and zipping her jeans closed. He sat her up like a ragdoll and stuffed her into the tank top.

Panting like a whipped animal, she regarded him with a kind of murderous respect. "*Now* can I have my food and a drink?"

He dug a soda and a sandwich bag out of a cooler, and Dana snatched them from his hands. When he bent to retrieve his water bottle, he caught a lightning move in his peripheral vision, and barely deflected the blow. Flint wrenched the red can from her, forced her to the mattress and cuffed one hand.

"I hate you," she said, and her voice was low and deadly.

"One Coke," Flint said and poured the can's contents into a paper cup. "One bologna sandwich with mustard."

Dana drank, laid the sandwich on her knee and dissected it.

"I hate this kind of mustard," she said scornfully. Then she rattled off a litany of complaints and questions while Flint drove. He opted for silence, hoping she'd run down, wear herself out.

Master Wu Chin had counseled that the temper of a woman is like a summer storm, violent but short-lived. The Master had never met Dana Madison.

Flint imagined the old man trying to reason with Dana, and he grinned in spite of himself. Dana Madison was not a woman. She was a force of nature, and Flint would have to reckon with her treachery for a hellish four weeks. His grin faded as he struggled to ignore the bulge in his pants that gave mute testimony to her bold sex appeal. Aside from the physical attraction, Flint would have to deal with her intelligence and defiance which issued a dangerous challenge to tame her.

Realizing he'd been speeding to reach the cabin, he slowed and rehearsed all the break-downs travelers suffered in the desert, all the stories of people trying to walk out of the inferno.

God help her if one of her unpredictable escape attempts worked, and she found herself in the badlands without him.

Chapter Two

"You know what your trouble is?" Dana leaned back and braced herself. She crossed her long legs at the ankle and stretched out on the bearskin rug before the fireplace.

Silent as a granite monument, Flint stared into the flames, hands relaxed on the arms of his chair. He said nothing.

"Did you hear me, Flint?" Her voice grew snide. "I'll bet that isn't even your real name. I'll bet it's some godawful wimp name like, like Lester or Cecil, isn't it?"

Slowly, Flint glanced down, his cool gray eyes examining her as dispassionately as a scientist might inspect a bug under a microscope. The inspection seemed to go on forever, until he resumed gazing into the flames.

He said nothing, the way he **always** said nothing when she sniped and needled, but once Dana started, she couldn't stop pouring out her fury and frustration. If he wouldn't give her attention, then she'd steal it, goad him until he retaliated, satisfying her ego, manipulating him into action.

"Well, I don't care about your phony tough guy name. After all, who'd be stupid enough to waste money on a hired gun named Petey or Ricky? Or are you working alone?" Her stomach twisted in embarrassment at her bitchiness. "But that wasn't the question, Mr. Strong Silent Type, now was it?" Dana got to her knees and jammed her hands on her hips.

As though speaking to an inattentive child, she repeated, "The question was, do-you-know-what-your trouble-is?" She was acutely aware of his nearness, of the virility he radiated, aware of the flush on her cheeks. Unbidden, a shocking thought intruded.

If it were a different situation, a different place, she'd recklessly abandon common sense and throw herself at this rugged male, luxuriate in his strong arms, let him make decisions, revel in the carefree confidence he inspired. But in this time and place, Flint remained cool and considerate, the model warden, the gentleman kidnapper. And Dana chafed under his reasonableness.

"I'll be glad to reveal your weakness, O great stoneman. You can't talk." Triumphantly, she plowed ahead. "Don't deny it. Those rare one-syllable grunts you produce hardly qualify as conversation."

As usual, Flint denied nothing, agreed with nothing, and Dana trembled on the verge of slapping his immobile, chiseled face and tearing out his thick black hair. Two weeks with him had been two weeks of pure hell, two weeks of virtually talking to herself, two weeks of continual surveillance. In the end he would drive her mad. And maybe that was his scheme.

A knot formed in her throat, and tears burned behind her eyes. She wanted to go home.

Flint rose, powerful legs flexing to support his huge body, all thick thighs and massive torso, and corded neck. Behind his fly, the snaps of his Levi's contained an enormous bulge, thrust nearly into her face when he loomed over her.

"Bedtime, Miss Madison," he said, a voice cold as his eyes.

"I'm not ready for bed, thank you very much for your concern, Flint. I am an adult and quite capable of deciding when I'm tired and when I need to go to bed." With a smug smile, she clambered into the chair he'd just vacated, and pretended to relax. But how could she? Flint had left the chair imprinted with his incredible heat, and it lingered, it disturbed her.

Dana hoped that she'd disturbed him, and sneaked a look at the black T-shirt hugging the slabs of his muscled chest and straining to cover his biceps. But his respiration was regular, under rigid control, like his emotional responses to her, clock-like. The guy was a robot, inhuman.

She'd never seen Flint sweat, lose his temper, overeat, or over-react. His responses were exact, automatic, icily perfect.

He never wasted a move, never squandered an ounce of energy, as though he had a fuse box installed. No overloads, no power surges flustered the Stoneman. And he could, she knew, maintain his steady gaze and comfortable stance for hours without the least show of anger.

Damn him. Why should she make his life easy? When her ordeal was over, if he wasn't caught, he'd be a million dollars richer, and, by God she'd see to it he'd earned every last cent. Clamping her arms over her breasts, Dana dug in and tightened her mouth.

Flint stood like a rock, courteous, patient to a fault and totally infuriating. He eyed her. "Miss, for the second time, please go to bed." More than once, she'd had a taste of what he'd do after he made a third request. The quick lift, the unhurried walk with Dana Madison manhandled like a side of beef.

"You're a hateful bastard," she snapped. Out of the depths of the deep low chair, Dana struggled to her feet, brushed past him, and stamped into the bedroom. She itched to slam a door, but ten days ago in his methodical way, Flint had extracted the hinge-pins and carted the door outside, a punishment for one of her tricks.

Now he propped his bulk in the threshhold and watched her march into the bathroom whose door he'd permitted to remain after replacing the lock with a hook and eye. Probably so he could kick it in, she griped. This tiny room was the last, the only private place left to Dana, and sometimes she was astonished Flint had had the decency to free her, ever so briefly, from his spying.

She shucked off her jeans and tank-top, poured water from the chipped pitcher into the ewer, and wrung out the wet cloth. In the mirror above the wooden counter, she studied her face. Too large blue eyes, full pink lips, flyaway blond hair, and a face her nanny had called elfin. "Now listen, my little elf," she'd say as she scolded Dana, "it is truly a sin to waste God's gifts, and your gifts are beauty and cleverness."

Dana heard Flint cough to hurry her along. Well, let him barge in and get a good look. She retreated to see more of herself, everything Flint would see. She dropped the cloth, and ran her hands down the body her aerobics intructor always said was "to die for."

Dana frowned. Creamy skin, generous breasts with marble-size, dusky pink nipples. Tight abs. She smoothed her hands over the firm flare of her hips, the curve of her belly, down to the nest of dark gold curls.

Karate hadn't worked on Flint. Neither had trying to run past him, climbing out the bathroom window (after that episode, he'd boarded it over), hitting him with an andiron, or grabbing a knife. Maybe this, her body was the perfect weapon.

"A guy like Flint, a weight-lifter type, handsome if you like 'em tall, dark and dangerous," she whispered, "a babe magnet." When was the last time he'd had a woman? A couple of weeks ago? Maybe the very night he'd snatched her?

The thought of Flint sweating between the legs of a woman pleased her, Flint losing his impassive expression, going wild. Images came of Flint taking a woman like a bull, his immense cock plunging in and out, in and out, Flint sucking that faceless woman's breasts as she cried in an agony of fevered tension. Yes, sex might be Flint's weakness.

Sex. Was he hurting for sex, hurting bad? As hungry for a hot joining as Dana herself?

To her horror, Dana saw her nipples standing erect, her hand foraging in her pubic hair, rubbing her clit. She leaped to the basin and washed her fingers.

"This has nothing to do with wanting him myself," she insisted. The woman in the mirror seemed unconvinced. "Sure, I have needs, cooped up like this. But so does he, and I'll use it to my advantage. And if push comes to shove, I can fake it."

Lure him, seduce him, yes, that was the ticket, exhaust him into the heavy, dreamless state of the drained male. Then, car keys in hand, she'd speed into the night, speed to the nearest police station, and then let Flint see how he'd enjoy life in jail.

Despite the trial and error of all her failed attempts to subdue him, to hide, and sneak and run, at last she'd crafted a scheme bound to work, a plan to control the invulnerable Flint.

Never before had Dana worried about controlling a man. Her father's fortune and her willfulness anesthetized her lovers. The eager yes-men, a string of polo players, an ambassador with erotic skills, and his young assistant whose lasting power had almost fooled Dana into thinking she was in love.

In the end, all of them wilted, brought to heel by her strong personality. "I want a man, a real man," she whispered. If she'd wanted a fawning, submissive dog on a choke collar and chain, she could buy one at a kennel.

The faces and forms of her rejected lovers receded and disappeared, overpowered by Flint's commanding presence.

In the mirror she watched her smile flicker and dissolve. Through half-closed eyes, she replayed her fantasy of Flint making love, but this time instead of the unknown woman, he held Dana immobilized and plunged between her legs. Flint the master, his dark dominance protecting her, making her feel safe in his arms.

She thought of his rigid decisions, his unwavering limits that stood up to her practiced pleadings and arguments. Dana shivered. For the first time in her life she knew boundaries and consequences. And she liked it.

≈꽃\(ʘʘ\)꽃≈

Flint heard her brushing her teeth, her white, white teeth, the brush moving between her rose lips. He closed his eyes, and imagined her naked, her top thrown aside to reveal her lush breasts, her jeans slithering over her long legs, slim ankles, dainty feet, gorgeously, completely naked, peaches and cream. And in that downy triangle, were the lips soft and pouting, was the clit a tiny button or a dark pink projection?

He fixed his stare at the paint peeling off the opposite doorjamb, and cursed himself for accepting this job. All the assignments in the past, guarding moguls, running down a crazed fan with a gun, even taking a bullet in the side for a rock star, every job had been a piece of cake compared to snatching Dana Madison.

Yeah, Flint, boxer, Navy SEAL, mercenary, he'd been around, had the expertise, the contingency plans, the quick improvs for extreme situations. But this, this grab and hold was the hardest thing he'd ever done, as hard and swollen as his cock. He took in a huge breath through his teeth, and thumbed open the first two snaps of his Levi's to relieve some of the pressure.

Pain, some new pain, would kill his desire. Flint stiffened and ground his spine into the crusty wood of the frame, forcing himself to inflict damage, a harsh rasp to cleanse himself of these distractions. But the sting of abrasion was numbed by the picture of her nakedness. He clenched his jaw. His sex grew heavier. He had to get her into bed right now.

Startled by how far he'd let his mind wander, he corrected himself. He meant he had to force Dana to go to bed now, by herself. Forget his pulsating cock, forget the damned thing, that, like an untamed, instinct-driven animal, fed on his fantasies and disrupted his coolness until he forgot his job and lasered his attention on his aching groin, on the sweetness between her thighs.

With an oath, Flint raked his hands through his hair, and looked up to see Dana in the bathroom doorway, silhouetted by the lantern behind her, the thin nightie rendered nearly invisible.

"Oh," she murmured, cupping her breasts, "I didn't know you were out here, Flint."

A lie. He'd stood in this exact spot every night for the past two weeks, supervising as she crept under the covers, turning out the Coleman. What the hell was she trying to pull?

He held his breath, willing away the throbbing. He limped into the bathroom, doused the light, and reclined on a thin futon outside her doorway. Stifling a groan, he raised one knee and stacked his hands behind his head. He hadn't had blue balls since he was sixteen.

"Flint? Flint, are you awake?"

Five feet away, Dana Madison was calling, and his cock was answering. Flint squeezed his eyes shut, as though her throaty voice could be banished by simple silence, and he remained mute.

"Flint?" She gave a little, apologetic sigh. "I'm sorry I was so bitchy. Forgive me, Flint. I—I want you to like me."

His eyes flew open. In the glow of the fireplace, the room seemed soft and feminine, the old paint and splintery furniture transformed into a romantic landscape by her voice. The cracked walls were hung with tapestries, the ratty sofa magically changed into a silk chaise where Dana clung to him, where she urged him deeper into her dripping, honeyed heat.

With a grim smile, Flint brought himself up short. He'd read the studies on the Helsinki Syndrome, the bizarre emotional state that linked the helpless hostage and the all-powerful perpetrator.

A spasm fisted his guts. The soft voice, the sweet apology seemed sincere. But was it the syndrome? Had Dana Madison, now totally dependent on him for every bite of food, every sip of water slipped into the captive's mentality?

Or was it that Dana needed his approval, and now hungry to please, craved his affection, as if any kind of relationship survived a captivity ordeal?

And he? He wanted to shake his head, to clear his libido of the contagious fantasy Dana was spinning.

Worse, he wanted to believe she had maintained her feisty independence and was engineering a ploy to lull his suspicions. Inexplicably, he preferred a fiery, trouble-making, take-no-prisoners Dana, busy plotting his ruin, to a psychologically-bent Dana who wanted him to love her.

"Flint, do you remember the night you kidnapped me?"

"Go to sleep," he growled.

"How can I sleep when I'm never tired? You never let me go out to exercise." She caught her breath and grimaced in the dimness. She had to walk a chalk line in her approach. "There I go again, complaining. I'm sorry, Flint. Talk to me a minute, like we're kids having a pajama party."

"Someone put me out of my misery," he said.

"Oh, Flint. That was a joke. I think." She giggled. "Now get serious. When you woke me that night, did you expect the karate move, the old snap-kick?" She heard him sigh.

"I surrender. If I talk for one minute, will you shut up and go to sleep?"

"It's a deal. One minute." Real excitement tinged her voice. In the dimness, she saw Flint set his watch alarm.

"All right, Miss Madison, tell me, that night, did you expect me to grab your ankle?" She saw him shift, prop himself on one elbow so he looked into her room. "Or pull you under me?"

"Nope. You were too strong, too fast, like a panther, on top of me, gripping my thighs between your legs. I thought you were going to rape me." Slip sex in at every opportunity, and try to lose my overactive imagination. "And me, taking those female empowerment classes. I beat up dummies every week, and guys wearing protective pads, you know, the fake mugger types." She gave a self-mocking laugh. "But when the chips were down…oh, Flint, I was so helpless and scared."

"Only sick jerks take a woman by force. I was on a job. Look, Dana, for your own good I had to get physical, tape your mouth, your wrists and ankles. I won't use sedative injections."

He'd called her Dana. She shivered with satisfaction. That was real female power. And she dicovered her moves were more than a game, and she needed to know his secrets, needed to break down the barricades this mystery man maintained so successfully.

"Ah, Flint, you trussed me like a Christmas package, touched my neck and the next thing I remembered was waking up on a mattress in your van next to all those boxes of supplies."

⁂

In his memory Flint had hoarded the natural perfume of her skin, the soft feel, the sweet weight and curves he'd carried as gently as he could. She'd fought furiously, wild blond mane whipping his face, her eyes wide with fear and hate, glimpses he'd caught in the flame-shaped light of a wall sconce. He'd put her out with his thumb on a pressure point on her neck.

"The way you touched me, somehow I knew you weren't going to hurt me. I trusted you. And, Flint, I still do." Her voice was a lover's voice, and Flint imagined his mouth slanting over her tempting lips that begged him for more.

Two beeps chimed. "Night, Miss Madison." Flint rolled onto his back, eyes open, listening to the sounds of Dana sighing, sliding those long, smooth legs between the sheets.

Three hours later, he checked Dana's even breathing, and, quiet as a cat stepped over the futon and slipped onto the front porch. Exasperated at himself, at the failure of all Wu Chin's emotional serenity teachings, Flint gave himself to the full moon.

He slipped into the first stage and meditated on his life, his detached, complete life that suddenly had developed a hungry yearning void in the place where he'd shielded his heart.

Chapter Three

"I won't stay here alone, you know." Dana struggled to keep her voice cool and reasonable, swirled coffee in her cup, and studied Flint's reaction.

But, of course, there *was* no reaction. As if he hadn't heard a word she'd said, he swallowed the last bite of his bread, wiped his mouth and pushed back his chair. After dusting his hands, he tossed the styrofoam bowl and napkin, and looked at her.

"Finished?"

"With lunch. But not with this discussion." Dana balanced her chair on the rear legs, and rested her hands on top of her head, an innocent gesture, and one that raised her breasts and brought her nipples to his attention. "So let's decide what to do."

She smiled to show him she was being both logical and sweetly submissive. It was her best move, the one she'd used without fail on a dozen men over the years.

"Finished?" His steel-gray eyes were inscrutable, yet almost electric in his bronzed skin. She detected the tiniest tic in his strong jaw. Dana knew when she'd got to a man, and as different as Flint thought he was, how invulnerable to her manipulations, she'd seen a chink in his armor.

With a sigh, she bounced the chair forward. Her lower lip quivered, and she covered her face with her hands. "Flint, please don't leave me here by myself. You know how scared I get."

He took her utensils and trashed them. "Time for bed, Miss Madison."

"No. I know what you're thinking, that maybe I ran away a couple of times, hit you, and, well, a couple of other things that make you believe I'm really tough. But Flint," her voice wobbled, "Oh, Flint, I'm not as tough as I look."

He held up two fingers. "Time for bed."

Dana's game plan crumbled, and she snapped. "Stop that ridiculous three-times-and-you're-out nonsense. I'm going nowhere until we talk about this." As soon as she tilted her chin defiantly, she knew she'd made a mistake.

"Time for bed."

He moved faster than any man she'd ever seen, all smooth speed and determination, and he had her in his hard embrace before she could get out of her chair.

"Then talk to me." She screamed and thrashed. But all it got her was Flint holding her higher and harder, her face in his throat, the sweat and tang of his maleness on her lips, the scent of sage and woodsmoke in her nostrils.

He carried her as if she weighed no more than a cat, and Dana fought the rising tide of her excitement, the stunning realization that Flint could do anything to her, even possess her body, and she was helpless.

But when he laid her on the quilt and released her hands, she managed a stinging slap to his face, directly on the jagged scar that sliced from his ear to the corner of his mouth. His gold-bronze skin burned with a rush of blood. And the scar stood, a bloodless vein of white, unchanged, impervious to any assault Dana mounted.

Sick at herself, she wilted. Calm, gentle, efficient, Flint clamped the metal ring on her left wrist, securing her to the bedpost.

"No one comes here. You're safe. I'll be back no later than four." Without consulting his watch, he said, "It's one o'clock. Three hours is adequate to stock up on food and water. Your water bottle is on the bedside table."

He swiveled and was at the door before Dana whimpered. "Flint, I'm sorry. Oh, God, your face." But the only answer was the screen-door banging shut, and then the engine turning over.

As the sound of the van died away in the hot afternoon, Dana wiped her eyes on a tissue and stared up at the cracked ceiling.

If only he'd talked, engaged her in conversation, she could've convinced him to take her along, then, on some pretense, slipped away, freed herself and run for help.

But no. Flint was like that scar. Impervious, unchanging, no matter what she said or did. A man hard-wired to be exactly what he seemed, the same outside and in.

Dana twisted, making herself as comfortable as she could. Flint. He was on her mind, and now that she'd been relieved of his heavy presence for the first time in weeks, she considered the mystery man.

The men in her life were nothing like Flint. Not even her father who could cause a panic with a raised eyebrow. But she, who people insisted was a chip off the old block, had always been able to twist her father around her little finger.

If girlish coaxing failed, pouting worked, or flashpoint temper, or the silent treatment, and then Dana had her own way.

Dana always had her own way. Until Flint.

She daydreamed about Flint, in a half-doze, imagining the origin of his fascinating scar. Maybe a historical setting?

She smiled at the thought of Flint duelling with sabres. Dark and bronzed like a fabled black knight, playing a waiting game with a blond Aryan **Ubermensch**, offering his cheek for the cut to gain advantage, to find the perfect opening to break the sabre loose and power his opponent to the floor.

Dana turned onto her left side and closed her eyes against the sunshine. Or maybe Flint as a Green Beret, caught in an ambush, missing having his throat slit by catching steel in his face.

Maybe something more romantic. New Orleans. Through slatted balcony windows, the music and laughter and songs of Mardi Gras filtered onto a dim bed draped with netting. Flint, controlled, on automatic pilot, pleasuring a fiery Cajun beauty with regular deep strokes, increasing his speed as her moans grew louder and faster. A violent climax, a cry splintering the reggae tunes, and then Flint rising to leave. The demanding lady, a glint of a razor, blood spurting from his cheek. Flint shoving her aside, walking out with a snowy kerchief on his wound.

Dana moaned like the Cajun woman, and slept.

When she woke, the sun had moved behind the mountains. She

stretched and drank from her water bottle. Idly, she picked up her watch. "Four-thirty," she said, a little groggy from her nap. "A diller, a dollar, a ten o'clock Flint."

He was late. She giggled. Another chink in the stainless steel armor of Stoneman Flint. She took both pillows and elevated her handcuffed arm, relieving some of the strain on her wrist. Then she slept again.

When she woke, the sunlight had disappeared. The window framed a clear black velvet desert sky winking with a million stars.

"Flint?" she called, yawning the sleep from her throat. No candle, no cozy blaze in the fireplace. No sound. The utter silence of the desert prevailed.

"Flint, if you're jerking my chain, it's not funny." But she knew she was fooling herself. Where was he?

A horrible scenario flashed into her mind. Flint killed in a crash, in his dying breath trying to tell the paramedics about Dana, Dana cuffed and helpless.

Flint, purchasing food, Madison's team of private detectives waiting, Flint running, the shots, the limp body hitting the dusty street.

Flint driving toward the cabin, rubbing his cheek, fingering the thin line of his wound, the wound she'd struck. Flint meeting his own eyes in the rearview mirror, and shrugging off Dana and all the millions her father would pay in ransom. Flint slamming on the brakes and hitting the accelerator, a perfect one-eighty. Flint barreling down the road toward civilization.

Dana licked her dry lips. The water was gone. She'd read a survival guide once. She could last ten days without food, three without water. And in the end, hallucinations and a blessed euphoria.

Dana screamed and jerked at her captive wrist. The cuffs were steel, the bedpost iron. She tried to unscrew the iron finial atop the post. It was welded on. Frantically she raced through options. Trapped animals chewed off the snared foot.

She shuddered. "Wreck the bed. Break the post. Drag the whole thing out behind me onto the road." Conserving her strength, she began to jounce, to rattle the bedstead. And just behind her determination to free herself lurked the mother of all screams.

Flint lay on the brakes and the van skidded to a halt. Dana's guttural screams rang out, screams from a raw throat. Once he had screamed like that, and he couldn't get to her fast enough. He hurled himself out of the car, flung open the screen door, and rushed into Dana's room.

"I'm here, I'm here." He lit the candle and unsnapped the cuffs. In the dimness, Dana lay panting and sweating, the fan of hair tangled from thrashing. Her eyes were glazed and she looked at him without recognition.

"Baby, baby, it's all right. I'm here now." He sat propped at the headboard and gathered her into his arms. "Dana, baby, I'm here. Flint's here, darling."

"Flint," she said. Within the shelter of his embrace, she looked up as though not believing her eyes. "Flint?"

He pulled her into his lap, brushed back hair damp with the sweat of terror, and kissed her brow. Flint stroked her face, drying the tears with his thumb.

She clung to him, shivering, and raised her hand. "I couldn't get loose. I couldn't get loose and you weren't here."

Flint, even in the semi-darkness, saw the dark bruise the cuff had burned into the sensitive flesh of her wrist.

The bruising purpled her pale skin, the delicate tracery of her veins.

Guilty and torn, Flint kissed the soreness gently. "Let's soak this. And make you some soup." He moved and Dana panicked.

"No. No, you'll go away again." She held him fiercely, and her voice trembled on the edge of hysteria.

"I'll stay right here with my baby," he whispered, and pressed her head into his throat. "We'll sleep now."

Twice during the midnight hours, Flint shifted, but she cried out in her sleep, and he relaxed, cuddling her closer.

At three, she woke and fondled his bicep. "Strong man," she murmured.

He squeezed her shoulder. "Even a strong man has to use the

head occasionally. How about you?"

She ducked her head, hid her face in his chest. He could feel the heat of her blush through his tee. Dana Madison, blushing? The woman who'd parade around naked rather than follow an order to put on clothes? Asked to choose between her naked beauty or the sudden, inexplicable modesty, he was stumped. Modesty sure as hell would make his life easier, yet to see Dana nude had been a saving grace of this assignment.

But Dana slid over his lap and padded to her bathroom. He got up and stretched, and headed for the kitchen. He heard water pour into the ewer, and combed his hair with both hands.

That damn fuel pump, the dumb jerks at the auto shop, no place to rent a car or even to hire a car and driver. He kept reaching for his center, remembering all the near-misses, the fringes of fatal mistakes in his adventurous life. Curiously, none of them mattered, none came close to his fear of terrifying Dana Madison with his long delay.

If anything had happened to her, if anything had happened to his sweet...

Flint cut off the renegade thought. Women were dangerous, women were mine fields in the kind of life he led. They made him feel things, want things he couldn't have and couldn't need. When he saw a guy and a woman and a kid, a lucky guy with a woman who cared where he was or if he was hurt, Flint's guts constricted with envy. Was love a forbidden luxury? Was Dana forbidden, too?

He built a fire and listened to his center. And when she came out, on tip-toe wrapping her arms around his neck, shyly burying her face in his throat, rubbing her warmth into him, he curled his fingers around her forearms and set her away.

Stoically, he met the hurt and puzzlement in her eyes and wore his mask. His voice was flat, monotone to conceal his pain.

"Time for soup, Miss Madison."

Chapter Four

For two days, Dana alternately teased Flint, nagged and sniped, and subsided into sullen silence. He had put up a wall, and in the quiet time after lunch, she suspected she knew why.

She was getting to him. The experience of being tied and abandoned had horrified her, but Flint's reaction had erased the residue of those bleak seven hours. Lovingly, Flint had held and comforted and cherished her while she nestled in his arms. He had kissed her. Not, she admitted, with passion, but with tenderness, and that was a start.

"Why don't you talk to me, Flint?" Dana sat Indian-style at his feet. "Lately you dole out about six words a day, and you know how I get bored."

Flint immersed himself in a paperback western and said nothing.

"I loved how you held me that night, made me feel safe and protected, Flint." She walked two fingers through the fur rug until they reached his boots. Compelled to make contact with him, no matter how fleeting, how trivial, she stroked the hard blackness of the boot.

Flint dog-eared a page and closed the book. "That was the point. That's what you do to a frightened person on the brink of hysteria." There was soberness in his voice, and a hint of guilt. "Even chimpanzees hug each other during a fright."

Dana hit him with a mocking laugh, and smoothed the hard leather. "Do they call each other *my baby* and *darling*, Flint? Do they hold each other for hours and kiss?"

"You're getting carried away," he said flatly. "In extreme situations, one does what's expedient. Here. Read an old Zane Grey."

Casually, he set aside his book and strolled out onto the porch. Dana restrained the urge to dive after him. Instead, she waited a few minutes and followed. Flint was leaning against the post that supported a rickety overhang. His powerful neck flowed into broad shoulders, the vee of his torso arrowing down to the lean curve of his butt. How many women had feasted on Flint's masculine beauty?

All women developed a low, juicy radar for men like Flint, an instinct for tracking hot, dangerous males. Oh, she'd seen women give out all the primping signals when a man like Flint swaggered past. Flirty tossing of the head, fingering hair, licking lips, dilating pupils, hordes of women must have put out the vibrations, must've thrown themselves at Flint.

With a yank to keep her tanktop taut, she sidled next to him. "I've never spent time in the desert," she offered. "It's very beautiful." Damn, she was lame. "Do you like the desert?"

"What do you want, Miss Madison?" Flint's incisive stare shut her up, and his coldness forced her to change strategies. Obviously he wasn't caving in, wasn't bowing to her seduction. Flint was as obdurate as his name, and his resistance hurt her. Dana smiled brightly as if the two had shared a joke. She wanted to cry, but as often as he'd bested her, Dana still had a few weapons in her arsenal. And now, ashamed she'd been rejected, the smart idea was to pretend they meant nothing to each other.

He'd shoved her back to square one. Then the one option was escape. But she couldn't escape her longing for his lips, her need to feel him buried in her welcoming heat, most of all, her desire to love him. Stupidly, she thought she'd seen signs that he'd cared. Her throat ached with unshed sobs.

"Can I sit in the van?" It came like a bolt out of the blue, an inspiration.

"Why?"

"A change of scenery, for heaven's sake." She reined in her testiness. "Just to **do** something. Please, Flint."

He shrugged. "Then go sit. I've got some firewood to chop." He sauntered off the top step, and vanished around the side of the cabin.

As soon as Dana heard the even thunks of axe on wood, she gave herself to the dry heat, meandered to the van, pausing to inspect a tiny lizard doing push-ups on a rock.

Flint left the car unlocked. After all, no one came here, no one spied. She left the door open to cool the suffocating interior, and climbed into the front seat. In case he'd bother with a quick check, Dana popped the driver's seat back, and rested her feet on the dash.

When the thunks continued, she jack-knifed, searching for the ignition wires. A few tears trickled down her cheeks before she took the final irrevocable step.

She held her breath, tore the strands loose, and twisted the ends together. Buster, her father's chauffeur, had taught her, always claiming that Dana could set up shop as a primo car thief when her father disinherited her.

Her heart pounded and her pulse raced. Escaping Flint, showing him she really was tough, that she didn't need him, that was the adrenalin rush.

A few fits and starts, and suddenly, wonderfully, the engine turned over.

"Eat this, Flint," she crowed. Dana kicked it into first gear and barrelled down the dirt road. In the side mirror, through the cloud of dust, she spotted Flint, both hands on his axe, like a dark statue.

"Oh, baby, if I'd met you on the golf course, or on a cruise, we might've set some sheets on fire," she said ruefully.

After all was said and done, Dana sported the same radar as the rest of her sex.

She sighed, peering through the windshield for the highway.

"Flint, Flint, the trouble is I'd never see you on a golf course, or on a cruise. I'd never have met you at all. And now how will I ever learn how you got that scar, how you became such a smooth criminal?" She lay on the accelerator. Somehow, the prospect of learning Flint's secrets from the police department, maybe the F.B.I. sent an uneasy shiver down her spine.

She kicked the accelerator and the speedometer zipped toward eighty. The needle had just hit its mark when the engine spluttered and coughed. "Dirt in the fuel tank," Dana said, whistling in the dark. She stamped on the pedal again, but slowly the needle swung back and the van slowed, gave a pitiful wheeze and cruised to a dead stop.

"C'mon, c'mon," Dana shouted. A red light on the dash gave her the bad news. "Empty," she moaned.

A glance in the rearview reflected an ominous sight. Her escape from Flint's clutches measured about three blocks. And worse, Flint was hiking toward her with a red gas can, a leisurely hike as though he had all the time in the world.

Dana shrieked in her fury and jumped out of the van. She looked right, left in the draining desert heat, and struck out for the highway as fast as she could. A hasty glance, the glance of the terrified prey, revealed Flint filling the tank.

She shrieked again, but Flint started the engine and poured it on, and when he jumped out and snared her, she was soaked with perspiration, coated with gritty sand.

In the van, amid a barrage of her "I hate you's," Flint locked the cuffs on her, and headed for the cabin.

"Then say something," she demanded.

"Why? You know what's coming." He seemed on the verge of laughing. "Bedtime."

Fired with frustration, she lunged and kicked at the back of his seat. "If you think you're going to tie me to that bed again —"

"You'll hurt your wrist," he interrupted in a conversational tone.

And fifteen minutes later, he stood outside the bathroom while she washed away the sand.

"Here's your costume for the day," Flint said. He stuck his arm in and dangled a clean pair of babydolls. "Put them on, and give me the road clothes."

"I won't!" Dana stamped her foot. "I am not a child, I will not be treated as a child."

"Put them on." He waved two fingers.

Panicked, she cursed at him and slipped on the outfit. At least it was clean and cool. She came strutting out. "Well, macho man, satisfied?"

For a second, his eyes clouded with hunger, and Dana knew he was anything but satisfied. Seductively, she arranged herself on her bed, lounging like an houri in a harem.

"I know you don't want to hurt my sore wrist with those metal things," she wheedled.

"I won't, so I made these." Flint tied her hands with strips of soft towels. Dana closed her eyes and wriggled her toes. Then Flint tied her left ankle, and her eyes flew open.

"What the hell do you think you're doing?" Outrage and temper sharpened her voice.

"I can't trust you. Starting now, I'll let you up every two hours. Then you can go wild." He side-stepped a vicious kick.

She sobbed and used her little voice. "I have to lie here twenty-four hours a day, alone? With nothing to do? Talk to me, Flint."

"I don't talk, remember?" He tied her right ankle.

Her howl followed him into the kitchen, out onto the porch, and behind the cabin where he chopped wood, trying to drive out the image of her oozing the promise of rich sex, bound, smelling of desire.

"Center yourself," he commanded and swung the axe higher, brought it down harder. Dana never let him or his cock forget her. She whimpered and cried between each strike of the axe.

With a mighty blow, Flint shattered the log. He only had to survive a few more days of the provocative Dana Madison. She was intelligent, but wasn't she smart enough to understand he could read her sexual overtures as clearly as the back of his hand?

She was her father's own daughter, clever, but without a sincere bone in her luscious body. She was just a job.

⁂

By the Coleman, Flint sat reading *Sports Illustrated.* A log sputtered and fell to ashes. He checked his watch and glanced at the futon rolled up beside her door. She'd been restless, talking in her sleep, and at 2:00AM, he'd given up and made coffee.

"Flint." A soft moan. "Flint, I need you."

He tossed the magazine, sprang up, and hovered at her bedside. Frowning with concern, he asked, "Feeling sick, Miss Madison? Water, juice, aspirin? Something I can get you?" He felt her forehead, and it was cool. "Something I can do?"

Her answer was a velvet whisper. "Oh, yes, Flint. You can do something." In the dim candlelight, she moistened her lips, and choked back her words. "No. I can't tell you." She turned her head to the side, avoiding eye contact.

He sat beside her and cupped her shoulders. "Tell me."

She faced him suddenly, and her eyes shone with naked lust. "It's been three weeks, three weeks without sex, Flint."

As though scorched by the touch of her flesh, he drew back. "You'll be home soon. One of your men—"

"Please, Flint," she wailed. "Make love to me. It won't mean anything, I promise. Please. I'm so restless, so tense. I'm having nightmares."

The bed creaked as he rose, and Dana began to cry, sobs that shook her slight frame.

"Look, I can't do it," he said. "My rule, no fraternizing on the job."

"You tie me up, watch me all the time. I can't even take care of myself." She trembled and wept until her breasts heaved. "I need it bad, Flint. Love me. Touch me there so I can sleep."

Flint's penis stirred and thickened. His guts twisted, and guiltily he reminded himself, this wasn't about him. It was about his hostage. The weeping Dana Madison, pinioned and writhing, was a wild woman used to indulging her appetites, a reckless heiress who'd been spoiled by getting everything she wanted, except escaping this abduction.

But he had bad news for the demanding Miss Madison. She wasn't getting a fucking, or a fondling, or even a quick kiss from him, not from Flint, her baby-sitter.

Her cheeks were streaked, the tears glistening as they flowed from those incredible blue eyes, from beneath the golden lashes. Her sobs hiccoughed. Damn, she'd worked herself within a hair's-breadth of hysteria.

Madison had given instructions about his daughter, but nothing about driving her crazy or depriving her of sexual satisfaction. And this was hardly a question an intelligent operative asked a father.

Dana moaned, so sweetly desperate, his cock strained even harder against his seams.

Flint sorted through Wu Chin's advice, but despite his respect and reverence for the old master's teachings, Wu Chin had never tied a woman to a bed and walked away while she pleaded for sex. He paced to the door, pivoted, and completed a stiff half-circle, trying to work off his anger and frustration.

Hell, he'd give in and give her what she wanted, this time. But he suspected when he got through with her, she'd never again depend on relief being just a finger away.

In the half-light, she lay, the sheer cotton nightie riding up, a veil over the lush, firm breasts. "Thank you, oh, thank you, Flint. It means so much to me." She smiled then, like an angel about to sin.

With his bandana, Flint dabbed at her tears. He cursed himself for a fool and reached for the candle.

"Please, leave it lit, Flint. I want to watch you play with me." Her voice, an intoxicating blend of shame and boldness, lured him like a magnet.

In the half-light, he sat beside her, and threw the quilt to the foot of the bed. No panties. The downy triangle was exposed. Beads of sweat broke out on his brow, and a trickle slid down his spine. He fought the urge to rip off her gown and drive into her. Flint suppressed a shudder of desire and rested his hand on her mound.

She hissed through her teeth and tensed her pelvis. "Yes. Please, Flint."

Holding his breath, he began toying with the soft curls, periodically sliding his hand away to brush the satin of her inner thighs. She wriggled, spread her legs wider, beckoning him with her body to return to her vulva, to her clit.

She was shivering now, jutting her dampness into his hand. "Oh, God, don't make me wait. Please touch me."

He covered her wetness with his palm, squeezed the pouting lips, leaned over and raised the candle in its china saucer high overhead, until it cast a distorted oval of light on her flesh.

"What, what are you going to do?" she gasped, shrinking into the mattress.

"You want to watch me play with you," he got out huskily, "and

I want to watch you come. But let's make it interesting." Deftly, he balanced the saucer on the curve of her belly. "Keep quiet, Dana. Hold still, no matter how good it gets." He smiled wickedly.

At first Dana concentrated on the dancing candle flame and the quivering of her belly. Then, desperately as she tried, she couldn't ignore the thrilling, insistent massaging. Flint's skilled fingers slid in her wetness, caressing the labia, finally transferring the slickness to her clit, his thumb circling the nub.

Wild sensation tore through Dana. Maintaining the candle's balance tormented her. She gnawed her lower lip and mewling sounds escaped from her throat. But the longer she held still, the longer she dammed the urge to release the fire pooling between her thighs, the longer she checked the urge to scream her pleasure, the more slowly he built the tension.

"Is this what you want? Mmm-hmm. Do you like me rubbing your cunt, Miss Madison, all open and hot and creamy?"

Dana shut her eyes, and lay silent, praying to fall over the edge, praying to drown everything in silence, to shut out questions and answers and let her whole world be the constant agony of his touch.

But Flint was having none of that. "Tell me, or I'll quit."

He stopped all movement, and Dana bit her lips and looked deep in his eyes. As always, he meant what he said. Hastily she swallowed and jerked her head.

"You know I like it. Oh, don't stop." Her words caught in her throat.

"I'd make you tell me exactly what I'm doing to you, what you like," he commented almost conversationally, "but I am not a cruel bastard."

Flint thrust a big, blunt finger into her sheath, plugging her, filling her, controlling the internal probing even as his thumb increased speed.

Hungrily, Dana called his name and arched up.

"I'm finger-fucking you. Do you want to come now, Dana?" he whispered. His eyes darkened and his nostrils flared.

Dana breathed the ripe smell of her sex, and knew Flint smelled it, too. She saw herself reflected in his eyes, two tiny Dana's spread-eagled, mercilessly teased by Flint's rough calluses, and she flexed her hips, trying to delay her spasms.

The candle tottered, the flame winked. "Let it burn me," she shouted, crazed for release at any price. But as soon as Flint felt the first powerful ripple, the milking of his finger, he lifted the candle, watching her watch him.

"Flint, Flint!" She shouted his name, wanting all of him deep inside her. Sobbing and pumping her hips, she thrashed, screaming for fulfillment. She froze then, impaled on his thick finger, feeling the pulse of her clit under his callused thumb.

Dana looked down when he placed his left hand gently on her belly and pressed as the spasmodic shudders gradually diminished.

Drenched with perspiration, she sighed. A few delayed contractions squeezed his finger, and he massaged her dewiness.

Dana groaned, exhausted and utterly boneless in happy relief.

Flint had made her burn, had built the blaze, and stoked it into a mindless, final conflagration of the senses.

"Feel better now?" He raised one eyebrow, and a very small smile quirked his lips.

"Was this a medicinal screw, an injection of Flint's finger sedative?" Dana tried to chuckle, but she was too dizzy, too mellow. Instead, she gripped the wrist ties, tensed her vaginal muscles and clung to his finger, but he slid it out, and drew her nightie over her wet curls.

Flint exhaled and rolled his shoulders. Tight-lipped, he untied the bindings. And Dana, heavy-lidded and dazed, still managed to detect the heat lightning of desire flicker across his impassive face, and the huge swelling in his groin.

Behind the bathroom door, she washed and read her total satisfaction in the mirror. By lantern light, she stretched, cat-like, gloriously loose, relaxed. Languidly as if in a dream, Dana basked in ripeness, fullness. Her nipples had softened, the aureolas smooth and content, courtesy of Flint and his educated hand.

When she drew a towel between her legs, the soft distended tissue protested, and she licked her lips. If Flint could bring her to the edge of the universe and spin her out into the void with one hand, what could he do with his mouth, his body?

She shivered and studied her expression. Oh, he was a real master of the art. She'd sleep great tonight. And it took no seer to predict that Flint would suffer from insomnia and a granite groin. For all his emotional distancing, she'd bet a million, Stoneman had a heart and a hard-on.

And for some stupid reason, she let the cynicism melt, trickling away like the mingled drops of sweat and water between her breasts. Her father had preached his motto. Take what you need, but do it with charm and style. If you have to work an opponent's weak spot, work it, but leave him smiling.

Flint wasn't smiling. She'd taken what she'd needed, an intense sexual experience her captor had given freely, believing that she was suffering. Dana draped the thin towel around her waist and leaned into the splintery wood, wishing for the first time she knew the secret of smoothing the hard lines of Flint's mouth, of bringing to his face the sloe-eyed look of satisfaction she wore tonight.

Chapter Five

From the porch, Flint counted stars, gazing at their cold perfection like his assignments, each encounter, each task clean, distinct and separate. And when the job was finished, all the ties were cut, all the feelings. The file was closed. And Flint followed Madison's next order.

In her bedroom, Dana lay sleeping, languid, perhaps drifting in a soft dream. He smelled her scent lingering on his fingers, closed his eyes, and pressed the ache behind his tight Levis.

Dana, magically golden in the candlelight, was the stuff of his dreams and fantasies. He'd looked at her as little as possible during the past three weeks, afraid of losing control, of dragging her to the floor, devouring those red lips, and taking her savagely. He'd spoken to her as infrequently as possible because her low, throaty voice spoke innocence, but his brain heard a phantom invitation, phantom moans of ecstasy while he dreamed his cock plunged and probed her wet velvet.

"Dana," he whispered. He re-ran the moments of caressing her slipperiness, fondling her quivering flesh as the candle glimmered. He'd read the wild shifts of lust and delight on her face as he varied his strokes and touches to bring her time and again to the edge, then forced her to retreat.

He passed his fingers over his lips, and inhaled deeply. Sea air and a heady bouquet. Dana. To be inside her was all he cared for, damn everything. Protect her, and love her and make love to her. Dana, in her strength and defiance, her open sexuality, an elusive mix of want and shyness, excited him more than any other woman.

Then he dredged up Wu Chin's homily on sex. "My son, what

hides between a woman's thighs is the most mysterious being on the earth," he'd intoned. "For it has no voice, yet calls to a young man constantly, has no brain, but schemes and plans, has no arms yet catches and holds with the strength of a giant."

"But, Master, what is a man to do? This?" Half-smiling in the dark, Flint remembered lifting his right hand to touch the crotch of his white cotton ghi.

"The boiling overflow of the life essence must be drained, and I tell you to answer the call of the being. Yet answer to a different call each time. Or one woman will bind you and know your secrets."

One woman, the only woman for him, the ultimate woman for him, lay asleep in her bed. She would never hear his words of love. And she was the only woman he could never have.

"Snap out of it," he ordered himself. Action, action was the prescription, not replays of the Master's advice.

He washed his hands in the outdoor basin, scrubbed them with harsh disinfectant soap, and poured the intoxicating odor of Dana Madison into the thirsty sand.

Flint ran for hours over the arid landscape. In the distance grotesque forms threatened until he approached and recognized twisted cacti, deformed rocks, the meshed bulk of tumbleweed.

Returning to the cabin, he bowed, grabbed his knees, and sucked in great breaths. The moon lit beads of sweat dripping from his face. He flopped on the weathered wood planking and let the cold night wind chill his face.

Wu Chin's advice was always correct. Grim and exhausted, Flint remembered the Master's emphasis on the *yang*, action and light and heat. "Exhaust the body, and reason shall mount and rule with the whip."

Flint splashed water on his face, pulled his futon to the middle of the room, and fell into a restless sleep.

❦❦❦

Cuffed again, Dana twined a curl around her index finger, and tried to focus on a dreary women's magazine. Seven A.M. and Flint was hacking at the wood pile. He had enough for twenty bonfires and a thousand barbecues and still he chopped away. Were they going to be holed up through winter? A tiny frisson of pure excitement and anticipation raced down to her belly, and she shook it off.

Surely, Daddy's men would track her down before long. A question nagged her. Why hadn't her father's top investigators found her, and frog-marched Flint into a black sedan?

She stiffened, and the picture of Flint subdued and arrested woke a sharp pain in her breast. No, she wouldn't let them take him, not the man who'd soothed and embraced her tenderly, the man who'd kissed her tenderly, and called her his baby, his darling.

That damnable Flint and his tenderness had muddied her motives, her purpose, her plans to escape. And he refused to sleep with her.

She sighed and glanced at the table of contents. What was this? **Getting Mr. Right into Bed, Three Steps**. Whoever wrote it had never tried to seduce Flint. Dana snorted and started reading.

During lunch and dinner, she commented about the weather and slumped into silence. Flint looked like hell. Tight-lipped, tense, deep violet shadows beneath his eyes. Dana shuttered her gaze and imagined kissing the shaded crescents, imagined the texture of his skin.

When night fell, he waved her into the bathroom. "I'll stay out here. Something I want to read." Over his shoulder, in a tone suggesting that he was having a tooth pulled, he said, "You were good today."

Dana hurried to the bathroom. "Give me a break," she whispered to herself, "my big reward, washing up without Flint on duty." Her last reward had been her father's donation of a quarter million to Dana's favorite charity. How she'd come down in the world! She chuckled, and plied the washcloth.

Moonlight drifted through the windows, painting everything falsely new. Dana, fresh from bathing, put on her nightie, picked up the hair brush, and ignored her bed. Playing close to the edge, she tip-toed into the big room to linger, to show herself in front of the fire and test Flint's mood. She bent from the waist and brushed the fall of her hair. When she sensed she'd stolen his full attention, she snapped straight to toss the mane down her back, thrusting her breasts for him to scrutinize. The abrupt intake of his breath, and the turn of a page were notes of his lovesong.

"Flint." It came out soft, wanting and compelling. And real. She wanted him, and all her scheming and conniving vanished in her need for his taut body, the heaven of his owning her, the sweet aftermath when he'd murmur —

"Forget it. Whatever it is." Gruffly, he rattled the pages of his magazine.

"I'm sorry if I've done anything to upset you. Why are you so angry?"

"Don't beat around the bush."

If Flint had ever blushed, he was doing it now. Boldly, Dana touched his knee.

"Sorry to disturb you, but it's time to tie me." She added brightly, "Of course, I could stay up late and chat."

"No. You should be in bed, all covered up." Slowly, he followed her.

Dana sashayed into her room, and lay atop the old quilt. "No quilt tonight, Flint, please. I'm so warm." If her range had fallen any lower, he'd need a hearing aid to catch it. She fanned her hair on the pillow, and stretched her hands up and over her head.

"Tie me."

The ties hung on the bedposts, but as Flint took the first one, Dana stroked his bulging crotch.

"Flint, do you want me?" Her lips were open and inviting, and she wet them with the tip of her tongue.

An image flashed in Flint's brain, Dana swirling that eager pink tongue around the head of his cock, Dana begging him to bury it deep in her mouth, then into her plush heat.

"No." He snared the trespassing hand, tied it, and leaned over the bed to trap the other hand.

"Flint, kiss me. I need you to kiss me."

"No." He delayed a fatal second, and she stayed free to massage his thickened groin. He groaned and rocked into her hand.

"Please, Flint."

He shook his head, and fell to his knees to protect his genitals from her forays. Another second and he'd be on her like a hawk on a dove. "You don't know what you're doing. You don't know what you're saying. So shut up." He fumbled for the tie and tried not to seek those lips, those eyes. He lost the struggle and knelt on the bed, memorizing sapphire and gold.

"Then kiss my breasts," she begged. Her eyes sparkled with desire. "Kiss my nipples. They're aching for you." She arched, displaying her erect, marble-sized buds. She eased his head to her, and, cursing himself as he did it, Flint instead met her mouth, probed it with savage kisses, tasted her, wanted her.

In a fog of lust, he barely felt her open his Levi's until his penis sprang free. She encircled him, squeezed and stroked his rigid length. "God, baby," he moaned, trailing a ribbon of kisses to her nipples, "do you like my mouth on you?" He glanced up, but she had no words, and he plumped the white globes and sucked until she writhed. He closed his teeth on her hard nipples.

His penis knocked against his belly, and Dana crooned and slid her hand deep to play with his balls. Then she brought his hand to her mouth, and suckled one finger. She panted, she raised her hips, she loosed a little cry of pain.

"Untie me, Flint, so we can make love."

I'm crazy. She's finally kicked what's left of my brain to the curb. Unsteady, Flint got to his feet, grabbed her left hand and bound her. Throughout, he was conscious of his cock nodding toward Dana.

"Good-night, Miss Madison."

"You pansy bastard, do you jerk off?" Dana delivered the accusation like a quick jab below the belt. Her eyes shone with contempt. She was furious, at once aroused and disappointed. "Don't you ever need a woman?"

"Yeah." He clenched his jaw and buttoned his fly. "When I need sex, I buy one. Anonymous. No one gets hurt. It's professional on both sides of the deal. And then we walk away."

Painfully, with a swollen groin bursting his seams and breath hissing through his teeth, he managed to reach the door.

"And from now on, Miss Madison, the lullabies are over."

"But I won't be able to sleep." Outrage drove her voice up an octave.

"Count cocks." He itched to slam the door, but of course, he'd
carted it away weeks ago to punish her.

When he let her out for lunch the next day, she slouched in her
chair, barefoot, hair a mass of gold tangles. Sullenly, she ate half
an apple, drank a few sips of water. Without prompting, she rose
and flung herself into her bed. She lay like a cream and pink statue,
unseeing. Especially not seeing him.

A spoiled bitch, so used to getting her own way, she goes into
shock everytime she hears no. When her stomach grumbles, she'll
eat quick enough. Despite his dismissal of her tactics, a sick cold
lump grew in Flint's gut.

As darkness fell, she'd lain silent, except for one quick bathroom
trip. She'd refused a Coke, turning away her head.

At suppertime, he hauled her to the table. "I cooked for us,
corned beef hash, and cactus salad." Sheepishly, he gestured at the
the candles he'd set out, and the styrofoam cup of dried flowers.
"Kind of like a date."

And he imagined Dana on a date, a stroll along Riverwalk, an
intimate dinner in a cool Mexican restaurant, a secluded booth where
she kissed him, tiny, loving kisses, promises of the gift she'd give
him when they wore nothing but music and bare skin.

He hung a towel over his arm, and brandished a bottle of Welch's.
"A touch of the grape, Madame?"

Dana stared into her plate, her hands in her lap.

Flint poured anyway and served the hash, buttered her bread.

After chewing a few times in the silence, he tried again. "Please
eat. You'll make yourself sick."

He ate his salad, and she watched her plate. "Just a little something," he coaxed. "One bite."

Nothing. Was she testing him, after all the times she'd tested and
lost, egging him on to the third request? He propped his elbows on
the table and steepled his fingers.

Dana picked up the white plastic fork. She ate nothing, drank nothing. But Flint, reminding himself he was a patient man, drank grape juice and pretended to ignore her.

The candles choked on melted wax. Her face was dimmed and illuminated by the dying and reviving flame. And still she sat, fork hovering over her plate, drink untouched.

A tic danced in Flint's jaw as he showed three fingers. "Last chance, Dana, before I stuff the food down your throat. Eat your dinner."

Quick as a flash, Dana was on her feet, wielding the fragile fork, jabbing at him. In the faint light, her eyes flashed with anger. "Let me go before I —"

Flint twisted her wrist until the fork fell. He kicked over his chair and, boiling with temper and fierce hunger for her, swung her around the table and lifted her.

She kicked and screamed, and threatened his eyes with sharp fingernails.

"Do it, woman," he snarled. "C'mon, give me your best shot." He threw her onto the bed. But instead of the hysterical rage he expected, Dana sprawled, legs spread, eyes bright not with fear but desire. She panted and licked her lips.

"Damn you, you hellion," Flint growled. He ripped off her tank top, tore off her shorts. In a frenzy, he skinned out of his clothes. Fully aroused, he roughly nudged her legs wider apart, slipped his hands beneath her thighs so they rested on his forearms. His big hands splayed over her belly, then her mons. His hard thumbs separated the lips, forcing her clit out and up, until it glistened and offered itself to his ravenous mouth.

"Flint, do it. Flint, please."

He ran his tongue between the lips and back down, holding her immobile against involuntary twitching and quivering. He licked faster and faster, the only sound her moans and the sound of wet flesh on wet flesh.

He stopped and blew tiny breaths onto the sopping cleft.

Dana made wanting noises, and locked her hands behind his head, futilely trying to bring his mouth into full contact.

"Are you asking me to do what you wouldn't do for me at dinner tonight? Talk to me, Dana."

She probably thought he was torturing her for holding back, but she couldn't feel the torture his need was extracting from his nerves while he prolonged the foreplay. He glanced up.

Dana was whimpering, her eyes half-closed, half-mad with lust. She could hardly get out the answer. "I don't remember, Flint. Oh, please, lick me." She tried to raise her wetness toward his mouth, but he applied pressure to her pelvis to restrain her.

"Ask me what I asked you to do." He flicked the tip of his tongue and withdrew again.

"Eat." She moaned. "You asked me to eat. Please, Flint, I've been good and answered the question." She was shaking now, pleading.

Flint buried his face in her, nibbled the sweet projection, and then released her so she jogged against his mouth, freezing as all her nerve-endings fired and she sang the ancient female song of desire fulfilled, of the male pleasuring her beyond reason or sense.

Flint straddled her chest and brushed her cheeks and lips with his cock. Dana turned her head from side to side, and opened her mouth, trying to capture him. Slowly he slid down to her waist, pressed her creamy breasts together and worked himself between softness and watched as she crooned, thrust out the tip of her tongue and lapped at the drops of clear fluid on the end of his shaft.

"Come inside me, Flint," she begged. "I need this —" she kissed the engorged head "— all of you so deep inside I —" She drew in a great breath.

Flint settled between her legs, lifted them over his shoulders and drove into her. A low moan erupted from her. He arched in the ecstasy of treading the edge of self-control, of sending his whole length into her pulsing heat, of feeling his balls against her wet crevice.

He pulled out and sank into her again. "God, so tight, so ready, you were made for fucking." He rocked, abruptly withdrew, and despite her protest at the cessation, her efforts to catch him in her cleft, he let her legs fall to the sheet, caught her shoulders and supported her head.

"Kiss me, baby," he whispered. "Taste yourself on me, and then I'll ride you till you scream." Dana extended her pink tongue and licked the pearly essence of herself on his stiff flesh.

From under half-closed lids, she met his eyes. "You're so good, so good for me." She fell back and put her hands on his biceps. Her eyes were blue diamonds, her mouth a sweet prison where his tongue was welcome. Flint braced himself above her, feeling her fingers guide his massive erection deep into her.

And he grew harder than he'd ever thought possible, delving into the hot velvet, her quickening cries of rising tension joined to his ragged breaths. His powerful pistoning slid her toward the headboard, and Flint grabbed her and pulled her down toward the middle of the mattress.

"Don't — don't stop, my darling," she cried. Her hips rose faster and faster to meet his thrusts, speeding the coming of the explosion, frantic.

Her blue eyes dilated, so wide they were black, and she clutched his shoulders, slipped her hands to his slick back and kneaded the rippling muscles laddering his spine. As her control shattered, she dug in her nails.

"Oh, Flint. Oh, darling, I love you," she screamed. And the bloodrush beating like her voice in his ears, Flint pounded into her, gripping her hips, melding her to him. He threw back his head, and slammed the final thrust home, coming like a sirocco breaking over the desert, his shout boiling up from his guts.

He held her through the smaller paroxysms that pulsed around his cock. She fit him like a custom-made glove, and he wanted her to be here with him. Always. Always with "I love you" on her lips. But he knew it was a lie.

The coming separation would destroy the interlude they'd shared. Flint brushed away a tear. He'd never believed that crap about broken hearts, yet his own drummed with physical pain. Just for tonight he'd fight to believe her lie of love would come true. Just for this one night. Possessively, fiercely, he banded her to his body, stroking the supple, woman muscles, counting her ribs, palming her breast. Learning her, engraving her on his memory.

Then Flint drifted in a cloud of exhaustion, a delicious half-dream more satisfying than he'd ever felt after the act. *Submerge yourself in feeling,* Wu Chin would advise. *And when the immersion is complete and you have taken everything you can use, erase it. Erase her cries of passion and the softness that fed your need.*

And Flint tried to slip into a river of dreams, into a perfect nirvana where sensation and thought and reason seeped away, leaving him to float mindless, empty, blank. He failed, and let the sharp questions pierce his conscience.

How many times had he brought women over the line to climax, heard them cry, "I love you, Flint"? Faceless, nameless women. And how many times had he skillfully extricated himself, ruefully slipping out of bed, dressing himself in black? How many times had he leaned over silk sheets to soothe a lady with his special *au revoir,* murmuring faintly apologetic excuses (he had to go), delivering the practiced good-bye consisting of a short tongue probe of her mouth, a lick on her breast, and a quick kiss on her mons.

All very tender, and more importantly, the ritual allowed him to slip farther and farther from her grasping hands, and let him exit without a messy final scene.

Dana didn't deserve that, wouldn't be soiled by those cheap tricks, ruses to oil his escape. He'd never told a woman he loved her, unless it was part of the job.

"Am I crushing you, Dana?" He hoisted his bulk an inch, and the suction created by their sweaty torsos gave way. "Want me to climb off?" His cock registered a no vote.

Dana ran her fingers through his hair, traced his jawline.

"Don't you dare, lover." Smiling, sleepy-eyed, she stretched, offering her breasts so he could nuzzle the softening nipples. "And don't let Flint, Jr., take a hike either." With a laugh she tightened her female muscles.

Flint flexed and came up on his toes, elevating his hips just enough to slide his hardness out almost to the head. "That critter has a mind of his own." He mouthed her breasts up to crests, teased her, poised while Dana complained deliciously and struggled to envelope his cock to the hilt.

"No, no." She wrapped her legs around his waist and urged him back inside.

Grinning, he sank deep in her again. Still connected, he rolled onto his back, and brought Dana over him. He locked his hands behind his head and worshipped her in candleglow.

First, Dana lay quietly on his chest, tickling his throat with tiny nibbles, brushing him with light kisses. Then she sat up, cradling him inside. She curled his black chest hair around one finger, trailed her nails around his nipples, lapped sweat under his arms, bit his shoulder.

"Oh, you taste so good, lover," she whispered, and ground her slipperiness into his pubic bones. "Recommended by *Dana's Guide to Five Star Restaurants*."

"Damn cannibal woman," he growled.

"Yep," she agreed cheerfully, "that's me. And to prove it, I'm going to eat you all up." She rotated her wetness around him and bent to graze his nipples with her teeth.

"You missed dinner, so I suppose you have to eat something," he mused. He bucked up into her, ready for round two. And before her delicious kisses and more delicious squirming rendered him unable to speak, Flint whispered, "All of me. Is that a promise?"

Chapter Six

In the fading moonlight before false dawn, Dana, sated, burrowed in his arms. Flint drew her close, kissing her, tender kisses, loving kisses and gentle murmurs. They were wrapped in a cocoon of dreaminess.

"You make me feel so safe, Flint." Her toes explored the wiry hair on his leg. She slid one foot from his ankle to his knee, parted her legs and pressed herself into his thigh.

"Yeah? You make me feel like an endangered species, strong and healthy until I fell into the hands of a ruthless exploiter and was screwed to death. But what a way to go." He cradled her and nibbled her ear. "I can't move."

Dana giggled. "Then what's that thumping on my thigh?"

"Involuntary muscle twitches. No pain, no gain, they say. Are we going to sleep now, sweet thing?" He brushed his lips over her temple.

Dana touched tiny kisses to his chest. The moon lay a white path across him, and she traced scars on his chest.

"How did you get these?"

"Knife."

"No, I meant *who*?"

"Look, Dana, there's stuff we can't talk about." His voice took on an edge, the old edge he'd used on her before they'd had sex.

"And what's this puckered thing on your ribs? It's horrible. Who did this to you, my darling?" Dana bent and kissed the wound. She wept for him and his pain.

She saw Flint blink when the tears watered his chest, felt him hold his breath when she caressed his scars and swept her long hair over the violent blemishes marring the perfection of his body.

"Bullets and knives. It's the past, babe." He spread his legs, making himself loose and open. Flint carried her hand to his swollen genitals. "Do me," he pleaded, folding her fingers around his cock.

"But I want to know—"

"Know this." He played in her wetness, found her clit, and concentrated on slow, circular movements until her hand moved in the same erotic rhythm on him.

She stroked him and gushed onto his fingers until her heart pounded, and she needed all of Flint's maleness. Hastily, Dana straddled him and high on her knees rubbed the plushy head in her heat. With a little cry, she shoved him inside and slid down the iron length. Flint gasped and grabbed her hips.

In the moonlight, she braced her hands on his shoulders and rode him slowly. "Tell me," she whispered, as he'd done to her.

"You trying to pump me for information?" Flint gave a strangled laugh. It wasn't funny, and he wasn't convincing. He was burning up in another fever of desire.

"No action until you talk." She gnawed on her lower lip.

"What's to stop me from throwing you on your back and having you whether you want action or not?" He gripped her more firmly.

"Because you wouldn't do that to me." Conviction rang in her voice.

"All right." He grimaced in the blue-white light. "The knife scars, top secret. I could tell you, but then I'd have to kill you. The bullet I took when a crazy dude shot at Billie Winkler on stage during his Save the Frogs Tour. Happy now?"

Dana straightened. "I love you, Flint. Please don't get hurt anymore. I couldn't stand it."

"Fuck me," he whispered, a dark angel coaxing her to fall.

And Dana rode him to ecstasy, arching backward, one hand buried between their linked bodies, massaging the base of his root.

In the fraction of a second when Flint, too roused and bullish to let her finish on top, powered her on to the sheet and spurted into her, Dana caught the moonlit glisten of his keys on the floor.

"Breakfast is ready, big man." Dana spooned fruit cocktail and melon chunks into his soup bowl. Half-listening, Flint fished under the cushions of the wing chair. Methodically, he'd searched his pockets, the van, and the house. Nothing. He went to the table where Dana served toast and bacon browned over a small fire on the hearth.

He ate and smiled. "Pretty good. In fact, five-star for a lady who doesn't cook, and had to make do with the fireplace." He leaned over the table and kissed the tip of her nose.

"Still can't find the keys?" Dana sipped tomato juice and wrinkled her brow. "And you only have the one set?"

In that second, Flint knew she'd stolen them. The next time she made a break for it, she'd have the advantage of a quick ignition. He gave her a curt nod.

"One. Even a careful man makes mistakes. Of course, I can always rely on your expertise to hot-wire my wheels."

"Going somewhere?"

Flint detected the lie in Dana's too-innocent question. She thought she was smooth and subtle, that her love-making had softened him, dulled his powers of observation. He munched on a hunk of watermelon and speared a cube of honeydew on his fork.

"Town."

"Ah, the weekly trip for supplies." Dana put down her glass and met his eyes. "Can I go along?"

"No." Had her voice revealed an edge of anxiety?

"Then take this." She dropped a small paper between the salt and pepper shakers. He saw a numbered list and gulped his coffee.

"Instructions? What do you want me to do, lady? Call the F.B.I.?" Flint forced a chuckle. "Or the Texas Rangers? Or Daddy? Or maybe stop by the Auto Club for a map?"

"Of course not, you suspicious critter." Dana rose, pinched the list and snuggled into his lap. "But I love you, anyway." Her body heat radiated her perfume, and the scent of roses brought back the night and scenes of the most intense joining he'd ever experienced.

He froze the urge to breathe deeply, to pull in her heady aroma. Flint concentrated on the keys and her slyness.

Hell. She did exactly what I would do in her place. He flashed back to a POW camp where he'd gradually loosened fencing, sustaining burns from electric shocks until he'd wedged his body through and made a successful escape.

Flint wanted to throw away that memory and replace it with Dana's turbulent love-making that had seeped into his very bones.

A POW's first duty is to escape. The first rule of capture besides restricting info to name, rank, and serial number. Why shouldn't it be Dana's rule, even her motivation for coming on to him?

"Penny for your thoughts, lover." She bit his lips. "On second thought, can't town wait another day?" Dana moved in his lap and woke his need again despite his suspicions. What mental trick could shield him from her delicious lure?

"Kiss me, lover," she whispered. "Take me to bed." And when her tongue traced the seam of his closed lips, he fought his rebellious body, got up and stood her on the cracked linoleum.

"Have to go to town. What's on that list?" He put a few feet between them by checking the paper. "Juice, meat, canned milk, fruit. Salad greens?"

"For tonight. I've got no way to make them last without a refrigerator." She leaned against him, brushed her breast on his arm, and his groin tightened. "If I can't go along, you're stuck doing the shopping, lover."

"Dana, the terrible thing that happened when I was late can't happen again." Flint folded and pocketed the paper. "Don't worry. I wrote a couple of notes with your identity and your whereabouts. One in my jacket, one in the car, one in a safe deposit box at the local bank. I'll need an extra hour today."

"Hurry, lover. I'll be waiting." She raised her wrist for his kiss. "Cuff me." Dana walked backwards into the bedroom as if she couldn't see enough of him. "The faster you leave, the faster you'll be back."

Watching her lie before him like a willing sacrifice to his power, Flint slowly tied her hands to the bedstead. When he bent for the good-bye kiss, her blue eyes filled with tears.

Stay, his body told him, and his emotions echoed the refrain. *Stay and hold her forever and make her your own.* But he knew what Madison expected, and it was not a complicated job.

Flint took her mouth in a bittersweet kiss that spoke of heat, love, and the final, inevitable detachment.

Flint pivoted and strode to the front door. He closed his ears to Dana's I-love-you's, and hot-wired the van. On the deserted, sweltering road to Brisco, he prioritized his errands.

First, the replacement of the ignition switch and new keys. While he waited, a call to Madison's lawyer in Portugal, and a quick stop at Hopkin's Super Foods.

He remembered the bleak and empty meals before Dana. Now he'd have to resume his meals eaten standing over the kitchen counter, or the silent, lone dining with a book or a newspaper broken only by a question from a waiter.

He'd never be the same. How could he go back to that empty life without her? The life of the cold, objective professional who lived everywhere and nowhere, who had no bond to anyone. An agony built in his throat, and, on the barren road, he threw back his head and howled like a wounded animal.

Dana had left a hole in his heart.

※≈⟨✿⟩≈※

When the van parked in front of the cabin, Dana woke from a doze. The sun was just setting, and he was early. Her stomach lurched with anticipation. "Flint," she cooed, waiting for him to bolt to her side, loosen the cuffs, and take her in a bone-melting embrace. She imagined his lips on hers, his hot tongue probing, his strong hands stripping her with an exquisite slowness to heighten her erotic excitement.

A flush of desire washed over her and her nipples stiffened, tingled, incredibly sensitive to her shirt's light cotton weave. At the apex of her thighs, creamy moisture flowed and collected. She writhed in her need.

"I'm so ready for you, lover," she called. She heard his slow footsteps. "Come make love to me before I dissolve." Her voice was steamy and inviting.

He came and leaned against the doorjamb. He looked at the bureau, at the brown braided throw rug, everywhere in the room except at her.

"Flint, what's wrong?" She strained against the cuffs. "Free me so I can love you."

"The loving is over, Miss Madison." He approached her bed.

When he freed her, Dana smiled. "I see. Anything to torment me. Come here, lover." Eagerly, she threw herself into his arms.

"It's over."

"Don't say that, Flint. Please." Fear colored her voice.

He held her and stroked her hair. "Hush, now hush. And listen. Good news. Tomorrow night you'll be going home. Happy?"

"Home?" She leaned back in the curve of his arm. Shock and bewilderment flickered across her face. "Why?"

"Hey." Flint gave her a little shake. "The deed is done. The job is finished."

"But you, me. The two of us —" She choked on the words.

"Baby, there never *was* the two of us." He gave her a quirky teasing smile. "You've been around the block. You know the story. A little stimulation, a little relief."

"No. That's not true. I love you."

"C'mon, Miss Madison. This is what you love." Flint laid her on the coverlet. Bracketing her head with both hands, he leaned down and opened her mouth with a tongue kiss, and lowered his face to her breasts. Through the thin fabric he worked on her nipples until she lifted herself for more. She sighed and moaned his name.

Flint raised his head and for a second he gazed deep into her eyes with naked hunger. Dana heart thudded erratically. "Flint, take me. I can't wait any longer."

With a fleeting kiss he touched her cleft. He clenched his right fist and caught the punch in his left palm. "I'll make sandwiches for dinner. After a couple of meals tomorrow, we won't have any food to throw out."

"What about me? You'll have *me* to throw out, won't you, Flint?"

She leaped off the bed and ran after him, jerking at his arm until he spun to confront her.

Dana screamed and beat on his chest, slapped his face in her fury and pain. Flint took it all, not catching her wrists or stepping away from the blows. A statue without feeling, a stone without pity, without remorse.

And Dana wept then, and crumpled, sliding down his strong, ungiving form, clutching him, embracing his knees. She sobbed and pressed her cheek to his thigh. "It had to mean more to you than sex. Please tell me it meant more to you than that. The way you touched me, the way you owned me, as though you could hold off all the bad things."

"Nobody can hold off the bad things, baby." Flint seized her by the elbows to lift her to her feet, but she shook her head wildly and clung to him with every ounce of her strength.

Flint disengaged himself. "You're making this rough, Dana. Use your common sense. *I'm* one of the bad things. I'm your kidnapper. Have you forgotten?"

Dana wilted and shrank into herself. She knew what he was seeing. He saw a small teary version of the defiant, brittle Dana, the overbearing princess who lived in a palace with King Madison. A woman who spoke and people snapped to, a woman whose heart had never been touched because she'd never given up control.

She hiccoughed a sob, and Flint hunkered before her. "Let me go, lady," he whispered. He cupped her cheek, and Dana tilted her head and snuggled into his palm.

"I can't," she said, miserable. "Not without being with you one last time." When Flint pulled her to her feet, she inhaled, preparing for a scream of despair.

But she was wrong, wonderfully wrong.

Flint swept her into his arms, the kiss he gave her blended tenderness and savagery and took her breath away.

"Promise me it's the last time, Dana." His gaze was fire and smoke. "Promise me this is over. Tonight."

Weak with joy, she nodded. She kissed the line of his jaw. "Does tonight last until tomorrow morning?"

Flint laughed. "That's my girl." But his laugh died away, and under her hand, she felt the drumming of his heart.

⁂

Hours of perfect connections played out in Dana's bed, an incredible partnering with positions changed, speeds modified, bodies squeezed and released, an instinctive dance of love in which Flint both led and followed.

"Does this feel good, this slow motion?"

"So good. Don't stop."

"Want my tongue here?"

"Yes, yes. For God's sake, you're driving me crazy."

The sound of fevered flesh meeting fingers. Licking and tasting and lapping, whimpers and groans. The bedstead creaking, faint in the still night. The slow, prolonged, deliberate working of stiff shaft in wet softness.

And finally, Dana taut and unmoving as a tightened string, her mouth open, and release that went on and on as Flint poured into her and the two joined in a duet of satisfaction and cruelly unfilled longings.

Braced on his forearms, he hovered over her, sheathed and content. He moved himself in her blood-hot cleft, eliciting tiny moans, tiny aftershocks.

"Come down on me, all of you," she whispered. "I want you against me this last time." She pressured his biceps.

Flint lowered himself, his bare chest covering her warm breasts. He kissed her throat, and rested his head beside hers. He was lost in her fragrance, wanted to submerge himself in a sweet exhausted sleep but worry kept him awake. Dana dreamed she could change the situation, change him.

For her own sake, she had to discard the notion that their meeting was somehow fated, that this had been a romantic tryst, a prelude to a heavenly forever-life together.

Reality, like a sharp knife, cut to the truth. He heard Wu Chin's sad commentary on failed love affairs. "The rift is not caused by what fools say, not the shape of the lover's eye suddenly grown displeasing, nor the laugh grown too loud. It is instead the way of life, the expectations of family and parents which intrude and crack the seamless shell."

Flint closed his eyes to blind himself to Dana's hair, silvered in the moonlight, her long lashes sweeping her cheeks, her eyes like the ocean off Tuamoto, stormy and calm and sultry by turn. He had to erase her beauty and her passion as though they had never existed.

Chapter Seven

"It's time, Miss Madison." Flint glanced at his watch as if his heart hadn't been counting the minutes whizzing by in the early dark.

Dawdling near the kitchen's dry sink, Dana scrubbed a plastic fork. "Finishing up," she said.

They'd sat at the old plank table, pretending to eat. He'd watched her moving chunks of tuna on her plate, and he knew she'd watched him covering his fish with a piece of bread.

And they'd glanced around the cabin. The fireplace, the shabby chair, the bearskin rug. He hoped a storm would destroy it, or a lightning fire. Then no token would remain of their sad little love story.

"We'd better hit the road. Don't want you hanging around the bus depot all night."

She carefully placed the fragile plastic in a drawer, as if putting things in their proper place was the magic charm to make the inevitable disappear. She wiped her hands on a paper towel.

"Guess we're finished."

He nodded, not trusting himself to speak, opened the door for her, and blew out the candle.

"Sit up front," he said. He slammed the passenger side door, and climbed into the van. He dug out his keys.

"Here." Dana dangled the missing keys before him. "It was a stupid trick to hold us in the cabin."

Flint closed her small hand around the key ring. "I bought a new ignition, different keys. Keep 'em as a souvenir." He hit the starter, a starter that ended what had only begun. Damn, if he kept up this philosophizing, he'd give old Wu Chin a run for his money.

The engine roared to life. The moon shone on Dana's solemn face. Flint gripped the wheel. A wave of tenderness rolled over him and he considered driving forty to prolong his time with her.

He kicked it up to eighty and held the redline.

❧⚬⟨♥⟩⚬❧

"Three blocks south of the intersection. You understand why I can't drive you to the door." He extended a packet. "I bought your bus and airline ticket. There's some cash for a cab if your father's not home to send a chauffeur."

"Is this how it ends, then? Tickets and a little cash? Of course, you remarked that when you needed sex, you bought it. Was I anonymous enough for you?" Dana curled her lip and lifted the papers from his fingers, avoiding his hand like a kid repelled by a snake.

Choked by furious urges to deny her accusations, to jump out and kidnap her for himself, to keep her close forever, Flint said nothing.

He'd been a fool. During the day, dreading the loss of Dana, he'd cut wood and slogged around the backyard desert. He had assumed she was making work for herself or reading or napping. But unpredictable as always, she'd been crafting an icy manner, a glacial good-bye. Under the street lamp, even her gaze was cold and dismissive.

"Hope you didn't knock yourself out entertaining me. But as you said, it meant nothing —" she unlocked the door and stepped to the curb "— a little stimulation, a little relief." She slammed the door and instantly ran toward the bus station.

Flint cursed. His acting had been too good. Did she really believe he wanted to let her go? He drove a parallel street, turned down an alley, and parked in the shadows across from the depot.

Dana appeared in the halo of the street light. Slender and compelling and desirable, she pushed the smeary glass door, and marched to the sleepy clerk behind the counter.

Flint threw the van into reverse and backed onto the parallel street. She'd seen nothing. Let her imagine he was so glad to dump her that he'd driven off and left her unguarded.

The love affair had ended with money, but it had ended the right way within the boundaries of a job. She'd scamper home to the loving arms of Madison. He'd counsel her not to publicize her mysterious disappearance, that he'd personally take care of the bold kidnapper.

Dana could return to high society, marry a well-connected man, and produce little Samantha's, Robbie's and Caroline's.

Flint might linger as a romantic memory for a while, but as the years passed, he'd be re-molded as a villain in her thrilling adventure. Finally, a white-haired Dana would reduce Flint to a big teddy bear who'd played tough guy, but had been brought to his knees courtesy of her cleverness.

By 2:00AM, he'd ramped onto the throughway and sped toward Louisiana. He had a couple of friends in Algiers, in old New Orleans where he'd conveniently disappear. He muttered names of parishes, saw himself driving the Causeway, drinking beer in a zydeco saloon, chugging rye whiskey shooters, getting a little wasted to dull the pain of losing Dana.

⁂

"Time heals all wounds. Out of sight, out of mind." Dana gave a cursory glance at the framed mottoes and separated the lace curtains of the cozy sitting room overlooking the curved drive. "It is better to have loved and lost than never to have loved at all. What lies." She made a choked, desperate sound, and stared at the gardeners manicuring the lawns.

She had an herb garden she should be tending, but two long months after Flint had released her, she had slipped into a shell of solitude. Her nightgowns had become a kind of uniform.

Not that she hadn't tried to resume the old life. Hadn't she attended the Madison Foundation's board meetings where she sat distracted? Two invitations to dinner from dear friends who seemed annoying and unreal. Their mouths moved, the laughter was tinny, the teasing dull.

With crusty politeness, Dana strolled the terraces, sipping from her champagne flute. After an hour or two, she'd migrate to the exit, offer thanks. "We must do this again some time," she'd said, the statement vague enough to be forgotten.

"C'mon, c'mon," she'd coax the parking valet, slip him a twenty, and roar home in her Lexus. Fast and faster. She'd wanted to be in her quiet bed, by the weak light of a candle stub reliving Flint's heady love-making, a happy captive in his arms.

Now the walls were drenched with sun, altogether too cheerful for her mindset. Dana skipped over the embroidered heirloom mottoes her mother had adored. Two made sense. She read aloud the tiny one speckled with bluebells. "There are no reasons that explain love, but a thousand that explain marriage."

A few tears betrayed her efforts to dismiss Flint from her mind, from her life. She'd stopped trying to find reasons for loving Flint. And what did it matter? No reasons explained love. And she had a hand-worked piece to prove it.

She studied another very old motto she agreed with. Worked on frayed silk, stags and does eyed each other from the four corners. "In hunting and in love you begin when you like and end when you can."

Flint and she had begun when they liked, but her heart told her that they hadn't found the end, that despite her release and his let's-pretend attitude, he loved her.

The crunch of gravel brought her to the window again. Buster must have taken the ancient Silver Cloud Rolls Royce for its weekly exercise. Idly curious, Dana frowned. What was he doing parking? Buster's routine ended with steering the old girl to the huge garage for a shower. Instead, he braked at the porch and leaped out.

Before he could reach the passenger side, the door opened and a man stepped onto the gravel. A big man, a towering man, a man in black with sable hair.

Dana's heart skipped a beat, and then pounded furiously. He had come for her. "Oh, God, thank you. Flint. Lover."

As though he knew she hid behind the curtains, Flint looked up. No smile, no wave.

In shock, Dana watched as Leon the butler appeared and soon he and Buster were talking with Flint. A man's man, Flint was charming the family retainers. She could hear faint laughter as Flint and Leon entered the foyer.

At the sight of herself in the mirror, Dana blanched. She was no charmer. Out of control hair, blue baby dolls at three in the afternoon, eyes red from weeping.

In five minutes, she'd thrown on jeans and a tank top, twisted her hair into a pony tail, and rushed down the backstairs. She followed the voices, Flint's booming baritone that made her knees weak, her father's imperious tenor.

She crept up and peered through the crack between the double doors of the den. Was he here for more money? No, that was irrational. He could be arrested. For her? Or Lord, she prayed, make him say he came for me.

If her father had chosen the site of the confrontation, he'd chosen badly. The massive mahogany furniture covered in brown leather diminished her father. On the other hand, the den seemed designed to scale for Flint who overpowered the huge chairs and reading tables.

Shock piled on surprise piled on confusion. The meeting had no hint of confrontation. Genially, her father was chatting with Flint like an old friend.

"Heard you were hanging out in the bayous, my boy. You look like hell."

"This job's over?" Flint sprawled in the largest leather chair and stacked his hands behind his head.

"Merger complete, my little girl home safe and sound. Job well done." Madison poured sherry. "Simple and clean, that's why I like your work."

"Give me some action, Madison. Get me out of here. Africa, South America, Singapore." Flint emptied the dainty sherry glass. "Nothing civilized, like paper sabotage. Maybe a take-down in Brasilia. Or give me stuff on the high seas. What's that poem? A ship with a hard-assed crew and a star to steer her by? But no more snatch and grab, Boss. And no more women."

No *more* women? Dana's stomach churned. Jealousy and love

and hate boiled over. Was making love to her an assignment, part of a job? Dizzy and sick, she leaned into the carved mahogany.

With the uncanny sixth sense of a hunter, Flint whirled and jerked open the paired doors. He arched one eyebrow and greeted her in a coolly impersonal tone. "Want something, Miss Madison? I was just telling your father —"

Dana stormed in. "If I had to choose which of you was the most despicable, I'd call it a tie." She was panting with fury. "You had me kidnapped, Father, consigned your own daughter to this animal, this throwback to prehistoric times."

"Now Dana, dear." Her father took refuge behind his desk and showed her his palms. "It was for your own good, little girl, your own safety."

"My safety? You weren't around to see this Neanderthal manhandle me. And now he walks away from his crime unpunished."

Desperate, Madison searched for support. "See, Flint, this turmoil was the very thing I wanted to avoid. If I'd explained, and asked her to leave quietly, she would've exploded. The merger —"

Flint casually moved between her and her father, as if she'd physically attack her own dad!

"You're a savage, Flint," she began when the idea came. How would Flint enjoy having the tables turned, Flint the hostage instead of the captor?

A tiny wave of anticipation rippled in her belly. Flint hand-cuffed and begging for sex. But even more, she envisioned her smile when she imposed his rule of three times and you're out. Why, she could plan a dozen tricks.

Caught in the scent and heat of Flint's presence, Dana trembled. She called up reserves of stubbornness to maintain her taste for teaching him a lesson.

But he had all the weapons, and her defenses failed in the face of his compelling gaze. He depleted her will power, and her body forgave him in spite of her anger. Her legs weakened, her dewy sheath remembered and cried for his sweet invasion. It was madness to think she could battle to get even when her every cell prepared for penetration. She licked her lips, and drummed up a crumb of resistance.

"All this for a merger?" she whispered.

"A merger," Flint said. "You do know what a merger is, don't you, Miss Madison?" Dana fixed her stare on the curve of his lips. If only he would slant them over hers in a scalding kiss, she knew she would surrender in a kind of erotic trance.

How could she concentrate when he smelled of pine and the sea and the familiar randiness of the man who had bedded her? Damn, she raged inwardly. It wasn't fair. Flint wasn't fair to make her want him so, not when she should give him a dose of his own medicine.

Sheltered from her father's gaze by Flint's broad chest, she mouthed, "Are we over?" She slid two fingers up the sleeve of his jacket, read his thundering pulse, looked into his hungry eyes. Dana quivered with a crazy exaltation. He still wanted her.

"Dana," her father said angrily. "Go upstairs, or for a drive as far as you can get from this man. Buster will be taking him home shortly."

"Daddy?" She side-stepped, adopting a cool, civilized demeanor, restraining herself from leaping into Flint's dark embrace. "I think you're in no position to order me around when you hired this man to hold me hostage."

"Dana, please let's talk about this later. You'll make yourself ill. Little girl, excuse yourself and rest. Flint and I have business."

"Yes, Daddy," she answered so meekly her father should've heard alarm bells. To Flint she whispered, "I need to see you one last time. The Morton tomorrow night at ten."

Dana pulled the carved doors together. Then she grinned and ran upstairs to plan. The dinner, the decor, the wine, and if she could get it, a special ingredient to pacify the panther, and subdue his objections to her cage.

※⟨☾⟩※

Dana paced around the penthouse suite of the Morton, checked the bouquets of old cabbage roses with their muddled centers, red and pink white, autumn damasks dense with thick perfume. To fool Flint into thinking this meeting would be their last, she'd even scattered rose petals on the seafoam green silk sheets.

Like a nervous hostess, she inspected the table swagged in pink linen, the candles reflecting on crystal and silver. She glanced at her watch and, like Victorian ladies, felt an awful compulsion to wring her hands.

For the hundreth time, she paraded in front of the mirror.

The sapphire blue silk, carefully selected to match her eyes and show off her nipples, plunged in a daring vee between her breasts nearly to her navel. She wanted Flint to lust for her as she ached for him.

"Damn, what are Leon and Buster doing now?" She'd expected the chauffeur and butler to call her as soon as Flint came into the hotel. When her cell phone finally rang, her heart flew up into her mouth.

"Miz Madison," Leon mumbled. "He come in, set at the bar. Dint go to no elevators a'tall."

"What? Where is he? What the hell's going on?" Dana said.

"Hold on, Missy. Worked out real good."

Dana's stomach took the elevator Flint had ignored. "Oh?"

"Yeah, me and Buster bellied up to the bar, started yakking, even bought Flint a drink." He was choking on his cleverness.

Dana filled her lungs and tried to stay calm. "You've got to get up here with the stuff so I can doctor the drink. And how can I do it when you've got it in your pocket and he's on a barstool?" Her throat hurt in her effort to keep from screaming.

"Done it," Leon announced proudly. "Slipped it in his beer when he run to the men's room."

With a clenched fist, Dana silently raged at the fates in the form of her father's bizarre family retainers. Why had she trusted them to do anything complicated? "What did you give him?"

"You don't wanna know, and we don't wanna tell. Herb don't hurt none, Miss, just make him a little woozy, but he'll be able to talk and walk and do what you tell him. Lasts about eight hours. You need him down for longer, you shoulda told us."

Dana grimaced. "Listen carefully, Leon. Walk away. That's right, let him get up here *now* before he goes down in public. And follow him, but don't let him notice you."

The few minutes dragged like the hands on a bad clock, and she jumped at the knock. As she opened the door, the space between them pulsed with excitement. The air was charged with electricity.

The man she loved wore his usual black, and had clubbed his midnight hair with a leather thong. Wickedly handsome, stern and powerful, he was the man she loved.

"Flint, Flint." Dana breathed his name and threw her arms around him. "Lover."

He turned so her kiss was wasted on his jaw. Flint gripped her wrists, brought her arms down, and kicked the door shut. "Dana, we've got to talk. Madison said the estate is off-limits, or he'll turn me in. You forget me, and everything that happened. He's right. To sweeten the pot, he's assigned me to jobs that I can't discuss with you or anybody else." His tone was honed and cutting as a samurai sword.

"He told me to forget you, never to see you again. Whether he sends you to the North Pole, whether he lays down the law, I don't care. Darling, I wanted to see you one last time. Please, Flint." She waved at the little table, the intimate setting for a romantic supper, a bittersweet final meeting.

Dark and rugged as a basalt statue on pink velvet, he paused for a second. Then he exhaled a long-held breath and pulled out her chair.

Flint's lips twitched as he uncovered the salvers. "Corned beef hash, cactus salad, oysters and a steak. A trip down memory lane plus eats to give a man staying power." He reached across the table and held her hand.

Dana captured his hand and pressed her lips to his fingers, the fingers that had known her so intimately. "I love you, Flint."

He rescued his hand and picked up the wine goblet. "Don't say that." Quickly, he scanned the room. "This was a mistake, only makes it harder for both of us, Dana."

"Ah, that's what I wanted to hear, that it's hard for you, too." Dana came around the table with her arms open, but Flint was too fast. He rose and put up one hand, as if to shield himself from her love.

"Don't touch me, don't try to kiss me. This is over. Now. It was over when I completed the transfer." His eyes were dark gray, the color of a storm.

"The transfer? You completed the transfer? Like you signed a lading bill for used cargo?" Dana heard the sorrow, the tears in her voice, gradually waking her resolve to make him pay.

"It's more than that, and you know it. This is dangerous for you, for me. Tonight in the bar —" Flint frowned and shook his head as if to clear it "— a couple of weird characters were hanging around." He rubbed his eyes, reached for the chairback and swayed. "They must've slipped something in my drink."

"Are you feeling all right?" Dana was scared, trembling as she led him to the bed. Quietly, he lay back on the pillows and rose petals. "Is there something wrong?"

"Something wrong," he said. He clung to her hand.

"Don't get up, darling. Stay here."

"Stay here," he repeated.

Dana thumbed the cell phone. "Leon. Back service elevator. Take him down like he's a drunk buddy."

It took less time than she'd planned, changing clothes, whisking Flint away, stuffing him in the van onto the mattress next to the supplies.

"Thanks. You're too smooth, guys," Dana said, thrusting the bills into their hands.

"Slick as grease on concrete," Buster said with a wink. "Now you drive safe, Missy."

Chapter Eight

When she'd driven twenty miles, compulsively eyeing the rear-view mirror, she started to breathe regularly. No flashing red lights had appeared, no sirens, no state troopers or F.B.I. to haul Dana Madison off to jail for kidnapping. Or at the very least, for plotting revenge.

Revenge. An awful ache beat in her heart, and she knew she was lying, and confused. She had to have justice, and she'd find it in subjecting Flint to the iron control he'd once wielded over her. Yet she had to have *him*, his lovemaking, his hot masculine determination to pleasure her, to bring her to completion. She missed his erotic skills, missed even more his strength and his sense of humor that glimmered at the most unexpected moments.

"Just this one last time, Flint." A renegade tear crept down her cheek. "Darling, one last time." In the dark, she followed the van's frosty headlights. "Then if I can't make you love me enough to stay, to stand up to my father, I'll let you go. Did you know you're the only man I love, the only one I've *ever* loved?"

She slammed on the brakes for a stubborn armadillo, and the sharp stop took her mind off Flint. A puzzle had niggled at her for the last couple of hours. Something she'd heard or seen out of place, not right. Something about Buster and Leon and Flint.

She rolled the prickly mystery around as she zipped down the highway toward the desert cabin, then shrugged it off. Every few minutes, she glanced back where Flint sprawled, open and utterly vulnerable.

Overwhelmed with memories, Dana first tried to separate them into two categories: delicious, wild sex with Flint, and the tenderness, the softness that spoke of love. But the divisions mingled just as the days and nights of isolation had blended into a seamless union, just as hot battles of dominance blazed and left a residue of glowing coals that could burst into flame at the least puff of desert air.

Dana mulled over their short past, how the chemistry had worked between them in the rough cabin. First, the powerful physical attraction that had drawn them together, later the growing intimacy, his comforting her in his arms, her weeping over his wounds. And then a tangle of caring and sexual thrills impossible to unravel.

Dana remembered the years when she was still waiting for the right man, for a man who donated to the fund for retired polo ponies and knew how to choose the proper wine, how to impress the maitre'd.

Oh, she'd met the men who did all the right things, carried the right name, suave and sophisticated. Dana had even imagined being in love twice. But neither eligible bachelor, no matter how hard he tried, generated the heat and desire Flint ignited with a single touch, a single scorching look.

Somewhere she'd read that the act of sex allowed communion, not abstract and pie-in-the-sky, but a real melding in the flesh. And she wanted now, more than anything, to have that union again with the man who made her feel satisfied and safe and complete.

She peered at him, the sleeping giant comfortably stretched out, muscular legs parted, exposing the meaty bulge in his crotch. His rugged face was relaxed in dreams, and she smiled, hoping the dreams were of her.

Far into the desert, she pulled to a roadside rest area and took a carton of milk from the cooler. When she knelt beside him and smoothed his hair, Flint stirred, propped himself up, and buried his face between her breasts.

"Thirsty, darling?"

"Thirsty." He fastened on her nipple and suctioned it until she gasped at the sweet pain. His teeth tugged, and shock waves of desire spread to her flowing cleft. A mere pulsebeat from urging him to take her, she pulled away from his seeking lips.

"No, no. Here." She slid the straw into his mouth. While he drank and Dana supported his head, foreboding shivered down her spine. What was romantic about Flint toying with her breasts when he didn't even know what he was doing?

She tossed the empty carton aside, and lowered him to his bed. "Sleep, lover."

"Lover," he repeated, like a warm robot.

Ashamed of herself, Dana said, "I love you."

"Love you," he muttered.

She clambered behind the wheel, and the few hours to the cabin were the longest in her life. When at last she set the brake, she hesitated before cutting the engine. Was she making a mistake, rendering Flint unconscious, giving him commands, putting him on automatic pilot? She palmed the thick leathery head of the stick shift and flashed immediately on Flint's heavy maleness. In her hands, in her mouth, down her throat.

Squirming, Dana had to whip up her resolution to force him to beg the way she'd begged for relief. In his docile state, Flint would be a pussycat, not the panther she knew and loved. Dana dragged open the sliding door, thumbed on the flashlight and led Flint to the porch through the cabin to the backroom. She propped him against the doorjamb and flapped the coverlet. A wee breeze, ripe with sagebrush, freshened the night and extended a welcome.

"Rest for a while, darling." She let him stretch out on the bed while she lit a candle.

"Darling," he murmured. In the glow of the flame, Flint smiled. Dana caressed his cheek with the back of her fingers, and had to tear herself away to bring in the supplies and food.

The newly pliable Flint was allowed up for a snack. And Dana slipped into the bedroom with a bag of surprises for the big man. She torched logs in the fireplace, not trusting Flint to do it in his drugged condition.

Meanwhile, the object of her obsession munched and drank and smiled. Beneath the heavy wings of his brows, his dark eyes studied her as if he'd forgotten her and waged a war to retrieve their secret passion.

"Darling," he said without prompting.

Uneasily,Dana brushed a stray curl off her face, checked her watch and grimaced. Buster had said the drug's life span was eight hours. Driving here had eaten up four. And now Flint was initiating comments instead of echoes.

Dana hurried, biting her lower lip. After all, it wasn't forever. Just a few hours to show Flint the cost of his playing the heavy, of forcing her to his will. Rapidly, she cleared the table while Flint stared into his glass.

"Well, now, lover." Dana leaned over the back of her chair. "Let's go to bed."

"Bed," Flint agreed. When he rose, he staggered slightly and draped one arm over her shoulder. In the dim light, she peered at his face. Was it her imagination, or had his weird complacency been replaced by the hint of a sparkle? The second before she turned him loose to fall onto the bed, she was almost sure she detected a slight squeeze on her upper arm.

❧⊶(✺)⊷❧

The pale moon shone in the window. Two candles threw light and shadows. Beneath his lashes, Flint enjoyed the sight of Dana skinning out of her shorts. Slowly, she unpinned the gold silk of her hair, a sweet act that raised her breasts. Wearing her pink tank-top and her black bikini panties, she straddled his hips. "Flint, should I make love to you? No or yes?"

"Yes," he mimicked.

"I could be mean to you, coax you to tear everything off and put you in strange positions. But I won't," she whispered hoarsely, "because I love you."

Flint kept his gaze blank, and ineptly poked her nipples as if they were a novelty. The buds were rigid, the size of large pearls, and he bit back his desire to pinch them between thumb and finger until she moaned.

"Do you like them?" Dana pressed his hands into her swollen breasts, and moved slightly on his groin. "Oh, lover, my nipples are so hard."

Flint sneaked a quick glance at Dana arching backwards in delight. Behind tightly closed lips, he gritted his teeth, and held the pressure on her breasts steady.

"I think *you're* getting hard, lover." Dana rocked forward, put his hands over his head, and kissed him. She nibbled his earlobe, and trailed her fingernails down his black turtleneck, past his belt, to the bulge straining his slacks. "What have we here?" She massaged him and he heard the tremor in her voice. "I like this. I want to see it. But first—" she stretched and snapped handcuffs on his left wrist.

Flint raced to make a decision, fast. Let her cuff him and have her fun, or tell her he hadn't been drugged, and end the game. But why spoil a good thing? Dana had to do all the work.

He held his breath, simulated relaxation and played along, suspecting he'd hate himself for giving up control, and encouraging her need for dominance. Hell, he'd save hating himself until the morning. When he got back to Leon and Buster, he'd kick butt for buying into this crazy scenario. Dana, he noticed, had been so busy immobilizing him, she'd forgotten to take off his clothes. He suppressed a grin.

"Oh, oh. I forgot something. Your shoes." She laughed and dropped them on the floor, and cuffed his ankles. Flint expelled his breath as she found her favorite spot on his zipper and wriggled.

Dana tilted her head and touched her lips with one finger. "It's so puzzling. Why do people have sex naked?"

"Naked," Flint repeated, putting real effort into his act and inwardly admitting he'd better not give up his day job.

"Do you know the answer, darling?" She stroked his zipper and Flint did multiplication tables. "Let's have sex with our clothes on. Ready?"

"Ready," he croaked.

Through his fine cotton sweater, Dana licked his nipple, sucked it, and took the tiny nub between her teeth. He swallowed a groan as his sensitive flesh felt each thread. Dana slid lower, working his nipples with her nails, and probing his navel with her tongue.

A devil peeped out of her blue eyes. She sighed and knelt between his knees. In a sad little voice, she said "I'd love to rip this shirt and play in your black hair. But dearest, should I keep the action above your waist, or" she palmed his erection "—do it?"

"Do it," Flint echoed.

She caressed his swollen genitals, and rubbed him through his trousers. "No," she declared. "Down here, I absolutely must feel the naked man. See it all. Should I get the candle?" She chuckled wickedly.

Dana tossed back her blond mane, and eyed him as she fondled herself. Then she slid the black leather through his belt buckle and undid the button. Carefully, she pulled his zipper, opened his shorts and with gentle hands lifted him from the protection of his boxers.

Flint strained to fight off the intense urge to beg her to mount him, to give him relief. He was sweating. Dana tickled his balls, explored them with her tongue, and tasted the tiny bead of lubricant on the head of his cock. She was squirming with need, but by-passed her body's demands at the cost of keeping him powerless. She licked him from root to tip, engulfed him in her warm mouth, and bobbed her head rhythmically.

Under his mask of composure, Flint was seething, in prime shape to explode. He jerked his hips and bucked up into her mouth.

"Damn it, woman, uncuff me," he roared, glaring down the length of his torso to where she crouched, driving him mad. His come boiled, and his need to sheath himself in her was torture.

Suddenly she stopped and looked up, feigning bewilderment. "Of course." She slapped her thigh. "Now I remember what's missing. What was it you said when you teased me? *I want to watch you come, and I want you to watch me watching you.* Where's that candle?"

Her laughter died on her lips, her seductive golden lashes slowly lifted, and Flint burned when he saw in her eyes a depth of desire matching his. Tenaciously, she returned to mouthing him, determined to humiliate him at the expense of her own sexual satisfaction.

Flint thrashed his head under the delicious titillation, and then fell still as a statue. He began with breathing exercises, the reduction of pulse rate, the gradual elimination of the stress Dana had cooked up. Thanks to the teachings of Master Wu Chin, he threw a mental shield over his genitals, numbing them to Dana's busy tongue. "Flint? Flint? Why are you so quiet." She gasped and released his wet cock. "My God, they poisoned you! I knew it." "Help," he said faintly. A sheen of sweat covered him. "Oh, my darling. Wait." She fumbled for the cuff key, alarmed and almost weeping in her anxiety. Flint pondered his original decision. Was this acting or was this acting? Maybe he *should* give up his day job.

When he was free, and lying with one arm over his eyes, Dana insisted on bringing water and making him lean on her while he drank. She kissed his cheeks, held his hands, and confessed to a hundred sins against him. He frowned and couldn't remember a damned one.

"I have to get up now," he said in his usual stony way. Dana squeaked and hopped out of bed quick as a cricket, her eyes wide, her mouth open in shock. Flint grinned evilly. Then he started to strip, his jacket, the turtleneck. By the time he thrust his thumbs under the waistband of his slacks, Dana was running for the door.

"You'd better run for it, lady," he shouted. He tore off his boxers and sprinted after her. He caught her in front of the fireplace. Flint slanted his mouth over hers in a long, deep, wet kiss, and her knees weakened. Without breaking the kiss, Flint lowered them to the bearskin rug.

In the firelight, he caught her wrists and pulled her hands over her head, and sucked her nipples through the pink top until she arched. "Strip me, lover," she spoke with great effort and her eyes were glazed with want.

Flint ripped the thin top off, and caressed her breasts until she moved restlessly. "I want you, Flint." He took his time, sliding his strong, blunt fingers beneath the black lace panties. The hot dampness surrounded by a nest of curls warmed his fingers and he worked them in and out of her slipperiness.

Flint gazed at her, from her wild mane of golden hair to eyes half-closed in lust to her perfect white breasts, to the honeyed delta he needed to sip from. "Dana, I'm going to mount you. Stay inside you all night, ride you till you forget any man you've ever had."

She shuddered and eased his access to her sleek treasure. Flint, on the edge of losing control, tongued her through the lace, tasting her salt, her sweet, feeling her fleece while she uttered a low purr of readiness.

"Take me, Flint," she moaned and raised her hips so he could pull down her panties. Then she lay before him, a lithe blond cat, stretching, luxuriating in the warm light on the furry rug. "Come inside me, please. I'm so hungry for you."

Settling between her legs, he pushed, filling her with one smooth stroke through the melting liquid velvet, and he groaned at the perfect fit of his rigid cock in her cleft. She wrapped her legs around his waist, and he rocked, slick, thrusting flesh urgently building spirals of higher and higher tension, to a mutual explosion.

Flint, still hard inside her, rested his head on her breast, and listened to her heart beating while he thumbed one nipple, and then reached down to their connection and stroked her clit.

She cried out and came and came again, squeezing his cock until he began pistoning in her, and she'd climax again, a sweet circle of cause and effect.

In the breaking dawn, at the final spurt of his juices, Flint shouted, "I love you, Dana. I'll love you forever."

After their spasms had subsided, Dana laced her arms around his neck, and sighed into his ear. "I loved you from the first time I met you, lover."

"Not a contest, woman," he said with a drowsy chuckle. "Go to sleep."

"You have to answer a question first."

"Give it to me," he groaned and rolled onto his back.

Dana snuggled under his arm. "You were drugged tonight. Yes. I'm guilty. Orders from me to the family's Buster and Leon. What do you think they slipped in your drink at the Morton?"

"Nothing. They're my buddies." He closed his eyes and cuddled her.

"What?" She propped herself on one elbow.

"Mercenaries in a private army together. They were already old then and I was just a punk kid. When we fell out of work, your father hired us to do a little spying. The old guys finally retired to being houseman and chauffeur. Now will you go to sleep?"

She lay touching his muscled length with her whole body. "Don't worry about Daddy. He's grouchy, but it's all an act. He'll probably make you head of security." She pulled a curl on his chest. "Look at me when I talk to you, Flint."

He opened one eye. "I'm looking. Now you look. Know what this means?" He raised three fingers.

About the author:

Sandy Fraser lived in Southern California, but recently passed away. Published in book-length women's fiction, she loved the opportunity to push the sensuality envelope and to tell the forbidden in **Secrets**.

Love's Prisoner

~❧❀❧~

by MaryJanice Davidson

To my reader:

I've always been intrigued by good guys who have to do bad, and werewolves are prime examples of that. It's tough to be a sensitive, 21st century guy when you turn furry, howl at the moon, and crave raw meat once a month. It's even worse if you're in love with someone who not only thinks you're delusional, but at times actively despises you. Stick two people like this in an elevator, add one power outage, and watch the sparks fly…

I hope you'll email me or visit my website to tell me what you thought about *Love's Prisoner*. I love to hear from my readers, and I like getting suggestions on what you think I should write next.

Chapter One

Engrossed as she was in *Glamour's* Do's and Don'ts, Jeannie Lawrence scarcely noticed when the elevator jolted to an abrupt halt. She *did* notice when the lights went out.

"Oh, come on!" she cried, slapping her magazine shut. Getting stuck in an elevator during a power outage was nowhere on her to-do list. Today, anyway.

"Not now," a voice muttered, and she nearly shrieked. She hadn't known anyone else was in the elevator with her. When she had her nose in a book or magazine, she wouldn't have noticed if Barney the Dinosaur was in the elevator with her.

"Well, this is a fine fix, huh?" she asked the voice. "Of all the days to drop my ad copy off early! I guess it's true—no good deed goes unpunished. What are you going to be late for? Me, I'm trying to beat the rush hour traffic to the bridge. I can't stand it when—"

"Hush."

The voice was a pleasant baritone, one she liked despite its abruptness. She hushed, not offended. Some people didn't like talking to strangers. Or maybe this guy was claustrophobic. Or—what was fear of the dark? Darkophobic? Whatever it was, he was clearly unhappy to be trapped in an elevator for who knew how long. Poor guy. She hoped he didn't get the screaming meemies. There was nothing worse than a grown man having hysterics.

"Sorry," she said, then added, "I'm sure we won't be here long."

She heard a sound and recognized it immediately: the man trapped with her had taken a couple steps back. Almost as if he was trying to put as much space between them as he could.

Exasperated, she said, "For crying out loud! I don't have cooties.

Anymore," she added, hoping to lighten the mood.

"Be quiet. And step into the far corner. Now."

"The hell I will!" She turned toward the voice. "Look, just be-cause you're feeling antisocial doesn't mean I—"

"*Don't*." No pleasant baritone that time. That one sounded like a growl, like he'd forced the word out through gritted teeth. "Don't come near me. Keep away. When you move, you stir around the air currents and I get more of your scent."

"And that's *bad*, right?" Great, she thought with grim humor. Trapped with someone who skipped his medication this morning. Why didn't I take the stairs?

"No. It's not bad." His voice, low in the dark, was a throbbing baritone she could feel along her spine. "It's... extraordinary."

"Gosh, thanks." Uh-huh. Clearly a nutcake, sexy voice or no. She hadn't had time to put perfume on after her shower. He couldn't smell a damn thing, except maybe a lingering whiff of Dial soap. "Do you have a special doctor you tell these things to? Someone you should call when we get out of here?"

He barked laughter. "I'm not insane. I'm not surprised that's the conclusion you've drawn, though. What is your name?"

"Jane Doe."

He chuckled softly. "What harm could it do to tell me your real name?"

"All right, but only if you promise not to freak out on me. More than you already have, I mean. It's Jeannie Lawrence." There were a million Lawrences in the greater St. Paul area, she comforted herself, so if he was a serial killer he likely couldn't track her down when this was over. "Now remember, you promised..."

"Actually, I didn't. Not that promising would have done any good." He sighed, a lost sound in the dark. Absurdly, she felt sorry for him, this perfect crazy stranger who talked so oddly and in the sexiest voice she had ever heard. "You smell wonderful."

"Don't get started on that again," she warned.

"The moon's coming. I can feel her." She heard him swallow hard. "There isn't much time."

"Boy, have you got *that* right." She put her arms out in front of her, feeling in the dark, then stepped forward and banged on the elevator door. "Hello!" she shouted. "Anybody up there? A nice girl and a raving lunatic are trapped in here!"

"You're ovulating," he said directly in her ear, and she shrieked and flung herself away from him, so hard that she bounced off the far wall and would have fallen had he not caught her. Even in her startlement, she was conscious of the easy strength of his hand, in his scent, a crisp, clean, utterly masculine smell that she liked very much, despite her sudden fear.

"You—" Her mouth was dry; she swallowed to force moisture and finished her rant. "You scared the hell out of me! *Don't* sneak up on me like that, for the love of—and you can let go of me, too." She yanked her arm out of his grip, her heart yammering so loudly she felt certain he could hear it. And what was that absurd thing he had said? Had he really said—

"It's too late. You're ovulating," he said, his voice a low rumble in the dark. "You're...in heat, to put it a little more crudely. And I'm too close to my change."

"Then empty your pockets," she said rudely. "Let your change out."

"You don't want me to do that," he said softly. "Oh, no."

She supposed some women would be reduced to panic at this turn of events, but this weirdo with the sexy voice and strong hands had no idea who he was dealing with. She had a black belt in karate, could drill a dime at fifty yards, and had once put a would-be mugger in the hospital with cracked ribs. If this guy tried anything with her, he was going to have a very bad day.

"Look, I'm sorry you're feeling... uh... unwell, but if you just stay calm, they'll have us out of here in no ti—"

With that same shocking suddenness, his hand was behind her neck, tilting her face up, and she could feel his mouth near her temple, heard him inhale deeply. "You're in heat," he murmured in her ear, "and the moon's coming up." He inhaled again, greedily. Frozen by his actions, she waited for his next words. "I'm very sorry."

Then his mouth was on hers. Pressed against the far wall of the elevator, she could feel his long, hard length against her body, could feel his hands on her, could hear his rasping breath. She had the absurd sense he was wallowing in her scent, glorying in it. And she came absurdly close to relaxing in his embrace, to kissing him back. Instead, moving independently of her brain, her hands struggled up and pressed against his chest, hard, but it was like trying to move a tree.

"Oh, Christ," he groaned into her hair.

"Don't—"

"I'm sorry."

"—stop it—"

"I'm very sorry."

"—before I break your—"

"Do you believe in werewolves?"

"—big stupid—what?"

"I'm a werewolf. And my change is very near. Otherwise I might be able to—but the moon's too close. And so are you."

"*What* are you talking about?" she cried.

"I'm trying to explain. Why this is going to... why this must happen. Don't be afraid."

"I'm *not* afraid," she hissed, shoving at his chest again. This time, it worked. Or he stepped back.

"You're a liar." Odd, how he could make that sound like an endearment. "I can smell your fear."

"I'm not sure how to break this to you," she said through gritted teeth, "but I'm not afraid of any man. And I *don't smell*."

"Not afraid. Anxious, then," he soothed. "I don't blame you a bit. If *I* was trapped in a box a hundred feet off the ground with a werewolf an hour from his change, I'd be out of my mind."

"About the werewolf fixation," she said, striving for a note of humor—she'd always had a perverse need to make light of any seriousness. "I confess this concerns me a bit. Perhaps there's a support group that can help. Men-who-love-werewolves-and-the-women-trapped-in-elevators-with-them."

He laughed, a throaty chuckle.

"Couldn't you have waited another hour to have your nervous breakdown?" she complained, pleased that she amused him. If she could keep him distracted, off balance, maybe the power would come back on and she could—

Then she felt his hands on her arms, gently pulling her forward. "I am sorry," he said, his voice heavy with regret. Again, she caught his pleasant, utterly masculine scent, and again she fought her unwitting attraction. Jeannie didn't plan to let him do anything he'd be sorry for. She took a deep breath and prepared to strike him, palm out, with all her strength. A crippling blow, and, if she nailed him on the bridge of the nose, a killing blow. She hoped she would get him in the forehead or cheek. She didn't want to kill the lunatic. That was her thought as she smashed her hand into his chin and felt him rock backward with the blow.

"Ouch," he said mildly.

She felt her mouth pop open in stunned surprise. She hit him, she *knew* she hit him! Her hand was numb from the force of it. He should be unconscious, or at least groaning on the floor.

"That was some punch," he continued, as if commenting on a drink and not a blow it had taken her four months to learn. "You've had training."

"You're out of your mind," she whispered. Or she was. Could it be true? Was he a—ludicrous thought—werewolf? She felt for him in the dark, sure he had to be bleeding, and her fingers encountered his smooth cheek. She jerked her hand away. "You're completely crazy, you know that?"

"No." She sensed him step close to her and threw another punch, no more fooling around—and her fist smacked into his open palm.

He had blocked her punch. In itself, almost impossible unless he was also a black belt. And what were the chances of being trapped in an elevator in the Wyndham Tower with a crazy man who was also a black belt? More worrisome, he had *seen her strike coming*. Whereas she couldn't see her hand in front of her face.

She felt his fingers curl around her small fist, felt his thumb caress the knuckle of her first finger. Her knees wanted to buckle, either from sudden, swamping fear or the sensation his warm fingers were calling forth. "Brave Jeannie Lawrence," he murmured, his voice so low it sounded like tearing velvet. "What a pity you didn't wait for the next elevator."

Then he deftly swept her legs out from under her and she was falling—but he was coming down with her and cushioned her fall and was on top of her in an instant, his mouth on her throat, his hands busy at her blouse. She shrieked in anger and dismay, raining blows on his shoulders, his chest, his face, and he took them all without being deterred from his task. She heard a rending tear as he ripped her blouse away, tugged at her bra... then felt the shock of it to her toes as his warm mouth closed over her nipple.

She tried to lunge away from him but he pinned her easily with one hand on her shoulders, while the other tore at her clothes. "I'm sorry," he was groaning against her breast, "don't be afraid, I won't hurt you... ah, God, your scent is driving me *out of my mind*." That last ended on a growl, an ominous rumble that filled the dark elevator.

She drew in a breath to scream the building down—and sobbed instead. He was too strong for her, she was punching him and clawing him and kicking at him and he was barely noticing. This... thing he meant to do, it was really going to happen. To her. Daughter of a cop and a Special Forces veteran, a man and woman generous with their teaching, who never wanted their daughter to be a rape or murder statistic. Jeannie could pick a lock and knock out most men with one punch. But she couldn't stop this man from taking her by force. Never mind the fact that her mind kept shrieking that this wasn't happening to her, this was not, was not, was *not*. It was.

"Don't cry," he begged, and she could feel his hands shaking as he gathered her against him. "We'll be done soon. It won't hurt. I'm so sorry to scare you."

"Please don't," she whispered, hating the way she sounded—so helpless, so frightened—but unable to do anything about it. "Please don't do this."

He groaned again and squeezed her in a rough hug. "I have to. I'm not mated, I don't have any control over this, just like later I won't have any control over—but you don't believe me, so we won't talk about that." His voice was still soothing, and now his hands were beneath her, stroking her back, forcing her chest up, and his mouth was buried in her throat, kissing and licking and even—very gently—biting.

She could hear his breathing roughen in the dark, heard another rip as her skirt was torn. She remembered herself and struck out at him again, blindly, connecting hard but with no apparent effect. He shredded her linen skirt like it was paper...Christ, he was strong! But his hands on her bare flesh were gentle, almost languid. They were everywhere, stroking her skin, sliding across her limbs, and she felt her nipples harden so much it was almost painful. When his lips brushed across one she almost wept with relief, even as she was pushing against his shoulders with all her strength. He rubbed his cheek against that same nipple, his stubble rasping across the sensitive bud, and her fingers curled into fists so she wouldn't touch him with tenderness. She couldn't give in to him, no matter how—

Stubble?

He had been clean shaven two minutes ago.

She shoved that thought away, hard. His rough tongue swept across her nipples, a blessed distraction that made her want to scream, made her want him, and she hated wanting him. She tried to remind herself that this man was raping her, but the only thing she could really understand was that he was making her feel as no one had ever made her feel. She was no stranger to sex, but the only man she had ever been intimate with was her college boyfriend, and that was almost three years ago.

In the back of her mind, a constant refrain: this isn't happening. It's not real. Ten minutes ago I was on my way home; now I'm having sex in the dark with a stranger. Thus, this is a dream. It can't be happening, *ergo* it's not happening. Tempting to believe that voice, to give in to the pleasure he could so skillfully offer her, to...

She realized she hadn't hit him in quite a few seconds. That she no longer wanted him to stop. That traitorous thought alone galvanized her into raining more blows on his head, until he caught her wrists and pinned them above her head with one hand.

"Enough," he said hoarsely, and she cringed, wondering if he was going to hit her back. "I don't blame you one bit, but... enough, Jeannie."

He pinned her knees apart with his own, kept her hands out of his way by keeping them above her head, and bent to kiss her. He jerked back and her teeth snapped together, bare centimeters from his mouth. He could apparently see in the dark like a cat.

Or a wolf.

She put the ridiculous thought out of her mind as quickly as she could. That way lies madness. That way lies...

His thumb was stroking the soft cotton of her panties. And moving lower. Her breasts were pressed against his chest, her knees were flat against the carpet, forcing her thighs wide apart, and now his damned fingers were—were—inside her panties. His breathing was so harsh in the dark, almost panting, and she could feel his body thrumming with tension, could hear his teeth grinding together as he fought—what? It was clear he was in the grip of urgent lust, that he wanted to surge inside her and thrust until he could no longer move, but something was holding him back. And now his fingers were delicately brushing the plump lips between her thighs, stroking so sweetly and tenderly... and then his thumb slipped between her nether lips while his tongue thrust past her teeth and she nearly shrieked, so intense was her pleasure.

He groaned into her mouth and then his fingers were spreading her plump folds apart and his thumb was slipping inside her and his tongue was licking, darting, and she sobbed with frustration and strained against him. His fingers danced across her slick flesh, sweetly stroking, probing, oh so gently rubbing a circle around her throbbing clit, a circle that got smaller and smaller... and then his thumb was dipping inside her again while his fingernail flicked past her clitoris, and she shivered so hard she nearly bucked him off.

He growled. The sound did not frighten her. It kindled her blood, made her want to growl back, made her want to sink her teeth into his flesh while his flesh sank into her again... and again... and again...

She realized dimly that he wasn't growling, he was saying her name, but his voice was so thick and deep she could hardly understand him. "Jeannie—let your—hands go?"

"Yes!" she screamed, wild to touch him, to feel his flesh against hers, to rip off his clothes as he had ripped hers. He released her wrists and in a flash her arms were around him, pressing him closer, she was tearing at his shirt, frantic to get the damned cloth off him and he was helping her and now her clothes weren't the only ones in shredded ruin, after all, what was sauce for the goose was sauce for the werewolf, and—

His hands were beneath her buttocks, raising her to him, and she could feel that long, hard, hot part of him nudging for entrance. For an instant, reason reclaimed her. Was she really going to do this? This crazy thing? She had no protection and without it, in this day and age, she was taking her life in her hands. And why was she cooperating in her own rape, for the love of God?

"Wait—" she said in a thin, high voice, but he drove forward, thrust into her with power and searing heat and her good sense left her; she threw back her head and screamed until she thought her throat would burst, screamed at him to never *never* stop and still he came, that hot hard length parting her, filling her, and it should have hurt, it should have, he was very large and she hadn't known a lover in years, but her need for him was as great as his for her, and instead of hurting, she needed more.

When he was seated completely within her, somehow, somehow, he made himself stop; he gathered her against him and she could hear the furious hammering of his heart. His hands behind her back were hard fists and he was shaking as though he had a fever, and still he stopped. When he forced the words out she could barely understand him.

"—doesn't—hurt?"

"No," she gasped, wriggling against him, his throbbing cock within her making her frantic. "No no no please, please you can't stop now you can't you can't you—"

"You're—very small—sure—doesn't hurt?"

"—you can't you can't please I please don't make me—"

"Don't—be afraid—tell truth." He took a deep, shuddering breath; his fists were still clenching beneath her and, very distantly, she heard carpet tearing. "Can try—wait—if you—"

"—beg, don't make me beg, please please please PLEASE!"

He pulled away but before she had time to groan her disappointment he slammed forward. His mouth covered hers, his tongue mating with hers as he took her again and again, as they made love so fiercely the elevator shook. And above it all, beyond it all, she could hear someone screaming with hoarse joy and dimly realized it was she making the noise.

Her orgasm slammed into her as he was, spasms so fierce she could actually feel her uterus contracting. He stiffened at the height of her climax, threw his head back, and roared at the ceiling in pure animal triumph.

For long moments, she didn't think she would ever be able to move. She could smell the scent of their lovemaking, could hear his heavy breathing, hear her own. Her pulse thudded in her ears and she was damp with sweat and... other things.

He pulled back and out, his hands frantically feeling her limbs, her neck. "Are you hurt?" he asked hoarsely. "Did I hurt you?"

"No," she said tiredly, ready to sleep for a week. A year. "No, it was a surprisingly painless rape."

She felt him flinch, and wondered who she thought she was fooling. It might have been rape for the first minute, but after that she had been an eager participant. Shame made her flush.

"Jeannie—I'm so very sorry. I don't expect you to understand." She felt his hand on her arm and cringed back, hating herself, hating him, and most of all, hating the fact that she wanted to do it all over again, right now. Right here. "I'm sorry," he said again, quietly. "My poor Jeannie. You were so brave."

"Don't call me that," she snapped. She tried to pull her shredded blouse together, but might as well have tried dressing with confetti. "Don't call me anything. Don't talk to me at all."

"We need to get you out of here," he said urgently, completely ignoring her order. "And quickly. The moon's almost up."

"Do *not* start that again," she ground out.

"Out," he was muttering, "Need to get you out. Not safe here."

"Brother, have you got *that* right." She started to stand and nearly pitched forward; she would have thought her eyes would have adjusted to the dark by now, but she was still effectively blind. And exhausted. And—how was this for the stupidest thing ever—she wanted him to put his arms around her and promise everything would be all right.

What if she was stuck in here with him all night? What if he decided to take her again? Could she fight him off? Did she want to?

She heard him stand, heard him bang experimentally on the elevator roof, then heard the groan of metal as he somehow forced the locked hatch. She shook her head at the sound, amazed at his strength. He could have broken my neck, she thought dumbly. Anytime he wanted.

"Why the *hell* didn't you do that twenty minutes ago?"

He gripped her waist and lifted her up, up... and through the small trapdoor. "I had other things on my mind," he replied shortly. "Like how badly I needed to touch you."

"Bastard."

"Yes," he said quietly. "But now I can think again. For a while."

"Don't flatter yourself," she mumbled, cautiously getting to her knees on top of the elevator. She heard him chuckle beneath her and then abruptly, shockingly, he was crouching beside her on the roof. Off the floor and through the trap door in one bound, apparently. It was almost enough to make her wonder...

But that was ridiculous. This was the 21st century, and there were no such things as werewolves, dammit!

"Why have we left the relative safety of the elevator, to teeter out here on top of the elevator, you nutcake?" she asked with saccharine sweetness.

"I'm definitely planning on falling in love with you," he said casually, in a tone he might have used to ask her to close the window. "Any woman in mortal danger who can tease her assailant after being terrified is definitely worth taking to mate. Just so you know."

"Save it for your parole hearing, pal," she said. Before she could elaborate on what the judicial system would do to him with her blessing, she heard their death warrant: the elevator cables groaning from stress. She belatedly realized she was in danger of more than forced sex this evening. "Oh, God," she said, abruptly terrified. Had she thought she was scared when Tall, Dark, and Horny had taken her against her will? She hadn't known what scared was. "Oh, God—what should we do?"

"Live," he said simply and, absurdly, she took comfort in that. She had to, because never was the dark more terrifying. She could hear his rapid movements, hear twangs as parts of the cable give way under the stress, hear the elevator doors two feet above her creaking as they were forced open.

"Be careful!" she said sharply.

"Always," he said, and suddenly his hands were on her again, and she felt herself effortlessly boosted and shoved. She reached out and clutched wildly, and felt the carpet in front of her. The building was as dark as the elevator had been, but she could tell he had held her up, almost over his head (no one is that strong) and boosted her through the elevator doors. In the pure dark, she could sense no one else around, which was just as well, given the shredded ruin of her clothes. Now his hands were on her heels, and he shoved, hard. She zipped across the carpet as if it was wet tile, her entire front going warm from the friction (he's not crazy, he really is a werewolf).

She turned around and crawled back toward the open doors, groping for the drop-off. "Come out!" she cried in the dark, hearing the sharp twang of more cable parting. "Jump out! Quick! You can do it, weirdo!"

"Stay back from the doors!" he said sharply. "You can't see a thing, you'll fall right back down here. Stay—"

She would obsess about that for weeks, that his last words were warnings to her. Because at that moment, the main cable parted and the elevator car plummeted five floors into the basement.

Her rapist had become her savior. And paid the price with his life. She shouldn't have cared. She should have been relieved. And she was relieved. So relieved that she put her face down on the dusty carpet and sobbed as if her heart would break.

Chapter Two

Of course, there were questions. There were always questions. And when she stopped crying, Jeannie tried to answer them. No, she didn't know the elevator passenger's name. No, she didn't know how he'd managed to break the hatch lock and lift her several feet to safety. No, she didn't know how he'd over-ridden the safety locks on the doors, forcing them open. No, she didn't need to see a doctor. No, she couldn't identify the body—when they found it—because she had never seen his face. No and no and no.

She supposed she could sympathize with the building's management. A half-naked, hysterical woman cheated death on their property and now only wanted to go home... of course they were loathe to let her go.

She had her chance to tell them what he had done to her, how he had forced her—there was even a lawyer in the room to take her statement (the building management's corporate counsel, doubtless prepared to beg her not to sue)—but she couldn't do it. As much as he had scared her, used her, she couldn't bring herself to lay charges against him. If the price for her life was forced sex and mind-numbing pleasure, she was going to count herself very lucky indeed.

She saw a doctor at their insistence, a doctor who raised his eyebrows at the shredded ruin of her clothes but said nothing, a doctor who could tell she had recently had sex but, after her rude replies to his carefully phrased questions, said nothing to the others. Probably assumed it's my nature to seek out quickies in elevators, she thought darkly, and at the thought of her "quickie" partner, crushed and dead, she nearly started crying again.

The doctor had tried to insist on an overnight hospital stay; she had been firm. Like mountains were firm. She would not stay, she would spend the night in her own bed, thank you, will someone call me a cab?

They gave her a cab voucher—her purse was at the bottom of the elevator shaft, along with her wallet, ATM card, credit cards…and her rapist/savior. The cab came. She got in. The cab dropped her at home. She got out. Went inside. Threw her clothes away. Showered for a long time. Wept for a longer time.

❧❨❀❩❧

Three weeks later, about the time she noticed her period was late, her martyred rapist/savior showed up on her doorstep.

Chapter Three

Michael Wyndham III stepped from the car, nervous as a bridegroom. Which, he supposed, he was. It had taken him nearly three weeks to track Jeannie down, weeks of frustration and guilt and worry. But now he was going to see her again. The thought of taking in her scent, maybe even touching her, made his pulse pound in his ears. Oh, he had it bad.

He grinned. It was marvelous, to find his mate. And in such a strange way! His father had tried to tell him, but Michael had never believed, had always figured one female was as the next. But he had found his mate through purest luck and, best of all, most wonderful of all, she was an extraordinary human! And *homo lupus*, unlike *homo sapiens*, mated for life.

Now to persuade Jeannie, who thought her future husband was nuttier than a granola bar.

Derik and Jon got out of the car and the three of them examined the apartment building before them. Minimum security—not that that would be a problem for three werewolves in their prime—and a pleasing location, right on the lake, with a park across the street. Best of all, less than a four hour drive from the Wyndham estate.

"Remember," he told his men. Derik and Jonathan were his closest friends, his fiercest protectors. "She was scared to death. I forced her, and she had to assume I died. She'll be terrified when she recognizes me."

"If she recognizes you," Derik reminded him. He was as blonde and fair as Michael was dark. "Her eyes aren't as good as yours. It was probably pitch dark in the elevator to her."

"If she recognizes me," Michael agreed. "I'm just reminding

you, you'll need—"

"Patience," Derik and Jon echoed, then laughed at him. Michael rolled his eyes and cuffed Jon in the back of the head.

"It's true," he said, "I might be repeating myself."

"Quit fretting, Michael," Derik said. "We'll not muss your mate."

"Do you think she's pregnant?" Jon asked with hopeful curiosity. He was a curly-haired redhead with boyish features. He looked all of sixteen, and was twice that. "The pack has been after you for a long time to mate and provide an heir. It would be wonderful if she—"

"Was pregnant and happy to see our pack leader, and embraced our lifestyle with open arms, and settled into the pack as if she was born to it?" Derik shook his head at his friends. "None of this is going to be easy, for her or for us. Better that she not be pregnant. Then Michael can let her go."

"Enough," Michael said sharply. Let her go? Let that witty, beautiful, sensual woman go? In his dreams, his ears still rang with her cries of ecstasy. Let her go?

Moot, he comforted himself. She was surely pregnant. Her scent had been all sweet ripeness, like a bursting peach. And beneath him, she had felt—

"Excuse me, o mighty king of the werewolves," Derik said dryly, "but you're about to walk into that pillar."

"I am not," he said, swerving at the last moment. He grinned at his friends, who rolled their eyes. Jon had taken a mate last year, and thus knew exactly what his pack leader was going through. Derik had not, and thus thought his leader was being foolishly sentimental.

"She was scared," he said aloud, remembering, "but she never showed it."

"I still think this is nuts," Derik said gloomily. "And bad luck. Of all the times to get stuck in an elevator—with an ovulating female who couldn't fight you off, who just happens to be human and not believe in werewolves—"

"Gosh," Jon interrupted with a grin, "what are the chances?"

Derik ignored his friend. "—who's going to go right out of her mind when we try to bring her home. Man, I hope she's not pregnant."

"It will work out," Jon said, but they both heard the doubt in his tone. "Humans mate with werewolves all the time, and vise versa."

'All the time' was a gross exaggeration ('once or twice a generation' would have been more accurate), but neither Derik nor Michael pointed that out.

"Jon's right, pardon me while I choke on that phrase," Derik said, giving his pack leader a friendly clap on the shoulder that would have felled a human male. "It'll work out. C'mon, chief. Let's go get your mate."

At least, Jeannie thought grimly, I don't have to worry about chasing anyone down for child support.

She was in her bathroom, staring at the double pink line which, the instructions assured her, meant she was positively pregnant. One bout of sex after going without a partner for three years, and she was well and truly caught.

Among other things, it was problematic that her baby's father had been a little unhinged. It was also problematic that he was dead. Jeannie had no idea—none at all, not even a smidgen of an idea—what to do now. Her mind, after taking in the double pink line (such an innocuous color for such a momentous event), had shut down, and the same thought kept cycling through her brain: now what? Now what? Now what?

There was a firm rap on the door and, annoyed at the intrusion, she went to answer it. She peeped through the eyehole and saw three large men standing quietly on the other side of the door. They were dressed in dark suits; the one in the middle was the tallest, with dark hair, and he was flanked by a blonde and a redhead.

What fresh hell is this, she wondered. Normally she would have at least asked for their names before opening the door, but the shock of that double pink line was still governing her actions, and she swung the door wide.

The one in the middle was almost enough to distract her from her news—he was, simply put, one of the finest looking men she had ever seen. He was tremendously tall, with longish, wavy black hair that looked thick and touchable; her fingers itched to see if it felt as lush as it looked. His eyes were a funny, gorgeous color—the pupils were large and dark, the irises yellow-gold. His nose was a blade, and his mouth had a sinfully sensuous twist to the lower lip. His shoulders were ridiculously broad; his coat was belted at a slim waist.

"Yuh..." She coughed and tried again. "Yes?" She glanced at his companions and they wouldn't lose any beauty contests, either. One blonde, one a redhead, both fair and green-eyed, powerfully built and even broader across the shoulders than the brunette.

All three of them were staring at her. She covertly felt her face to make sure ants weren't perched on her nose or something equally disgusting. "What's up, boys?" They must be selling their hardbody calendars door to door, she thought, that's the only explanation for the abrupt arrival of three gorgeous men on her—her!—doorstep..

"Jeannie," the brunette said. With that one word, she recognized his voice—that deep, velvet voice—and went cold to her toes. Forcing her expression to remain neutral, she raised an eyebrow at him.

"Yes?" she said, with just the right amount of impatience.

His shoulders slumped a little and the blonde man shot him a look of compassion. Mouth drawn into a sorrowful bow, he said haltingly, "I—ah—this is difficult, Jeannie. You probably don't remember me... whurggggh!"

He said 'whurgggh!' because she had hoisted her sneakered foot into his testicles with all her strength. His breath whooshed out in an agonized gasp and he crashed to his knees. She shouldered past the astonished redhead and bent over him, shaking a finger in his face.

"You bet your demented ass I remember you! A) Thanks for saving my life, and B) drop dead! Again, I mean! Now get lost, before I lose my temper—"

"You haven't lost your temper yet?" the blonde asked, aghast.

"—and forget that you saved my life and remember that you *raped* me in an elevator that was about to *plummet* into a basement.

If you'd taken five more minutes to get your jollies, we'd both be dead! You're lucky I don't call the cops on you!"

"I don't think he feels lucky right now," the redhead said, staring at the rapist/savior, who was clutching himself and writhing on the floor in an undignified way.

"And as for you two," she said, rounding on the redhead, who took a step back and covered his crotch with both hands, "your friend here has some serious psychological problems. He thinks—"

"—he's a werewolf," the blonde said from behind her. She whirled, part of her not liking the way the three of them, purposely or not, had boxed her in very neatly.

"You know about the delusion?" Now might be a good time, she thought uneasily, to step back into my apartment and close the door.

"We share the same delusion," the blonde said, smiling at her with very white, very sharp teeth.

"Well, *great*," she snapped, concealing her unease… which was rapidly turning to fear. At her tone, the blonde's eyebrows arched in appreciation. "Maybe you can share the same shrink, too. You—what are you doing?"

He was sniffing her, like a dog. He didn't touch her, but he got entirely too close and sniff-sniff-sniffed her neck. "Shit," he said, right before she shoved him hard enough to rock him back on his heels. He turned to her felled giant, who had been helped to his feet by the blonde. "She's pregnant."

The brunette grinned in triumph, and he stared at her with a gleaming gold gaze, a gaze too proud and possessive for her taste.

"Congratulations," the redhead said politely, "to both of you."

To her astonishment, the blonde reached out and put his hand on her flat stomach. "Here grows the next pack leader," he said respectfully. "Congratulations, ma'am."

She gritted her teeth. "Hand. Off. Now."

He complied hastily. Before she could think of what to do or say—nothing had been controllable since that double pink line—the brunette spoke up. His color was coming back, and he had recovered from a ball-stomping much faster than she expected. "Jeannie, the short version is: I'm a werewolf—as I believe you heard—the pack leader, you're pregnant with my heir and successor, I have enemies who would steal my mate and unborn child so it's not safe for you to stay here, you have to come home with us."

Without a word, she turned around and went into her apartment, firmly closing the door in their faces, twisting the deadbolt with a click. Once inside, she started shaking so hard she looked around for a place to sit down.

"Jeannie?"

It was the brunette, calling her from the hallway. Sure, like she'd open the door and say, 'Yes, dear?'

"Jeannie, get away from the door."

Having seen his strength before, she had a good idea what was coming, and went at once to the small chest on the living room endtable. There was a tremendous thud and her door shuddered in its frame. She flipped the top of the chest and grabbed her .9 mm Beretta, cursing herself for being so paranoid about gun safety that she kept the clip—fully loaded—in her bedroom. No time to go for it now—

THUD!

—her door had just been kicked off the hinges.

She turned, her palm cupping the handle of the gun to conceal the emptiness where a clip should be, and leveled it at him, sighting in on the hollow of his throat. The brunette—odd, how she still didn't know his name—stepped across the threshold into her home. His friends, she was relieved to see, were nowhere in sight.

"You're going to shoot the father of your child?" he asked with honest curiosity. He picked up the door and set it neatly aside, then strolled toward her.

"In a New York minute," she said coldly. "Stop. Turn around. Go now."

"I can't imagine your rage and hurt and frustration." His tone was serious; he never even glanced at the gun; his gaze was locked on her face. "I told you I had no choice, and I hope someday you'll be able to see me as more than a conscienceless monster."

"Kicking down my door wasn't a good start to that end," she said curtly. "Last chance, Romeo."

"Sorry."

Before she could figure out how to keep bluffing him, he had zipped forward, so quickly she couldn't immediately track the movement. He slid forward, under her gun sights, across her prized hardwood floor, and tackled her around her knees. With one hand he cushioned her back as she fell to the floor; with the other, he pulled the gun from her grasp. Hefting it, he knew at once it had no clip, and he smiled at her. "Good bluff. I never doubted you." He tossed it over his shoulder.

"Get off me!"

"I will. Wait. Tell me now, while we have some privacy—you weren't hurt that night? After, I mean? I had to be rough when I threw you out the elevator door. There wasn't time to—"

Part of her anger—a tiny part—diminished. He was a wanna-be kidnapper and a rapist, but he was awfully concerned for her well-being. She remembered his concern that night, too, after he had taken her. Him on top of her, both of them still panting, and his hands running over her limbs, checking for injuries, making sure she wasn't hurt.

"No," she admitted through gritted teeth. "I wasn't hurt. Not even a skinned knee. They told me you died."

His gold eyes twinkled at her. "Just a couple of broken legs. But I'm a fast healer. Were you sorry? When you thought I was dead?"

"No," she said stiffly, remembering her sobs, the way it had taken her an hour to stop crying after the elevator fell down the shaft.

"If I had died," he whispered, leaning in close, nuzzling her ear—to her annoyance, her entire left side started tingling. "If I had died, I would have taken a beautiful memory with me. I would have died sated, knowing my seed had found a home, knowing the bravest woman I ever met was going to mother my child."

"Shut up," she said thinly, bringing her hand up to push his face away—he went easily, and she had the feeling he went because it pleased him, not because of anything she had done. "Shut up, I hate you, I wish you *had* died."

"I know," he said sadly. "Your opinion is not about to change." Abruptly, he shifted his full weight on her, and she felt his fingers

come up and settle on the junction between her neck and shoulder...
and start to squeeze. Black roses bloomed in her vision and she felt
herself fading, fading, using up precious strength to get him off her
rather than trying to drag his fingers away from her neck and what
the hell was that, anyway? Was that—

Chapter Four

She woke in an unidentified bedroom… and came to consciousness yelling. "What the hell was *that*? Did you actually use the Vulcan Neck Pinch on me, you freak?"

Then she realized she was alone. The bedroom was small—the bed took up nearly the entire room, and paneled with pastel-striped wallpaper. There were two large windows on each side of the bed, and…

And the bedroom was moving. She bounded off the bed, swaying for a long moment as a wave of dizziness swamped her, then lurched to the nearest window.

The bedroom was on a highway. Traveling roughly seventy miles an hour.

There was a short 'rap-rap' on the door, and then Tall, Dark, and Weird stuck his head in. "Are you all right?"

She whirled on him and he grinned as she snapped, "I am *so* sick of hearing that question from you—usually after you've done something horrible to me! *No*, I'm not all right! I'm a rape victim and a kidnap victim and a—a pregnancy victim and a Vulcan Neck Pinch Victim and now I'm in some sort of mobile bedroom—"

"It's an RV," he said helpfully, easing into the room, keeping his hands in sight. She felt like a rabbit, easily spooked, like she might bolt any second. Apparently he had the same impression, because his voice was low and very soothing. "I wanted you to be comfortable for the trip."

"How very fucking considerate of you," she said with acid sarcasm. "Why, I don't know when I've been kidnapped by a nicer man."

His smile faded. "Jeannie, I have enemies who would kidnap you and take your baby from you and then kill you, all so they could raise the next pack leader and have a voice of power. How could I let that happen to you?"

She took a deep breath and forced calm. On top of everything else—the physical power, the sexy voice—did he have to be so handsome? If she'd gotten a look at him in the elevator before the lights went out, he probably wouldn't have had to force her. Much. "Look. I'm not saying you're a liar, okay? I'm not saying that. I'm sure you believe all this stuff."

"Thanks," he said dryly.

"But the fact is, you can't force women in elevators and then show up and yank them from their homes and take them who-knows-where. You *can't.* Don't you know it's wrong? Don't you care?"

He sat on the edge of the bed and nodded soberly. "I do know it's wrong. By your laws."

She threw her hands up in disgust. "Oh, here we go."

"I do care," he continued. "As angry and humiliated as you are, I'm as embarrassed to find myself having to play the villain. But it's far worse to use you for my pleasure and then never give you another thought. Especially when I knew you were ovulating, knew there was an excellent chance I'd made you pregnant. How could I turn my back on you after using you? How could I never look in on you, make sure you were out of danger?"

"Fine!" she shouted, stomping toward the bed. "Look in on me! Tell me you're not dead! You could have apologized for forcing me and scaring me and—and other stuff, and I could have thanked you for saving my life, and then you could have gone your way and I'd have gone mine. Instead you do *this*." She gestured to the RV bedroom. "I loathe rooms on wheels," she hissed.

"There was the small matter of my enemies finding you," he reminded her calmly.

"Very small—you knew my name and it *still* took you three weeks to find me."

"Even if there was only a chance in a thousand you were in danger, do you think I'd risk you for an instant?" he asked sharply.

"You're angry with me now, but what if I had never come back in
your life...but my enemies had? You would have died cursing my
name. I couldn't have borne that."

"Oh, please." She turned her back on him. "You don't give two shits
for me. I was a piece of ass you couldn't resist. That's—aaah!"

He had come up behind her with that liquid, silent speed she
had seen before, startling her badly. His hand fell on her shoulder
and he turned her toward him. His eyes, locked on hers, were gold
and blazing. "Do not say that again," he said with an icy calm that
terrified her, even as it fascinated her. "It's disrespectful of me, as
well as yourself. I'm not in the habit of forcing unwilling females,
despite what you must think."

"Sorry," she said quickly, through numb lips. Then, despising
her fear, she added coldly, "Remove the hand."

His hand fell away. "And now I've frightened you," he said with
real regret. "Forgive me, Jeannie."

"It's just that, since you don't even know me, I don't see how you
can claim to feel anything for me," she said carefully.

His hand came up slowly, carefully, and when she didn't flinch,
settled on her cheek like a dove's touch. "I do know you," he murmured. "There is much more to you than beauty."

She flushed; against her hot skin, his hand felt cool. "I'm not
beautiful."

He laughed. "With all that curly blonde hair?"

"It's frizzy," she corrected him.

"And all those adorable freckles?"

"Ugh."

"And that pale skin, like the richest cream?"

"When I go to the beach I look like a fucking vampire, thanks
very much, and could we get off my looks, please?"

"Then we'll just have to talk about your intelligence and courage
and razor wit," he said with faux regret. "What a bore."

She laughed; she couldn't help it. And immediately bit off
the sound.

"I've never heard you laugh before!" he said, delighted. "Do it
again."

"I can't laugh on command. Look," she said briskly, getting back to business, wondering how long he was going to be touching her face, "let's talk facts, here. *Facts*, not delusions and you're the king of the werewolves and you've got enemies out to get me even though they don't know me—cold hard facts. Where is your home?"

"Barnstable, on Cape Cod," he said, amused.

"Ah, yes, Cape Cod," she said sarcastically, "a hotbed of shape-shifters. I always thought so. The tourists had to be going there for some reason..."

He laughed again, and his hand slid down, toward her collarbone. She knocked it away and backed up, so fast that she hit the far wall. Startled, he went after her, politely backing off when she kicked out at him.

"*Don't* touch me there again. Ever. Ever *ever*. If you do, I swear I'll—" She couldn't think of something bad enough. "I'll do worse than rack you in the 'nads."

Understanding dawned. "I wasn't going to knock you out again," he said. To her amazement, he actually sounded hurt. "I just like touching you."

"I don't give a shit! You're contemptible, showing up uninvited, pinning me down and pinching me until I was out cold—"

"I had a feeling," he said dryly, marching to her and dragging her, kicking, out of the corner. He shoved her gently to the bed and then walked around it, standing on the far side of the room. "I had a feeling you wouldn't cooperate in your—uh—removal. Steps had to be taken. But think about this—think about the things I could do to you if I didn't cherish your well-being."

She'd been trying not to. She had realized in the elevator he could have killed her, crippled her, as easily as stomping a spider. If he wanted to hurt her, he'd had ample opportunity. Hell, she'd visited upon him the worst pain a man can know... and there had been no retaliation.

"It's still wrong," she said firmly.

He shrugged. "You had more questions?"

"What happens when we get to Cape Cod?"

"You'll stay at my family home."

"Until?"

He hesitated. She gritted her teeth and repeated the question.

"Until you accept your destiny and freely agree to stay with me. Us."

"Forever?" she asked, aghast.

He nodded.

"You've kidnapped me forever? Unless I escape or blow the place up or whatever?"

"Yes." He paused. "I don't expect you to agree right—"

She launched herself at him. It was time to take advantage of the fact that he wouldn't hurt her, and do some major damage. Her first punch missed—he caught her wrist in time—but her simultaneous kick hit the mark, and he winced as her foot cracked into his shin.

"I hate you!" she was shouting, raining blows down on him. He held her wrists and took her kicks stoically, only blocking the ones to the groin with his thigh. "You can't do this! It's not my destiny, you weirdo, it was just *dumb luck!* I won't stay with you, I won't! I have a *life!* And it does not include hanging out on Cape Cod with a creep who thinks he's a werewolf!"

"Understood. But it doesn't matter; you're staying." At her shriek of rage, he continued. "And while we're talking, I don't like being hit, or kicked," he said calmly, wincing as she brought her foot down on his instep with all her strength, "so there will be consequences in the future."

"Fuck your consequences!" She brought her head forward in a devastating head butt; he jerked his head aside and she ended up banging her forehead into his neck.

"Starting now," he said, and pulled her too him so sharply she lost her breath. Then his mouth was on hers in a bruising kiss that stole the strength from her knees. He pinned her arms to her sides and, when her teeth clacked together in an attempt to bite him, contented himself with gently nibbling her lower lip.

"Don't," she managed, and when her mouth opened his tongue slipped past her teeth.

He pulled back before she could gather the sense to bite him again. He was breathing hard. Almost as hard as she was. His effect on her was infuriating and she practically gnashed her teeth in rage.

"So," he said coolly, but his eyes gleamed, "now that you know there are consequences, feel free to punch away. Because, afterward, I can put my hands on you without feeling a bit guilty, under those conditions."

"You should die of guilt," she choked out. "I hate you."

He was staring at her mouth, his own a line of sadness. "I know."

He left, slamming the flimsy bedroom door behind him. Jeannie sat down before her knees betrayed her.

Chapter Five

"This," Tall, Dark, and Disgusting said to the fifteen or so assembled people, "is my wife-to-be, Jeannette Lawrence."

"Ma'am," the small crowd said in respectful unison.

Jeannie opened her mouth to tell them exactly what she thought of what's-his-name, but the black-hearted bastard beat her to the punch.

"She's here entirely against her will," he went on, "and isn't happy about it. She's also pregnant by me—"

A happy gasp from the crowd.

"—and not happy about it. It happened, as some of you probably guessed, during the last full moon."

Nods. Sympathetic glances. She bit her tongue, hard, so as not to shriek with embarrassed rage.

"Thus, she will be rude, throw things, and do her best to escape," he went on casually, as if she wasn't standing at his elbow and hearing every word. "She doesn't understand her vulnerability and can't appreciate her delicate position. And she won't thank any of you for pointing it out." He paused. "Be patient with her."

Jeannie rolled her eyes. At the edge of the crowd, a petite, elfin blonde woman saw it and winked at her.

"Moira, if you'll show Jeannie to her rooms?"

The small blonde nodded and stepped forward at once. Psycho Boy turned to her and asked with ridiculous politeness, "Did you have any questions, Jeannie?"

"Just one." She paused. He waited, the crowd waited, expectantly. "What the hell is your name?"

Score! He flushed a little, and there were a few outright laughs in the crowd. Moira giggled, and quickly choked off the sound as he glanced at her with a frown. "Ah—that's right, we never got around to that, did we? It's Michael. Michael Wyndham."

"Great," she said, unsurprised. After the month she'd had, nothing could surprise her. The Wyndhams controlled a vast shipping empire and were reputed to be slightly more wealthy than God. The father of her child owned the tower she'd taken the ill-fated elevator in, probably owned the magazine she worked for. It figured. "Psychotic *and* rich."

"I'm afraid so," he said with an irritatingly sexy smile. She looked away, disgusted.

Moira led her out of the yard, into the astonishing mansion she'd glimpsed from the RV. After her last confrontation with Tall, Dark, and Wyndham, she'd cried herself to sleep. And when she woke, they had been pulling up to the most beautiful manor home she had ever seen. She was so stunned at the home's size and majesty, she hadn't said a word when Michael gently led her out of the RV and introduced her to the household staff who, the redhead (whose name was Jon; the blonde had introduced himself as Derik) had assured her, all shared Michael's "delusion."

She was so impressed with the ocean-side mansion, she could hardly fret about being kept prisoner by fifteen people who were all as nutty as Wyndham. True unease would come, she had no doubt, in time. Like as soon as her shock and surprise wore off. Then there'd be hell to pay. Then there'd—

"I hope you'll come to like it here," Moira was saying, leading her through a home that made *Gone With The Wind*'s Twelve Oaks look like a claim shanty. "We've been waiting for you for a long time."

"Waiting for *me*?"

"For our leader to take a mate," Moira explained. She was a lovely, delicate blonde with eyes the color of the sky, and skin so pale it was almost translucent. She was tiny; almost a head shorter than Jeannie, and Jeannie herself was five-ten. "He needs an heir. It's just unfortunate that…" She trailed off, seemingly embarrassed.

"You don't know *how* unfortunate," Jeannie said dryly. "Look, Moira, I don't suppose there's any chance you'd help me—"

"Don't even ask, ma'am," she said firmly. "I'd die for Michael. Any of us would."

"In other words, don't waste your breath asking anyone else to crack out of this pokey," she finished.

"Your 'pokey', ma'am," Moira said with a grin, throwing open a set of mahogany doors. Jeannie stepped into the most beautiful room she had ever seen—all gleaming blonde wood floors, lush throw rugs, a fireplace large enough to roast two pigs, and several doors. And the bed! A king-sized monstrosity, large enough to comfortably sleep a family of six.

"Bathroom, closet, closet, balcony," Moira was saying, opening all the doors.

"Whoa!" Jeannie said, staring, goggle-eyed. Moira giggled again. "Okay, so, this place ranks high on my Top Ten List Of Places To Be Held Prisoner. But it still sucks, you know."

"Hmmmm?" Moira said, turning down the bed.

"Being held here against my will," Jeannie reminded her impatiently. She waited for Moira to blush, to acknowledge guilt, to do something...something besides shrug and look unconcerned, dammitall. Then a thought struck her, and she asked sharply, "Where does Wyndham sleep?"

"His is the adjoining room," she said simply.

"Over my dead body!"

"You'll have to discuss that with him, ma'am."

"And stop calling me ma'am! I'm not ninety!"

"As you wish, my lady."

"Out!" she hissed, and to her relief and surprise, Moira obeyed at once. Jeannie threw herself on the bed, which enveloped her at once in an eiderdown embrace. She was too mad to cry again, which was a relief—she'd done entirely too much crying lately. Now was the time for action!

"Would you like to have something to eat before you try to escape?"

It was Wyndham, poking his head through the doorway that doubtless adjoined his rooms to hers. She'd like to slam that door shut, watch his eyes pop out as his neck broke.

She glared up at him from her bed. "I want to go home."

"Yes, I know."

"Now!"

"Sorry."

She reared up in the bed, tottering to stay balanced on her knees amid all the fluff of the quilts. His mouth twitched as she struggled to right herself. "Wyndham, I'm telling you this for the last time: I won't stay here with you. I won't have anything to do with you. You're a criminal *and* a jerk, a miserable combo."

"You're not afraid," he said with a satisfied sigh. "I knew you wouldn't be."

"Don't flatter yourself. I'm too pissed to be afraid. Listen, dickhead: there are going to be some horrific consequences if you try to keep me here. We're talking broken bones and FBI raids. I'm out of here the second the opportunity presents itself."

He actually looked alarmed—at the chance of losing his sex toy? Or a deeper reason? Then his expression cleared. "There will be consequences if you try to escape," he said simply, stepping into her room and softly closing the adjoining door. He had changed from his suit to khaki shorts and a white t-shirt, and if possible, looked yummier in casual clothes that showed off his finely muscled legs and upper body. He was ridiculously tan, ridiculously handsome. "Are you going to try to escape soon?" he asked, as if inquiring about the temperature in her room.

"You—you—" She sputtered wordlessly at his absurd question. "You're not supposed to *want* me to get away."

"You won't get away. We'll catch you. I don't want you to leave—it's dangerous. So, as I warned you earlier, there will be consequences if you try and escape."

"What consequences?" she asked, but had a sinking feeling she knew.

His gaze was level. "Elevator consequences."

Her mouth went dry, even as her heart sped up. "Seek help, Wyndham. As quickly as possible."

"Do you think I'm pleased with this scenario?"

"Yes! I think you're very pleased," she said bitterly.

The bum actually looked hurt. She couldn't believe his nerve. "It's the only way I can think of to keep you from trying to leave," he sighed, "since you don't believe me about the danger."

He walked to the bed and stared down at her. A blind woman could have seen the hunger in his gaze. "I won't lie—part of me wants you to try and escape," he husked. "Don't misunderstand—I'm sorry about the circumstances that brought you here. And I'm sorry you don't like my home."

"I never said I didn't like your home," she interjected sharply.

"But if you try to escape, just as if you try to hurt me again, I can take you without guilt."

"You—"

"I can hardly stand to be this close to you without touching you," he said, and for a moment she saw such pain and longing in his gaze, she had to glance away. "Having you sleeping just a few feet away is going to drive me mad. But I won't take you again by force, Jeannie—except as a deterrent. Because," he added sadly, "as much as I long for your touch, I know you can't stand to be near me, that you despise me. So lovemaking relieves my hunger while punishing you." He turned away. "I wish it could be different between us," he said without turning around. "I'd give anything for things to be different."

"You know what *I'd* give anything for?" she asked sweetly, groping behind her for something to throw at him, and finding nothing more deadly than a pillow.

He laughed shortly, and left the room. The pillow smacked into the door and fell to the floor with a fat thump.

Chapter Six

Since Wyndham, the sadistic cretin, was panting at the thought of her escape, and since he'd alerted the household she was an unwilling guest, Jeannie decided to stay put for a while, provided her situation didn't change (read: Wyndham didn't decide she was in heat again, or Moira didn't spike her milk with broken glass).

So she took lunch with Wyndham and his staff, who were obviously more friends than employees, in a dining room that had more windows than a solarium. Sunlight splashed across the table and gleamed from the blonde wood floors. She sat in the finest dining room she'd ever seen and commented on how delicious everything tasted. They had all been watching her expectantly, and seemed disappointed when she didn't throw things or leap across the table through the French doors that led to the beach.

"How long have you known you were expecting our leader's child?" Derik asked, sliding the bread basket toward her.

She helped herself to another piece of the sun-dried tomato and basil loaf and looked at her watch. "About six hours and fourteen minutes."

Wyndham looked up from his soup. "You did one of those home tests? You haven't seen a doctor?"

"I had an appointment for this afternoon. Which I missed. Guess why, King Psycho."

He remained unruffled, though she saw a few of the staff hiding smiles. "Well, then, you need a doctor. Moira, see to it." He glanced at Jeannie with a frown, then added, "A female physician, if you please."

"Yes, sir."

"Like there are *so* many werewolf doctors to choose from?" Jeannie interrupted sarcastically. "What, is there a directory or something?" As the others laughed, she had a sudden thought. "Oh, will we have to go to town for that?"

Derik, seated at Wyndham's left (she was at his right), snickered. "Nice try. The doctor will come here."

"Well, goody for him."

"Her," Michael corrected sharply.

Jeannie raised her eyebrows, said nothing, and ate her chicken. Wyndham was jealous? Of a male doctor? Ridiculous. Still, that might be a handy button to push. She filed the thought away.

"Are you mad because you think we're all crazy, or because you're here against your will?" Jon asked curiously.

"I don't think that's a fair question," Michael said reproachfully.

"Yeah, I mean, there's so many reasons for me to be furious at all of you, how can I pick just one?"

"I meant," Jon said, flushing a little, "the full moon is in three days. And you could watch some of us change, or even one of us change, and then you wouldn't think we were crazy anymore, so it might be easier to accept—um—are you okay?"

She could actually feel the color draining from her face, could feel the trembling in her hands. She dropped her spoon in her soup and fled the table, running, running, for her rooms.

Michael caught up with her on the stairs. She wrenched away from him and kept going. Never one to take a hint, he followed her into her bedroom.

"The full moon?" she asked, hating the shrill, panicky note in her voice. He shut the door to assure some privacy; she barely noticed. "The full moon again? I can't go through that again! I can't go through that *craziness* with you again! *Don't you touch me!*"

He had been reaching for her, ignored her shriek and pulled her, struggling, into a firm embrace. "It's all right," he said into her hair. "I had planned to leave the grounds when my change came. I wouldn't have forced you again. I promised you I wouldn't force you, except as punishment."

"What good is a promise from you?" she choked, resting her

forehead against his shoulder. He smelled so good. It was as comforting as it was irritating.

"I've done many things to you, Jeannie, but when have I broken a promise?"

She shrugged sullenly. Then stiffened, remembering. She leaned back to look at him. "But what about the others? They all think they're werewolves, too, they all—"

"You have nothing to fear from the females, because as my mate, you're alpha female. No, listen, Jeannie—if it's a delusion, at least we all have to follow the same rules, right? And the males won't—can't—touch you without my permission." His voice hardened. "And I won't give it. Ever. So you have nothing to fear."

She choked on a laugh.

"You really don't," he said, pressing a warm kiss to her brow. "Now come back and finish your lunch. You don't want the baby to starve, do you?"

"No," she sighed. She glanced at him again; he had put an arm around her shoulder and was steering her out the door, back to the dining room. A thought struck her—late, but her thought process was continually being thwarted by shock upon shock. "What do you think? About my being pregnant, I mean? I never got a chance to ask you. Not that I care either way," she added hastily.

"I'm thrilled," he said simply, giving her a warm smile. He leaned close and she had the sense he wanted very much to kiss her. Something—belated concern for her feelings?—held him back. "I love children. The pack needs the continuity of succession. And I get to keep you now, don't I?"

His voice ended on a teasing note, but she wasn't amused. "For a minute there, I was almost liking you," she said evenly, pushing his arm away. "Thanks for turning back into a creep."

At the dining table, the other werewolves—people—were still glaring at Jon, who was miserably embarrassed. "I'm really sorry," he said at once upon seeing Jeannie. "I shouldn't have reminded you about the full moon. I forgot that—" He paused, glanced at Michael, blushed harder. "I have no excuse. I'm so sorr—"

"*Please* stop," she said, rolling her eyes and sitting back down.

"I'm the one who should apologize. I can assure you it's not my usual M.O. to drop cutlery and flee for the bedroom when the word 'moon' is introduced into the conversation."

The others laughed, Michael harder than anyone. Jon smiled at her with pure gratitude. And Derik forked another chicken breast onto her plate.

࿔ৡৄ౦ৄ৾

"How about a tour, Moira?" she asked briskly, after the lunch dishes had been cleared away. "Might as well check out my new home."

"She'll try to escape," Derik warned, finishing the last of his peach sorbet.

"I know," Moira said defensively. "You don't have to tell me everything, Mr. Right Hand Man."

"Bring her to me once you've found her again," Michael said casually, but his eyes were gleaming in a way Jeannie didn't much care for.

"Hello!" she shouted. "Prisoner still in the room, here! Can you have this conversation where I can't hear you?"

Moira giggled, and extended a hand. Surprised, Jeannie took it. "Come on," she said. "We'll start with the gardens. If you cosh me over the head to escape, try not to muss my hair."

"For God's sake," she muttered, but obediently followed Moira out the door.

She had, in fact, decided to escape in the next day or so—well before the full moon. Michael's assurances aside, she had no intention of sharing a home, however sprawlingly luxurious, with twenty people all sharing the same delusion. And she didn't plan to be in the same *state* with Wyndham when he went through that again. She wasn't afraid of being forced, so much as being forced to pleasure. Her cheeks burned with humiliation every time she remembered how he had made her scream in ecstasy. In a flash she was back in the warm, dark elevator, Michael's cock surging between her thighs, her fingers digging into his skin, wordlessly urging more, more...

She shook herself, and concentrated on the tour. Now was no time for daydreaming. Now was the time to plot and plan and eventually escape these crazies.

In the rose garden, Moira said in a low voice, "We don't blame you. For being upset, I mean. It must have been..." She trailed off, then asked timidly, "Was it very awful?"

"Huh? You mean being stuck in the elevator with your boss? Well, the lights went out, so we couldn't read my *Glamour*..."

"It's kind of you to joke, but... I can't imagine how it must have been for you—a pure human, and an unbeliever, besides. Tearing clothes and scratches and bites, and being forced on your knees and taken without so much as a 'please'...I suppose you had to see a doctor." She looked as though she was going to burst into tears. "I suppose you—you tore and...and—no wonder you hate him. Us."

"Uh...yeah. Yeah, it was an unending torment. What's that building over there?"

As Moira obediently showed her the gardener's shed, Jeannie's mind whirled. What Moira imagined hadn't been at all what happened. Michael had gone out of his way to soothe her, to bring her pleasure, to make sure she was ready for him. He'd had that much control, at least. What would sympathetic Moira think if she told her it had been the most exciting, pleasurable sexual experience of her life? What did that mean, that he'd been nearly out of control, but cared for her enough to do his best not to hurt her, even to bring her pleasure?

In a flash, she was back in the warm, dark elevator—

Jeannie pushed the thought away with a firmness she didn't feel.

"You can't leave the grounds," Moira was saying casually, "until we kill Gerald. But after that, it should be all right."

"What?" She nearly fell into a rose bush. "Now you're talking about killing someone so I can leave?"

"Didn't our leader explain about Gerald?"

"Frankly, I tend to tune him out when he's babbling about all the reasons it's okay for him to break the law where I'm concerned."

"Your law," Moira pointed out calmly, "not ours."

Jeannie bent to sniff a rose so gray it was almost silver. "Okay,

I'll bite. What is your law?"

"Safety of mates and children first, above and before *everything* else. Michael has to keep you safe. Because he knows it's right, and because he must set an example. How could the rest of us follow someone who can't even protect his own mate?"

"I'm not his mate," she said sharply.

"Yes," Moira said simply, "you are."

Jeannie stewed over that one for the five minutes it took them to walk from the rose garden to the beach. "How does Gerald fit into all this?" she asked at last.

"He's our enemy. He went rogue five years ago. His mate was giving him nothing but female cubs and he wanted an heir, someone he could train to challenge the pack leader. He's too cowardly to try a challenge himself; he wanted a son to do the dirty work." Cute, delicate Moira spat in the sand to express her disgust.

"Whoa, whoa, watch those loogies." Jeannie took off her shoes and wiggled her toes in the surf, scanning the horizon and judging the wisdom of swimming to England to escape. Still, this was a fascinating delusion. "His mate was giving him daughters? Did the creep never crack a biology textbook? Sperm chooses gender."

"Gerald is… old-fashioned," Moira said reluctantly. "He represents the pack before the Wyndhams took over. Savage, undisciplined. Gerald killed his mate after the birth of his fourth daughter. Michael would have killed him, but for the intercession of Gerald's other daughters, who begged their leader to spare their father's life. Michael did, but banished him. Now Gerald's rogue, and the only way he can come to power is if he gets his hands on the pack leader's child."

"Thus, I be kidnapped," Jeannie said dryly.

"If you ever crossed Gerald's path, he would kill you to revenge himself on Michael—for what is worse than the loss of a mate? Or he would keep you until you whelped, take the child from you, and then kill you. And he would be well-revenged indeed, for he would be as father to the next pack-leader, and come to power quickly. And we would be back in the days of savagery and blood." Moira turned an unblinking, wide-eyed gaze to Jeannie. "It would be the end of all of us." Pause. "You can't leave while Gerald lives."

Despite herself, Jeannie felt a thrill of fear. Determinedly, she pushed it away. It was all part of their delusion, it was a way for Michael to justify kidnapping her. She wouldn't believe it.

There had to be a way out of here.

❧⟨(꙰)⟩❧

Exhausted—either from the wild events of the last few hours, or fatigue brought on by an early pregnancy—when Moira brought her back to the mansion, Jeannie went straight to her room and stretched out on the bed to nap. The bed was ridiculously comfortable, her room astonishingly beautiful, and if she wasn't being held here against her will she'd probably be having the time of her life.

Hell, she thought drowsily, watching the light play against the rich gold wallpaper, there hadn't been anyone in her life since college. Under different circumstances, she'd gobble Wyndham with a spoon. *She'd* rape *him*. Gorgeous, rich, intelligent, and a gentleman—when he wasn't raping and kidnapping. A real catch. And those eyes… those eyes…

Yes, she could definitely wish things had been different, that they had not met in such drastic fashion. But, as her mother used to say, done can't be undone. Her mission was not to play nice with the lunatics, it was to get the hell out of here.

With that unsettling thought, she drifted into sleep. And found herself in the elevator again—for the last month, she'd stumbled into that elevator two or three times a week. Only this time, Michael didn't save her. This time, he used her and left her, turned his back on her and left the elevator in one bound, leaving her in the car, in the dark, and there was a terrifying Snap! as the cables parted and then the sickening sensation of free fall, her feet left the floor and her head banged on the ceiling and her stomach climbed into her throat and she screamed all the way down, screamed for him to save her, and—

"Jeannie… hush, Jeannie, it's all right. You're safe here."

"Ha," she said weakly, opening her eyes. To her surprise, while she dreamed she had been pulled into his embrace. He was sitting on the edge of the bed, holding her in his lap like the world's biggest doll.

As she rested her head against his chest, she was absurdly comforted by the thud-thud of his heartbeat in her ears. "Do you dream about the elevator often?" he asked, his voice against her ear a deep rumble.

"No," she lied. In a moment she would have to pretend outrage and shove him away. In a moment. For now, it was too damn nice to be held with tenderness. Even if he was crazy. Even if he'd landed her in more trouble than she'd ever been in. "No, never."

"I do, too," he said softly, as if she'd told the truth. "Only, in my dreams, I can't save you. And down you go. And I wake up with a scream in my throat."

She shuddered against him, closing her eyes. He stroked her back and murmured to her; she caught no words but was comforted by tone. "In mine," she whispered, "you leave me. You use me and leave me and the elevator falls into the basement and they scrape what's left of me into a jelly jar."

He tightened his grip. "Never. I'd die myself before letting that happen to you."

"I know," she said and, to her surprise, she knew that as a fact, as she knew her own name. "You proved it, didn't you? But I can't help dreaming about it."

"Nor I," he agreed.

She noticed his right nipple, which was about two inches from her mouth, was stiff. Probably from her; every time she opened her mouth, breath puffed across it. She had the absurd urge to kiss it. To taste it. Run her tongue across it and test the texture. Her mouth had actually gone dry from her sudden, startling need to take part of him into part of her.

He was rubbing his cheek against the top of her head and she could feel that odd tension in his body, as she had felt it the night in the elevator. He wanted her, she realized with a bolt of excitement. But he was afraid to do anything, afraid she'd fight him, scream the house down, call him names. He wanted to preserve this temporary peace between them as long as he could. What would he do, she wondered with a strange, thundery joy, if I leaned over and kissed his nipple? And slid his shorts down to his ankles and took him into my mouth?

"I came to get you," he said, and she thought his voice sounded thick, "because the doctor is here."

In a flash, she remembered herself: she was pregnant, by him, against her will, in his house, against her will. She sat up and shoved him away. Christ, she mentally groaned, standing up and walking out the door, what was I thinking? I've got to get out of here before I forget I hate this creep.

The doctor, who introduced herself as Rose Madison, was waiting for them at the foot of the stairs. Jeannie greeted her with, "Nice to meet you, I'm Jeannie Lawrence, they're all crazy and they're holding me prisoner, mind getting me out of here?"

The doctor, a small brunette with whiskey-colored eyes, was all commiseration as she explained she, too, was a werewolf, and she was very honored to be tending to the pack leader's mate as well as her future pack leader, and would my lady mind peeing in this cup?

Jeannie snatched the plastic cup out of Dr. Madison's hand, shot a sizzling glare toward Michael, ignored Derik's smirk, said loudly, "I hate every one of you," and marched into a nearby bathroom.

Within half an hour, Dr. Madison had confirmed her pregnancy and handed her what looked like—yes, it was. An ice cream bucket full of pre-natal vitamins.

"What the hell?" she asked helplessly, hefting the bucket and astonished at its weight.

"You'll need at least four a day, due to your increased metabolism," Dr. Madison informed her.

"Sure I will," she said, humoring her. Dr. Madison let that pass, cautioned her about her diet, and told her she would see her again in two weeks.

Sure you will, Jeannie thought. She glanced around at Michael, Moira, and Derik. Now or never. If any of them came with, she was toast. "Dr. Madison, can I talk to you in private about—uh—a female thing?" she asked, feigning embarrassment.

"Of course," the doctor said quickly, even as the others did a respectful fade. "Come, walk with me to my car."

Once outside, Jeannie glanced around again, saw no one, and followed Dr. Madison to her car, a nifty little Ford Taurus. "Uh—the werewolf thing. Should it turn out to be true, will I have a litter? Will I have a puppy?"

Dr. Madison laughed kindly. "No, you won't have a litter. Two, at the most—and that is rare for our kind. And werewolves don't change until puberty. He or she will seem like a perfectly normal-looking child until, oh, about age thirteen or so." She grinned. "Then all hell is going to break loose. Don't worry about being human mother to a werewolf, though. Our leader will help you. We'll all help you."

"It takes a village to raise a werewolf," Jeannie said wryly, casually hefting the huge container of pre-natal vitamins. Who ever heard of taking four a day? The doctor had given her enough to last ten years.

"To raise the next pack leader, certainly." Dr. Madison turned to look at her with a serious gaze. "One thing, though. Your child will be highly prized. Not only because of his status in the pack, but because often the child of a human/werewolf mix is able to control their Change. To turn into a wolf at any time, not just during the full moon."

In spite of herself, Jeannie was fascinated by the complexity of the fantasy. "Is that why the others don't resent me? I'd think, if anything, a human would dilute the strain."

"Not in this case. Human mothers are prized. Smart, courageous ones even more so. Every time you snap at Michael or crack a joke, or make a determined effort to hide your fear, they like you more. *He* likes you more."

"Oh," Jeannie said, completely mystified.

"Well," Dr. Madison said reasonably, "who wants a dishrag for a consort?"

"Not me," she said, and swung the heavy container, hard sidearm, at Dr. Madison's head. The blow knocked the small woman into the car, where she bounced off and hit the gravel drive, hard. Jeannie prepared to step over Dr. Madison's unconscious body, and was astonished to see the woman was still clinging to consciousness.

"Don't," she slurred, trying to get to her feet. "It's too dangerous.

Gerald will kill you."

"Sorry," Jeannie said, and she was. The doctor was almost a foot shorter, after all. But tough as hell. Jeannie jumped into the car, starting the engine with one twist of the keys conveniently left in the ignition. "Christ," she muttered, slamming the car into first gear, "hit her over the head and her only concern was for me. Damn." If she wasn't careful, she'd get attached to those loonies.

She was down the lane and out the gate before the alarm was raised.

Chapter Seven

Knowing better than to outrun them—who knew how many fleets of cars, choppers, and what-have-you Wyndham had at his disposal—she screeched to a halt in front of the Barnstable Police Station. Sprinting up the stairs, she burst into the station and yelled, "Help! I've been kidnapped by a group of nuts who think they're werewolves!"

The three people in the room—the desk sergeant, an off-duty patrolman, and a plainclothes detective—turned to stare at her. "Quiet town," Jeannie mumbled, keeping an ear cocked for the sounds of pursuit.

"I'll take this one," the detective said. He was a large man, a good four inches taller than she, with mud-colored brown hair, eyes the same color, and fists the size of bowling balls. He gestured to a door at the end of the hall. "C'mon, honey. Tell me all about the big bad wolf."

"Werewolf," she corrected him, walking down the hall. At his nod, she pushed through the door and found herself outside, in a small alley. Surprised, she turned—and ran smack into the detective's chest. To her shock, he shoved her away, hard.

"You've got Wyndham's stink on you. You must be his new bitch," he snarled, snuffling her ear. She jerked away, appalled. His tongue flicked out and ran across his thick lips; he looked about as evil a creature as she had ever seen. "And is that his little bitty babe I smell *in* you?"

"Are you Gerald?" she asked dumbly.

"I was. Now I'm going to be stepdaddy to the new pack leader." His big fist came looping through the air toward her; she ducked under it, darted forward, and snatched his sidearm out of his holster. In a flash she had the barrel jammed into the soft meat of his throat.

"Guess again, Detective Stupid," she growled. "Christ, has everyone gone crazy? Am I the only sane person in an insane world? Can it be that—?"

"If you're going to kill me, get it over with," Gerald grunted, "but don't make me listen to you whine."

"Oh, shut up," she snapped. "Who else on the force thinks they're a werewolf?"

"*Thinks* they're a werewolf?" As she dug the barrel deeper into his flesh, he added, "Three others. They're all on Wyndham's side. Too bad for you they're on patrol, eh?"

"Guess again, rogue," a cool female voice said. Jeannie snapped a gaze over her left shoulder and saw two uniformed patrolmen and another plainclothes detective—this one a woman—pointing guns at them. At Gerald, hopefully.

"Our leader told us you'd probably stop here first," one of the patrolmen said, almost apologetically. "Step away from Gerald, please, ma'am."

"You might want to mention to Michael that I had everything under control," she said, obeying.

"If I were you, ma'am," the detective said, not taking her gaze off Gerald, "I would not mention that I had even met this man, much less drew down on him."

"Good advice," Jeannie mumbled. She tucked the piece into the back waistband of her jeans, ignoring Gerald's burning glare. "I like to keep souvenirs," she told him, then let herself be escorted to a patrol car.

In the back (feeling like a POW, to tell the truth), her curiosity impelled her to ask, "Are you guys going to get in trouble? For pulling a piece on a fellow cop, a member of the brotherhood, that sort of thing?"

"Pack business is private," the lady detective said, turning around to look at her through the mesh. "And Gerald doesn't outrank *me*." Her buddy behind the wheel laughed at that one, and Jeannie shook her head, wondering what the joke was.

To her surprise, the cop-werewolves let her keep the piece. To her further surprise, upon return to the mansion she was not instantly dismembered. Instead, Dara, the chef, politely asked if she wanted to eat and, upon declining, Jeannie was escorted to her rooms and locked in. That was it. No yelling, no threats, no thunder-voiced Michael promising doom. No Michael, period.

"Well, hell," she said, looking at her watch. She'd been free for all of twenty-seven minutes. She tucked the pistol away in a bedside drawer and prepared to kill a few hours.

She amused herself watching daytime reruns (*The Brady Bunch* and *Wings* were particular favorites) until dinner time. Moira, pale and quiet, brought supper.

"What's up with you?" Jeannie asked, pouncing on the covered plates. She lifted the lids to reveal prime rib, baby red potatoes, green beans. Bliss, except for the green beans—blurgh. "And why hasn't your lord and master been in here to play 'Jeannie is a bad girl'?"

"He's so angry," Moira practically whispered. "He's staying away from you until he calms down. When he heard Gerald had his hands on you—the builders are coming tomorrow to fix the holes in the wall."

The bite of prime rib stuck in Jeannie's throat. With an effort she swallowed, coughed, and said, "So, the cops ratted me out, eh? Fascists. Did they mention when they came on the scene, Gerald was saying hello to the barrel of his gun? Held by me? Because I got the drop on the overconfident son of a bitch?"

Moira flashed a smile, which eased the tension lines around the smaller woman's eyes. "They did. They practically fell over themselves assuring our leader you were never in any danger. You made quite an impression on them."

"You should see the mark on Gerald's neck, you want to see impression," she chortled, forking down another bite of the delicious prime rib.

She was halfway through the meat before she realized it was raw. She waited for the urge to puke, or faint, but it didn't come. Moira saw the look on her face and quickly explained, "It's normal, my lady, don't fret. You're growing a werewolf, after all. You'll crave raw meat throughout your pregnancy."

"My God!" Jeannie said, putting down her fork. "I'm catching your delusion!"

✶❀(❁✿❁)❀✶

Hours later, she was soaking in the tub—which was more like a miniature pool—when the bathroom door opened and Michael said, quite calmly, "You put yourself in danger. You put my unborn child in danger. On purpose."

She swallowed a mouthful of water and sat up, looking behind her to see him standing in the bathroom doorway, stone-faced. She opened her mouth, but before she could speak he said, "Finish your bath," and walked out.

An hour later, she was still in the tub. Wrinkled and shivering, but defiant. He wasn't the boss of her, dammit! She'd get out of the tub when she was damned good and ready, thank you very much—

"Jeannie. If I have to remove you from the tub, you won't like it."

—and that was right now. She climbed out of the tub, dried, and shrugged into the clothes she'd been wearing earlier. She wrapped her soaking hair in a towel and padded into the other room to take her medicine.

Wyndham was apparently a helluva boy scout, because he'd kindled a respectably-sized fire in the fireplace. He was crouched before the flames, balancing on the balls of his feet, and she had the impression he'd been in that position some time, waiting for her. He turned his head when she entered the room and came to his feet at once.

"Why aren't you wearing a nightgown? There are plenty of clothes for you to wear."

"They're not my clothes," she pointed out. "You stocked up before snatching me, didn't you? Bought a bunch of stuff in my size? I saw it earlier. Well, forget it. I'm wearing my own clothes."

By firelight, his eyes were yellow. His voice, though, was still cool and calm, which reassured her somewhat. "Everything in this room is yours."

"This *room* isn't mine. Nothing here is mine. Now, about this afternoon." She swallowed and lifted her chin. "I admit to some remorse about cold-cocking the doctor, but..."

He crossed the room and tore the shirt off her body, ignoring her outraged squawk, then leaned down and tugged at her leggings until they, too, were shreds. "Your old life is over!" he shouted as he dragged her to the bureau. He yanked open a drawer, found a nightgown, thrust it at her. "You belong to me, and you will wear my clothes and stay in my home and be safe and you will damned well like it!"

Shocked at his rage and loss of control, she couldn't grab the nightgown and it floated to the floor. "You weren't this out of it in the elevator," she said, brushing the scraps of t-shirt off her arms, hating the way her hands trembled. "What's your problem?"

"My *problem*," he said with savage sarcasm, yanking the towel from her hair and furiously towel-drying the soaked tresses, "is a willful mate who doesn't care about her own safety or, apparently, my child's."

"I'm not your mate!"

"You *are*. And all your protests won't change the fact. Werewolf law is a hell of a lot older than human law, Jeannie, and as such, you're mine, as the child is mine, forever and ever, amen." He finished drying her hair and tossed the towel at her. "So I strongly recommend you *get over it*."

"I hate you," she said hopelessly, furious at herself for not being able to come up with anything better.

"I suggest you get over that, too," he said carelessly. He pulled his t-shirt over his head, unbuttoned his shorts, let them drop, and stepped out of them.

"Wrong," she said, and oh God, her throat was so dry. "Not in a thousand years, pal. Never again."

"I'm not your pal," he said coldly, but his cheeks were flushed with color and his gaze was hot. "I'm your mate. It's time you were reminded of the fact."

"And you can't wait, can you?" she hissed. "All day you've been hoping I'd escape, so you can *rape* me. Again. Well, I did try, and now you get to play—or at least you think you do—so why are you so mad?"

"I never expected you to end up in Gerald's literal grasp," he growled, stalking toward her. She took a great, clumsy step backward and nearly tripped over an endtable. He was there to steady her, his hand on her arm surprisingly gentle. "Jesus! He could have torn your throat out and you wouldn't have known it until you woke up in the afterlife!"

"The only one in danger of throat trouble was Gerald," she retorted, and swallowed to get the lump out of her throat. "I had his gun. I—"

"There was no bullet in the chamber, you idiot!" The heat of his rage baked her face; he shook her so hard her hair flew into her face, her eyes. "The gun wouldn't have fired! Gerald knew it, he could have killed you at any time! Now he knows your status, knows where you are, knows if he gets you he gets the next pack leader. You've been reckless and you might have paid the price with your life, if my people hadn't gotten there in time, you stupid, stupid…" Then she was crushed to him in an embrace so tight it drove the breath from her lungs. His chest heaved and he shuddered all over, trying to force calm. "How could you have risked yourself? Risked our baby? Frightened years off my life?"

"I didn't—I didn't—"

His mouth was suddenly on hers in a bruising kiss even as he moved, pulling her with him. The backs of her knees connected with the bed and she twisted away from him, gasping, only to have him casually toss her on the bed. He stripped off his undershorts and she couldn't help but stare at him, at the thing that had gotten her into this mess. Fully erect, almost curving under its weight, thrusting from a lush nest of black hair, she looked for a long moment, almost spellbound. Then her gaze was drawn upward until she was staring into his gleaming gold gaze.

"I can't," she whispered, but oh, part of her wanted to. "Not with you. Not again."

"You will. Only with me."

He climbed onto the bed, easily avoiding her kick, and then his chest was settling against hers and his hands were in her hair, tugging, forcing her head back. He dipped his head and inhaled her scent, seeming almost to savor her, but she could feel that hot, hard pressure against her lower stomach and knew he wasn't going to be satisfied with just her natural perfume.

"Don't."

"I can't help it. I've always loved your scent."

"*Don't!*" she said, almost gasped, as he licked her throat. "I don't want you. Don't do that!"

"It doesn't have to be punishment," he said, and sounded almost—could it be?—desperate. "Let me make it good. I want *you*, not your body. I don't want to take by force what you could share with both of us."

"Don't you understand?" she screamed at him, startling him, startling herself. "I *can't*! The qualities that make you like me also fix it so I can't... give... in." No matter how much I want to, she thought desperately. "Now leave me be!"

"Please," he said again, and his eyes were haunted. "I'll overlook what happened. I shouldn't have backed us both into this corner. Just let me—" He dropped a soft kiss to her throat. "You'll like it."

That's what I can't bear, she said to herself. Oh, God, anything but that—anything but me begging him again. I'd rather be taken in anger than reduced to humiliating screaming and begging, shouting myself hoarse while I come so hard I can't think straight...

And he was *wrong*. He was wrong to keep her here, Gerald or no Gerald. Her outraged pride could never escape that fact. Nobody held Jeannie against her will, God damn him.

"I'll escape again," she said through gritted teeth, as he licked the underside of her left breast. Her nipple rose, a taut pink rosebud, and he rubbed his cheek against it. She whimpered, the tiny sound escaping before she could lock it back.

He smiled at the sound. "I was so afraid," he said quietly, pressing his mouth to her cleavage for a brief, sweet kiss. "So terrified. When they told me who you'd run to. When they told me that mate-killing bastard had actually put his hands on you." His head dropped to her shoulder. "Jeannie, I was so scared for you," he said, so low she could barely hear the words.

She wanted to comfort him. She wanted to thank him for his concern. And she hated every tender feeling he was calling up in her. Forcing on her. Better to be forced, better to be victimized, than a willing prisoner. Anything but that.

"I think I could get a better deal with Gerald," she said with cruel casualness. "As soon as I escape again—and I will—I'll have to track him down. At least he'll leave me alone until the baby's born."

He froze against her and she held her breath. He raised his head and gave her a long, level look.

"I *will* leave," she said evenly, and felt shame, and felt anger at feeling shame. "I won't stay here against my will. Let me go now, tonight, or I'll find Gerald just as soon as I can." A bluff—she wasn't going near Gerald on a bet—but Michael wouldn't know that.

He said nothing. Instead, he calmly rose and padded out of the room, stark naked. She went limp with relief, unable to believe she'd gotten off so lightly.

She rose from the bed and put away the nightgown he'd thrown at her earlier. She'd meant what she had said, about not wearing clothes he'd picked out during his shop-for-my-future-prisoner spree. It wasn't to be borne, not any of this male-domination bullshit, and if he thought she was the type to...

He was back, carrying something.

He kicked the door shut behind him, his face dark with anger, then he unscrewed the top to the tube, squeezing a handful of—of something onto his hand. He rubbed the handful all over his turgid cock, until his member was shiny and slick with lubricant.

She watched this cold procedure—his expression never changed—with her mouth hanging ajar. Then understanding hit and she turned to run...somewhere. But his hand was on her elbow before she'd even taken a step. He thrust her, screaming her denial, face down on the bed. She scrambled to her knees and he let her, then he grasped her hips and plunged inside her. She shrieked again at the shock of it, the brutal intrusion, the taking of her for punishment.

He reared behind her, plunging and withdrawing, and her screams of anger—for, in truth, this didn't hurt, but it couldn't exactly be called pleasurable, either—gave way to furious weeping. He never missed a stroke, and after a minute he was shuddering behind her.

He let go of her hips and she dropped to the bed, which shook with her sobs. He let her cry for a long moment, then put a hand on her shoulder and eased her on her back. She couldn't look at him.

"That was for what you just threatened to do," he said hoarsely. "Never *think* of going near him. He'll kill you. I couldn't bear that."

He left her on the bed, going around the room and shutting off the lights. She tried to get a grip on herself, tried to stop crying, but it was all too much—the stress of the last three weeks caught up with her, not to mention the stress of the last minute and a half.

When he eased into bed beside her she cringed back, expecting to be used again, but he shushed her and pulled her, oh so carefully, into his arms, as if he thought she might shatter if handled too roughly. His large warm hands stroked her back and he pulled her face into his throat. In the dark, his voice rumbled against her cheek, sad… almost lost. "You wouldn't know this, but…that's how a werewolf punishes his mate. Using her but withholding pleasure. You had frightened me so badly, you weren't listening, I—I couldn't think of what else to do." Pause. "And I was very angry, tremendously angry." He licked the tears from one cheek and, when she didn't cringe or flinch, but just sobbed softly and steadily, he licked the tears from the other. He licked the ones that had dripped to her chest, chasing one errant tear all the way to her nipple.

He trailed soft, sweet kisses down to her naval and she could feel herself stiffen beneath him. He paused, obviously expecting a protest, but the agony of her recent humiliation was too great, and she was afraid to stop him. "It's all right," he said sadly, reading her mind, or perhaps smelling her fear. His tongue flicked out, caressed the cup of her navel, moved lower. "No matter what you do or say, I'm done with cruelty for tonight. I've found I don't have the taste for it when you're involved. Do you want me to stop? Leave?"

Wary of werewolf tricks, she said nothing, but couldn't stifle a gasp of protest when he settled himself between her legs. He started lapping the inside of her thighs, cleaning his seed from her, and a treacherous warmth began to spread through her limbs. She could feel herself relaxing by inches when long minutes went by and all he did was nuzzle and kiss and lick her inner thighs. When his tongue brushed her clitoris, there and gone again, she didn't even have time to squirm before he was back to tending to the less sensitive skin of her thighs. Then his tongue was delving inside her, darting, flicking, probing... and then back to her inner thighs.

Soon the trips to her inner thighs were shorter, and all his attention was on her cunt, which had began to throb in delighted abandon. She tried to bite back a groan, but he heard the muffled sound and murmured, "It's all right to like it."

Not with you, she thought despairingly, and nearly groaned again when he suckled her clit, swirling the impudent bead with his tongue. Then she felt his finger ease into her and her back bowed off the bed, her teeth biting her lips bloody in her efforts not to show him how his wonderfully skilled touch was affecting her.

Everything clenched within her, and suddenly her orgasm was blooming through her like a dark flower. Even as sweet aftershocks made her limbs tremble, he was pulling her toward him, and then he was on his back and she had straddled him. Murmuring encouragement, he took himself in one hand, nudged her thighs a bit further apart, and then his tip was in her, while she braced her hands on his chest to keep from falling.

He stopped. She looked at him in the near dark.

"Go ahead," he urged softly, hoarsely. "Take me inside you. Or not. This time, it's your decision."

Still she didn't move, wary, wondering what he was up to, wondering if he was going to punish her again, the black-hearted (he's never hurt you) bastard, oh, how she hated (you were no match for that crooked cop) him, wished him dead, hated him for humiliating her (if the cavalry hadn't shown up, you'd have been toast) and then bringing her pleasure. He was contemptible, and she was trapped (you don't really think they're all crazy, do you?).

She shut out the despicable voice and abruptly, hatefully, let her weight drop on him, slamming him all the way inside her, until she could feel his tip touching her womb. Then she lifted...and dropped again. And again. Beneath her, Michael gasped, a ragged sound. "Jeannie—"

Lift. Drop. Again.

"Stop, Jeannie, you're not—this is all for me, you're not getting any—"

Again.

"—*please*, stop it, stop it, let me help you come again, don't do this—"

Again.

"—don't do this, don't, don't—"

Again. She kept it up, riding him with savage intent, ignoring his pleas that she slow down, that she allow herself pleasure. She used him as he had used her, and from the look on his face, her expression was every bit as mean and ugly as she felt. After an eternity, he threw his head back, his protests ending in a ragged groan. She felt him pulse within her, felt her muscles grab at him greedily, milking him, and hated herself almost as she hated him.

Without a word, she climbed off him and curled up on her side, away from him.

I'm trapped, she thought with dull despair. They're all nutty, the whole town's infected, they're all in on it, they'll help him keep me. I can't get away, and if I try again, there's more of...of this.

I can't get away.

I can't stay.

She wept again, silently, ignoring Michael's soft entreaties that she look at him, that she forgive him, that she try to understand.

"You're pregnant with a child who will grow up to safeguard and lead some 300,000 werewolves across the globe. That's bigger than your pride, Jeannie. Your safety has to come before everything. I'm—"

"Don't say you're sorry again," she said coldly, and he shut up.

Chapter Eight

"You've broken her!"

The accusation brought Michael wide awake. After leaving Jeannie, he'd paced his room for hours, wondering what, if anything, he could have done differently. Werewolf discipline had been a mistake—or had it? If it kept her from fleeing to Gerald, it was worth the tears and hatred. He'd rather she hated him forever than love him and die tomorrow.

It all came down to their natures, to the fact that he had different rules than she was used to, but she couldn't accept this because she couldn't accept them. She thought they were all deranged. Perhaps Jon's suggestion had been correct. If she saw them Change, even one of them Change, she could look at her situation in an entirely new light.

But oh, she would be terrified, would expect to be forced again. Could he put her through that, even though he knew he was right?

Was he right?

Finally, he'd dozed off at dawn, only to be brought awake by his door slamming open and Derik shouting at him.

"What?" he asked fuzzily, blinking sleep out of his eyes. He looked out the window...and was startled to see it was mid-afternoon. "What's the matter?"

His boyhood friend slammed the door so hard, a splinter the length of his forearm jumped off the frame and landed on the floor. "You've broken your mate, that's what's the matter. She's been curled up in the window seat all damn day, won't speak a word to anybody, won't eat a thing—*naked*, for God's sake, she won't get dressed, won't talk, won't eat—"

"You're repeating yourself," he said sharply, quelling the dart of worry that made an instant appearance at Derik's words. "Is she hurt? Has anyone seen to her?"

"She's not hurt," Derik said, aggravated, "I keep telling you, she's broken. You smashed her spirit. And we think that rots." He paused, coughed. "Sir."

"We?" he asked, sliding from the bed. "My loyal staff and pack members, you mean?"

"I can smell her all over you," his friend said quietly. "You took her again, didn't you?"

"When I heard about Gerald—that he'd actually had his hands on her—"

Derik groaned and collapsed on the bed. "Not mate-punishment, tell me, *tell* me you didn't take a human for punishment?"

Silence.

Derik sat up and glared at his pack leader. "Jesus, Michael, she's delicate! She's *human*. You shouldn't have done that, no matter how badly she scared you. You can't treat her like a werewolf, even if she is your mate."

A low growl got Derik's attention, and he dropped his eyes at once. "Okay, hell, I'm upset. I shouldn't tell you how to handle your female." He paused, then burst out angrily, still keeping his eyes respectfully downcast, "But you'd better get up there and fix it, O mighty king of all werewolves, because your mate is in a sorry state and it's all your fault. She's got to eat. And it would be nice if she got dressed, too."

"I can't go near her," he said, pacing the same stretch of carpet he'd walked so many hours last night. "I'm part of the problem. She doesn't understand our rules, doesn't understand—"

Derik looked up. "Then make her understand," he said, clearly exasperated.

"I'm *trying!*" Michael managed to restrain himself from kicking a hole in the dresser. "I'm trying, but how do you teach a blind person how to look at things? How do you tell a deaf person what a symphony sounds like? You can't make them. You can only hope they get it... even though your worst fear is that they never will.

You know she's my mate, and I know... and we both know she's alpha female, and a valued member of the pack. But she doesn't understand any of that. It's too soon. A month ago, she'd never met me. A month ago, I had no idea I'd—I'd—"

"Fall in love?" Derik asked quietly.

Michael groaned. "How could everything turn to shit so *quickly*? She hates me, Derik, and I can't blame her for that. I've been a disaster for her since I stepped on that elevator. The worst thing is, even if she saw me Change, if she knew we weren't crazy, she'd be terrified."

"But what's the alternative?"

The pack leader had no answer.

꧁༺ღ༻꧂

"Please, ma'am, please... Jeannie...try some of the bread. Dara saw how much of it you ate yesterday, she made a whole loaf just for you, won't you please try just a piece?"

Moira's entreaty became a soft drone as Jeannie looked out her window, out to sea. The ocean looked exactly like she felt: grey and stormy. The weather matched her mood; it was a perfect day to stay inside and brood. Even the sand looked cold and forbidding, like dirty snow. She'd give anything to be a weredolphin, a weregrouper, a wereminnow, anything that could swim the sea and never never come back to this crazy place. Her stomach, which had been gnawing and rumbling most of the morning, had finally quit and was now a still stone in her abdomen. Vanquished. Defeated.

The way she'd like to defeat Michael Wyndham.

They'd tried to get her dressed. Moira and another woman, one she didn't know, had come in and gently pulled her from her window seat, and dressed her in clothes that weren't hers, clothes Michael had bought for her when he was dreaming about stealing her. She tore them off her, not as spectacularly as Michael had torn hers, but enough to get her point across and then, naked, she had gone back to the window seat, resting her forehead against the panes and wishing she were a wereguppy.

Moira whispered that she understood, she could smell Michael all over her and understood completely, but why punish the baby for the sins of the father, and wouldn't she please try some of this soup?

Somehow, the day passed. Jeannie was thinking harder than she had in her life (ha) but couldn't see a way out of the trap (except to quit letting your pride call the shots).

Night came, and she dozed off in the window seat, ignoring the cramping in her legs. And there came a point in the dark when she was gently lifted, carried, and placed in bed. She roused herself enough to catch Michael's scent and tried to fight all the way back to wakefulness, to get back to the window and look out at the sea and freedom, to get his hands off her, his wonderfully comforting hands...

"Go back to sleep, Jeannie. The window will be there tomorrow."

Reasonable advice, she thought muzzily, and sank back to sleep.

Michael, keeping uneasy watch out Jeannie's window, turned when she sat up. He saw at once she wasn't really awake; her dreaming, wide-open eyes looked right past him.

She got out of bed. Having a good idea of her destination, he followed her out the door, steadying her on the stairs when her sleeping feet stumbled. Jon, back from a late-night hunt, passed them in the dark, his eyes widening appreciatively at Jeannie's nudity. Then he saw she was asleep, saw Michael behind her, and passed on after a polite nod to his pack leader.

She wandered aimlessly on the lower level, until he gently steered her toward the kitchen. Once there, he opened the fridge for her and saw the small plastic container with her name on it. He popped the lid and caught the rich, savory scent of raw ground beef mixed with raw eggs, onion, and lots of salt and pepper.

He handed the container to Jeannie, who did not hesitate to grab a fistful and eat it. She ate until the container was empty, and while he shut the fridge and put the container in the sink, she delicately licked the raw meat from her fingers. He watched her without words.

Then she woke up.

He saw it at once; her dreaming gaze became clouded, then utterly astonished. She looked down at herself, then looked around, saw him, saw where they were.

"I—thought I was dreaming."

"You were hungry," he said simply. "So you sleep-walked down here to feed the baby."

"I ate—I ate all that raw hamburger?" She touched her mouth, revolted. "I can still taste it."

"You were hungry," he said again. "And I think the taste in your mouth is good to you. It's just the idea of it that tastes bad. Jeannie… can you see me? Do you know where we are?"

"We're in a kitchen. Yes, I can see you." She added, with a snap of her old fire that heartened him, "Ask another stupid question."

"It's pitch dark, Jeannie. A month ago, in equal darkness, you couldn't see anything."

A long, strained silence, broken by her whisper. "What's happening to me?"

"You're pregnant with a shapeshifter," he said simply. "You share a blood stream with the baby. You'll eat raw meat and see in the dark and probably get stronger before you birth the baby. It's natural."

"It is *not* natural. None of this is." She rubbed her face. "Oh, Jesus, I'm catching your delusion, you've all got me turning as crazy as you are…"

"That's not true," he said, reaching up and stroking her shoulder, lightly, a butterfly's touch. "And I think you're coming to know it."

"It has to be true," she said, almost moaned. "What's the alternative? That everything you said was right? That everything you—e verything you did to me was understandable? Okay, even? That's not acceptable, I won't tolerate it!"

"Jeannie…"

She broke away from him and ran out of the kitchen, navigating her way past boxes and stools without hesitation, though most people would have been effectively blind in such utter darkness.

He came to her room the next morning to find her huddled in the window seat, looking out at the near-full moon with a dazed, almost hypnotized expression.

"Jeannie," he began, and then trailed off helplessly. His fingers itched to touch the smooth skin of her back; luckily, his hands were full. His lack of physical control had gotten her into this mess. Christ, he was like a pup around her, only thinking about physical pleasure, about the sounds she made when she... "I'm glad you ate your breakfast."

"Starving myself doesn't work," she said hopelessly, not turning around. "It just makes me sleepwalk and search out raw meatloaf, for God's sake. Better to have my scrambled eggs, please go away."

He decided it would not be prudent to mention her cravings would get worse, not better, before she gave birth.

"I brought you something."

She didn't answer.

He set the suitcases down, bent, unsnapped all four catches. At the sounds, she snuck a glance over her shoulder, then came off the window seat in astonishment. "My clothes!"

"Some of them," he confirmed, while she elbowed him out of the way and took a closer look. "I went to get them last night. I can't have you running around naked for the next eight months, can I?"

She grinned at him, so wide and natural he actually felt his heart catch: ka-THUD! "Thanks!" She made an aborted movement with her arms; for a moment of pure astonished happiness, he thought she was going to hug him. Then the moment passed and she was wriggling into panties, shorts, and a sweatshirt.

Well, what did you expect, fool? he asked himself bitterly. That she'd kiss you and say, 'Hey, PsychoBoy, I forgive you for the whole raping thing—twice—and love you and want to stay with you forever, thanks for the clothes.'

He turned to leave.

"Michael," she said tentatively.

He turned around, hope jumping in his chest like a rabbit. A continuously lusty rabbit hopelessly infatuated with someone who hated him. "Yes, my—my dear?" He'd almost called her 'my own mate', a common werewolf endearment he was positive she would not appreciate.

"Michael... can I ask a favor?"

He waited. She looked out the window at the moon, nearly full, the moon which would ripen tonight and call to his blood. Her eyes were wide with distress, dilated with fear. "Can I please stay somewhere else tonight? I promise I won't try to get away. I'll—I'll do whatever you want, if you don't make me stay in the house with—with all of you tonight."

"It's not safe for you anywhere else," he said, as gently as he could. "And I'm still planning to leave. You don't have to worry about a repeat of what happened last month." She didn't have to worry no matter where he was, he thought but did not say, because she certainly wasn't ovulating this time. What he would likely want to do in wolf-form is hunt food for her, then stay close. Following her from room to room, drinking in her scent, worshipping her with his eyes. She'd be terrified... or hate it—him... or both.

He closed his eyes against the pain that thought brought, then opened them as she did something he never thought she would do... never thought she was capable of.

"Please!" she begged. "I don't feel safe *here*! It's beautiful here, but I don't feel safe in your home." Every word was a knife in his heart, but she didn't notice, just rushed on in her agitation. "Every minute that goes by, I feel like something terrible will happen, something I'm in the middle of! Please, *please* let me stay somewhere else. I'll do anything, Michael, anything you want."

"Don't beg," he said thickly, "I can't bear it," but she wasn't hearing him. She crossed the room in an instant and flung herself into his arms; he hugged her to him automatically, stepping backward with the force of her assault. "Jeannie, listen. It's not—"

He quit talking because her frantic mouth was on his, her hands were pounding on his chest and then scratching the fabric of his shirt, her scent—orchard ripe, succulent peaches—overwhelmed him. The force of his return kiss bent her backward. "Anything," she hissed into his mouth. "Anything."

The man in him managed, 'Wait! She's giving herself to you

for a favor, she thinks if you take her, she can leave tonight. Stop, idiot!' before the wolf took over, yanked her sweatshirt over her head, divested her of her shorts, tore her panties in his haste, tossed her on the bed. He was on her, her limbs were entwined with his and everywhere was her scent and he couldn't get enough, could never get enough of her. He buried his face in the sweet slope of her throat, cupped her breasts with their impudent velvet nipples, kissed her so hard they were both panting when he pulled his mouth from her.

Part of him thought, even as he put his hands on her, his mouth on her, that she must be frightened indeed to give herself to him, a woman who had starved herself and gone without clothes to show her contempt for him. He made a last, heroic effort. "You can't leave," he growled, then bit her earlobe, and wondered how he could make himself leave her with his cock on fire and her musk in his nostrils. "It's not safe."

She bowed her head, resting her forehead against his shoulder. "I know. I knew you wouldn't let me, but I was desperate. I've been watching that damned moon and getting upset and now I'm... oh, God, I'm so ashamed."

He kissed the slope of her breast. "Don't say that."

"I am, though." She seemed content to let him nuzzle her breast; one hand was in his hair, almost absently. He gloried in her touch, in her temporary acquiescence, even as he craved more.

"Because you used your body to try and get what you want?"

She didn't answer, but he felt her swallow hard.

"It doesn't make you bad. It makes you formidable." He chuckled. "The remorse, now, *that* makes you human." He licked the underside of her breast, then nipped the sensitive skin. She jumped and he heard her swallow a gasp.

"I think," she said carefully, trying to ease herself from beneath him, and, because he wasn't cooperating, having no luck at all, "that since you won't let me leave, there's no reason for us to finish this."

"You're not going to send me away, are you?" He probably looked as horrified as he felt, because she got a downright devilish look in her eyes.

"Yes," she said, "I am. You promised you wouldn't force me unless it was to punish me. I haven't done anything wrong—"

"Today," he interrupted dryly.

"—so you have to go," she finished triumphantly. He could tell she was loving it, loving the power she had over him, and was curious to see if he really would leave her, when they could both feel the throbbing below his belt.

"Jeannie, I am *begging* you."

"No," she said, pouting, but she was watching him, watching, and he caught the sharp scent of her wariness. He groaned theatrically and stumbled from the bed, adjusting his jeans to ease the stiffness between his legs.

"About that promise…"

"Out!"

The last thing he saw before leaving was the delighted, surprised look on her face.

Chapter Nine

Jeannie spoke around a mouthful of chocolate. "What do you mean you're all leaving?"

Moira had made the bed, over Jeannie's protests that she 'didn't need a maid, dammit'. Now she was clearing her mistress's lunch plates, and looked up. "Only the females, my lady."

"Why?"

"Because you want us to," she said simply.

"But I never said—besides, Michael's the boss of you guys, not me."

"The alpha female has expressed distress to her mate at the thought of being around us this evening. Thus, we depart." Moira shrugged. "Simple."

"But *I'm* not the—" At Moira's look, Jeannie reversed herself. "Okay, say I am. I never told you guys to go. I only told Michael."

"Werewolf hearing," Moira said with a smile, "is very acute. Besides, we can smell your torment. We don't want to add to it."

"You're really leaving your home tonight? For me? Even though I didn't ask?"

Moira just gave her a look, something along the lines of, 'yes, dummy'.

"Of course," Jeannie said slowly, "you could just be leaving so I don't see you're not werewolves."

"After everything you've seen? Felt? Eaten?"

"Ugh, don't remind me."

"You still think we're crazy? Half the town? And everyone in this house? *And* the father of your child?"

Jeannie harumphed. "Well, I'm not saying you're not convincing…" But she squirmed under Moira's stern regard.

"Well." Moira picked up the tray. "As it is, we're leaving. I'll see you tomorrow."

"Wait!" She bounded to her feet and fought the urge to pluck at Moira's sleeve like a child. "You said the females are leaving. What about the guys?"

"The 'guys'," she said dryly, "think you should get over it. But we won't go there."

"No," Jeannie shouted at Moira's retreating back, "we certainly won't!" She kicked a pillow across the room.

There was a tap on the adjoining door, and Michael poked his head in. "We certainly won't what? And stop kicking that pillow, it's a hundred years old."

Jeannie, bending to retrieve the pillow, dropped it like it was hot. "The girls are all leaving," she said in an accusing tone.

He frowned. "Yes. They told me they were. They've gotten quite loyal to you in…" He checked his watch. "Seventy-two hours."

"But the men *aren't* leaving."

"No." Seeing the confusion on her face, he added, "The females will do what the alpha female wants, period. The males will do what is best for her. Not always the same thing."

"Fascinating. Really, and I mean that." She yawned theatrically, and rubbed her eyes, feeling sudden, surprising weariness she didn't have to feign. Then she looked at him and said, no screwing around, no wise cracks, "I'm afraid."

"I know."

"Why do you have to sound like that?" she asked crossly, rubbing her eyes again. "All loving and nice."

"Because I have great admiration for you. Not just, as you think, your physical charms." He paused, then said, as baldly as she had stated her fear, "I love you."

She choked in mid-yawn, and stared at him with wide eyes. "No, you don't."

"No?" He smiled, that slow, sexy smile that always charmed her.

"You just love the way I smell. Michael, be reasonable," she said, trying to sound reasonable herself, "you don't know me well enough to love me." Thinking with surprised, giddy joy: He loves me! He loves me!

"Yes, I do," he said casually.

"Michael," she said slowly, wanting to cross the room and touch him, but unable to make herself take that step, "if you really love me, why'd you—why'd you shame me like that?"

"Are you going to run away and find Gerald?"

"No!" She shouted the word before she thought, then blushed furiously. "I mean, yeah, maybe, what's it to ya?"

"*That's* why," he said simply. "I didn't want to punish you. I wanted to take you, but I wanted you to enjoy it. I hated having to scare you." To her astonishment, she saw his hands were shaking. "I hated every second of it," he added with savage emphasis, "but I would do it a thousand times if it meant you would keep away from Gerald."

There was a short silence while they looked at each other. "Um... thank you? I guess," she muttered.

He smiled a little. "Are you tired, sweet?"

"No," she said defiantly, but her eyelids felt ridiculously heavy. "I want to keep talking about this so-called love."

"Talk while lying down," he said, taking her arm and pushing her gently onto the bed. Before she could turn around or sit up, he had slipped into bed behind her, snuggling against her, spoon-style.

"I don't want to nap with you," she said, wriggling against him.

"If you don't stop moving," he warned, his breath tickling her neck, "you won't be napping."

She went rock-still, and yawned again. "Seriously, though. Why should I reward you for—" He loves me, she reminded herself. "Oh fine, stay then," she grumbled. "See if I care."

His rumbling laugh was the last thing she heard.

❧⟨☺⟩❧

It was dark when she woke, but she could see everything in the room quite clearly. She refused to think about what that meant (you've been doing lots of refusing to think this week, huh, babe?) and instead focused on Michael, who was pacing at the foot of the bed. His face was sheened with sweat and he kept running his fingers through his hair. In the gloom, his eyes were a tortured gold. He must have fallen asleep, too, she realized, and now there isn't time for him to leave before... before...

"Michael?" The word practically stuck in her throat. He didn't turn, didn't even glance at her. "Are you all right?"

"Fine," he muttered.

Abruptly, she decided: no more fear. She couldn't fear rape if she was the aggressor. And, to be completely honest, the bastard had a touch like nothing she'd ever felt. She wanted it. At night, in her lonely bed, she *craved* it.

"No more fear," she announced, and stood up in the bed. Then she leapt at him.

He caught her, as she had known he would, and staggered back so hard his back slammed into the wall.

"My thinking is," she said into his astonished face, as she looped her legs around his waist, "I've been terrified of a repeat of the elevator scene, right? All week, I've been worrying about it. Hell, I even tried to seduce you so you would send me away. Well, if *I* rape *you*, there's nothing to be scared of. Then I can go back to sleep."

"Are you out of your—"

She kissed him. Then she bit his lower lip. He groaned and staggered with her.

"Jeannie—"

She snaked her tongue inside his mouth. His own met hers in a frantic duel before he wrenched his face from hers. "No! It's not like earlier, it's not—this close to my Change, if you change your mind I won't be able to stop." He set her down and shook her. "I won't be able to stop! And I can't bear to force you again, even for punishment. If I find out in the morning that you were frightened, hurt—no."

She ripped open his shirt.

He spun away from her, panting. "*No.*"

"For God's sake," she muttered, and jumped on his back. Looping her arms around his neck, she ignored his hoarse demand that she stop this at once, took his ear in her teeth, and bit. He howled and grabbed for her head, trying to pull her away... then changed his mind and pressed her face into the side of his head, hard. She bit him again and he groaned, "I will never understand you."

"Tough luck," she said sympathetically, then bit the side of his neck, and licked the spot.

He staggered to the bed and dropped, pinning her beneath him. She released her legs and he rolled over, shoving her sweatshirt to her neck and burying his face between her breasts. "Last chance," he moaned.

"My thought exactly," she grunted, pulling the shirt over her head, wriggling to get free of her shorts. He helped her with hands that shook and in moments they were both nude.

She started having second thoughts when he turned her over and eased her on her knees. "Michael," she managed as he kissed the base of her spine. "Anything else—any other way—but I'm not sure I'm ready for this yet."

He didn't answer, and she was about to try again when she felt his tongue flick past the opening of her vagina... then delve deeply. She bit back a moan and thought, What the hell am I hiding from? I love it, and he knows I love it.

When his thumbs spread her wide and his tongue lapped at her exposed flesh, she groaned so loudly she was fairly certain Moira, wherever she was, could hear her. He laughed at the sound, a rumble of unbridled delight, and then his tongue was inside her again, darting and wriggling.

In less than a minute she was rocking back against his sweetly busy mouth, keening softly, feeling the familiar delicious warmth start in her stomach, feeling the all-over tightening that meant her orgasm was approaching...

...then she felt the tip of him, engorged with blood, the head so like a delicious plum, ease into her... and then he shoved forward, the quick, hard thrust instantly jolting her into orgasm.

She shrieked his name and rocked back, meeting him thrust for thrust, on a roller coaster of pleasure, one swooping orgasm instantly merging into another. His low groans, so like growls, fired her blood and made her want to bite something.

She felt his teeth on her shoulder, gently, and then felt him pulsing within her. She thrust back once more, greedily, then felt him slide from her.

"Oh," she said, almost sighed.

"Christ," he groaned, and flopped face down on a pillow. She giggled, and he reached out, snagged her waist, and nestled her against his side. "Tell the truth," he rasped, and when he looked at her, she saw his pupils were huge, his irises only faint rings of gold. "You're trying to kill me, right? Wearing me out before I Change?"

She laughed again. "Does that mean you're not up for seconds?"

He didn't smile at her jibe. Instead he reached out a finger and touched her mouth. Then his rough palm was cupping her cheek. "Don't be afraid," he said, his voice so deep it was difficult to understand him. "I couldn't bear it if you were afraid."

"The funny thing is," she said seriously, "I'm not. The thing I worried about most... I *made* it happen. I had to throw myself at you—literally. But I didn't mind, because it's easier to be scared if you're the passenger, not the driver."

"Don't be afraid," he said again, panting. "I can't hold it off anymore."

He began to Change. And it happened so quickly, if she had blinked she would have missed it. His features and limbs and body seemed to shift, to melt, shrinking into a furred, four-legged wolf with a lush black coat the exact color of Michael's hair, and deep gold eyes. There wasn't a smell. There wasn't even a mess. She had just witnessed a physical impossibility.

"Guh," she said, blinking, staring, before the wolf gave her a sloppy lick on her cheek. The large, furry head bent and licked her stomach, where their child nestled. "Michael, oh Michael," she whispered, reaching out a shaking hand and touching the luxurious pelt. When the wolf—Michael—didn't move away from her touch, merely sat calmly, she gave her delight and curiosity free reign, running her hands over his strong limbs, his tail, stroking the noble head, even burying her face in his rich, black coat. She realized dimly her face was wet as the pent-up emotions—fear, anger, despair—departed as easily as Michael had shed his human form.

It was all true. They weren't crazy fools. She was the fool, for blinding herself to the truth. He was pack leader, she was his mate, she carried the next pack leader. She was in danger as long as Gerald wanted power. Michael had been right to track her and bring her to his home. She had been wrong to escape.

"Michael," she whispered into his fur, "I love you."

She didn't know if he could understand her in his lupine form, but all the same, he made a deep, rumbling noise in his chest, quite like a purr. She hoped he understood. On the other hand, she had a lifetime to repeat the phrase.

The rumbling abruptly shifted in pitch, from purr to growl. She pulled back from him, instinctively knowing Michael was incapable of hurting her in whatever form he took, but still wary. He sprang from her side and arrowed at the balcony doors, slamming into one of them hard enough to crack the heavy glass.

"Whoa!" she said, scrambling to her feet and running for the door. "You want out? No problem, just a second." After a moment she had the door open and Michael dashed past, scrambling up the railing and then fearlessly leaping into the dark.

Behind him, Jeannie watched him drop two stories, landing in a crouch on all fours. "Well, hell," she breathed, "no wonder the elevator fall didn't kill you."

She was still staring, mouth open like a rube idiot, when another wolf darted out of the cover and went for her lover's throat. This wolf had mud-colored fur the exact color of Gerald's hair, and she knew at once who the wolf had to be... and who he had come for. Michael avoided the attack, and the two powerful males squared off and charged.

He's nuts! was her first thought. Taking Michael on in his own territory? Maybe Gerald had heard all the females were gone, and assumed Jeannie would be easy for the taking... maybe he'd also heard Michael had planned to be gone this evening. And probably figured, tonight, or not at all...

Her thoughts were interrupted by a noise; she turned in time to see a buttercotch-colored wolf with Derik's green eyes rocket past her, straight over the balcony railing. Four other wolves had by now surrounded the snarling, fighting males, and Derik unhesitatingly went for the throat of the closest traitor.

Jeannie turned and went at once to the endtable drawer where she had so carelessly dropped Gerald's gun—was it only yesterday? She popped the clip, noted with grim pleasure that it was full, then slapped the clip back in, pulled back the slide, and ratcheted a load into the chamber. So Michael was right, she thought distractedly, walking back out on the balcony. Gerald's gun wouldn't have fired, and he could have killed me then. Well, well. Note to self: apologize to lover, after saving lover's ass.

A distant part of her reminded her that the room was pitch dark and there was not enough starlight for her to see by. Still, she could make out everything as clearly as if it was noon: the wolves' coloring, the lush green of the grass, even some of their eye colors. *Thank you, baby werewolf*, she thought, and then sighted in on Gerald, who had, she noticed with detached rage, just taken a chunk out of her lover's shoulder. She had no idea how Gerald expected to hustle her off Wyndham property in his wolf form. Maybe he was part human and could control his change. Regardless, she wasn't about to stand by and let him damage others—Michael!—in his quest for power.

The two wolves were locked together in an age-old battle for territory and females, and Jeannie, whose cop mother and Marine father knew a little something about battle, waited for her chance. In the meantime, Derik had chased off his opponent and, though one leg was bloodied and one ear gone, was turning hungrily on another.

Gerald reared back and went for Michael's throat. Instead, Jeannie got his—two shots, right where she guessed the adam's apple was on a werewolf.

"How about *that*, Gerald?" she shouted down. She picked off Derik's newest opponent with a clean head shot, and Derik jumped back from the newly-dead werewolf with a yip that sounded suspiciously like a laugh. "In case you didn't realize, trespassers will be shot!" Thinking: thank goodness, the stories about silver bullets aren't true.

The other traitors froze, and looked up at her, except for Gerald, who was coughing out his life on the lawn.

"This is the alpha female speaking," she said, and as the fatally wounded Gerald made one last try for Michael, she put four into his head. "Playtime's over."

The other traitors—only two, now—took off, Derik hot on their heels. Michael looked up at her, coiled, and made a clumsy jump for the balcony. She gasped when she saw his wounds.

"Lucky for us you're a fast healer," she said, and popped the live round out of the chamber. She put the gun away, then went to tend to her mate.

Chapter Ten

In bed, she could hear them chatting at breakfast, even though they were a floor below her.

"And then Michael's trying to keep Gerald off his throat, right?" Derik said. She could picture him holding the group spellbound, talking with his hands, eyes gleaming with suppressed excitement. "And I've got my hands full with those other two assholes. And Michael and I are both thinking, Cripes, are there more on the grounds? Can we take them even though the girls aren't here to help? And we're assuming Jeannie is just about out of her mind, right? I mean, *I* would have been scared at the sight. Then—ka-blammo! Close enough to singe Michael's fur, Gerald's got a couple holes in his throat, and we all look up and there's our pack leader's mate—naked, no less—holding a smoking gun and yelling at Gerald, who's been causing trouble since he was whelped."

"Then what?" Moira asked excitedly.

"Then she drills my guy, puts a few more in Gerald, binds Michael's wounds, and ate a big supper at 2:00AM."

"I knew it! I knew Michael had chosen wisely! And *you* said she'd never fit in, Dara."

"I did not. I said after a few months, she'd never fit in her clothes. That's all."

Hearing her staff speak of her with such admiration brought a warm flush to her cheeks. And really, she hadn't done all that much. Just saved the day.

The thought made her laugh out loud. Beside her, Michael was sleeping deeply, and stirred at the sound. She hushed at once and examined his shoulder. The wound looked months old, and she again thanked God for werewolf metabolism.

She touched her stomach lightly, with love. There was a were-wolf growing inside her, which should have scared her—should have creeped her out at the very least—but instead, she was filled with a joyful acceptance of her future. She didn't know much about werewolves, but she was going to learn, oh yes. Michael would help her. Her pack would help her.

A large brown hand covered hers, and she looked into Michael's golden eyes. "My own mate," he said slowly, savoring the words, "and so brave. Even when we were in the elevator, you were brave."

"Well, of course. You weren't going to let anything happen to me."

"As you, apparently, won't let anything happen to me," he said wryly. "Remind me to instruct you on the finer points of werewolf etiquette. Number one: never interfere with a Challenge." But he was smiling as he said it, and she knew that, though his male pride might be a bit ruffled, he was pleased with her.

"And number two?"

"Always take a human to mate," he said, and pulled her to him for a long kiss. When he pulled back, she was breathless, and his eyes glinted with satisfaction. "Before we were so rudely inter-rupted last night, you told me something. I very much want to hear the words again."

"So you *can* understand me when you're a—"

"The words, Jeannie."

"I love you. Dork. What, you think I'd shoot a man for just anybody?"

"For a while," he said seriously, "I wondered if you might shoot me."

"I was an idiot," she admitted. "A blind fool. It was all right in front of me, and I wouldn't accept it."

"You were perfect," he assured her, "considering the circum-stances. The words again, Jeannie, please."

"I love you."

"Let me show you how *I* feel," he whispered, and kissed her.

Their lovemaking was slow and almost dreamlike, and for Jean-nie, who had only known fierce, fast, couplings with this man, it was like discovering a whole different side to her mate. He took his time, touching her with skilled reverence, gaining pleasure from her own. Even when she was begging him to enter her, tugging on his shoulders and whimpering pleas that made his eyes narrow with lust, he held back. "No," he said, almost moaned, "this time, I want it to last."

Shuddering with pleasure beneath his hands, she had the sense that he was finally touching her as he had always longed to, and she gloried in it. When he slid into her she shivered in his arms and gasped her love, and he closed his eyes in gratitude, deeply moved. He opened his eyes and she stared into his curious gold gaze. "Oh, Jeannie," he breathed, "I love you, too, my dearest, my own mate."

They rocked together, both of them creatures of savagery and passion, and cried out until they were hoarse. And when they were done, and drowsing in each other's arms, Jeannie had time for one thought before she spiraled down into sleep: *Thank God I didn't take the stairs.*

About the author:

MaryJanice Davidson is the author of several romance novels. She's been writing since she was thirteen; **Love's Prisoner** *is her first erotic romance. She lives in Minnesota with her husband and two children, loves reading, and has a soft spot for werewolves. You can email her at alongi@usinternet.com or visit her website at www.usinternet.com/users/alongi/index.html.*

The Education of Miss Felicity Wells

by Alice Gaines

To my reader:
    At a time when all is forbidden, all will be desired...

Chapter One

Marcus Slade had seldom seen a young woman quite as frightened as the one who stood in his study at this moment, alternately biting her lip and toying with her reticule.

"Miss…," he said, greeting her as best he could without knowing so much as her name.

"Wells. Miss Felicity Wells," she supplied. "It was on my card. But then, you didn't get my card, did you? That is, there wasn't anyone to take it, not a butler nor a servant anywhere." She stopped mid-babble and gave him an uncertain smile. "Oh, dear."

"Won't you sit down, Miss Wells?" he said and indicated an upholstered armchair.

She sat very delicately in it—or perched, rather like a bird ready to take flight. He sat on the matching love seat, crossed one leg over the other, and studied her. She wasn't a particularly handsome woman, but neither was she unattractive. Her wide-set brown eyes and other regular features—straight nose, forehead neither too sloped nor too lofty—made her someone who could easily disappear into a group of women of a similar age and station in life. The healthy glow to her skin and the absence of suspicion in her aspect marked her station in life as one of wealth and privilege. One that cossetted its females and kept them safe from any harsh wind.

In short, she was exactly the sort of young woman who would have been warned away from men like him with scowls and clucking tongues and warnings of debauchery. No doubt that explained her fear, but why had she come here at all? And unaccompanied.

"May I be of service to you somehow?" he asked.

Her gaze darted around the room and then lit on his face. She leaned toward him. "Are we completely alone, Dr. Slade?"

"Completely," he answered. "As you observed, I don't have servants. I treasure my solitude."

"Good." She took a breath. "I need your help with a delicate matter."

"You intrigue me, Miss Wells."

She appeared taken aback at that, as her mouth formed a little O. She had an appealing mouth, actually, almost out of keeping with the rest of her ordinary features. A generous mouth with lush, moist lips that curved up at the corners. Yes, a very appealing mouth.

"I intrigue you?" she said on an intake of breath.

"It isn't often I get a visit from a proper young lady of Boston's Brahmin class. I'm a notorious libertine. Or maybe you didn't know that."

"And a researcher of some note in... how shall I put this... the intimate arts." She bit her lip again and gazed at him as if she couldn't be sure whether he was her salvation or a danger. "That's exactly why I've come to you."

"That intrigues me." He steepled his fingers together and looked at her over the tips. "Innocent young women don't come to my house, especially not unescorted. You are innocent, aren't you?"

Her back stiffened at that. "Of course, I am."

"Mama didn't warn you off men like me?" he asked. "Your chaperon didn't refuse you permission to come here?"

"No one knows I'm here."

"Slip your tether, did you?"

"All right, you find this amusing, Dr. Slade. I understand that. But I really do need your help."

He did find her amusing, but he hadn't lied about finding her intriguing, either. Unfortunately, whatever she wanted, he'd have to send her away without it. Too many young girls sought him out when they experienced the first flush of their own sexuality. Society didn't prepare a girl for the animal side of her nature, and her mother usually made matters worse if the child even dared to ask about the flutterings in the pit of her belly.

No, he'd vowed to keep all virgins safely at arm's length. He'd succumbed to the first innocent who'd turned to him, and he'd lived to regret it. If he hadn't let the girl's father wing his arm in a duel, thereby saving face all around, things would have turned very ugly, indeed. He wasn't about to make that mistake again.

"I'm afraid I can't help you," he said.

"But you don't even know what I want," she objected.

"You come unescorted to the house of Boston's most celebrated hedonist to ask for help with a delicate matter. What else could you want but a good frigging? I'm sorry, Miss Wells, but I'm not in the business of deflowering virgins."

He cheeks turned bright pink, and her full lips parted as she took in a sharp breath. "But I don't want to be deflowered," she said. "Oh dear, this is very complicated."

He crossed his arms over his chest and watched her as she rose from her chair and walked to the fireplace. She rested her hand against the marble mantelpiece and gazed into the flames of the small fire he'd built to keep away the chill of an early Spring afternoon.

"I'm to be married soon," she said.

"Congratulations," he answered. "Then the sex will take care of itself, won't it?"

"That's just the problem. It won't take care of itself. I have to take care of it, and I don't know how."

"But surely, if you love the man..."

She turned toward him. "Love?" she said. "What does love have to do with marriage?"

"Isn't that what modern young women insist on now? Marrying for love."

"That may well be, but I have no plans to marry for love. Why in heaven's name would I want to give a man that kind of power over me?"

"Power?"

She looked at him as if he were a perfect idiot. "Loving him. Love makes a woman weak. It makes her vulnerable. I don't intend to fall in love with my husband until he's proven himself worthy."

"Oh, really?" He couldn't quite manage to stifle a chuckle at the thought of some poor male having to make himself worthy of the unremarkable Miss Felicity Wells. "And what will you offer your husband as a reward while he's struggling to win your love?"

"Lust," she answered. "I intend to satisfy his lust."

Marc laughed outright at that. What did this woman, with her whalebone stays and the proper set of her posture know about a man's lust? What did she know of desiring and needing and holding back until the woman's cries begged him to take her? Of sweating and groaning and straining for release, only to need more almost immediately? Of a steel hard cock, throbbing to the point of pain, aching to drive itself home in a woman's flesh?

She couldn't know about those things, but he did. And damn him if he wasn't responding to her right now, Priapus growing thick in his pants as he watched the prim Miss Felicity Wells stand at his hearth and talk of a man's lust. His reaction to her was laughable. Preposterous. Out of the question. He wouldn't give in to it. But he could amuse himself with her for a few more moments without harm.

"Men are lustful creatures," she said. "Completely at the mercy of their baser natures."

"You know that from experience, do you?"

She glowered at him, the expression turning her lips into a tempting pout. "Never mind how I know it. I just do."

"And you want to learn how to use a man's baser nature against him."

"No, no, no. You're deliberately misunderstanding me."

"Then, please explain to this lustful beast what it is you *do* want."

Her cheeks flamed again, but she stood her ground and faced him. "I want to be very, very good at... at..."

"At sex," he supplied.

"At the marriage act."

"At sex," he repeated.

"All right, if you insist, at sex. I want to satisfy my husband's every whim. I want him to desire no one but me. That isn't so bad, is it?"

"It's quite admirable," he answered.

"Well, there you are, then."

"And quite impossible," he added. "Monogamy is unnatural,

especially for men."

She walked back to the chair she'd vacated and rested her hands on the back, her fingers digging into the crimson velvet of the upholstery. "I don't believe that. I won't believe it."

"Study nature as I have, and you won't find exclusive mating relationships anywhere. Males compete with each other to rut with as many females as possible."

"I don't see how crude language helps this discussion."

"You wouldn't," he replied. "The female is every bit as profligate as her male, although somewhat more subtle in her tactics. No, my dear Miss Wells, monogamy doesn't exist in nature. It's a human invention conceived to make us all miserable."

"What a cynical view of things."

"I? Cynical? You're the one who's come to me to learn how to please another man. A man who'll trust you to be innocent. How cynical is that?"

"I only want to please him," she cried. "Really, that's all I want."

"And what do you get in return?"

She didn't answer but turned her face away. A slight tremble of her chin told him she was trying to contain herself. She badly wanted to cry but wouldn't let him see her tears. What in hell had he said that would make her cry? Oh, damn it all.

He rose and walked to her side. "Miss Wells, I don't mean to be unkind, but you have no idea what you're asking."

"I would if you'd tell me, Dr. Slade," she answered in a small voice. "I'm a quick study. All my teachers have said so."

"This is different." He reached out and turned her face to him. His fingers looked perfectly huge against her delicate chin, and unshed tears added a luster to the warm brown of her eyes. "The physical side of love isn't something that can be taught like history or literature. It has to be experienced."

"I understand."

"We'd have to engage in behavior that society frowns on outside of marriage. Even some things society frowns on within marriage."

"I'm willing to do all that," she said, looking up at him with a clear entreaty in her eyes.

"I'm not. As I told you, I won't take your virginity."

"And as I told you, I don't want you to take my virginity. I only want you to teach me how to satisfy a man."

He ran a thumb over her lower lip and watched as a tiny tremor ran through her. Fear, perhaps. Excitement, definitely. He moved his hand to skim the tips of his fingers along her jaw and then down the soft length of her throat to where her jacket closed very chastely over her collar bone.

"I'll give you one lesson in love right now," he said.

"Please," she breathed.

"Nothing excites a man more than passion in his partner. If I'm to turn you into an irresistible temptress, I'll have to urge your own lustful nature into full blossom."

"Oh," she whispered, and her skin became hot beneath his touch.

"It wouldn't be entirely unpleasant for you." He bent and put his lips next to her ear. "Would you like for me to do that?"

"Yes," she whispered. "Yes, I think I would."

He nuzzled the space behind her ear with his nose, breathing in her fragrance. Something innocent. Rose water and soap. "We'll both become very agitated. We'll both want full consummation. We'll want that very badly."

"Yes," she repeated.

He nipped at her earlobe with his teeth, and she gave out a little cry. "Do you think you can resist?" he asked.

She rested a hand against his chest and pushed herself away from him. "I'll have to."

He looked down into her face. "Are you sure?"

"I'm sure," she answered. "And what about you? Are you sure you can resist?"

He laughed. "Oh yes, Miss Wells, I'm sure."

"Then that's settled," she said. "You will take me as a pupil? I can pay you well."

"I don't want your money. I have plenty of my own."

A look of alarm crossed her face, as though she feared he wouldn't give in. He shouldn't, really.

She'd still be a virgin when he was through with her, though. Still quite marriageable, with no need for her father to come gunning after him. She'd go off and marry her fiancee, and everyone would be happy. But what would he gain in exchange? Nothing. Unless…

"Very well," he said. "I'll serve as your guide to the sensual if you'll do something for me."

She raised an eyebrow. "What would that be?"

"As you mentioned, I've made a study of the human sexual drives. I'd like to use our encounters to observe your sexual responses systematically."

Her eyes widened. "How would you do that?"

"I'd ask you to report—in great detail—everything you're thinking and feeling when I touch you. When you touch me."

She gave a sigh of relief. "Of course, I could do that."

"Think a moment what I'm asking of you," he said. "No dissembling. No hiding anything from me. Your thoughts, your dreams, your fantasies—I could demand them at any time, and you'd be obliged to supply them."

She took a breath and looked him straight in the eye. "I could do that."

"Good." He extended his hand toward her. "Then, you have a teacher, Miss Wells."

She took his hand and gave it a firm shake. "I take my constitutional on Monday, Wednesday, and Friday afternoons. Except when it rains. I'll visit you then until I'm satisfied that I can be a good lover to my husband. Agreed?"

"Agreed."

"Until Wednesday, then."

He gestured toward the study door. "I'll see you out."

"No need," she answered. "I can find my own way."

"As you wish."

Since she hadn't removed so much as her hat or reticule, there was nothing for her to gather up. She simply turned and walked briskly from the room, leaving the scent of rose water in her wake. Marc watched her go and only then realized that he had an enormous, aching erection.

Although comfortably soft and smooth against Felicity's bare skin, Dr. Slade's shirt nevertheless rubbed her bosom in a frankly disturbing way, the friction irritating the peaks of her breasts. Although if asked, she'd have to admit that the feeling wasn't entirely unpleasant. In fact, the sensation stirred something deep inside her—a hodge-podge of feelings and urges that reached all the way to the pit of her stomach. The very idea of that made no sense at all, of course, and the whole of the experience left her rather breathless and confused. But then, she'd never before sat in a man's study wearing nothing but his shirt, so maybe her reaction was entirely normal and to be expected.

The man himself sat across the desk, making notes in a book as though he entertained nearly-naked women every day. He scratched out a few more lines, and the sounds of his pen somehow resonated through the fabric of his shirt to chafe her breasts even further. Oh dear heaven, that last was truly ridiculous. She shifted in her seat, but the movement only made matters worse.

He looked up and studied her face for a moment, a light of intense curiosity in his blue eyes. "First I want to know about your sexual history," he said.

"I don't have one, I'm afraid."

"Nonsense, everyone has had some lustful adventure or other by your age."

"I've lived a very sheltered life."

He set his pen aside and cleared his throat in a stern manner that a minister or headmistress might have admired. "We agreed that you'd reveal everything to me, Miss Wells. It was the one condition I made to tutoring you."

She clutched his shirt around her, even though she'd taken great care to button all the buttons. The action only increased the friction against her nipples, and she shifted again, trying in vain to make herself comfortable. "I'm not holding back, Dr. Slade. I just have nothing to report."

"All right then, let's approach this more methodically." He lifted his pen again. "You've never had full knowledge of a man?"

"I beg your pardon."

He huffed again. "You've never been screwed. You've never taken a man's staff between your legs."

"Of course not," she answered. But oddly enough, just the thought made her tingle in the place where her thighs touched the leather upholstery of her chair.

"Has a man ever touched you there?" he went on. "Has any young fellow ever slipped his hand inside your drawers and fondled your nest?"

"No," she exclaimed.

"You needn't sound offended. This is exactly the sort of discussion we're to have during our sessions," he said. A light flush of anger appeared over his high cheek bones, coloring the pale skin that made such a contrast against his near-black hair. "You'll never learn to accept your lascivious nature if you become shocked at any mention of your pussy."

"My pussy?" she repeated.

"Your pussy. Your cunt. The seat of your husband's delight. Do you understand?"

She looked down into her lap but only found her own naked legs and the hems of his shirt. "I understand."

"Coyness won't serve us here, Miss Wells."

"I know that."

"In fact, you should realize what so few young girls do. Coyness isn't appealing. It's irritating."

"I'm sorry," she said.

"All right, then." He wrote a few more lines in his book, and she studied his face. The flush was still there, although less pronounced, as his gaze stayed fixed on the paper in front of him. His long, black eyelashes cast shadows over his cheeks, softening what were otherwise rather harsh, angular features.

"Has a man ever touched your breasts?" he asked without looking up.

"No."

"Has a man ever kissed you?"

"No."

He glanced up at her, disbelief written in his expression.

"I'm sorry, but that's the truth," she said. "You don't want me to invent stories, do you?"

"No," he answered, his expression gentling. Slightly. "Has anyone else ever kissed you?"

"Anyone else?"

"A boy, another girl... anyone."

"No," she said. "Oh, wait... that's not true. My cousin Henry did once. It was Christmas, and our families were visiting. He came upon me all alone and forced me to kiss him."

"Go on," he answered, bending to his writing again. "How old were you?"

"I was twelve, I think. Yes." She closed her eyes briefly, trying to capture the details in her mind—the cold wind of that December day, the sounds of the horses in their stalls, the feel of the planking against her back as Henry had pressed her back against the wall. "Henry had been looking at me oddly all through dinner, and his foot reached out under the table to touch mine a few times. I'd never liked him, with his fat cheeks and squinty eyes. I escaped as soon as I could and ran out of the house, but he followed me."

"How old was he?" Dr. Slade asked.

"Sixteen and very much enamored with himself. He told me that he'd become a man and that I'd soon be a woman and that he could show me what went on between men and women."

"And what did you say?"

"I told him that if I couldn't do any better than him when I *did* become a woman, I'd stay an old maid. I ordered him to let me go back into the house, but he didn't. He grabbed my hair, pulled me into the carriage house, and kissed me."

"What do you remember of the kiss?" he asked.

She looked at him. His expression held neither approval nor censure, just curiosity as he studied her evenly. "It was wet and unpleasant," she answered. "He pressed his mouth against mine, crushing my lips against my teeth. Then he parted my lips and tried to put his tongue into my mouth."

"What did you do?"

"I bit it."

He smiled at her. "Good girl."

"Good?" she repeated. "I was hardly an obedient female."

"We're not her to teach you to obey, Miss Wells. We're here to encourage the passionate side of your nature."

She reached down and toyed with the hem of his shirt. "And we're going to touch each other in order to do that?"

"Certainly."

She took a breath, a none-too-steady breath. "Do you plan to kiss me?"

"Yes, I think so," he answered. "This very afternoon. I won't put my tongue into your mouth unless you want me to."

She did her best to calmly digest this bit of information, despite the furious beating of her heart. Dr. Slade wasn't her cousin Henry. He wouldn't force himself on her, wouldn't handle her roughly or awkwardly. He was a fully-grown man with a great deal of experience in the boudoir, if any of the stories were true. Kissing him really ought to prove far more interesting than kissing cousin Henry.

"What are you thinking?" he asked. "Right now."

She gazed at him, her attention rivetted on his mouth. His lips appeared gentler than the angles of his face and jaw. But neither were they particularly soft. Would she find them hard? Would the kiss be wet and unpleasant as Henry's had been? Or would it be as exciting as she'd heard kisses can be?

"What are you thinking?" he repeated, putting more force into the demand.

She felt heat rise over her cheeks. "I was thinking that I'm looking forward to you kissing me."

His eyes widened almost imperceptibly for just a moment, and then he looked down to write some more in his book. She could easily learn to dislike the sound of his pen as it scratched over the paper. Here she'd confessed to some desire for him, and instead of saying anything in reply, he'd simply written her wishes down. Still, she'd agreed to this. She sighed.

"In good time," he said. "I'll kiss you after you've answered a few more questions."

Oh, dear heaven. He'd mistaken her sigh for impatience. No matter how great her curiosity about the texture of his lips, no matter how persistent the ache in her bosom, she had no urgent need for his caress. He was only a man, and not even the one she intended to share the marriage bed with. She only needed him for her purpose. Surely, he realized that.

"Dr. Slade," she began.

"In good time," he repeated.

What a ridiculous, impossible situation. She crossed her arms, but that only pushed her breasts upward, showing that the peaks had hardened into stiff, little nubs. When had that happened?

He noticed them, obviously, because his gaze came to rest there and lingered. Then he wrote something else down, damn him. The whole encounter had grown ridiculous and only promised to get worse. She really ought to tell him she'd had enough for one day, get up, dress herself, and leave. If only she could rely on her legs not to tremble.

"Has anyone ever touched you between your thighs?" he asked abruptly.

"I told you no one had."

"You told me no man had. I'm asking if anyone else had."

"Cousin Henry didn't, I can tell you that much."

"There's no need to get waspish, Miss Wells," he said. "You wanted to be tutored, if you'll remember."

"No one has ever touched me between my thighs, Dr. Slade," she said and felt her cheeks positively burn with mortification.

"No little girl school chum sharing your bed?" he said. "No groping under the coverlet?"

"No. The very idea. Another girl."

"It happens all the time, and there's nothing wrong with it," he said, glaring at her.

"It never happened to me."

"Have you ever touched yourself?" he demanded.

"No." Oh dear, except for that one time. "I'm sorry. That isn't quite true. I'd almost forgotten."

"Tell me about it."

Vague memories came back to her. Lying in her bed in the middle of a rainy night. She'd been half-awake, warm and dry. No, hot. So hot there. Surely, he didn't need to know about that. "I'd rather not discuss it."

His ice blue gaze focussed on her face. "I'd rather you did. As part of our agreement."

"Oh, very well." She took a breath and allowed the images to fill her mind. "I'd been asleep, having a very strange dream. In my dream, I'd been riding a horse." She hesitated. "Astride. Without a saddle."

"Go on."

"It was a very singular horse. Warm, chestnut brown. And large. Very, very large."

He didn't comment on that, but made a few more scratches with his pen. After a moment, he looked up at her. Expecting her to continue, no doubt.

She cleared her throat. "The beast was so impossibly huge—his back so broad—that I had to spread my legs as far apart as I could to stay seated. And he kept running and running, and the muscles of his back kept bunching and rolling under me. Faster and harder. Until something happened inside me—some kind of aching. It woke me up."

God help her, it was all happening again. That throbbing between her legs. Right now as she shifted in the chair, the leather rubbing against that part of her body.

"And you touched yourself then?" he asked.

"When I awoke I discovered that my hand was pressed against myself there. So, I moved my fingers, squeezing."

"And…?" he said.

Sweet Lord, she didn't have to tell him all this, did she? It had all taken place so long ago. What could it have to do with her current problem?

"And…?" he repeated, insistent now.

"It sent such a shock through me. It frightened me. I could scarcely breathe."

"Was this shock painful, unpleasant?"

"No, it was very pleasant. But too strong. Frightening. Over-powering."

"What did you do?" he asked.

"I moved my hand to pull the covers under my chin. Then I lay very, very still until I could fall back asleep again. It seemed to take hours."

"Thank you," he said. He set his pen aside and reached toward her. His fingers touched the top button of the shirt she wore, and she jumped nearly out of her skin. "I'm not going to hurt you," he said softly. "I only want to look at your throat."

She took a steadying breath and tried to relax as he unfastened the button and moved the fabric aside. He peered intently at her skin, at the violent flush that covered her neck and shoulders. Then he moved his hands to where the pulse beat at the base of her throat. He must have liked what he discovered there, because a tiny smile crossed his lips. He closed the shirt and studied her. "You're embarrassed."

"Yes."

"Is it only that? Or is there more reason for you to color like this?"

She could lie. Anyone would be embarrassed to tell a story like that. He'd believe her if she lied. "There's more," she answered. "Much more."

He made no comment but merely rose from his chair and walked to a book shelf, leaving her to sit where she was. Miserable and ashamed and excited beyond any reason. She hugged the shirt around her and moved once again, trying to find some release. But everything she did made matters worse.

After a moment, he returned with a large volume bound in leather. "I want you to look at some pictures and tell me how they make you feel."

He resumed his seat and set the book in front of her. "What do you know about the male anatomy?"

If it was possible for her skin to grow even hotter, it did. She could feel the blush to the roots of her hair. "I've seen my cat groom himself. I know there's something that grows stiff on a man the same way it does on my cat."

"But you've never seen a man in that state."

"No. Cousin Henry did push his hips against me that time, and I felt a hardness there. I assume that's what that was."

"Charming fellow, your cousin Henry," he said. "You're not marrying him, I hope."

"Certainly not. No one in my family can abide him."

"Good." He opened the book, looking at the pages upside-down. "Look at this picture and tell me what you see."

She glanced down and found a picture of a naked man and woman sitting on a blanket in a sunlit grove. A very distinct protuberance stuck straight out from the man's body. "It looks like a shaft, I imagine," she said. "And there's a rather large, reddened tip on the end."

"Does it frighten you?" he said.

"No," she answered. "That is, yes, a little. But it's not unattractive, either. It's compelling in an odd way."

"Look at some more pictures," he said.

She turned a page and found a brown-skinned couple, both partially clad. The man was fondling the woman's breast while she stroked his shaft. Both appeared to be enjoying themselves immensely. She turned another page, and a little cry of alarm escaped her lips before she could stop it.

"What's wrong?" he said.

"This man," she managed to gasp, looking down at the picture. It showed a man and woman in Asian dress. Preparing to couple, no doubt. But oh dear heaven, no one could be proportioned like this man. His thing was as thick as a woman's forearm and almost as long. "It isn't possible. No man could be built like this."

Dr. Slade looked at the page and laughed. "That's *shenga*," he said. "A Japanese form where the size of the man's cock is exaggerated for stylistic purposes."

"So, it isn't real?"

"No." He turned the page and glanced at another picture. "This is more realistic for the average man."

She studied another depiction of a male nude, his thick cock standing proudly erect. The proportions of this man seemed much more possible, but he was still very imposing, indeed. A woman was supposed to take something this large inside her body?

"May I ask you a question?" she said, looking up and meeting Dr. Slade's gaze straight on. "You're made the same as these men, aren't you?"

"Yes."

"Are you as big as this man?"

He looked again at the picture briefly. "Rather larger, actually."

Oh dear heaven.

"You'll see for yourself soon," he added. "All I'd need to do is stand before you now, and you'd get a very good idea of the size of my rod from the bulge in the front of my pants."

She raised her hands to her lips. "You're in that, um, state now? Even as we sit here?"

"I've been fully erect since you told me about your dream." He smiled at her, more than a hint of challenge in his eyes. "Would you like to see for yourself?"

"Oh, dear," she gasped, too terrified and too fascinated to say yes or no.

He rose and walked around the desk until he stood right in front of her. He parted the sides of his jacket, and true to his word, an enormous bulge distended his trousers. She stared at it and swallowed hard. Heaven help her, her fingers ached to touch the thing. To stroke him and see what he'd do. But she didn't. She just sat and gaped at him.

After what seemed like several minutes, he reached out a hand toward her. "Come."

Chapter Two

Felicity had no idea where Dr. Slade would lead her, but given the fact that she'd put herself in a position where she could refuse him nothing, she could hardly start making demands now. So, like a good, little marionette, she put her hand in his much larger one and rose from her seat. He didn't take her far. Only to a settee at one end of the room, where he sat, spread his legs apart, and patted one knee. "Sit," he said.

"On your lap?"

"You wanted me to kiss you, didn't you?"

"Yes."

"We can do that in a different position," he said. "But this is the easiest."

She stepped between his legs, into the sphere of the warmth of his body and the smell of his shaving soap. He reached up and put his hands around her waist, finally guiding her down onto his knee. She kept her bare toes firmly anchored in the carpet and looked downward, away from his face.

Unfortunately, her gaze settled on the front of his pants. His jacket had fallen open when he sat, giving her a clear view of the bulge she'd seen before. She really ought to look away, but the thing held her gaze. It wasn't shapeless, really, but rather a ridge—long and thick—starting at the base of his torso and straining up toward his waist. Exactly like the shafts she'd seen in those paintings. She could almost make out the contour of the head.

Her heart beat faster just looking at him that way. But no matter how engrossing she found his body, she would have to remember always that she had refused him one thing. He would not put that impressive instrument into her, no matter how much they both wanted it.

"Do you like what you see?" he asked.

She looked into his face and found amusement in his eyes. "'Like' is a silly word, don't you think?" she replied.

"A good answer, Miss Wells. What word would you use?"

"Compelling. A little frightening. Quite removed from my experience so far in life." She looked straight into his face. No matter what, she would not allow him to catch her staring like a startled doe at that part of his body again. "Am I to touch you there?"

"Not today. Today we concentrate on your body."

"Oh." The sound rushed out of her before she could compose herself. He might have interpreted that one syllable as disappointment, when in fact, it was more surprise. The mere thought of him concentrating on her body had made her even more aware of the pressure of his shirt against her breasts and the heat between her legs where her bare flesh met the wool of his trousers.

He didn't react to her utterance but merely studied her face intently. "What are you feeling, right now?"

Her cheeks grew hot with embarrassment, but she'd made this bargain with him, and she planned to keep her part. "Breathless," she answered. "I feel as if the air is fluid somehow and I can't get enough into my lungs."

"Kiss me," he commanded softly.

"How?"

"However it pleases you. Just touch your lips to mine for a start."

Sitting on his lap, her face was at the same level as his, and she only needed to lean toward him to bring his mouth within reach. He did the most amazing thing as she approached. He closed his eyes, almost the way a cat does when it's being petted. She brought up her fingers to stroke the angular line of his jaw before she covered the last distance and kissed him.

His lips were warm and dry as she tasted them, and although they yielded to hers, they made no movement of their own. He was leaving all the choices to her, it appeared. Letting her decide where to take the kiss. That knowledge warmed her heart, banishing any fear. She took a breath, savoring the scent of him and then closed her own eyes and gave herself over to kissing him in earnest.

Sweet, so impossibly sweet, this touching of mouths. That made no sense, and yet it couldn't be denied. She sampled his upper lip and then his bottom one, nipping at it gently. Tasting his nectar. A sigh escaped her, and she slipped her arms around his neck to pull herself to him.

Finally, he responded. His lips parted and he moved them against hers. At first gently, tentatively, and then with more authority—joining hers in a dance of sorts. Urging and teasing and cajoling. All the while, his hands roamed over her back, warming her and bringing her breasts against the solid muscle of his chest. Reality dissolved, leaving her with nothing but his kiss and his warmth. And the ache that radiated out from her bosom to places below.

He made a soft groaning sound in the back of his throat and ran his tongue over her lower lip. The light rasping sent a tremor through her, and she let her own tongue venture out to find his. When they met, the contact created such a jolt of pleasure, she cried out.

He pulled back immediately. "I'm sorry. I promised I wouldn't do that."

"If I didn't want you to," she answered in a voice that had grown oddly strained. "I was only surprised that it felt so good."

He smiled, and the expression gentled his features, as did the softness of the lips she'd so thoroughly kissed and the drowsy look in his eyes. "You were right, Miss Wells. You are a very quick study."

She blushed at the compliment and also at the rush of unfamiliar sensations. How could simple contact with a man she hardly knew set her heart to racing? And why had her skin grown hotter than any amount of embarrassment could have caused? And why was she throbbing between her thighs when he hadn't even touched her there? Yet.

"Yes," he whispered. "You're an apt student. A perfect delight to instruct."

He pressed his mouth to the base of her throat, where he'd earlier tested her pulse. She let her head fall back in pleasure while he nipped and kissed a path up her throat to her ear. He nibbled on the lobe, and his breath slipped into her ear, making her own breath catch loudly.

"What are you feeling?" he whispered. "Tell me."

"I feel as if my flesh is on fire. As if flames were licking at me instead of your tongue."

"And now?" he murmured, as his lips skimmed the line of her jaw.

"Oh," she cried. "I can't say. That is... it's all so... oh... overpowering."

He pulled his face back and gazed into her eyes, his own eyes heavy-lidded and hungry looking. "But you're not afraid."

She took a shaky breath. "No, I'm not afraid."

"Good. We'll explore further." He reached for the second button of the shirt she wore—the top one still undone from before. She watched in fascination as his fingers worked at that button. And then the next. And the next. Any modest girl ought to stop him. Any decent girl would swoon from mortification. And although she did feel faint, it was only from pleasure and delicious anticipation of what would come next.

Finally, he had them all opened, and he gently pushed the shirt open to expose her body to his view. He appeared as fascinated with her as she had been earlier with the swelling in his pants. She looked down at herself and tried to picture what he saw.

Her skin had turned a bright pink, but then, she'd guessed as much by the way it felt. Her breasts rose and fell with her rapid breathing, and the nipples had turned into hard, little peaks surrounded by rosy flesh. Below lay the curves of her belly and hips. Would he think them too fat? And there between her legs sat the thatch of brown curls that hid her sex.

"What will my husband see when he looks at me?" she asked. "Will he find me acceptable?"

"Acceptable?" he answered. "My dear Miss Wells, any man who finds you anything less than exemplary is a fool."

"You like what you see?" she asked.

"'Like' is a silly word." He moved a hand under one of her breasts and tested its weight. "These are small and perfect. Firm like ripe fruit. My mouth waters at the prospect of tasting them."

"Please do," she breathed. Heaven help her, but she ached to have him do exactly that.

"In good time." He moved his hand lower, over her belly to her hip and the outside of her thigh. "Your legs are long and graceful. Your thighs delightfully plump."

"Not too plump?"

"Just right to warm a man's ears during gamahucherie."

"Gama…"

He smiled—an endearing expression she could learn to love if she weren't careful. "Later," he said. "Much later."

"Are we to put everything off until later?" she demanded, sounding petulant even to her own ears.

"Lust shouldn't be rushed, my eager student. It's most delicious if savored. Besides, I haven't even described your most charming attribute—your cunt. You'll want my opinion of your cunt, won't you?"

Her cunt. That place between her legs that craved him, his touch. "Please," she said.

"Your little cunny is delightful," he said. "Its nest warm and inviting and the lips puckered and begging to be frigged."

"You won't," she said. "You can't. You promised."

"Not with my cock, although he's more than ready and up to the job. My poor ramrod will have to be disappointed today."

"Not today," she said. "Not ever."

"I'm a man of my word, Miss Wells. But there are things I can do that will leave you a virgin. And right now your sweet pussy is weeping against my trousers. I must touch it."

Dear heaven, what such language did to her. She ought to cover her ears and run from the room, but the mere thought of his hard cock—eager and straining to be inside her—made her want to stroke him there. And he had spoken about her pussy weeping. Somehow she'd grown quite wet between her legs, hot liquid burning her flesh. Whatever was building inside her, he could cure it with his touch. She knew that even though she had no idea how she knew.

"May I touch your cunt, Miss Wells?" he whispered. "May I press against the nubbin there and bring you relief?"

"Yes," she gasped. "Please."

He did, and she nearly shrieked with delight, it felt so good. He stroked her fur and then separated the lips and stroked at her core. She clung to his neck as he rubbed and rubbed. "Dear Lord, I'm going to swoon," she cried. "I don't swoon. I never swoon, but oh heaven..."

"You're going to spend," he answered. "Give yourself up to it."

As though she had any choice. The pressure of his fingers, the insistent friction against the seat of her pleasure. The stroking, the fire, the lightening building there. She couldn't endure it. Surely, it would kill her.

If that weren't enough, he bent and covered her breast with his mouth. A whole new set of sensations rushed through her, connecting with the heat at her core. She gasped in her delight as he sucked there. Without knowing what she did, she squeezed her legs together around his hand, sending her ever closer to the something. Something she couldn't name and couldn't avoid.

"Yes, my sweet," he muttered against her bosom. "Yes, that's it. Come now, give me your cream."

He rubbed her even harder, faster. She responded deep inside, the pressure coiling and building. She rested her head against his shoulder and shut her eyes as her hips moved against his hand, seeking out his rhythm and finding it.

Finally, it was on her. A wave of fire, starting where his fingers played with her and radiating out to her breasts, her heart, her very being. She contracted and then convulsed—spasm chasing spasm—as she cried out in delirium. Over and over and over. Oh, heaven, so sweet. So powerful.

And then she felt spent, weak and helpless. She hung on his neck, her head still on his shoulder, and sobbed out her joy. He removed his hand from her nest and brought it to her face as he tucked her head under his chin. Her own scent clung to his fingers—musky and warm. He stroked her hair and made comforting noises in his throat while she felt the life slowly return to her limbs.

"Still not frightened?" he said.

"No," she whispered, her throat quite dry. She licked her lips.

"That was… that was… oh dear."

"That was what?"

"That was wonderful," she sighed.

He chuckled and slid his arms around her, pulling her close to his chest. She surrendered to him, to the comfort and peace of his embrace. The feelings were every bit as delicious as the passion he'd just aroused but far more dangerous. In fact, as her brain started to understand what had just happened to her, she realized one more thing. No matter what, she could not give her heart to him. For her very survival, she must not come to love this man.

Marc sat and watched Miss Wells pace around his study like a caged cat. She wore his shirts easily now—always buttoned, but never all the way up to her throat. Sometimes she even kept on her boots, stockings, and garters so that he had to make some effort for a glimpse of smooth, white thigh. Today she was barefoot and quite put out with him, if he correctly read the over-the-shoulder scowls she sent him as she padded across the carpet this way and that. Good. He'd planned for her to want a great deal more than she was getting from him, and it appeared his plan had worked.

"The soles of your feet must be burned from so much friction against my carpet," he said. "Why don't you come over here and sit down?"

"Whatever for?" she replied.

"We can talk more easily without so much distance between us."

She snorted, for not the first time that afternoon. "Talk. Is that all you want to do? Talk?"

"Hardly," he answered. "We do a great deal more than just talk."

She huffed and crossed her arms beneath her breasts. The action bunched up those two delectable mounds of flesh and stretched the linen of his shirt over their rigid peaks. By now she had to know that the sight of her that way inflamed him. And sure enough, she glanced at him out of the corner of her eye, her gaze resting point-edly on where his fully engorged member presssed hard against the front of his pants.

She'd turned into quite a coquette in the four weeks he'd been instructing her. But she hadn't learned to win her way in everything yet, and she wasn't going to on this particular afternoon, either.

"'Talk' hardly describes our afternoons together," he continued. "I've worked hard to bring you to completion on your every visit. Sometimes more than once."

She didn't answer but stared intently at the wall opposite her.

"I've been a very diligent paramour, haven't I?" he said.

Still stony silence from the very obstinate Miss Wells.

"Haven't I?" he demanded.

"Yes," she answered finally.

"But you want more, don't you?"

"Yes."

"You want my cock where my fingers have been, don't you?"

This time chagrin held her tongue, as her cheeks and throat turned a furious red. Dear God, her blushes of embarrassment were almost as appealing as the flush of passion on her skin just before she spent. If she managed to keep that innocence while also indulging her lascivious nature, she'd make the most glorious wanton the world had ever seen. If he were ever to shackle himself to one woman for a lifetime, it would have to be such a woman.

"You promised to hide nothing from me," he said. "You want my cock where my fingers have been, don't you?"

"Yes," she answered in a small voice. "And it's impossible."

He patted the settee beside him. "Come and sit and talk to me."

This time, she obeyed. She crossed the carpet and dropped down beside him. He reached out to stroke her cheek with the backs of his fingers. She sighed in pleasure, the way she always did when he caressed her. The simple trust inherent in her response always touched something inside him, and more and more he found himself stroking her whenever he had the chance.

"Tell me of your impending marriage," he said. "When is it to be?"

"Four months from now."

"You'll have all you could want of a man's cock after that," he said. "Surely you can wait that long."

"I suppose so," she said, but she didn't sound at all convinced.

Poor thing. He really would feel sorry for her if he didn't know beyond any uncertainty that he'd planned the very best introduction to the male appendage that she could hope for. Few men realized how intimidating a stiff rod could be to the uninitiated female. Especially one as large as his own. They simply reached into their pants and pulled out long tom, expecting the girl to swoon with delight.

Miss Felicity Wells wouldn't get a view of him naked, much less a touch of his stiff sex, until she wanted nothing more in the world than to fondle him. Unfortunately, that meant that every Monday, Wednesday, and Friday afternoon he had to allow his cock to swell to almost painful stiffness—a state it had no difficulty achieving at all—so that she could look but not touch.

All would work out for the best for both of them. If the waiting didn't kill him first.

"Tell me about your fiancé," he said. "I don't even know his name."

"George Wilmont," she answered. "Of the textile Wilmonts."

"Very wealthy," he said. He moved his hand to beneath her chin and began to stroke her throat. "Do you love him?"

"I told you I didn't."

"And does he love you?"

She grasped his hand and lowered it from her neck, toying with his fingers. "Why does that matter?"

He settled their entwined hands in her lap where he could burrow his fingers under the tails of his shirt and fondle her thigh. "It seems sad to marry someone you don't care for at all."

"We both know what sort of partnership we're entering. We've been very specific about what we expect."

He slid his fingers down toward her knee and back in the direction of her sex. "And what is that?"

"I'll be a model wife for him. The sort of wife a man in his station deserves. And he'll be a devoted husband."

"You mean, he won't let his affections stray."

She looked at him, a light of defiance in her eyes. "You've told me your opinion of marital fidelity."

"It's impossible. We're all designed to seek gratification where we find it. From as many willing partners as possible."

"I won't," she answered, her expression positively radiating anger. "I wouldn't do that to someone I cared for or even liked."

"Women stray as often as men. Or at least they would if the penalty for being caught weren't so much greater than it is for men."

"No," she insisted.

"It's human nature," he said. "You may try to pretend you're different, but after a while, you'd find yourself noticing other men, wanting them. No matter how happy your husband makes you."

"No!" She started to rise, but he held her with firm but gentle pressure against her thigh.

"Why does this upset you so?"

"Because I've seen what happens. I've seen the damage, the misery."

"Tell me what it is you've seen."

She stared down in her lap and bit her lip, looking for all the world as she had on that day of their first visit. When she'd been near tears. He took her chin in his hand and turned her face to him. "Tell me, Felicity."

"My mother... that is, my father. He's been such a beast over the years. Everyone knows how he is. I couldn't even have a friend home from school without him trying to molest her in our own house."

She stopped speaking and searched his face for something. He held very still, letting her decide whether to trust him with her story.

"He's always had other women—high born and low. He takes them out in public sometimes. As though he wants us to know what he's doing. As though he intends to hurt us. I hate him. I'll never forgive him for what he's done. Never."

"He's acting out of selfishness, not lust," Marc said. "That's domination, imposing one's will on everyone weaker."

"You can call it what you want, but it's nearly killed my mother. Sometimes I've been afraid she'd harm herself—anything to escape the humiliation." She took a shuddering breath. "That won't happen to me. I won't let it happen."

"And so that's why you came to me—in hopes that I could make you so desirable to your husband he'd always be faithful."

She looked back into her lap again. "Don't laugh."

"I'm not laughing." The poor child had set herself an impossible task. She'd even brought herself to a complete stranger and offered the most embarrassing intimacies in hopes of winning what no man would ever give—perfect fidelity. If anyone deserved what she wanted, it was Felicity Wells. If ever he were to devote himself to one woman, it would have to be someone like her. But that wasn't the nature of men.

Oh, well. The only thing he could do was teach her what he could. And perhaps their amorous sessions would make pleasant memories that would help her through the unhappiness when the inevitable happened.

"Kiss me," he said.

She studied him intently but didn't move toward him. "Will you let me touch you?"

"You touch me all the time."

"Not your face or your chest," she said. "I want to touch you...there."

Great progress. She'd come out and asked point blank for what she wanted. Next she'd have to name it. "Where?"

She looked down at the front of his pants. "There."

"My rod?"

"Yes."

"Say it."

She took a breath. "Your rod."

"My cock?"

"Yes."

He sat in silence, waiting for her to repeat the word.

"Your cock. Your yard. Your sex. I want to touch your prick. I want to fondle your erection. Is that good enough?"

"Very well done, indeed," he replied.

"So, may I finally touch it?"

"No," he said. "You're not ready."

"Damn." She pushed aside his hand and rose from the settee. "Damn you," she cried as she paced toward the desk.

"Such language, Miss Wells." He watched her begin her pacing again and did his best to stifle his amusement. Where before he'd seen a flush of embarrassment, now he found one of pure fury. The woman was magnificent in all her moods. If only she knew how Priapus strained against his trousers aching for just what she wanted to give him.

"You hold back from me exactly what I need to know to accomplish my goal," she said. "You expect me to sit obediently next to you and expose all of myself so that you can toy with me."

"I've never toyed with you."

"I have to tell you everything—my dreams, the unholy fantasies I have about you, every sensation while you take me apart with your fingers. And what do you give back? Nothing."

"I give you those sensations."

"It's not enough," she declared. "I've opened myself up to you completely. I must have some part of you in exchange."

"You're right," he said. She stopped dead and stared at him as if he'd started speaking some foreign language. "You have made yourself open to me, while I've remained hidden," he went on. "It's time for me to reciprocate."

That seemed to take some of the starch out of her anger. "Thank you."

He patted the settee again. "Come and sit down, and I'll tell you one of my favorite fantasies."

She quickly joined him again. "Should I sit on your lap while you tell it?"

"No," he said. "I think it safest that you sit there."

She settled her hands in her lap and waited. How in hell was he going to get through this telling without begging her to give him some relief? Bad enough to tell her his favorite lascivious daydream, but lately she'd played the major part in it. And there was nothing he could do but tell her.

"I imagine I'm at the opera," he said. "With a lady whose body I crave desperately but with whom I'm alone for the very first time. From the looks she gives me throughout the performance and the way she moves against her chair, I can tell that the feelings are mutual.

After some time, I become bold and start to caress her throat and bare shoulders with my fingers. When she doesn't object, I lower my hand to her bodice and press it between her breasts."

"And no one else sees you?" she asked.

"It's a private box."

"But they don't have walls all around. Someone could see you."

"It's a fantasy, Miss Wells. I don't plan to actually try this."

"I'm sorry," she said. "Please continue."

He closed his eyes for a moment, letting his mind wander to the images that inflamed his lust more and more often now. Felicity Wells sitting next to him in a brocade chair as he fondled her breasts below the bodice of her gown. As he felt her nipples harden and listened to her breathing grow uneven.

"Eventually, she becomes adventurous, too," he said, opening his eyes again. "She reaches over to the front of my pants and strokes my member. At first slowly and then faster, until I'm quite beside myself and ready to explode."

"I'd like to do that," she said, her voice husky. God in heaven, he'd like her to do it. Right now. It wouldn't take much to make him come. Oh hell, how was he ever to survive this exquisite torture?

"What happens then?" she asked.

"I somehow manage to get my hand under her skirts and up into her pussy. When I realize she isn't wearing drawers and had planned a seduction ahead of time, I almost spend on the spot. But I hold on to my control until I can feel her growing wetter and wetter and I know that she's as desperate to couple as I am."

"Oh, my," she gasped.

"Somehow by mutual understanding, we both know that we can wait no longer. She rises from her chair and lifts her skirts while I unbutton my pants and let my engorged cock spring free. Then, I put my hands around her waist and lower her slowly onto me. Both of us nearly scream with the pleasure, but just then the music is reaching a crescendo, covering our cries. I plow into her as fast and as hard as I can manage, and she rides the length of me until we both spend, the music washing over us in our bliss."

She licked her lips and stared wide-eyed at him. "That's...oh, my…very…um…very…"

"Yes, it is."

Without warning, she reached her hand to him and covered the thick ridge of his flesh with her palm. A jolt of pleasure raced through him, and he groaned. Another moment, and he'd have no control left. He could deny her nothing. But somehow, he managed to grasp her fingers and stop her. "It's time," he managed between his clenched teeth.

"I know," she answered.

"No," he tried again. "It's time for you to go home."

"But I don't want to."

He stared into her face. "If you don't go right now, I'll detain you. And you'll be late, and your mother will miss you."

"I don't want to go home," she said. "I want to stay here with you."

He didn't answer but just glared at her. Didn't she know he didn't want her to go home, either? But what choice did they have?

"Oh very well," she said finally, staring right back at him. "But I'm coming back in two days, and I will look at you and touch you then. I will know you. Do you understand?"

"Go home, Miss Wells."

Chapter Three

Marc knew instantly that it was a dream, but the knowledge in no way decreased the intensity of the images. Felicity Wells lay on a bed of cushions, surrounded by wild flowers, in a sun-drenched meadow. She was wholly and completely naked, her arms outstretched toward him in invitation. God knew he'd seen her unclothed before. He'd often held her in his arms and opened one of his own shirts to expose her perfection to his view. He'd watched her flush with excitement and then surrender to the force of one orgasm after another. And yet, he'd never seen her quite as wanton as she looked right now as she lay there, stretching and turning, her lips parted in a silent plea.

Please, Marc, her mind called to his. *Please, Marc. Take me. The need, the hunger. I can't bear it all. Take me.*

"But, I can't take your virginity. You told me that," he answered.

This is a dream. You can have me in a dream, she said. *Hurry, please.*

She held her arms up toward him, showing him her breasts. How many times he'd kissed them. How many times he'd taken the rosy nipples into his mouth and teased them to hardness. He could do that now. He could devour every inch of her body. He could drive into her, bring himself the completion he'd craved for so long. He could do all that now. But for some reason, his feet wouldn't move.

She reached down and stroked the insides of her thighs, parting her legs. *Please, my darling. Please, my Marc. I need you here. Please.*

He watched her and wanted her and couldn't move. God help him, something always stood between him and the satisfaction she could give him. Even in his dreams.

Come to me, she begged. *I want you as much as you want me.*

I know you want me.

"I can't," he said.

You're so beautiful, so magnificent. I want to touch you. I want to stroke you, pet you, make you come.

"I can't," he cried.

Your cock says you can. He wants me, I know he does. He's so big, so hard for me.

Marc looked down at himself and realized that his clothes had disappeared. He was as naked as she was and hopelessly aroused for her inspection. His member had grown to mammoth proportions, as if in *shenga.* He touched himself and nearly came apart. He was going to spurt into his own hand in a moment because he couldn't have her. No matter what, he couldn't have her, and the loss was going to kill him. "I can't," he gritted. "I promised you, and now I can't move."

I release you, my darling. I release you. Come to me.

Finally, his feet moved, and he went to her and dropped down onto the cushions beside her. She immediately grasped his throbbing cock. She stroked him, her slender fingers pale against his reddened sex. He grew even harder and bigger. Impossible, but true.

My pretty man, she crooned to his rod. *So large, so stiff, so hot. You'll find peace soon enough.* She lay back against the cushions and looked up into his face. Her expression made his breath catch. Innocence and lust. Vulnerability and hunger. Her eyes widened, until he felt he could fall into them and lose himself inside her soul. Instead, he'd lose himself inside her body. He positioned himself between her welcoming thighs and drove his sex into hers.

She let her head fall back as a cry of pure, animal pleasure escaped her throat. He pulled almost out of her and thrust back in until his cock was buried in her flesh up to the hilt. She arched her back, meeting his thrust, and her breasts pressed into his chest. So beautiful, she cried. *So beautiful. Oh, my darling.*

He'd made love so many times, and it had never been like this—blood pounding in his ears and fire burning in his groin. Impossible and inevitable. He would have her, over and over. He would make her writhe beneath him. He'd make her spend and spend all over his member until he joined her in bliss.

Only, he couldn't. He'd promised.

In an instant, Marc was awake and lying in his bedroom. He had quite a cockstand pressed into the bed, and in a moment he was going to shoot his sperm onto the sheet. Nothing could keep him from coming, and he might as well make it as good as he could.

So, for the first time since his youth, he took his erection into his hand and began to stroke himself, closing his eyes in hopes of re-joining Felicity in that field. Instead he imagined her in his study. He and Felicity together on the Oriental carpet in front of a fire, and he took his furious member out of his pants and drove it into her pussy. She spent immediately, throbbing all around him, milking his sex with her spasms.

Oh, God, just that image. He bit the pillowcase and kept stroking with his fingers until he could stand no more. Pressure built at the base of his spine, then rushed through his groin to his cock as he spent. Wave after wave of his sperm spilled out of him as he came into the sheets. Finally relieved, he collapsed, gasping for breath.

God, what she did to him, even in his imagination. He'd never wanted a woman so badly in his life. That made no sense, of course. As modest and quiet as she'd been on her first visit, he'd never have noticed her if she'd passed him on the street. Quiet, little things with unremarkable brown eyes and hair had never excited him before. So, why did she have him so at his wits' end?

She wasn't modest anymore. He'd seen to that. She pouted and flirted. She demanded more and more from him, just as he had hoped she would. She'd learned how to take pleasure with great enthusiasm—a trait that would make her husband a lucky man, indeed. The fact that Marc wouldn't take personal gratification from her education didn't make him happy, but it couldn't be avoided. Felicity Wells required nothing less than marriage and total fidelity—things he couldn't possibly give her. So, he'd give her pleasure and take her impressions and feelings for his own pursuit of knowledge. They'd both agreed to that. Why didn't it seem enough now?

Oh, hell. He didn't have to be a martyr in all this. He'd promised to teach her how to satisfy a man, and he could best do that by showing her how to please him. She'd been insisting on access to his body for some time, and he'd only held back to make her want him enough to overcome her shyness. She had fewer and fewer reservations now, and he might as well let her get over the last of them. She was ready to see a fully-grown and fully-aroused man and learn how to please him.

At their very next meeting—two days hence—she'd get her wish finally. He'd bare himself and let her see exactly what happened when a man reached fulfillment. He could think of several ways that didn't involve harming her virginity.

He might have her press her breasts around his cock while he thrust himself between them. He'd spend that way, sure enough. Or he might undress them both and then position himself behind her so that he could press his rod between her thighs. She could reach down and stroke the head while he pumped until he came into her hand. Perhaps he'd have her wear a glove while he did that. Perhaps a black glove so that he could watch over her shoulder as his sperm went onto the fabric.

Damn, what an image. He'd become hard again, just thinking of it. His hand was still closed around his member, and he could feel it growing thick all over again. If she were here now, he'd be ready to take her, to roll her onto her back and bury himself in her and go again. How could that be possible?

Of course, he could stroke himself again and give his body ease. But he already had quite a mess to clean up before he went back to sleep. He'd save this erection for Miss Wells and her education. Yes, indeed, she wanted to see him aroused. She'd have her wish and more. She'd learn about the male body on her very next visit.

❦

Dr. Slade greeted Felicity in his robe de chambre the next time she visited him. His lack of clothing startled her so badly that she almost went back down the steps and up the street before she remembered that for the past several weeks she'd been insisting he disrobe for her. Now she had what she wanted, and she hardly knew what to do with it. He was so tall, so broad-shouldered, so imposing.

Well, she wasn't about to let him see her hesitation, not after all the effort she'd put into getting him to expose any part of himself—physical or emotional. So she squared her shoulders and gave him what she hoped was a confident smile.

"You were expecting me, I trust, and not some other fortunate female," she said.

"This is our appointed time," he answered.

She studied his face but, as usual, could read little there. His ice-blue eyes looked back at her intently, one might even say hungrily, but he gave no hint of pleasure or displeasure at seeing her. Would she ever fathom the man?

"Shall I have my lessons on your front stoop today?" she asked. "Or would you prefer your study?"

That at least brought an embarrassed smile to his face. He stepped back, pulling the door open. "Please come in."

She walked in front of him and along the foyer she'd crossed so many times now. But today it seemed like a very long walk, indeed. Almost as if she were headed toward her own execution. Dear heaven, what a preposterous idea. She'd nearly begged for this encounter, and now her knees felt like water.

He didn't say anything as he followed her into the study. She turned and gave him another smile. "Shall I undress as usual?"

He gestured toward the screen. "Please."

She noticed the fire in the grate then. A pleasant blaze, although totally unnecessary for the weather. Maybe he'd meant it to comfort her. He'd set some cushions in front of the fire, too. Their trysting site for the day. It looked very inviting.

She glanced at him and found the same even gaze trained on her. As his robe fell more loosely around his person than his trousers, she couldn't even tell if he was aroused. That would come later.

She stepped behind the screen and proceeded to undress as quickly as her trembling fingers allowed. She was already working on her small clothes when he finally spoke. "How long have you been coming here?"

"Six weeks, I think. The weather's been good, so I haven't missed many of our afternoons."

"Have you enjoyed them?" he asked.

Enjoyed? She'd hadn't begun this for her own enjoyment. She'd come to him to learn, and learn she had. She continued removing her clothes. "Have you enjoyed them?"

He laughed, although the sound came out strained. "They've tried me sorely, but I think I'll enjoy today's session."

"Then, I will, too." She took off her drawers and found his shirt where it hung on the regular hook. She slipped into it and stepped around the screen.

He stood in the middle of the room, tall and handsome and as inscrutable as usual. His robe still gave no clue as to the state of his sex, but one way or another she'd find out soon.

He stared at her for a moment and then took a deep breath. "Have I told you how beautiful you are?"

Her heart stumbled in its rhythm. What an amazing thing for him to say. "You've complimented various parts of my body," she answered. "I don't suppose that's the same thing."

"I don't suppose it is."

"Then, no, you haven't told me I'm beautiful."

"Men can be asses. You needed to learn that lesson, too." He stretched out his arms toward her. "Come to me."

She walked into his embrace without hesitation and wrapped her arms around his neck, reaching upward and bringing her body against his chest. He bent and took her lips for a kiss, and she surrendered to the heat of his mouth. Before his clothing had always separated them, and although he still wore a robe and she still wore his shirt, they were nevertheless closer than they'd ever been before. His warmth and his scent surrounded her—an intoxicating combination. As his lips and tongue worked their magic on her mouth, she reached to his chest and parted the robe so that she could slip her fingers inside against his skin.

He was solid and hot under her palms. She smoothed her hands against the curling hairs and moved the robe upward toward his shoulders and then down his arms, baring his chest and watching her palms stroke him. He held perfectly still, but when she rubbed his male nipples with her thumbs, he trembled ever so slightly.

"Dear heaven, you're stunning," she sighed. "I never imagined."

"Not even in your dreams?"

"Not even in my dreams." She reached up and nuzzled the underside of his chin then planted a path of kisses along his throat, downward until she could run her tongue over his collarbone. "I want... oh dear heaven... I want so much."

"What?" he demanded. "What do you want?"

She smoothed her hands over the muscles of his upper arms and marveled at the steel-under-satin feel. "I want to devour you, Dr. Slade. One inch at a time."

He groaned—a deep, animal sound in the back of his throat. "I do believe you'll be the death of me, Miss Wells."

She looked up at him. "You won't deny me today, will you? I may have my way with you, mayn't I?"

"Oh, God," he moaned.

"I'll assume that means 'yes.'" She unfastened the belt of his robe and pushed it off him completely. Underneath, he was totally and magnificently naked. And aroused. She could only stare at him in awe.

"What are you thinking?" he said. "Right now."

She looked down at him, at his erect cock where it stood rigidly out from his body. She licked her lips. "I'm thinking that you didn't exaggerate. Not one little bit."

"You're not frightened?"

"No. But if I thought you were planning to use that to take my virginity, I'd be terrified."

"I'd be as gentle as I could," he said. "If I were going to do that."

"But you're not going to do that."

"I've given you my promise more than once," he said.

True, he had. And he'd never done anything to suggest he'd changed his mind. So, why did she fear that so constantly? Because it was something she wanted? One of the many things she'd learned during these sessions was to be honest with herself, and now she had to face the fact that she wanted him to know her fully. She wanted him to take her virginity and make her his. She wanted that desperately. But she couldn't have him in that way. She could, however, have everything else.

No, not everything else. She couldn't have his love. She couldn't even have his exclusive amorous attentions. If she wanted Dr. Marcus Slade, she'd have to share him, and she would not share the man she loved with anyone.

The pressure of his fingers against her skin brought her back to reality. He had reached to her throat and was now pushing his shirt over her shoulders. It slid down her arms and fell to the floor at her feet, leaving her just as naked as he was.

He stared down at her body, his expression heated and his breath coming fast and shallow. She pressed herself against him again, and he closed his arms around her. Of all the things she'd experienced since coming to him, this was the most remarkable. Standing in his embrace with nothing whatsoever between them—the peaks of her breasts pressed against his flesh, the heat of his body encircling her, the evidence of his arousal pressed into her body. If heaven could truly exist on Earth, this must be it. She ran her hands up his back and then down again, stroking his buttocks and pulling herself against his distended cock.

He shuddered in response. "Go slowly, Miss Wells, please."

"I don't want to go slowly."

"But you must, or this will all be over before it gets started."

She looked up at him. "I don't understand."

He gritted his teeth together in an expression that might have been pain or a tremendous inner struggle. "You will soon. Only now, don't rush things."

"Instruct me, then."

He bent and picked her up in his arms as if she weighed nothing at all. A few strides brought them to the hearth, where he lowered her onto the cushions and joined her.

In an instant, he was kissing her, setting fire to her being. His hands moved over her, pulling her against him, shaping her to his body. She let her own hands answer, measuring the width of his shoulders and testing the muscles along his arms. He was so much larger than she and so much more expert in his movements. She could only answer his caresses and pray that she could give him half the pleasure he gave her.

He slid along her body until his mouth found a nipple and closed over it. She arched her back and ran her fingers into his hair, stroking him while he sucked and teased until she could scarcely catch a breath. He moved to the other breast and took that as well. She'd grown so hot being with him like this—his body covering hers, flesh whispering against flesh. The throbbing started between her legs, and helpless to fight it, she squeezed her thighs together. Once, twice, such heavenly friction.

He put his hand there, separating her legs. "Impatient, little thing, aren't you?"

"Hurry, please," she gasped. "I'm burning."

"You have one more surprise coming," he said, and he slid his body lower. He nuzzled her navel with his nose and rained little kisses over her belly. Then his mouth moved lower and lower. Toward her sex.

"You can't," she cried. "You can't mean to kiss me there."

"That's exactly what I mean to do," he answered. "I'm going to devour your pretty cunny until you spend against my mouth."

"Oh, dear God."

"That's right, Miss Wells. Call out to your maker while I show you Paradise."

He lifted her hips, bringing her to his face, and her traitorous thighs parted for him. She reached out her hands for anything to anchor her to reality as he closed his mouth over her sex and licked the bud that was already throbbing for his touch.

He couldn't be doing this, but he was. She couldn't be responding to his caress, but she was. She turned her head and stared into the flames, trying to fight the fire in her belly. Useless. She couldn't fight something this powerful, and she'd die rather than have him stop. He nibbled and sucked and drove her mad with his tongue. She was going to spend. She was going to scream out his name and spasm against his mouth. No power on Earth could prevent it.

She closed her eyes and yielded. Beside her, the fire crackled and sent heat onto her body. She cupped her breasts with her palms and squeezed as he continued his assault. She couldn't stand much more.

Another moment and she'd shatter. He nipped and then sucked and then nipped again and she was lost.

The spasms started deep in her belly, and she tossed back her head and screamed with the pleasure. She pulsated inside as the world went crimson with lust. She came and came and came, sobbing and crying, until he finally released her and she fell back against the cushions.

He joined her and pulled her into his arms. Such heaven to be with him this way—sleepy and sated and comforted by the softness of his skin. Without opening her eyes, she reached out and grazed his lips with her fingers. He caught her hand in his and kissed her fingertips. "What did you think of that?"

"Oh, my," she answered. "Will my husband do that?"

He tensed. Just the slightest stiffness to his bearing. She would have missed it entirely if he'd been wearing clothing. "He'll do it if he's a considerate lover," he answered. "Many men don't like to gamahuche their wives."

"Gamahuche?" she repeated. "That's what it's called?"

"The vulgar term. It's also called cunnilingus."

"Can women do that for men?"

His only answer was a groan. She opened her eyes to find that same expression she'd seen before. Pain or struggle, she couldn't tell which. Or maybe pleasure. "Can I do that for you?" she asked.

"Oh, God, you really will kill me."

"I can make you come that way, can't I? Is that what you're afraid of?"

"I'm not afraid of coming with you," he answered.

"Then, why do you resist it so?"

"I'm not. It's only…"

"Only nothing," she said. She reached down and grasped his sex. He shut his eyes and trembled violently. She stroked him, rubbing her fingers along the velvet of his shaft until she reached the head and ran her thumb over the very tip.

He lay back, his eyes still shut, his teeth clenched together. "You don't know what you're doing to me."

"Then, tell me. Show me. I want to make you spend."

He took several gasping breaths and opened his eyes. She almost lost herself in their blue depths as he gazed at her. "All right," he said finally. "Do what you want to me."

"May I kiss your cock?"

He groaned again. "If you want. Only remember, if I tell you to stop, do so immediately or you'll get a surprise I don't think you're ready for."

"What surprise?"

"Never mind. You'll see soon enough."

She took a breath. "What should I do?"

"Kiss my poor Johnnie," he said. "Lick it. Suck on the tip while you stroke the shaft."

She reached to his member and began to stroke. "Like this?"

"Yes. Oh, God help me. Like that." He placed his hand against her cheek. "When I tell you to stop, move your mouth and finish me with your hand."

"Very well."

"I mean it. I won't be able to tell you twice, and I want you to watch what happens."

He rested back against the cushions, and she lowered herself until she was face-to-face with his glorious member. It was long and thick—so thick at the base that she couldn't get her hand all the way around it. It felt smooth and hot in her hand. She squeezed gently and heard a breath catch in his throat. Slowly, she lowered her head and kissed the very tip. Then, bolder, she took the entire head into her mouth and sucked.

His hips bucked upwards, and she had to grasp his shaft to guide it toward her mouth. The sensation was pleasant, really, as she was taking only as much of him as she could. And his surrender, his total vulnerability, the trust it showed—they all warmed her to her core. For once, she held him in her power and she could pleasure him the way he'd done for her so many times. How she loved the feeling.

She stopped sucking and licked around the head, dipping her tongue behind and beneath it. His breath grew loud and labored, and he moaned over and over. His hips continued to move, and she had to work to keep up with him. She sucked him again and stroked and stroked until she felt him tense.

"Now!" he screamed. "Stop now!"

She obeyed immediately, releasing him from her mouth while still pumping with her hand. His body thrust upwards, once and twice, and then a hot liquid spurted out of his cock in waves. He spilled his essence into her hand while he cried her name.

Finally, he collapsed and she moved to him and took him into her arms as he had just done for her. "Was that good?" she whispered into his ear.

He half-moaned, half-laughed. "My dear Miss Wells, you have no idea."

"To the contrary, I have a very good idea."

"Your future husband is a very lucky man."

George. Odd, she hadn't imagined doing that to George. Of course, that was the whole point of this exercise—learning how to please George. But somehow she couldn't picture George surrendering himself to her in the same way as Dr. Slade had. George Wilmont would never allow himself to be that vulnerable.

Dr. Slade pulled her against him and burrowed his nose into her hair. "You've progressed remarkably, Miss Wells," he sighed. "In fact, there isn't much more I have to teach you."

She stared into his face, at the softness of his features with his eyes closed and an angelic smile on his mouth. "You're not sending me away, are you?" she asked. "I may come again, mayn't I?"

"Yes, please." He rested his head against her shoulder. "Please do come again."

Chapter Four

An entire week, and she hadn't returned. Marc stood at the window and stared up the rain-slicked street in the direction from which Miss Wells usually came. She was twenty minutes late already and no doubt wasn't coming at all. Damn this storm.

The weather had to be keeping her away. He wouldn't even consider the other explanation—that she simply didn't plan to return at all. True, he'd told her he couldn't teach her much more, but she'd asked to come back, and he'd agreed. She couldn't have decided to quit their relationship. God only knew what went on in women's minds sometimes, but Felicity Wells had a great deal more common sense than most females her age. She wouldn't take it into her head to leave him without even a good-bye, would she?

He stared out the window at the pelting rain and the leaves whipping around on the trees. The scene was bleak, desolate—just like the void inside him. At least today he hadn't undressed fully but had only removed his suit coat. The previous afternoons he'd stripped and put on his dressing gown, only to wait and wait for her, pacing his empty study. Waiting and wanting like a school boy in the throes of his first love.

For God's sake, two days ago, he'd almost gone looking for her. Imagine her parents' horror if the notorious Dr. Marcus Slade had appeared on their oh-so-proper doorstep looking for their oh-so-virginal daughter. At least that might have amused him for a while. But it wouldn't likely win him a place in Felicity's heart.

In her heart? Damn, he'd better stop thinking in that direction immediately. This had everything to do with her body and nothing to do with her heart. Still, where in hell was she?

He was just about to give up when he spotted her walking quickly up the street. She held an umbrella into the wind, obscuring her face and head, but he knew her body well enough to know it was she. Even with her skirts flapping around her legs in the storm, he recognized her quick tread. It was Felicity. It had to be.

He waited until she reached the base of his front steps and then ran into the hallway to greet her. He had the door open before she could lift the knocker. In fact, she hadn't even raised her hand to knock. She stared up at him, her eyes wide and her hair matted against her head, despite the umbrella. Her clothes were soaked into her skin. She looked cold and bedraggled and infinitely desirable.

He took her into his arms and pulled her into the foyer. She tossed her umbrella aside, and he managed to close the door without letting go of her. He kissed her—hard—pushing her up against the wall and pressing his body into hers. It had been too long. Too damned long.

She caught his face between her hands and pressed kisses first over his eyelids and then his cheeks. "I couldn't get away before," she said. "It rained and rained and rained."

"I thought you were never coming back," he answered. "I thought I'd never see you again."

She devoured his lips with an urgency that took his breath away. Over and over, she kissed him as if she'd never get enough. "I couldn't leave you forever," she murmured against his mouth. "Not that way."

He pulled her sodden hat from her head, sending hairpins everywhere. Her hair fell over his hands and around her shoulders. He pressed his face into it and drank in the smell of rain and woman.

"I thought I'd go crazy waiting," she said. "It never stopped raining, and I wanted so much to be with you."

He worked at the tiny buttons of her jacket. Thoroughly soaked, they resisted the efforts of his fingers. He tore at them frantically, even ripping one off, before he could remove the jacket and start in on the even tinier buttons of her blouse.

She had more luck with his waistcoat and had it open and over his shoulders in an instant. "I wanted to come to you," she gasped. "I missed you, missed your touch. But it just wouldn't stop raining."

"I wanted you, too," he murmured as he removed her blouse, revealing her breasts above her corset. He bent and kissed the soft flesh of her bosom. "God, how I wanted you."

"I couldn't think of any way to get free of the house," she said. "Oh, don't stop. That feels so good."

He slipped a hand into her corset and freed one breast so that he could take the nipple into his mouth. She gave a little cry and tipped her head back. "Oh, Marc. Marc. Don't stop."

Stop? He could no sooner stop than he could stop breathing. He brought his hands down her back and pulled her against him. His cock was fully engorged, and it wouldn't take much to make him spend, but he had to make her come first. To do that, he needed her naked. He unfastened her belt and then her skirt. They both fell into a heap on the floor as she removed his shirt and stroked his chest.

"I finally couldn't stand it," she said. "I told them I was going to the library."

"Thank God you came," he said as he unlaced her crinolines and finally had her down to her small clothes.

"They tried to forbid me, but in the end, I just left," she said. "Oh, please hurry."

"Why did you have to wear so damned many clothes?"

She gave out a strangled laugh and reached to her corset cover, finally pulling it up and over her head. That left only her corset and drawers, aside from her stockings and shoes. But they presented no obstacle. Just the corset and its infernal ties. She removed his shirt and tossed it to the floor. She had him naked from the waist up, and he still had to deal with her corset.

She reached down to the front of his trousers and curled her fingers around his erection. "You'll make me come," he cried.

"I want you," she answered. "I want you between my legs. Hurry."

He caught her hips and lifted her off the floor, pressing her back into the wall behind her. She slid her legs around his waist and pulled him against her sex. Even through his pants and her drawers, the heat of her pussy burned at his cock. He moved, rubbing his throbbing erection against her cunt, and she cried out her pleasure. Over and over he thrust, bringing himself to the edge of madness.

Oh God, he couldn't take her like this. Not partly dressed and in his front hallway. He mustered every bit of control he had and stilled his movements. "Inside," he gritted. "I want to feel your flesh against mine as you come."

"Then, hurry," she answered. "I can't wait much longer."

With his hands holding onto her buttocks, he carried her across the foyer and into the study. She kissed him as he went and moved her hips, rubbing against his member. Up and down and up and down. He had to set her down somewhere and finish undressing her before it was too late for both of them.

He carried her to the desk. "Push those things aside," he ordered.

She reached out with one arm and swept the contents of his desk top to the floor—papers fluttering and the crystal inkwell spilling its contents onto the Oriental carpet. As hot as she'd made him, he didn't care a damn about the rug. He set her onto her back and pulled her drawers down and over her legs. As he did, she fumbled with the buttons of his trousers. Just that pressure nearly unmanned him, but he clenched his teeth and struggled for control.

Finally, she reached inside and freed his prick. Helpless against his own lust, he pressed himself against her naked cunt. He hadn't managed to get rid of the corset, and now he couldn't wait.

He pressed his cock against her so that the shaft thrust between the lips of her sex and the head pressed against her clitoris with every movement. Heaven, or almost. Heaven lay inside her, but he couldn't have that. He moved his hips over and over, listening to her cries grow as her head thrashed in the delirium leading to her orgasm.

"I want you there," she cried. "Between my thighs."

"I am."

"Oh dear heaven, not like that." She shifted, bringing the entrance to her grotto into contact with the tip of his sex. "Inside me. I want you inside me."

"I can't." Oh, God. He'd never wanted anything so desperately than what she was offering, but he'd promised.

"Please, Marc," she begged. "The throbbing there. It's torment. I can't stand it."

He didn't answer, couldn't answer. His cock ached to bury itself in her, to take possession of her and feel her come all around him. What torment, feeling the fire build in his loins and not daring to take what he craved.

"I've dreamed about you," she gasped. "Hot and hard inside me. Moving. Oh, please don't deny me. Please."

"No," he shouted. "I promised you I wouldn't."

"Never mind that. Take me. Now."

He stood as still as he could, his prick ready to claim its prize. One thrust would put him into her. One thrust would let him fill her, would give him everything he'd ever wanted.

"I release you from the promise," she said. "Damn you. What do I have to say to make you give yourself to me?"

"Felicity," he cried, the sound erupting from his chest in agony.

"Now, Marc. Please. Please!"

God help him. He grasped her hips and pushed into her. Past the barrier and into her wet heat. Her virginal muscles clamped around him. Tight, so tight. He was going to come. Any moment.

"Yes," she cried. "Oh, yes, my darling. This is what I've dreamed of."

He held still, fighting for control. His legs trembled, and his knees almost gave way. He had to make this good for her, had to take her to heaven.

"What a feeling," she said. "I never imagined."

Slowly, cautiously, he pulled back and then thrust forward again. Her hips rose to meet him, burying him completely into her flesh. She'd turned wanton and shameless, and her lust inflamed his own, bringing his arousal to almost intolerable levels. He slipped a hand between their bodies and found the pearl between her thighs. When he touched her, she gasped and bucked so hard he had to hold on tightly with his other hand.

"Yes, that way," she cried. "Oh God, I can't hold back. Now. Oh, now."

She was going to spend at any moment. And he could join her in ecstacy. He thrust more deeply, plunging into her over and over again. She sobbed and gasped. He gave in to every urge he'd denied. Deep and hard and fast, he went until he felt her tense around him.

The climax hit them both at once. Her spasms started just as he felt the hot essence spurt from him. One powerful explosion. Then another. And another.

When they were over, he'd grown so weak he couldn't stand. He rested his body over hers while her cries trailed off into soft sighs. He closed his eyes and heard her heartbeat returning to normal. Never, never had he found such completion, such total fulfillment.

❦

It was several minutes before Felicity could do anything but listen to Marc's breathing. His head lay on her breast, his face moist with sweat. Evidence of the violence of their coupling. Even now they were connected, with his sex still buried inside her.

Oh, dear heaven, she'd given herself to him when she'd sworn she wouldn't. He'd owned her heart for several weeks, and now she'd given him her body, too. How would she ever learn to live without him?

She lifted her hand and stroked his face, pushing his hair back out of his eyes. She kissed his forehead and then the tip of his nose. He looked so helpless, even innocent, like a sleeping child. Of all the ways she'd seen him—distant, amused, on fire with lust—this was the way she'd remember him through the years to come.

He opened his eyes and stared into her face, his expression dazed. After a moment, he took a few breaths and then raised himself onto his elbows. "Oh, dear God, what have I done?"

You've loved me, she wanted to shout. But he hadn't. He'd made love to her, and that was different. He regretted his actions already. He'd never really wanted her, but she'd made him take her virginity, and now he regretted it. She bit her lip to keep it from trembling. Crying would make her humiliation complete.

He straightened, and the action parted their bodies. She didn't even have that connection any more. Worse, his expression looked completely bereft, as though he'd made some terrible mistake. As though he hated himself for making love to her.

"I'm so sorry, Felicity," he said.

"It wasn't your fault," she answered, trying to keep the tears out of her voice. "I provoked you."

"No, I'm the more experienced. I should have controlled myself."

"Let's not discuss it," she said. "What's done is done."

"This should never have happened." He reached into the pocket of his trousers and pulled out a handkerchief. Dear heaven, she hadn't even pushed his pants over his hips. She been so eager to have him inside her, she'd just released his sex and begged him to drive it home. He'd made her that shameless.

He shook out the handkerchief and gently wiped her thighs. The linen came away bloodied, evidence that she'd crossed a threshold with him, and she could never retrace her steps. If he were capable of giving himself to her exclusively, she wouldn't care. She'd happily live the decadent life right here in his house, married or not. She'd thumb her nose at the world by day and share his bed by night.

That couldn't happen, though, and the tenderness he showed her now—the utter concentration with which he touched her sex—only underscored what she was about to lose. This very afternoon.

He stopped and stood, looking at the stained handkerchief in his hand. "I'm sorry, Felicity. I'm so damned sorry."

"Stop saying that."

"I hurt you."

"It's only the blood from my maidenhead. You didn't hurt me."

He gazed into her face, and the pain she found there tore at her heart. "I shouldn't have taken your maidenhead. This shouldn't have happened."

"Stop saying that, too."

"It's true."

Damn it, she knew that was true. But she couldn't bear to hear it. Not after the bliss they'd just shared. Why couldn't he just tell her he loved her, tell her he'd make everything right, tell her that she meant more to him than any other woman? Why couldn't he want her and no one else?

Tears welled up behind her eyelids and pressed for release. She was going to cry like a spoiled child, and she couldn't let him see it. She couldn't let him see how much she cared. She cleared her throat. "Do you suppose you might find my clothes?"

"Of course." He touched her cheek—more gentleness that threatened to unravel her heart. She bit her lip and willed her chest not to release the sobs choking her.

After a moment, he turned and left the room. She slid to her feet, but her legs wouldn't really hold her, so she rested against the desk and glanced down at herself.

What a spectacle she made. She was still wearing her stockings and shoes and even her corset—although that had been pushed askew during their lovemaking. Her breasts hung over the top of the corset, the nipples still wet from his kisses. She hurt between her legs, and her chest had grown tight with misery.

One sob escaped her, and she clamped her hand over her mouth to stifle it. He'd be back at any time, and she wouldn't let him find her in tears. She'd hold all the feeling inside until she could get home and into her own bedroom. She had to get out of here. Now.

She adjusted her corset as best she could, found her drawers on the floor, and slipped into them just as he re-entered the room. He walked toward her slowly, holding out her clothing. He'd put his shirt back on but hadn't buttoned it. There was no sign of the ruined handkerchief. Lord only knew what he'd done with that.

She took her clothes from him and held them up against her chest. "Thank you."

"What are you going to do?" he asked.

"I thought I'd get dressed and go home."

"That isn't what I meant, and you know it."

No answer came to mind, so she just stood and stared at him, clutching her clothes to her breasts.

"What are you going to do about what happened here today?" he said.

"Dear heaven, can't you even name it?"

"I took your innocence. We have to decide what to do about that."

She knew what she wanted to do about that. She wanted to throw herself into his arms and beg him to love her—only her. Beg him to keep her with him always. But that wouldn't work, and she'd already lost everything but her pride here today. She'd keep that somehow.

"The decision will be mine to make, I think," she said.

"What are you going to do?" he demanded.

"I don't know," she shouted. "I don't think I can lie. Maybe I'll tell George what happened. Maybe he'll marry me, anyway. If he doesn't, I'll manage somehow. There are worse things than spinsterhood."

"A woman of your passions a spinster?" he replied. "A sinful waste, if you ask me."

He'd made her that way. He'd given her those passions, and she only wanted to share them with him. But she couldn't tell him that, no matter how much she wanted to. "I don't know what I'm going to do. I have to think about it."

"If the man's too stupid to have you because of one indiscretion, I'll marry you."

Indiscretion. Oh, dear Lord. Indiscretion. "What a lovely offer, Dr. Slade. You take my breath away."

"Damn." He ran his fingers through his hair. "I didn't mean it to come out that way."

"I know how you feel about marriage," she said. "About fidelity."

"I'm not your father. I would never disgrace you publicly."

No, he wouldn't. He'd have his affairs discreetly. She probably wouldn't even know who his lovers were. She'd have to suspect every woman she met of sharing intimacies with her husband. "I want to go home."

"You're upset. We'll talk later."

"Fine." Only, there wasn't going to be any later for them, but she didn't want to discuss that now. She'd only end up bawling like a child.

"Get dressed," he said. "I'll bring the buggy around and drive you."

"I can get home on my own," she answered.

"Like hell," he answered. "I'm not going to take my pleasure with you and then send you out into a storm."

She looked into his face and found steely determination there. He wasn't going to let this be simple. He was going to make her ride with him to her house. She sighed. "Fine. Get your buggy."

Felicity let him drive to within a few blocks of her house and then told him to stop.

"But you don't live here," Dr. Slade—Marc—answered.

"It's not far, and the rain's letting up."

"You don't want to be seen with me?"

"It's better this way."

He didn't look pleased at that answer. In fact, he looked rather as if he'd bitten into something sour as he gazed around them at the puddle-strewn street. But at least the rain was slowing to a trickle.

"All right," he said finally.

She moved to climb out of the buggy, but he caught her arm. "I will see you again," he said.

"Of course," she lied.

"When?"

"I don't know."

"We're not through with this," he said. "We still have to talk."

"About what?" she demanded. "You've apologized. You've told me how much you regret our indiscretion. You've offered to marry me if my fiancee won't have me. You've even promised not to humiliate me—at least not publicly. What's left to discuss?"

"A little matter of pregnancy," he replied. "What to do if you're carrying my child."

Oh God, a child. His child. How could she have been so stupid? She'd wanted him for so long—thought of nothing but having him, even dreamed about having him—that she hadn't thought of the consequences. Now, she loved him, might even be carrying his child, and she couldn't have him without dooming herself to the very fate she'd been hoping to avoid from the beginning.

"Felicity," he said softly, as he reached up to stroke her cheek, "what if you're going to have my baby?"

His tenderness undid her. She could have withstood anything but that. Anger, sarcasm, blame, maybe even indifference, but not tenderness. A sob escaped her, followed by another and another. Her shoulders shook, and tears blurred her vision.

He gathered her into his arms, resting her face against his chest. "Don't cry," he whispered. "I won't abandon you."

"I know," she managed. "I know you wouldn't."

"And I'd never ignore any child we conceived," he said. "We'll be married, of course, if you're pregnant."

"No," she sobbed. "I can't."

"Don't be silly. I will take care of you and the baby, if there is one. You have no choice in the matter."

She pulled away from him and swiped at her eyes. No one was on the street because of the rain, but Lord only knew how many people could see them from the neighboring houses. She must look exactly like what she was—a woman who'd ruined herself and was now suffering the consequences. She had to get away from here, calm herself, and go home. With any luck, no one she knew had seen them.

"Let's not argue, please," she said. "We don't even know if there's anything to argue about."

"I must insist. I won't be put off about this."

She lowered her face into her hand and took a few breaths. "Fine. I believe you. Now, really... I have to go."

"When will you know?" he demanded. "When are your menses due?"

She looked up at him and felt her cheeks turn hot. She never discussed *that* with anyone. But how could she feel shy with a man who'd made love to her less than an hour before? "It should be in about three weeks. I'm usually fairly regular."

"I'll expect to hear from you in three weeks time, then."

"Three weeks," she repeated and moved to leave the buggy.

Once again, he stopped her with a hand on her arm. "Either way, I'll expect you to visit me then."

"All right," she said, glaring at him.

He glared right back. "If you don't come to me, I'll find you. And your parents, if necessary. Do you understand me?"

"I understand," she cried. "Now, let me go."

"Three weeks, Felicity."

Chapter Five

Callie Houseman looked every bit as plump and appealing as ever, but somehow today her charm wasn't working. Marc looked down into the sweet smile she always gave him after their first kiss, and he wanted to want her—desperately. But somehow he just couldn't manage any real passion.

"Why don't we go into my study?" he said.

She looked at him out of her twinkling blue eyes. Despite her "advanced age" of almost ten years Marc's senior, Callie still could turn heads. But she only indulged herself with Marc. He'd find that a bit overwhelming if she didn't have such a wonderful independent streak and sense of humor.

Right now one of her eyebrows went up, making her appear amused and a bit perplexed. "The study, not the bedroom?"

"I haven't seen you for months," he answered. "I want to hear what you've been doing. Where you've been. What—and who—you've seen."

"You want to talk?"

He gestured toward the study door. "Let's."

She shrugged and walked across the foyer into the study. He followed and found her standing by the love seat, pulling off her gloves. Her reticule already lay on the table nearby.

"So," she said. "Who've you been entertaining?"

"I beg your pardon."

"Someone's tired you out," she answered. "Usually we head straight upstairs on my visits."

"Really, Callie, can't we have some intelligent conversation? You're worth more than just a tumble, you know."

She removed her hat and stuck the pin into it then cocked her head and studied him. "Uh-huh."

"Do you find that so hard to believe?"

She set her hat on top of her gloves and reticule. "Not at all. We always have things to tell each other, things to laugh about together. Afterwards."

"Perhaps I feel like showing some restraint today. Perhaps I've matured."

She laughed at that. "Marc, sweetheart, this is Callie. We know each other better than that."

Damn, he should have known not to try to fool Callie. She'd been married for twenty years and had no doubt heard every excuse a man had to offer. But did she have to choose today to become so perceptive? "Alright, then," he snapped, "if you're so hungry for me, let's go to bed."

She laughed ever more loudly at that. "Now, I am curious, love. Some woman has tied you in knots, and I want to hear all about it."

"Don't be ridiculous."

She sat and patted the cushion beside her. He joined her and took her into his arms. If Felicity had him in knots, he didn't have to surrender to the knots. A delightful roll in the hay with a dear friend was exactly what he needed to make him forget the fact that it had been three weeks and two days since he'd seen Felicity.

He pulled Callie against him and bent to kiss her. She responded instantly, as she always did, opening to him and offering her softness. She made such a delightful armful of womanly curves, he usually grew hard and hot instantly. But somehow today she wasn't enough. The sweetness of her breath didn't satisfy, not as it usually did. The scent of her perfume seemed merely pleasant and no more.

She pulled back from the caress and studied him. "There is something wrong, isn't there?"

He dropped his arms to his sides and smiled at her. "No, really. You're making something out of nothing."

"I know nothing when I see it, young man," she said, sounding for all the world like any stern schoolmistress. He'd never heard her sound like that before. "This is far from nothing," she continued. "And I want to know what's bothering you."

He took a breath and searched for an answer. How could he tell anyone—even Callie—that an innocent young woman had come to him for help and he'd taken advantage of her? How could he admit that he'd taken the young woman's virginity, may have gotten her with child, and he didn't even know what had happened to her? He could hardly say the words aloud to himself. How could he tell anyone else?

Three weeks and two days. He should have heard from Felicity by now.

"I've been very stupid, I'm afraid," he confessed finally.

"A woman."

"What else?"

"Who is she?" Callie asked.

"No one you know."

She reached up and stroked his face. "Whatever you've done, you'll fix it."

"I'm not sure that's possible."

"I know you, Marc. You'd never do anything cruel. Anything else can be fixed."

He took her hand in his and lowered it to his lap. "I appreciate your faith in me. I'm not sure it's deserved."

"Come, come. Tell Callie everything. How bad could it be?"

He didn't answer, but just looked into her face.

After a moment her gentle smile turned to a frown. "You didn't get her with child?"

"I may have."

"Darling," she said. "You didn't use a French letter?"

He couldn't bring himself to admit exactly how idiotically he'd behaved, so he merely shook his head.

"But that isn't like you. You'd never lose your head like that," Callie said.

Damn it, he knew that. He'd always protected the woman and himself in the past. Always. But that afternoon with Felicity—three weeks and two days ago—had been different. He couldn't have waited to get a French letter or anything else. He'd played the encounter over and over in his head ever since then, and he kept coming back to the same answer. He'd needed her *then*, not a day from then or a minute from then. As hard as he tried, he still couldn't make sense out of how he'd felt that day.

"Marc?" Callie prompted.

He rose and crossed the room, running his fingers through his hair. When he reached the desk, he turned and faced Callie. "I can't explain it. I lost my control. Completely."

She looked at him for a moment, and then a smile crossed her lips. For God's sake, he'd just told her that he was the world's greatest idiot, and she was smiling at him.

"I can explain it," she said, sphinx-like. The way women acted when they were at their most irritating.

"Then perhaps you'd like to try."

"You've fallen in love."

"Oh, for heaven's sake, Callie."

"You have," she declared. "That accounts for everything. Why you're so morose…"

"I am not morose."

"Morose," she repeated. "Distracted. Why you have no interest in bedding me."

"What makes you think I have no interest in bedding you?"

She laughed again. Normally he loved her laughter, but this particular afternoon it grated on his nerves. To make matters worse, she looked pointedly at the front of his pants. She couldn't help but notice his total lack of an erection. Damn it, she saw entirely too much.

"I do wish you'd stop laughing at me," he said. Oh hell, now he sounded petulant.

"I'm sorry, darling. It isn't funny, is it?"

"No, it isn't." Damn, that sounded even worse.

She rose from the love seat and walked to him, finally reaching out and taking both his hands in hers. "Falling in love isn't funny. It's deadly serious and the most magnificent thing that can happen to anyone."

Could Callie be right? Could he have fallen in love with Felicity Wells? Timid, virginal women like Felicity didn't even appeal to him. But then, she'd gotten over her timidity during her tutelage, and he'd disposed of her virginity well enough.

Still, he didn't believe in love, at least not in the way society had invented it. Love restricted people unnaturally. It blocked the natural expression of the sexual drives. Only fools believed in that idea of love.

"I knew this would happen one day," Callie said, "and I couldn't be happier for you."

"I don't feel very happy."

"You will, darling. You'll make things right with the young woman, and you two will have a lifetime of happiness."

"How can you say that?" he asked. "You and your Robert loved each other, and you didn't have a lifetime of happiness."

"We had over twenty years. Not nearly enough time, but I wouldn't trade a moment of it for all the pearls in the ocean."

"That's fine for you, Callie," he answered. "But I'm a scientist, a researcher. My intellect tells me that love doesn't exist."

"Pig's piddle," she declared. "What does your cock tell you?"

More of her blasted perceptiveness. How could she know that for the last three weeks and two days he'd wanted no one but Felicity Wells? He'd tried imagining himself with other women—had even welcomed Callie's visit to prove to himself that he wasn't hopelessly smitten with his wanton, little Brahmin. Now he had to face the fact that his member was interested in one woman only. But where was she?

"I thought so," Callie said. She squeezed his hands. "I'll miss our afternoons together, Marc."

"Who said anything about ending our afternoons?"

She clucked her tongue at him. First laughter and now tongue clucking. She could be a real nuisance if he didn't like her so damned much.

"Marc, darling," she said. "You need to find the woman you love and be with her. Marry her, for heaven's sake. It wouldn't kill you."

"This whole conversation is ridiculous."

"You know I'm right." She waved a finger in his face. "Now, you go and make things up with her. Today."

He took Callie's hand in his. "All right. I do need to find her, in any case."

"Good, then. I'll expect an invitation to the wedding."

He slipped his arms around Callie and squeezed her. "I'll miss you."

"And I you." She smiled at him——- that delightful combination of sweetness and mischief that he'd grown to love. "But I've been thinking it's time for me to open myself to love again."

"Any man would be lucky to have you."

"You've been wonderful for me, Marc. Just what I needed after Robert died, but it's time for both of us to move on, I think."

"Perhaps you're right."

She backed out of his arms and walked to the table where she'd deposited her things. "I'll see myself out, then. You go do whatever you have to do to win your lady back."

"Thanks, Callie, I will." Only how in hell was he going to do that?

⁂

Marc's door wasn't locked, not even latched. When Felicity raised her hand to the knocker, the door swung open on its own, so she stepped inside and listened for some sound of life. Except for the ticking of the grandfather clock, the house was silent. Surely, he wouldn't go out and leave his door ajar.

She ought to just close the door behind her and go home, but she'd spent all last night and this morning readying herself for this visit. If she ran away now, she'd might never have the courage to come back. Courage indeed—the news she had to share would end things between them for good. After today, they'd never have any reason to see each other again.

She stood for a moment, doing her best to commit the hallway to memory—the stairway that curved out of view, the mahogany wainscoting of the walls, the plush carpet runner that passed the door to the study and disappeared into the back of the house. The study door itself stood half-open. She could go in and take one last look around. If Marc appeared, she could simply tell him that his front door had been open and she'd let herself in. She could chide him for his carelessness. She could look at him one last time.

Dear heaven, melodrama wasn't going to win her anything. She'd go back outside and knock properly. If he wasn't home, she'd come back tomorrow. She turned to go, but a sound stopped her. A sigh, from the direction of the study door. Someone had sighed. Marc had sighed.

She took a step in that direction and stopped. She'd heard him sigh before—when she'd kissed him. When she'd caressed him so intimately she could hardly bear to remember it. Was someone else in the study with him?

Lord, this was why she'd vowed to protect her heart from him. Why hadn't she kept that promise to herself?

He sighed again, and her cheeks grew hot with humiliation.

"Felicity," he whispered.

Her name. He'd whispered her name.

"Felicity," he said again. "Damn, where are you?"

She walked to the study door and looked inside. Marc sat on the settee, alone. He was bent over, his elbows on his knees, his head in his hands.

"I'm here," she said.

He looked up, his eyes wide, and rose immediately. "Where have you been?"

"I told you I wouldn't come back for three weeks."

"Three weeks were up two days ago."

She shrugged. She ought to tell him that she could have come several days before, but if she told him that, he'd ask for the answer to the unspoken question between them, and then she'd have to leave. For just a few seconds, she wanted to drink in the sight of him.

He'd always looked calmer than he did today. More in control. Today he wore no jacket, and his waistcoat hung open. He'd rolled his sleeves up, exposing dark hairs over his forearms. With no cravat and with his hair all askew, he appeared positively wild, and the angles of his face seemed even more pronounced than usual. He was so different from the Dr. Marcus Slade she'd first confronted in this very room, but he was still every bit as mysterious and beautiful.

"If you hadn't come today, I would have gone looking for you tomorrow," he said.

"I'm sorry."

"For all I knew your parents had packed you off somewhere, and you'd left without a word to me."

"I wouldn't have done that," she answered.

"You might not have had any choice." He ran his fingers through his hair, demonstrating how it had arrived at its present state of disarray. "You can't imagine what's been going through my mind. I might have lost touch with you, with my own child."

That did it. As much as she couldn't even bear to hear the words, she could avoid them no longer. "There isn't any child."

"Oh." He stared at her blankly for a moment and then ran his hand over his chin. "Oh."

"My monthly ran its course. A little early, in fact."

"Oh," he repeated.

Is that all the man knew how to say? She'd come to tell him that he was free, and all he could say was "oh"? Well, she'd planned to keep this light, and his terseness could help in that regard.

"I suppose you're relieved at this news," she said, doing her best to smile.

"I should be," he said.

"Well, I should say so. We can both get on with our lives now. You can do your research, and I can be married." She didn't add that she hadn't yet told George that his fiancée was no longer pure. That was her own personal hurdle to face, if she decided to marry George at all. The idea became less and less appealing the longer she stood and gazed at Marc Slade.

"That's it, then," he said. "The problem is solved, and you'll marry someone else and just forget about our…"

His voice trailed off, and he looked away. As though he couldn't face her.

"Our what, Marc," she demanded. "Our research? Our indiscretion? Our what?"

"You'll forget about me."

If only she could. If only she could forget the way he'd made her feel, the way his touch had made her come alive. The way his kisses had set her free to soar. She wasn't likely to forget any of that. Nor would she forget the way he looked right now, as if he was lost in a mist of pain and confusion. Damn him, why couldn't he just give her a cheerful good-bye and let her go home to try to recover from loving him?

"I don't understand you," she said. "I thought you'd be happy at my news."

"Happy?" he repeated.

"Relieved. I've released you from any obligation."

"Obligation."

"Would you stop repeating what I say and tell me what's wrong with you?" she shouted.

"I wanted you pregnant," he said. "I wanted you to have my child."

"Why?"

"I thought that way I could talk you into marrying me."

She stood and stared at him. He looked like the Marcus Slade she'd been visiting these past weeks. He had the same broad shoulders, the same high cheekbones and pale skin. But this man made no sense at all.

"You're exactly the man I can't marry," she said. "I won't live my mother's life—worrying who my husband is bedding every time he's out of my sight. And you can't be faithful to one woman. You've told me that over and over."

"I know I told you that," he answered. "But can you believe I've changed?"

She'd love nothing more than to believe he'd changed. She'd give anything for that. But she didn't dare delude herself on this point. It was too important.

"These weeks without you have been hell," he said. "I haven't been able to sleep or eat. All I could do was think of you and how much I wanted you. Only you, Felicity."

"Oh, Marc." The words rushed out of her before she could stop them. "You don't know how much I've wanted to hear you say that."

"It's true. I've been such a fool—trying to deny what was happening inside me. I might as well try to will the sun to orbit the Earth. I love you. I can't live without you."

"I love you, too. Oh God help me, I do. But can I trust you?"

"An old friend visited today," he said. He squared his shoulders and gazed at her straight on. "I'll confess this, and it will be the last confession I'll ever have to make to you, I swear."

"Please."

"She and I have enjoyed each other many times. I thought we would again today, but I had no interest in her whatsoever. She saw instantly what I've been hiding from myself for weeks. You're the only woman I want—the only woman I'll ever want, for the rest of my life."

"Oh, my love." She opened her arms and went to him. He took her in an embrace, clasping her tightly to his chest. How she'd missed the feel of him, his scent, his warmth. She tipped her face up to his, and he kissed her—desperation mixed with tenderness mixed with love. She answered in kind until the world spun around them.

After a moment, he pulled back and stroked her face with the tips of his fingers. "And what about you?" he asked. "Have you changed?"

"I don't think so. I've loved you from the very beginning."

"But you said you'd never marry for love. That you'd never give a man that much power over you."

"Oh, that." She toyed with a button on his shirt. "I don't know what sort of silly fool would say something like that, do you?"

"The sort of silly fool I'd fall in love with, that's what sort."

She gazed up into his face. "I don't suppose I have any choice in the matter, anyway. You own my heart, and that gives you the ultimate power over me. Use it carefully, please."

"I'll only use it one way. As your husband." He looked down at her with such devotion and tenderness in his face that her heart almost stopped beating. "Will you have me?"

"Oh, yes. Oh, yes, my love. Oh, yes."

"Good," he said, smiling at her wickedly. "Because I have the most tremendous cockstand just now, and Priapus will accept no one but you. Can you accommodate him?"

"I think so." She reached down and fondled his erection. Even through the fabric of his trousers and her gloves, she could make out the hardness and the length of it.

He sucked in a harsh breath. "Mercy, woman. It's been over three weeks. For once, I'd like to keep enough control to make love to you properly. In a bed."

"Then, take me to your bedroom."

"Our bedroom," he corrected, as he took her hand and led her into their new life together.

About the author:

Alice Gaines also writes as Alice Chambers for Leisure Romance. Her next full-length book, **Always a Princess**, will appear in May of 2001. Alice loves to hear from readers. Contact her at algaines@pacbell.net or write her at: Alice Gaines (or Alice Chambers); 5111 Telegraph Avenue, PMB #197; Oakland, CA 94609. Or visit her website at http://home. pacbell.net/halice.

A Candidate for the Kiss

the Kiss

❧✺☙

by Angela Knight

To my reader:

I was watching James Bond do something impossible in one of his movies when I thought, "This would be a lot more believable if he was a vampire." And just like that, this story was born.

Thanks to Alexandria Kendall for letting me play in her Secrets sandbox with my handcuffs and handsome hunks. And thanks to the readers who said, "When are you going to do another vampire story?"

Well, here it is.

Chapter One

If they caught her, they'd kill her.

Dana Ivory looked out the window of the rotting treehouse, peering down at the four men gathered around the bonfire below. She knew that if they discovered her, they'd put a bullet in her brain and dump her body so far out in the woods nobody would ever find anything but bones.

But if Dana could keep the four from catching her, she'd live to blow their plans to hell and make her own reputation. All she needed was guts and luck. Guts she had. Luck... well, she'd see.

Her hand shaking, Dana angled the microphone further out the window to better pick up the conversation going on below.

"Nothin'll put the fear in the mongrel races and traitor whites like killing the President they all elected."

"Shit, they'll piss themselves wonderin' where the next bullet's coming from!"

"And right-thinking whites'll flock to our banner. It'll finally be the start of our holy war."

The voices carried clearly in the warm summer air. Dana just prayed her tape recorder was picking them up half that well.

She swallowed against a queasy blend of terror and excitement. This time tomorrow, her byline wouldn't just be on the front page of *The Adamsburg Weekly Tribune*. Once the national wire services picked up this story, the words "By Dana Ivory" would be on every paper in the country.

And four white supremacists would be in jail for plotting the assassination of the President of the United States.

All thanks to Dana and their ringleader's nephew.

Jimmy Satterfield had sidled up to her just that morning to whisper that the local chapter of the White Aryan Brotherhood was meeting in the woods outside town. That in itself got Dana's attention, because Jimmy was so terrified of his uncle, he'd normally never breathe a word about anything Joe Satterfield or the WAB was up to.

"I ain't no snitch," Jimmy whispered, his voice hoarse and earnest with terror. "But this thing is so fuckin' big, anybody who even knows about it could go to jail. And not in no candy-ass state prison either. Hard time. Leavenworth time. Time I ain't gonna do for no Hitler-lovin' bastard, even if he is my uncle."

"But what are they planning?"

"Hide in the old treehouse just before sunset. You'll find out."

Dana had gone to the sheriff, of course. Steve Hannah should have jumped at the tip; he already suspected Joe and his crew in a string of convenience store robberies and drug deals he'd never been able to prove in court.

But instead of mobilizing his men for a raid—or even sending a deputy with Dana to investigate—Hannah had given her a verbal pat on the head and told her the elementary school was holding a nice pageant she ought to do a story on.

Well, she'd already written that story, dammit. Six times in the six years she'd been at *The Adamsburg Weekly Tribune*. What Dana hadn't done was an exposé that would send the WAB straight to jail, leaving the crime rate of Adamsburg, S.C. to plummet for at least a decade.

So she'd headed for the treehouse a couple of hours before the boys were due, picked her way over the rotting pine boards to a relatively solid spot, and started setting up her microphone, tape recorder and camera.

The treehouse wasn't the most comfortable perch in the world. Neighborhood kids had built it in the limbs of the old oak more than ten years ago, cobbling together pine plank walls and a sloping roof now pocked with several fist-sized holes. The whole thing smelled damp and unpleasant from the rot, mildew and wildlife that had moved in over the years.

But if the ambiance wasn't exactly Martha Stewart, it also wasn't enough to keep Dana away from a good story. She'd pushed a desiccated mouse carcass aside with the toe of her running shoe, swept off a relatively clean patch next to the opening that served as a window, and sat down to wait.

The four WAB boys had showed up just before sunset, jouncing through the woods in a rusted white pickup, one man holding on for dear life in the back. As they got out of the truck, Dana recognized them as a fairly sinister quartet she knew from covering various bond hearings over the years.

There was round, snake-mean Bill Mason, who put his wife in the hospital once a month; Skeeter Jones, a tall man who reminded Dana of a ferret with his long body and narrow head; and buck-toothed Tony Brown, who grew marijuana out in the woods and guarded his crop with a sawed-off shotgun. But the worst of the bunch was Donnie Anders, hulking, bearded and fresh out of prison for beating a buddy to death over a bar tab. Oddly, there was no sign of Joe Satterfield, the leader of the Brotherhood chapter. Dana wondered where he was.

They'd built a fire, rolled a couple of joints, and started working their way through a couple of twelve-packs as they told lies about women and who'd told whose boss to go to hell. Dana began to suspect she was courting the attentions of the area's chigger population for nothing.

Then the conversation wandered to President Daniel Grayson's upcoming speech at the University of South Carolina. Dana was just wondering what possible interest the boys could have in that surprisingly intellectual topic when Skeeter Jones drawled, "This'll be bigger than the time we bombed that church."

She almost dropped her mike. The Mount Zion Baptist Church in nearby Newberry had blown up on Christmas day last year, killing the African-American pastor who'd come in to open up for services.

"No kidding, asshole," Anders said, spitting a spray of tobacco juice into the fire. "Putting a bullet in the President is definitely bigger than blowing up a preacher."

"Too bad the damn bomb went off early," Mason grumbled. "We coulda got us a whole church full."

Being a pastor's daughter, Dana was so horrified they'd bombed the church that the assassination plot took a moment to register. By the time she'd recovered from the shock, the four were already discussing the expert they were bringing in to murder Grayson.

Oh, God, Dana thought, as her heart began to lunge in her chest. *These bozos are actually planning to murder the President of the United States.*

She spent the next half-hour listening in appalled fascination and planning the biggest story of her career.

Now Anders popped the top on his beer with a violent gesture of one grimy hand. "It's a helluvalot of money to give some bastard from out-of-state. I still say we should do it ourselves and keep the cash."

Mason hooted. "Yeah, right. We'd have the Secret Service so far up our ass we'd be pulling badges out of our teeth. This guy is good. Hell, Joe said he's the one that did that judge in Alabama..."

"Maybe he's good. Maybe he ain't." Anders' little black eyes gleamed in the firelight, feral and mean over his scraggly beard. "And if he ain't, maybe he gets caught and sings to the Feds about what we hired him to..."

Something growled.

A rush of blackness detached itself from the night and snatched Anders off the ground, then swung him around like a rag and slammed him against the nearest tree.

Dana jumped.

Anders must have tipped the scales at well over two hundred pounds, but now a man held him pinned so far up the trunk his cowboy-booted feet swung six inches from the dirt.

"Let's get something straight, asshole." The man's voice was cold, calm and so deep it seemed to rumble in the bones. "I do not sing for the Feds, I do not tap dance for the Feds, I do not provide the Feds with entertainment of any kind. And I sure as hell don't tell the Feds who hired me to do a job!"

That was the assassin?

Anders' square face twisted with rage. But as he met the stranger's narrow gaze, his expression slowly changed, eyes widening until the whites showed. Wheezing from the pressure of the big hand pinning him to the tree, he gasped out, "I didn't mean nuthin'."

Dana blinked. Anders had just done five years in prison for voluntary manslaughter. What had he seen in the other man's face that was nasty enough to make him back down?

True, the stranger was big, with a good four inches on Anders' six feet. Thick biceps shifted and bulged in his extended arm as he held the ex-con pinned, and the black T-shirt he wore molded to the curves of a powerful chest. But Anders was pretty beefy himself, despite the layer of fat covering his muscle, so it wasn't just the other's brawn that had him sweating.

Gazing at the stranger, Dana silently admitted he could make her sweat a little too. His profile looked as if it should be stamped on a Roman coin: handsome and arrogant, with an aquiline nose, high forehead, starkly masculine cheekbones and a square chin. The only soft thing about him was the wavy dark hair that brushed the tops of his broad shoulders.

But handsome or not, he stared at Anders with such menacing intensity Dana felt the hair rise on the back of her own neck. She was relieved when Joe Satterfield stepped out of the woods, his smile placating. "Uh, Jackson, you can turn him loose now. Donnie's harmless."

Like hell, Dana thought, but the assassin stepped back and let Anders drop. As the ex-con stumbled and tried to regain his balance, Jackson turned his back and walked away. An act of either courage or ignorance, considering Anders had hit the last man he'd killed from behind.

"So let's talk business." Accepting a beer from Skeeter, Jackson popped the top and took a long swallow. "Jonah said you want me to kill somebody big, but he didn't say who."

"How do we know you ain't wearing a wire?" Anders demanded, sullen hostility growling in his voice as he stumped toward the fire. Dana tensed, suspecting he'd feel compelled to do something nasty after the way he'd been humiliated.

Jackson shrugged, handed his beer back to Skeeter, and reached for the hem of his black T-shirt. In one easy gesture, he pulled it over his head.

Oh, my.

Why the hell was the man making his living with a gun when women everywhere would have paid just to look at his body?

Broad expanses of fluid muscle formed Jackson's pecs, and his abdomen and ribs were sculpted in tight ridges that could have been chiseled by Michelangelo. Dark chest hair grew in a silky ruff across his chest, narrowing to flow downward toward the snap of his jeans. When he turned his back, the firelight gleamed across smooth, rippling contours that formed a beautiful V from broad shoulders to narrow waist, drawing attention to a pair of buns clad in black denim that were as tight and round as cantaloupes.

The man could have played the lead in one of Dana's guilty fantasies.

God, she thought, *it's a shame he's a racist pig.*

When Jackson faced around again, he lifted a thick brow. "Is that enough, or do I have to drop my pants?"

Satterfield gave an uncomfortable laugh. "Hell, boy, I think you've made your point."

A small voice in the back of Dana's mind whispered, *Damn!* She winced in guilt. Here she was, ogling a killer. No matter how sexy he was, his job description included sniper scopes and grassy knolls. Her parents were probably spinning in their graves.

Jackson shrugged back into his shirt with a lithe twist of his torso, reclaimed his beer, and sat on the ground next to Skeeter, stretching his long legs out in front of him. "Now that we got that settled—who am I killing?"

Satterfield wandered over and eased his considerable bulk onto a fallen log, his checkered shirt straining over his belly. He splayed his jeans-clad legs far apart to balance his gut and scratched the two-day growth of gray stubble on his chin. "Like I told you on the phone, what we got for you ain't gonna be easy. But Mr. Howard says you're the man to do it, and that's good enough for me."

Dana frowned. Was he talking about Jonah Howard, the Idaho

racist who'd founded the White Aryan Brotherhood?

Jackson sipped his beer. "Yeah, I've done a lot of work for Jonah."

Which answers that question, Dana thought.

And what kind of "work" had Jackson been doing? A magazine article she'd read a few months back had called Howard "the suspected mastermind behind the WAB's domestic terrorism." Had Jackson been involved too?

"Well, now you can do something for us." Satterfield leaned forward and looked Jackson in the eye. "We want you to execute Daniel Grayson as a traitor to the white race."

Jackson's beer hesitated in mid-tip. "That is big." The assassin resumed his sip. "And you're right—it's not going to be easy. Not gonna be cheap, either. What do you have in mind?"

Satterfield told him about the President's planned trip to South Carolina. Dana listened, barely breathing, her hand sweating on the barrel of the boom microphone, her mind buzzing with questions and half-formed plans.

Should she call the FBI or the Secret Service? Did the Secret Service even have a South Carolina office? Could she get an agent to meet her so she could turn over the tape? She'd have to make some phone calls and find out.

Then, while the Feds were rounding up the WAB and their handsome assassin, Dana would write the exclusive of a lifetime. No more living on chicken salad sandwiches and driving a ten-year-old Mazda. No more working for a small town weekly for slave wages. This was her ticket to *The New York Times*.

" ...really think you can do this?" Bill Mason asked. Dana snapped back to attention.

Jackson propped his beer can on his flat belly. "It's gonna take some planning." He slanted Satterfield a look. "And money. Figuring out the best time and place to hit him..."

"We thought you could do it in the Carolina Coliseum as he gives the speech."

Jackson snorted. "I'd never get out of there alive. It'll have to be before that, while he's on the way. Or after."

"Could bomb the Coliseum," Tony Brown suggested as he picked his buck teeth with a match.

The assassin shot him a scornful look. "What, you think the Feds are going to let me park a tractor trailer full of fertilizer on the lawn? Get serious. I'm gonna have to work on this awhile, use my contacts in the Service." He turned to meet Satterfield's hopeful stare. "And you're going to have to make it worth my time."

"A real patriot would do it for free." Anders spat into a pile of dead leaves.

Jackson smiled, his teeth flashing white in the firelight. "Even a patriot's gotta eat."

"We got money." Satterfield nodded at Mason, who pulled a suitcase into the light and flipped it open with a flourish.

Jackson leaned forward to peer at the bundles of green inside. "Quite a stash."

"We been raising cash for months," Satterfield told him. "Robbed a couple banks, a few convenience stores, sold a lot of dope. We was planning to buy a truckload of fertilizer and fuel oil, maybe blow something up. But then I heard Grayson was comin', and I thought—here's a chance to make a real difference."

"We'll be famous!" Skeeter said happily.

Satterfield shot him a look. "I hope to hell not. That would mean we got caught, and I ain't getting caught. Some other fool can be Lee Harvey Oswald."

Jackson got to his feet and stretched, putting one hand to the small of his back as he arched his spine. "No, he's right. Y'all are gonna be famous." In one smooth gesture, he pulled out a flat black case and flipped it open on something that glittered in the firelight. Something that looked a lot like a badge.

His white teeth flashed in a malicious grin. "I'm a federal agent, and you assholes are busted."

Dana's jaw dropped.

Safe, she thought, dizzy with relief. *I'm safe. And so is the President.*

"I knew it!" Anders howled, exploding off the ground where he'd crouched in a sullen knot.

"Freeze!" a strange voice barked. "Federal agents! Throw down your weapons and raise your hands."

There was a concerted rustle, the crunch of feet stepping on leaves. A ring of men stepped out of the darkness, bulky and menacing in black body armor, their assault rifles leveled.

Donnie froze, staring wild-eyed at the muzzles ringing them.

"You heard the man, y'all." Jackson grinned mockingly. "Dump the guns and raise your hands."

As an assortment of hardware began thudding to the ground, it occurred to Dana that she'd better reveal herself to the Feds as quickly as possible. Especially if she wanted an interview with J. Edgar Gorgeous down there. Which she did.

God, what a story this was going to be. And it looked like she'd even live to tell it.

Trying to decide when to draw attention to herself, Dana watched as the agents handcuffed their prisoners. Anders was being his usual charming self—cursing, demanding a lawyer, refusing to lie on the ground so he could be searched. Frustrated, the agent guarding him stepped closer, gesturing with the muzzle of his gun.

Then all hell broke loose.

An agent moving to help Anders' captor tripped on a root and fell against his comrade. The first agent automatically braced him with one hand… and Anders struck like a snake, grabbing the man's gun and ripping it out of his grip. The guard snatched for it, but Anders jumped back, bringing the weapon to bear on both men. Even as everyone else swung to cover him, he opened fire in a thunderous explosion of sound. The two agents went down in a heap.

Before Anders could fire again, Jackson was on him with a roar of rage, smashing the gun out of his hands as he grabbed the ex-con by the hair.

Dana was still wondering how anybody could move that fast when the agent opened his mouth—*were those fangs?*—and dove, growling, straight for Anders' throat.

What the hell is he doing? Dana thought, incredulous.

Anders grabbed Jackson's head to try to force him back, but his jaws were locked tight. Blood poured down the ex-con's throat, black and wet in the firelight.

"Let go, you bastard! Somebody get him off me..." He clawed at Jackson, who ignored him, jaws working. Anders' voice spiraled into a shriek. "Shit! *He's drinking my blood!*"

Jackson growled like a rabid wolf.

Around them, the other agents watched while their prisoners stared in horror. One of the Feds made an abortive movement toward the two, but none of the agents seemed surprised by Jackson's bizarre behavior.

Dana fumbled for her camera. She didn't know whether the photo would even come out in such poor light, since she didn't dare use a flash. But she damn well wanted a shot of a Federal agent trying to rip out a prisoner's throat with his teeth. Bringing up her Canon, she started clicking off shot after shot.

"Archer, they're all right!" an agent yelled at Jackson as he knelt beside the two men who'd gone down. "He caught 'em in the body armor. Looks like broken ribs. Somebody call EMS!"

Jackson—Archer?—stiffened, then jerked up his head and shoved the ex-con away. An agent began yelling into a radio, calling for medical assistance.

Anders stumbled back, clamping a hand to his bleeding throat as he stared at Jackson. "You were drinkin' my blood! What kind of sick motherf..."

"Go to sleep!" Jackson roared.

Anders dropped as if somebody had put a bullet in his brain.

Dana blinked at the ex-con, sprawled flat on his back in a bramble bush. She hadn't even seen Jackson hit him.

There was a long, long silence, broken finally by Anders' gentle snore.

"Jesus." Satterfield lifted his head off the ground to stare at Jackson with an expression of wild-eyed horror. "You're some kinda fuckin' vampire!" He rolled his eyes at the agent crouching next to him, naked terror on his face. "We knew there was Jews running the government, but nobody said nuthin' about no vampires..."

Vampires in the FBI, Dana thought. *Yeah, right. That hood you like to wear must cut off the circulation to your brain.*

As for the fangs she'd thought she'd seen when Jackson had grabbed Anders—well, that had obviously been a trick of the light.

"You ain't gonna get away with this," Satterfield babbled. "I'm gonna tell my lawyer. There's laws against drinkin' people's blood..."

Jackson looked at the white supremacist coldly. A smear of red glistened on his mouth, and he wiped it away with the back of his hand. "You too, mastermind. Sleep."

Satterfield's eyes rolled back, and his head hit the ground.

Dana gaped. This time she knew Jackson hadn't touched the white supremacist; he'd been all the way on the other side of the clearing. The agent had just... commanded Satterfield to sleep, and he'd slept. Like magic. As if Jackson really did have a vampire's psychic powers.

But that was impossible.

The man who crouched beside the fallen agents got to his feet and walked over to Archer. "You always go out of your fuckin' mind when one of the men gets hurt." He shook his helmeted head. "It's a good thing you're magic, or we'd never be able to explain this kind of shit."

"Yeah, well, the smell of blood makes me cranky." Archer shouldered past him to kneel beside the two injured agents, who'd just begun to stir. "How you doing, guys?"

"Ribs feel... like I got stomped... by the Dallas Cowboys," one of them gasped. "What the hell happened?"

"You got lucky. It could have been your head." Archer rocked back on his heels. "You want me to do something about those ribs, Roberts?"

The man winced and took a deep breath. "Yeah. I'm not... feeling particularly macho at the moment."

"Okay, look me in the eye." He bent close to the injured man and gentled his tone. "Feel the pain drain away, George." His voice was a low, hypnotic croon. "Going. Going. And gone."

Roberts let out a sigh of relief and relaxed, the white lines around his mouth smoothing. "Thanks, Archer. You're better than Demerol any day."

Hypnotism, Dana thought desperately. *He's not a vampire, he's some kind of hypnotist.*

Yeah. That made sense. The vampire thing… well, that was just plain ridiculous.

"You're welcome." Archer straightened. "But I still don't want you jumping up and running around until you get the ribs taken care of. You could hurt yourself without knowing it." He glanced over at the other man. "How about you, Stevenson?"

The second agent licked his lips and looked uncomfortable. "I'll pass, boss. I'm not that bad."

"Don't be a dumbass." Roberts sounded annoyed. "Archer's not gonna hurt you. I know you haven't been with us long, but…"

"It's his choice, George." Archer shoved to his feet. "Stevenson, if you decide you want help after all, don't be too proud to let me know."

"It's not that I don't trust you," the agent said hastily. "It's just the idea of somebody else being in my head…"

Jesus, Dana thought, stunned. Maybe this guy actually does have some kind of psychic powers.

Uneasily, she flashed on the image of Archer's teeth buried in Anders' throat. Could it be true? Could he be a vampire—the kind of soulless demon her fundamentalist father had always said was abroad on the earth?

No. No way. This was getting too much like an episode of *The X-Files*. She didn't know what was going on here, but it couldn't possibly be what it looked like. There had to be some kind of perfectly logical explanation for all this that didn't involve capes and coffins.

There'd better be. Otherwise the only paper that would touch this story would be *The National Enquirer*.

Licking her lips, Dana aimed the camera at Archer and prepared to take another photo—just as he lifted his head, looked straight up at her and called, "Get any good shots, Ms. Ivory?"

Dana froze.

"Who the hell are you talking to, Archer?" The agent who'd checked on Roberts and Stevenson moved to join him, looking up at the treehouse over their heads.

"Remember the newspaper reporter the sheriff warned us about? She's up there taking pictures." Propping his fists on his lean hips, Archer stared upward. Dana knew the treehouse window was shrouded in utter blackness, yet he looked as if he could see her clearly. But that was impossible. Unless...

Jesus, she thought, unable to deny the weight of the evidence any longer. *He really is a vampire.*

"She's been up there with a microphone since before we arrived. I can hear her breathing and the tape recorder running." Archer shook his head. "Then she started snapping photos, though God knows why—she's not using a flash, and there's no way in hell they'll come out."

"Oh. Well, you can handle it." The agent looked around at his comrades. "Come on, let's load these morons up. Where the hell is EMS?"

"Dispatcher said they're on the way," somebody called back.

As Dana watched, frozen, the men hauled their prisoners to their feet. It took some sharp calls and shakes to rouse Anders and Satterfield, both of whom staggered and blinked once they were finally upright, disoriented as drunks.

"Look, Ms. Ivory, nobody's going to hurt you," Archer called, his tone patient. "You can come on down now. I just want to talk to you."

And then he'll look me in the eyes and make me forget the whole thing ever happened, Dana thought.

Like hell. She wasn't losing the story of a lifetime to some vampire's mental magic, badge or no badge.

Dana looped the camera strap over her head, then grabbed her tape recorder and mike and jumped to her feet. Wheeling for the door, she took a single lunging step forward.

Her left foot smashed through a rotten floorboard.

Dana fell, equipment tumbling. She caught herself on her hands and one knee, only to feel her ankle twist with an agonizing wrench of pain.

Biting back a frantic curse, she tried to jerk free. All she got for her trouble was a jagged board digging more deeply into her trapped leg. Dana gritted her teeth, grabbed her thigh in both hands and pulled. The board dug deeper, bringing tears to her eyes. Something hot rolled down her ankle.

Great. Here she was, trapped and bleeding with Tall, Dark and Toothy waiting to pounce.

"Calm down. You're just making it worse."

Dana looked up to see the vampire standing silhouetted in the door of the treehouse.

Chapter Two

He could see the reporter plainly with his vampire night vision, though Gabriel Archer knew the room must be pitch black to her.

"So," she demanded as she glared up at him through her platinum blonde bangs, gray eyes narrowed with a mixture of fright and defiance. "Are you going to bite me next?"

Archer killed the impulse to purr, "Oh, could I?" Instead he gave her an easy smile. "I wasn't planning on it."

"Well, that's a relief." But she didn't look relieved as she crouched there on the floor, one long, slim leg caught in a jagged hole in the rotten wood, her full breasts quivering with every agitated breath.

She was young, Archer judged. In her mid-twenties at most. And lovely, with a narrow, delicately angular face and a thin nose that tilted just slightly at the end. Under that shaggy mop of moonlight-pale hair, her eyes were the misty gray of clouds after a storm, wary and wide. It was the kind of face you'd expect to see peering out from beneath a mushroom—except there was nothing fairy-like about those centerfold breasts.

Or that courtesan's mouth, Archer thought with a stir of hunger. Her lips were full, pouting and exotic, parted slightly to reveal straight, white teeth. There was a wealth of erotic potential in that mouth.

Her feminine scent only added to the temptation: gently musky, blending with the sharp copper of blood to set Archer's appetite burning. She must have cut herself in that fall.

God, he'd love to kiss it and make it well.

Looking at her, scenting her, Archer felt a ravenous heat. He might consider himself a professional, but his body was a creature of sex, blood and seduction. A woman like her could feed all his favorite hungers.

Unfortunately, the middle of a mission was not the time to indulge.

While Archer worked for self-control, Dana's features smoothed as though she were reaching for calm herself. She sat back, bracing her hands behind her. The position arched her spine, and Archer took shameless advantage of the darkness to eye her breasts. She was wearing a bra under that cotton shirt, but he was willing to bet it was little more than a veil of lace over her tempting flesh.

"Just how many vampires does the FBI have on the payroll?" Dana asked, sounding as cool as Sam Donaldson grilling the President. A real feat considering the rapid heartbeat he could hear slamming out her terror.

The question startled an admiring laugh out of him. "Damn, you've got guts. No brains to speak of, but guts to spare."

"Just doing my job, Agent. And you didn't answer the question."

"I'm not with the FBI. It's another federal agency altogether."

"Called?"

"I could tell you." Archer smiled slowly as he put his own spin on the old spook joke. "But then I'd have to bite you."

"I could guess, and you could nod," Dana suggested boldly. "The Bureau of Vampire Intelligence? The Central Vampire Agency?" Her full mouth twitched in an impish smile. "Fangs 'R' Us?"

"The Federal Office of Inquiry and Analysis." She wouldn't remember it in ten minutes anyway.

"Never heard of it."

"I'd be worried if you had."

"Sounds more like accountants than vampires."

"That's the idea."

"How long have you been a vampire, anyway?"

Archer shook his head. "I can't believe you're trying to interview me. Not thirty minutes ago, you watched me come close to tearing out a man's throat. Most people would be babbling right about now."

"I'm babbling on the inside. How long have you been a vampire?"

"Two hundred and twenty-six years." He just wanted to see her reaction.

She didn't give him one. "How long have you been working for the government?"

"Two hundred and twenty-three."

That stopped her, but she rallied. "So what were the Founding Fathers like?"

"That thing about the cherry tree is a myth, Washington's teeth were ivory rather than wood, and Congress was just as big a pain in the ass as it is now."

"That doesn't surprise me."

"Nothing much does, does it?"

She smiled slowly, ambition and confidence in her eyes. "I mean to play in the big leagues, Mr. Archer. I can't afford to be taken by surprise."

I'd like to take you. Slowly. "Why don't you come down to the fire where we can see each other better, and we'll continue this conversation," he said, his voice far more husky than he'd intended.

"Where we can see each other better. Right," she said, sounding surprisingly tough for somebody with that face. "Translated: where I can look deep into your eyes and you can put the vampire whammy on me. And suddenly all my questions will disappear."

Archer grinned. "Smart girl."

Her tempting lips peeled back from her pretty white teeth. "You're not messing with my head."

"Don't you think it's best all around? It's not like anybody will believe you."

"They won't have to." Dana snorted and gingerly pulled at her trapped leg. "What kind of moron do you think I am? I'm not blowing my chance at a national story because of your overbite."

He walked lightly across the rotting flooring to kneel beside her. She shrank back, but Archer ignored the movement and reached down to twist the broken length of board away from her calf. "It won't hurt you to forget a detail or two. You'll still get your exclusive."

"Forget it. I'm not thrilled about having somebody else edit my copy. I sure as hell don't want you editing my head." Dana pulled her leg free with a tiny gasp of pain, then cautiously felt for the wound in the darkness. He could see it wasn't serious, though she could probably use a tetanus shot.

Archer sighed and stood, reaching down to pull her to her feet. "Ms. Ivory, I'm afraid you've missed the point. I'm not giving you a choice."

Dana narrowed her cloud-gray eyes in anger. He could almost see her busy little brain working out her chances of escape. The results evidently didn't please her; her shoulders slumped. Then she mustered a glower. "You've got no right to rape people's minds just so you won't be inconvenienced."

"Inconvenienced?" He snorted. "Ms. Ivory, if people knew what I am, they'd hunt me down like a rabid dog."

"So what about government officials? They've got to know about you." Dana bent and started to feel around in the dark for her camera.

"Only the few who need to. To others, I'm just another operative. The rest have never heard of me at all. And I keep it that way." Archer scooped up the camera, microphone and tape recorder, then handed the whole armload to her.

"Thanks," Dana grumbled. He took her elbow to guide her toward the door, where she ended up giving the pile back to him so she could climb down the treehouse ladder.

She moved stiffly as she crouched to feel for the first rung with her foot. Archer suspected her injured leg was hurting, but when he offered to help, Dana aimed such a cold look up at him that he shrugged. Delicate jaw set, she began to descend, her long, slim hands white-knuckled as they gripped the rungs. He climbed after her, holding her gear in one arm.

When Dana reached the ground, she immediately turned her back on him. Archer smiled in reluctant admiration, recognizing her stubborn determination to make his job as difficult as possible.

The clearing was empty except for the dying fire. His men had gone, headed for the sheriff's office and the nearest jail to book their prisoners. His unruly body immediately began to see the possibilities, but Archer reined in its eager leap with his habitual self-control. Business first. He wanted to change her memories and be done with it; he'd had enough of her pricks to his conscience.

But he'd make it up to her, Archer told himself. As soon as he checked on his men, he'd give Dana an exclusive about the arrest and finish up the paperwork.

Then, once duty was served, he'd turn his attention to seducing her.

Archer loved a good seduction. The sweet, hot quest to discover what aroused a woman most, the erotic dance of temptation once he found the key to her heat. Especially when the woman had this one's fire and will—not to mention edible little body. She'd be both a challenge and a pleasure.

He dumped her equipment on the ground and moved up behind her. "Look at me, Dana." Softly, he added, "I promise I won't hurt you."

Dana whirled on him, gray eyes snapping in the firelight. "The hell you won't."

"Then I'll be quick." Archer locked his gaze on hers, the way the Countess had taught him two centuries ago, and reached for her mind with his own. He expected the usual easy tumble into alien memories, feelings, hopes and fears.

Instead he felt... Nothing.

Her gray eyes didn't widen, didn't glaze, didn't falter from his in their cool, defiant stare. It was as though she looked at him through a glass shield.

Archer felt a quick spurt of delight at the unexpected resistance. He forced it down. He'd gotten his hopes up before when he'd encountered this kind of mental barrier, only to be disappointed again and again. If he pushed a little harder, her mind would yield to his control the way all the others had.

He gathered his considerable psychic power and stabbed it like a rapier straight between those wide gray eyes.

There. He waited for her to open to him...

"Are you going to do whatever it is, or not?"

God. Archer stared at her, staggered. His mental thrust should have punched right through her resistance, opening her mind to his. But it hadn't.

She was a candidate for the Kiss.

Finally, after two hundred and twenty-six years, he'd found a woman who could survive rebirth as a vampire.

Maybe, Archer cautioned himself. She had the psychic strength, but there was more to it than that. Much more. He needed time, time to examine and probe. Time to decide what to do.

Suspended between hope and wariness, Archer stared at her. She met his gaze stubbornly, her features set in rebellion.

Candidate or not, he realized Dana Ivory was going to be a problem.

For one thing, what was Archer going to do about her knowledge of his vampirism until he decided whether to change her? He had no idea if she could be trusted. He'd survived in his country's service all these years through ruthless secrecy, but Dana could force him into the glare of a national spotlight even if she never used the word "vampire." Once her story hit the Associated Press wire service, he was screwed. There was no way he could influence all the thousands of editors who used the AP into killing the story.

He had to get her under control.

Fortunately, Gabriel Archer had two centuries' practice in controlling women.

At first it was all Dana could do not to shake when she met his gaze. Archer's eyes looked so blue and cold and merciless as he stared into hers. And so knowing, as if he were immensely old. Looking into that immortal stare, she finally *believed* he was a vampire.

Her father's religious teachings stirred uneasily in her mind. If he was a vampire, didn't that make him some kind of demon?

Yet a demon would have helped the kind of men who bombed churches. Archer had jailed them. So he couldn't be a demon.

But what was he?

As she stared up at Archer, Dana suddenly realized his expression had softened, becoming less ruthless, almost seductive. His lids lowered, pupils expanding into dark pools set in his crystalline blue irises. The tight line of his mouth relaxed, taking on a sensual curve, and his nostrils flared as if scenting her. He took one step closer, then another, until he was so close his big body seemed to surround hers.

Her mouth went dry as she remembered the way he'd looked with his shirt off, the intensely male contours gleaming in the firelight. She took a step back.

"Are you afraid of me, Dana?" Archer murmured, closing the distance between them again.

God, his chest was broad. It seemed to fill her vision. And the T-shirt fabric clung, so she could see all that fascinating masculine topography. Like the way the black material tented over the tiny nub of his left nipple. She wet her lips and resisted the impulse to look down, see if something else might be protruding beneath his jeans.

"You shouldn't be afraid," he said, his velvet and whiskey voice curling around her senses. Archer lowered his head toward hers, his hair falling forward. Dana watched, hypnotized, as strand slipped over dark, gleaming strand, tumbling in slow motion against the stern rise of his cheek. She wanted to touch his hair, feel its silken length slip through her fingers.

"I have no desire to hurt you," he said softly. "There are so many better things to do." His breath gusted over her lips, warm and smelling faintly yeasty.

"Beer," Dana blurted, groping for a way to resist the lush spell he was spinning around her. "I didn't think vampires drank anything but blood."

"Don't believe everything you hear." Gently, Archer reached up and smoothed her own tumbled hair back from her forehead. His fingers felt warm, almost feverish. Wasn't a vampire's skin supposed to be cold? *Another myth shot to hell,* she thought, fighting dizziness.

"Don't be afraid of me, Dana," he said, his voice a deep, seductive rumble. "I'm one of the good guys." His eyelashes cast long shadows against his elegant cheekbones as he lowered his head. "Very, very good."

And then his lips touched hers, hot silk, brushing once, then clinging, slowly drawing her lower lip into his mouth to gently suckle. His tongue slipped across it, wet and clever, tempting her to open her own mouth, let him inside.

Her head went into a long, slow spin. What was happening to her?

He was touching her now, gentle little strokes, here on her shoulder, there on her cheek, a fingertip dance on her waist, slipping into a caress of her hip. How could a man who could throw Donnie Anders around with brutal strength touch her with such delicacy?

Dana dragged her mouth away from his and gasped. "I thought you were supposed to hypnotize me, make me forget."

"Oh, I want to make you forget." His mouth moved to her ear, nibbled, breathed. "I want you to forget how to say no."

Dana tried to brace her hands against his chest to hold him back, but she couldn't seem to summon the strength. And that alarming weakness spread quickly, rolling from her arms to her knees. She tried to stiffen her legs and stand erect, only to find herself leaning into his chest, surrendering to those hot, seductive hands.

One of them had discovered her bottom. He traced the curve of a jeans-clad cheek with long fingers, then slipped into the cleft to exert a suggestive, wicked pressure. Dana tightened reflexively, unintentionally thrusting forward against his groin. Where she felt the thick, hard length of his erection jutting against the zipper of his jeans. He rolled his hips, letting her feel the massive ridge. She gasped, and he purred a laugh in her ear.

He's got me acting like a skittish virgin, she thought, appalled. "Stop that. Aren't you on duty?"

"I'm taking a dinner break," he whispered, and bit her earlobe. One of those quick hands found its way under her shirt and slid upward toward her breasts. "How about it, Dana. Wouldn't you like to be dinner?"

The hand captured her, slipping over her breast to encircle it with long, possessive fingers. She caught her breath as the sensation unfurled along her nerves. He squeezed gently, his heat searing her skin through the lace of her bra. "No," Dana protested. It came out as a tiny, helpless whimper, sounding arousing even to her ears.

"But you'd make such a lovely feast. And I'm so hungry." He delicately pinched her nipple, which drew into a tight, tingling peak at his touch. "I could spend hours devouring these beautiful breasts. Let me see them, Dana."

"You've done something to me," she moaned.

"Not yet." He grabbed her shirt and ruthlessly pulled it off over her head, then dragged the bra down. "But I'm going to."

Dazed, Dana looked down to see her own bare breasts glowing pale in the firelight, the nipples hard, rosy points. Then Archer's head covered one breast while his hand claimed the other. His mouth sucked and bit as his fingers tormented until need jerked tight in her belly.

Dana's feet went out from under her. She yelped, grabbing at Archer for support, only to realize he'd swept her up in his arms. Still suckling greedily at her helpless nipple, he lowered her to the ground. Dry leaves crunched under her bared back.

For a moment Archer loomed above her, his massive shoulders edged in moonlight before he descended on her to continue his leisurely feast.

Dana twisted helplessly at the sensation created by his swirling, lapping tongue, then groaned as a hand slid between her legs, pressing into her cleft through her jeans until she thought she'd burst into flames. She panted, past protest now, her body yowling for him, for his mouth and his fingers and his erection.

Distantly, she heard the erotic whisper of her zipper sliding down. Then his hand touched her silk-clad belly, slipping past the waistband to search out wet curls and tight, soft lips. One long finger dipped inside, gliding through the thick cream of her arousal to slowly pump. Then another joined it, and another, filing her full. She moaned.

It had been so long.

This was just like her fantasies, Dana thought, in helpless, shamed excitement—the ones she never told anyone about because they were so sinful. Being taken by a stranger in the woods, letting him touch and taste and bite.

Bite.

The word stabbed her with a sudden realization that sliced through the heat in her mind like a dagger of ice.

He wasn't just any stranger. He was a vampire.

And this wasn't about love or even sex. He intended to feed on her.

"Stop it." Her voice was low and determined. "Now."

Archer froze, his mouth filled with hard nipple, his fingers buried in tight, lush sex. He was triply erect, fangs and cock, lust searing his veins until he ached.

But he didn't ignore that tone. Ever.

"I said get off me!" Her hands pushed at his shoulders.

"All right, dammit!" He jerked away and shot to his feet, retreating several paces as Dana jumped up and began to jerk and zip at her clothes. Aching, frustrated, Archer watched her pale breasts bounce as she scooped her shirt off the ground and shrugged into it.

"I thought you were supposed to be one of the good guys," she said bitterly.

"You weren't complaining a minute ago." Archer barely managed not to snarl. Showing fang at a time like this would be too much like a threat.

Dana jerked her head up. Her gray eyes swam with betrayed tears. "You said you would make me forget you're a vampire. You didn't say anything about making me sleep with you."

He gaped at her. "You think I did this with psi?"

"Didn't you?"

"I'm a seducer, not a rapist," Archer snapped. "I'd never use psychic influence to get a woman into bed."

Dana fisted her hands on her hips. "Oh, right. One minute you're going to hypnotize me, the next, I'm on the ground letting you suck my nipples. But you didn't use 'psychic influence.'"

"I'm *good*," he snarled.

"You're a vampire," she hurled at him. "You couldn't be good if you tried. You're damned by God."

For a moment Archer couldn't believe she'd said the words. This was the twenty-first century, and she was giving him the same line he'd heard in the eighteenth. "God and Satan have nothing to do with vampirism. It's a virus. You catch it."

That stopped her. Her pale brows drew down over those cloud-gray eyes. "How?"

"I'm not in the mood for another fucking interview," he ground out.

"I've just been rolling on the ground with you. I think I'm entitled to know."

She had a damn good point. "You have nothing to worry about." *At the moment, anyway.* "You can't catch the vampire virus from a kiss. Or a toilet seat, or a sneeze. You'd only have to worry if you drank my blood."

She wrinkled her pert nose at him. "Ugh. Well, I'm certainly not going to be doing that any time soon." There was a long, tense pause. Finally Dana drew herself upright, evidently deciding to defuse the moment. "When are you going to do your psychic amnesia thing?"

"Already tried." He shrugged. "It doesn't work on you."

She blinked. "Why not?"

"I don't know." A lie, but she wasn't ready for the truth.

A relieved smile spread across Dana's face, winsome and sweet. "Well, in that case, I'll just be getting back to the paper. I've got a story to write." She turned on her heel and started out of the clearing.

"No." He couldn't let her leave. Not now.

She whirled back to him, eyes widening. "But I told you, I'm not going to use any of the vampire stuff. Nobody would believe me anyway."

"I'm not even talking about the 'vampire stuff.' I just don't want this story out right now."

"Too bad. It's out."

"Dana, I flushed Satterfield's plot by using psi on the WAB's founder and ordering him to recommend me to anybody planning something big. If you report this, Jonah Howard will get suspicious, and he won't let me get close enough to influence him again. And I have reason to believe the WAB is planning other terrorist actions."

Well, it sounded plausible, anyway. In reality, Howard would have a hell of a time keeping Archer away no matter how suspicious he was. All Archer had to do was walk up to him in the grocery store, look him in the eye and give him an order, and Howard would do whatever the hell he wanted. But Dana didn't know that.

She shook her shaggy blonde head. "Archer, those men were going to assassinate the President. You can't keep something that big a secret."

He laughed. "Oh, I've kept much bigger secrets than this."

"But…"

"I am not letting you go, Dana."

She bared her teeth at him. "You can't keep me."

Archer reached into his back pocket and pulled out a pair of handcuffs. "Can't I?" He started toward her. "You have the right to remain silent…"

Dana backed up. "But I haven't done anything!"

"How about interfering with a federal investigation?"

"Interfering, hell, I'm just reporting it. Or did they repeal the First Amendment when nobody was looking?"

"Sorry." Archer grabbed her shoulder and spun her around. Catching her slim wrists, he pulled them behind her, trapped them in one hand, and snapped on the 'cuffs.

"I want a lawyer, you toothy jerk!" She turned her head to glare over her shoulder at him, her gray eyes snapping. Those moonlight pale curls framed her face, and her full mouth looked mutinous, kissable. "Now."

"You'll get a lawyer when I say you get a lawyer. In the meantime, you'll stay in my custody." Temper simmering, Archer leaned close to her delicate little ear and whispered mockingly, "How *do* you feel about bondage, Dana?"

Her heartbeat leaped.

"Ahh." A smile of delight spread across his face. "Does innocent Dana have a guilty secret?"

As he watched, a tide of red flooded from her cleavage right up to her hairline.

And he knew he had her.

Chapter Three

Dana picked nervously at a hole in the vinyl seat of her chair, then realized what she was doing and forced herself to stop. She was in enough trouble without destroying the property of the Adams County Sheriff's Department. Guiltily, she looked around the office, but none of the detectives were watching her.

And Archer and his handcuffs were nowhere to be seen.

Thank God. An hour had passed since he'd hit her with his wicked suggestion, but her skin still felt hot from that blush. Damn her misspent adolescence anyway. And damn big brother Mark and his stash of Victorian erotica.

She slumped. At least Archer'd had the courtesy to take the handcuffs off before he'd escorted her into the building. It would have been mortifying to be cuffed in front of the deputies she'd been working with for the past six years.

Unfortunately, he'd killed the spurt of gratitude she'd felt by leaning over and whispering in her ear, "They go back on... later."

That last "later" was spoken in such a tone of velvet suggestion that she'd felt the blush roll right back up to her hairline again.

Dana glowered, remembering the curious looks her red face had gotten from the deputies as they'd walked in. She'd promptly blushed even hotter. She just wasn't equipped to keep her cool in the face of Archer's sophisticated games, not with her upbringing.

From the day Dana had turned thirteen, her evangelist mother had exercised her considerable talent for fire and brimstone preaching on the subject of sex. "Intercourse," as Helen Ivory called it, was powerful and innately corrupting, and should only be risked under the protection of marriage for the purpose of begetting children.

Anything else was sinful.

Helen also laced her lectures with well-meant misinformation: the AIDS virus would go right through latex condoms, and abortions would leave you sterile and suicidal.

Dana's outrage when she'd discovered she'd been lied to was one of the reasons she'd gone into journalism, the business of spreading truth whether anybody liked it or not.

But that strict upbringing also left her hungry for any knowledge whatsoever about sex. So the day she discovered her brother's hidden porn cache in the attic when she was sixteen, she'd pounced on it.

At first Dana had been horrified at the stories, with their blatant misogyny and streak of cruelty. But she'd been equally excited by their eroticism. Even though guilt had quickly driven her out of the attic, fascination had repeatedly lured her back. She'd spent hours up there on a discarded couch, reading in the light from a tiny attic window as she caressed herself in guilty excitement.

From then on, her fantasies revolved around wickedly handsome rakes and bound virgin prisoners. Hell, she still had those fantasies, and she still felt guilty, not so much out of a fear of brimstone as the knowledge she shouldn't be aroused by the idea of submitting to anybody's domination.

Unfortunately, her libido didn't seem to have a social conscience. And it loved Archer, archetype of wickedly seductive dominance that he was. The man was the sum total of every fantasy she'd ever had: handsome, built like a Roman gladiator, and gifted with enough erotic skill to make a woman get down and beg. Dana would bet her last notebook Archer had actually *been* a Victorian rake. He certainly seemed to sense her darkest fantasies, knowing just how to drive her right into a frenzy.

Yet he'd stopped when she'd said no and meant it.

Unfortunately, he was also planning to book her on some pretty serious federal charges.

Dana slumped, discouraged, and braced an elbow on the battered desk beside her. Brooding, she turned her attention to the federal agent who was typing with two fingers on a small black laptop. He must have brought the computer with him; God knew the Adams

County Sheriff's Department couldn't afford any tech that high.

"Did Archer really fight in the Revolutionary War?"

The agent looked up and gaped at her, then glanced around hastily for eavesdroppers. Seeing none, he whispered, "He told you that? And let you remember it?"

"His psychic thing doesn't work on me. Did he?"

He frowned. "His psychic thing always works." Hazel eyes focused on her, sharp in the agent's middle-aged face. He was in his fifties, Dana estimated, with tired, lived-in features and thinning sandy hair, but his body was as hard and lean as a teenager's in its black fatigues. "No comment."

"But..."

"I'm not telling you a damn thing, lady," he interrupted, his voice cold. "Especially not if Archer's psi doesn't work on you."

"Fitzroy," Archer said from the doorway.

"Yes sir?"

"I need to talk to you a minute. And you." He shot Dana a hard look. "Quit trying to interview everything that moves."

She slumped down in her chair with a sigh of disgust.

※⚶(♥♥)⚶⅏

Michael Fitzroy followed Archer into the interview room and shut the door. "How'd it go?"

He closed his eyes and rubbed his temples. Repeated psychic sessions always gave him a murderous headache. "They'll cooperate fully for the next forty-eight hours or so. You'll need to gather all the evidence they'll give you before my influence wears off."

Fitzroy lifted a graying eyebrow. "You sound like you don't plan to be there."

Archer shrugged. "You can handle them. Besides, I've got another project." *Which should be a lot more fun.* "By the way, I want you to do a full security check on Dana Ivory—the works. I want to know her bank balance, her work history, her parents, her shoe size, what her third grade teacher thought of her and who gave her that first kiss. Everything, right down to the ground. The same check we give prospective agents. Then e-mail the data to me. I'll be at the house in Charleston."

Fitzroy stared at him, gaze sharpening. "Why? What the hell's going on, Archer?"

"She's a candidate, Fitz."

"For the *team*?" He looked horrified.

"More than that—for the Kiss."

"You want to make her a vampire?"

Archer gave him an annoyed look. "Would you hold it down?"

Fitzroy moved closer and dropped his voice to a hiss. "Shit, Arch, are you getting Alzheimer's? She's a kid. She can't be more'n twenty-five. You can't seriously mean to give her your kind of power. Besides, she's a *reporter*."

He said the word in a tone of such deep loathing Archer had to grin. "It's not a dirty word, Fitz."

"The hell it's not. Look, Arch, this little bimbo makes a living telling morons things they've got no business knowing. And you want to hand her the biggest secret in U.S. history? Why not make a fuckin' sixty-second commercial and run it during the Super-bowl!"

"Once she joins the team, she won't tell anybody anything." Archer scrubbed both hands through his hair, trying to make his second-in-command understand. "Look, I believe Dana has the strength to become a vampire without going insane. And I have never met anyone else I could say that about in my entire life, including you. That makes her a potential intelligence asset we can't ignore." He looked up and caught his friend in a determined stare. "I have to check her out."

Agitated, Fitzroy turned and began to pace. "What if you change her, and she misuses the power?"

"Then I'll kill her."

The agent snorted. "Oh, you are so full of shit. You hate hurting women, up to and including psychopathic terrorists. This kid would just look at you with those big gray eyes and you wouldn't be able to lay a finger on her. And we'd all be fucked."

"I said I'd handle her," Archer snapped. "Look, I'm not going to change her unless I'm sure she'll work, all right? Besides, she may not even agree."

Fitzroy threw up both hands. "Fine. You do whatever the hell you think best. You always do. But you'd better damn well be right."

Archer set his jaw. "Don't worry. I know exactly what to do."

Dana looked up as Archer stalked back into the detective's office and gave her a smoldering look. "Come with me."

She rose to her feet, eyeing him warily as he strode over to grab her by the elbow. "Where are we going?"

"You'll find out." Archer pulled her around and propelled her out of the office and down the hall toward the front door.

"Am I under arrest or what?" Dana tried to set her feet, but his relentless strength kept her moving. "Look, you haven't booked me, which means I haven't been charged, which means you have no right to hold me. I could report you for this. Who's your supervisor?"

He angled her an amused look. "Don't try to bluff me, Dana. Even if you did file a report, do you really think I'd let anybody take action against me?"

Damn. She hadn't thought of that. She could scream bloody murder clear to the President, and all Archer would have to do is whisper in the right ear to make it all go away. True, she could go to the press—he couldn't use his psi on everybody – but he could have the right people declare her a nut, and she'd be written off. Maybe even hospitalized.

A sudden chill skated Dana's spine. *He could do anything he wanted to her, and nobody would ever say a word.*

Feeling helpless, she stumbled after Archer as he pushed open the department door and pulled her out into the dark.

"What are you going to do to me?" Dana licked her dry lips.

He laughed, a low, seductive rumble. "I don't know yet. I'm still trying to make a list." With a flex of his arm, Archer swung her around the corner of the building. Her foot slipped as a piece of gravel rolled under it, but before she could smash into the brick, his big hands caught and steadied her. Then he planted a palm between her shoulder blades and gently pressed her face-first against the rough surface of the wall.

"Let's start with a frisk, shall we?" Before Dana could jerk back, Archer kicked her feet wide, then moved up behind her. She gasped as he slid his muscular thigh up between her legs until it pressed against her sex, forcing her to ride him. She was just gathering the breath to protest when his big hands began to explore her body as if he owned it.

"Archer, what the hell are you doing?" she gasped. "One of the deputies could drive up!"

"It's so dark back here the only one who can see a damn thing is me." His breath gusted warmly against her ear as he dragged her back against his powerful body, then cupped his hands around her breasts. His thumbs strummed her nipples through her shirt. She felt them harden. "Hell, you can't even see what I'm doing, can you? But I can. You've got beautiful breasts, Dana." His tongue flicked out, tested one of the straining cords of her neck.

"Archer..."

"Ever been strip-searched?" Archer's voice was so darkly suggestive, she shivered. "How about a body cavity probe? We could play pretty little hooker and bad, bad cop. I'll bet you'd like that."

Dammit, how did he do this to her? How did he know just the right notes to hit? Thirty seconds, and he had her creaming. It was humiliating. "I'm not interested in playing anything with you," Dana gritted.

"It's against the law to lie to an agent of the Federal government, Dana." He brought his leg up higher, lifting her off the ground and forcing her sex hard against his thigh. Heat scalded her. "Do it again and I'll have to pull down your pants and spank you."

It was all she could do not to writhe as she rode his leg. "This isn't right," Dana gasped. "It's just a game to you, isn't it? It's a role. Dominant male."

"It's what I am," Archer purred in her ear, fingers plucking her nipples through the thin fabric of her shirt. "There are too damn many of you and only one of me. I've got to dominate you or I'm dead."

He pressed closer until Dana could feel the entire length of his body against her back. She licked her lips as his rigid erection ground against her bottom. "I've got to find out what you need and give it to you, so you won't notice when I steal what *I* need. And what I need is you spread wide and wet under me, ready for my fangs and cock." He pressed her against the wall until she could feel every thick, powerful inch of him. "And Dana, you're going to give me just what I need."

"No," she moaned.

"Oh, yes. Over and over, every way I can think of." Slowly, Archer rolled his hips against her bottom, forcing her to imagine what it would be like to be at the mercy of his power. "On your belly with your ass in the air and your hands cuffed behind you. Tied spread-eagle to my big tester bed while I lick and taste all that creamy white skin. On your knees, sucking my cock until I shoot into your mouth."

"I won't!" Dana gasped, hot cream flooding her sex.

"You will," he retorted, his voice rich with velvet menace, his strong hands kneading her breasts. "Again and again. And you'll love every minute of it while I show you just what a vampire can do to a bound and naked woman."

"You'll have to use force," she said, trying for toughness.

"Oh, I will." He twisted her nipples. "Just the way you've always dreamed."

Shame and excitement stung her. "You don't know a damn thing about my dreams."

"I know how your heartbeat speeds when I talk about what I want to do to you. And I can smell how wet you are right now. I'd like to take your jeans down and lap you all up while you writhe and beg." He took her earlobe between his teeth and gently bit. "But you'd love it even better if I handcuffed you first. Admit it."

"No." She swallowed.

"At night in your lonely bed, you dream of being at the mercy of a man like me. Bound and spread and helpless. Ready to be fucked."

Humiliation shafted through the languid desire he'd roused. It was as if he'd eavesdropped on her darkest fantasies, the ones she hated to admit even to herself. "I'm not a toy, damn you!" Dana cried, her voice ragged with shame. "Don't treat me like one!"

Archer froze. She felt the hot wind of his breath gusting hard against her ear, heard him swallow. "No," he said, his voice hoarse. "You're not a toy."

Then he was gone, releasing her so quickly she would have fallen if he hadn't caught her again. He spun her around, gathering her wrists in one hand. She felt the touch of something cool around one of them, heard a snap, a musical rattle.

He was handcuffing her again. He was going to take her right here in the parking lot.

"No!" Dana fought to pull away, but he was too strong. "Not like this. Please, Archer!"

"Calm down," he said roughly. "I'm not going to do it here."

Panting, she subsided. He led her to the passenger side of one of the big, government cars parked in the lot and bundled her inside. Dana sat there, dazed, while he leaned in to buckle the seatbelt around her. His hair brushed her face as he snapped the belt together. She remembered what he'd said about smelling her wetness. She shivered in arousal and shame.

Archer pulled away from her and closed the door with a solid thunk. A moment later the driver's door opened, and he got in. The car started with a well-mannered growl.

"Where are we going?"

"Charleston. I have a house there." He threw the car into reverse and began to back up.

"Charleston. That's a two hour drive." Two hours in the car with him. Alone. And then they'd be at his house.

Alone.

She just wished the idea didn't make her feel so hot.

※❧(ℭℑ)ℰ※

There was something about Dana that made him lose control.

Archer had planned to take it slow, play the dark master of seduction until he had her begging. It was a part he'd acted for countless partners until he knew every leisurely step, every stylized gesture.

So when he'd pushed Dana against the wall, he'd intended nothing more than the opening act. Then he'd touched her, tasted her skin, scented her growing arousal, seen her blend of trembling desire and shame. He'd taken those full breasts in his hands, and hunger had roared over him in a wave so strong he'd come within a hair's-breadth of ripping her jeans down and taking her. Right there against the wall.

But the game was not supposed to affect Archer this way. He was supposed to be in control—of her and himself. An actor, playing a role. That was, after all, what he did best: act, whether the part was white supremacist assassin, Nazi S.S. officer, or demon lover. Whatever it was, Archer wrapped himself in the role, but he never lost sight of his goal and never forgot he was acting.

Yet somehow, Dana Ivory made him forget. This game was about gaining control of a potential vampire agent, yet he was the one who was being seduced. She kicked his hunger so high and so hot that all he wanted was to sweep her up and take her. Take her body, take her blood, take her heart. Take her and own her, until she was his without question, without possibility of escape.

And Dana responded deliciously, but she also fought that response, refusing to simply go along with the game. Archer wasn't sure he understood why. Usually women were more than happy to let him play the demon lover, never questioning what his real feelings were. He suspected they thought of him as nothing more than a fantasy given delicious life. And nobody cared about the feelings of a fantasy.

Yet Dana seemed to want something more. He had no idea what, or how to give it to her. Or even if he should.

Still, she responded to his demon lover. And that would have to be enough—for both of them.

❧✦(♥)✦❧

She should be afraid of him, Dana thought.

For God's sake, the man was a vampire. He'd handcuffed and abducted her for sex and bondage. He could even kill her and make sure no one ever caught him. Yet she felt no physical fear of him at all.

Paranoia stirred. Maybe she was under some kind of spell after all.

But... She stole a look at Archer's Roman coin profile as he drove. There was, despite every wicked thing he'd threatened her with, a basic core of decency under that dominant male mask of his. There wasn't even any real cruelty. He wouldn't hurt her. Not physically.

Emotionally, she wasn't so sure about. Dana didn't like the way he was getting to her, the way he'd figured out her darkest fantasies and turned them against her.

"How do you do it?" She asked the question before she realized she was going to. "How do you always know how to make me respond?"

Archer looked at her. His eyes reflected a glow of red in the light of a passing car, making her heart leap at the eerie shimmer they gave off. Dana expected him to give her another one of those suggestive lines of his, but his tone was serious when he answered. "I've been at this two centuries and more, Dana. I serve my country out of duty, but I seduce to survive."

"Why?" she demanded, not sounding nearly as cool as she wished. "Why does it matter to you what my fantasies are?"

Archer turned his head again to watch the road. "A vampire feeds on strong emotion as much as blood. The higher, the hotter, I can get my partner, the stronger the psychic charge she gives me in her climax. I learned a long time ago how to read the needs a woman can't speak, that she can't even allow a lover to guess. When I feed that hidden need, the response is explosive."

She stirred uneasily against the leather seat. "Then what? You just walk away? You've been fed, and that's it? What about how she feels?"

"You imagine a trail of broken hearts in my wake?" Archer snorted. "Women don't fall in love with a guilty fantasy. Generally they can't forget me fast enough."

Dana frowned, studying his profile in the dim, soft light of the dashboard. Was that a flash of vulnerability? "Are you the one with the broken heart, Archer?"

He laughed, a short, bitter bark. "Demon lovers have no hearts, Dana. We fuck, we feed and we walk, and everybody's happy."

"Are you?"

"Ecstatic." A flash of red. "You can't imagine what it's like, seeing a beautiful woman stretched out in chains, helpless and writhing and hot. Knowing that in a moment I'm going to possess her, sink my cock and my fangs into her delicate flesh..."

Archer tormented Dana like that for the next half-hour, until she finally blurted out, "So how do you become a vampire?"

It was such a transparent attempt to change the subject that he had to smile. Still, talking dirty to Dana was just a little too stimulating, so Archer decided to play along. "Are you asking about me in particular, or vampires in general?"

She licked her lips. "In general, I guess."

Archer eyed her. She looked flushed and flustered, he noted with satisfaction. Not exactly the cool reporter who'd started grilling him the moment they'd met.

"You'd need a weakened immune system, then you'd have to ingest a large amount of infected blood." Nothing like talking about infected blood to wilt an erection. "All of which would probably kill you anyway, but if it didn't, the virus would move in and change the DNA in your cells. That in turn would change your muscles, your bones, your nerves. You'd become enormously strong, and your immune system would be able to heal almost any injury."

Dana frowned. "I thought viruses weakened their hosts, not made them stronger."

"This is more of a symbiotic relationship," Archer said, repeating the explanation a CIA researcher had once given him. "It has to be. The vampire virus is so weak it only survives by making the few who do catch it practically immortal."

"Huh. I'm surprised the government's not infecting people in droves."

Archer winced, remembering one of the CIA's more boneheaded stunts. "They tried. Once. They had this program going in the Sixties, during the Vietnam War. It was so secret even I didn't know about it. They took samples of my blood when I went in for surgery to remove a few bullets. Then…"

"Infected somebody."

He nodded. "I found out about the project when I had to kill the vampire they made, and I made sure they never tried it again."

"You killed him? Why?" Archer could almost see her taking notes in her head. "How'd you stop them?"

"You never quit hunting a story, do you?"

"Nope. Why'd you kill him?"

"He ripped out the throats of the research team." Archer grimaced, remembering the battlefield gore he'd seen in that lab. "One by one. Then he killed the strike force the CIA sent in after him. Twenty-three people died before they finally called me to take care of the problem." He shook his head. "The crazy son of a bitch almost got me, too. God, I was pissed. You can't just pick somebody at random and infect them."

"Why not?"

He glanced at her and told her a crucial truth, knowing she wouldn't recognize it until later. "Because very few people can handle the change. You become aware of the thoughts of others, the beat of their hearts, the blood in their veins—blood you're desperately hungry for. If you're not one of the very few who can generate a psychic shield, you go mad. And it takes another vampire to recognize a potential survivor."

"So they dropped the experiment?" Dana looked uneasy, as if she didn't quite buy it.

"I told them that if I ever found a candidate, I'd let them know. Don't worry, nobody's got a lab somewhere turning out vampires. Not in this country, anyway."

"I can't tell you how relieved that makes me feel," Dana said, rolling her eyes. She was silent a moment, mulling over everything he'd told her. "There must not be very many of you."

"I've met only two, other than the one the CIA spawned. About thirty years ago, there was a Soviet agent named Pavel Andronovich…"

"The Russians have vampires too?"

"Not anymore."

"Oh." Whatever Dana read on his face kept her from asking for the details, thank God.

"Then," he continued, remembering a fall of silken dark hair and hungry eyes, "there was the Countess Isabeau de Vitry, who gave me the Dark Kiss in 1774." Catching her puzzled expression, he explained, "That's what she always called making a vampire, the Dark Kiss. I don't know if that's a universal phrase with vampires, or just another example of Isabeau's French hyperbole."

She eyed him, frowning. "Why not just ask her?"

"The Countess has been dead two centuries." Archer paused, remembering the day of guilt and grief when he'd gotten that last letter from Isabeau's steward. "A French mob took her head during the Terror."

A long, dark pause went by as he fought off black memories, until Dana said, her voice gentle, "It must be lonely."

"I have my work. I have my co-workers." He smiled slightly. "I have women, though usually not for long." Glimpsing Dana's appalled expression, Archer grimaced. "Quit believing everything you see in bad movies. There's something like two gallons of blood in the human body; I couldn't drink it all in one sitting if I tried. On the other hand, I can give someone a good case of anemia over time, so I tend to go for one night stands."

"No girlfriends? Couldn't you…" She gestured. "…Not bite? At least not every time?"

"Yeah, I could. And I do. Or rather, don't." Archer shook his head. "But it's best not to form close relationships with my partners. It's not fair, it's not practical, and after awhile, it becomes painful." His eyes caught on the delicate curve of her face. "I outlive people, Dana. I'm tired of grieving."

She glanced away. "Yes, I can see how you would be."

"Besides," Archer added wickedly. "There are so many more interesting things to do…"

Dana groaned as he started describing them.

By the time they pulled into the long, winding driveway, Dana had her legs tightly crossed against the wet ache between them.

Archer had spent the rest of the trip into Charleston describing the things he'd done to eager female victims, recounting acts of sensual decadence in that deep, drawling velvet voice of his until she was squirming and dry-mouthed.

Still feeling dazed, she looked across the darkened expanse of lawn to see a sprawling brick mansion with thick square columns and wide wings stretching out to either side.

"My father built it," Archer told her as he parked the car in a spacious garage. "Of course, I've made some additions." As he opened the driver's door, he flashed her a wicked smile that showed his fangs. "Manacles in the bedroom."

"Daddy would have been shocked," Dana said as he came around to open her door and unbuckle her seatbelt.

"Not really," Archer said, pulling her out of the seat and into his arms with easy strength. Another flash of those teeth. "We owned slaves."

Dana stared at him, so caught between fascination and revulsion that she forgot to protest as he picked her up. "You're kidding."

"Nope." He straightened, cradling her. "Don't look so self-righteous. I freed them all after the war ended." He shrugged. "It didn't feel right, keeping slaves after we'd just fought the British over natural rights. But God, it pissed the neighbors off."

Archer turned and started across the garage, still carrying her like a child. For a moment the novel sensation stunned her, and she froze in his arms, feeling the warm power of his body, breathing his exotic scent. He smelled faintly of sandalwood and spice, male and tempting. Too tempting.

Sudden panic rose, and she kicked out, trying to squirm her way from his powerful grip. "I can walk!"

"Only if I put you down." He ducked his shoulders so he could open the door without turning her loose, then swept her inside.

She subsided reluctantly. "You are such a high-handed bastard."

He shrugged. "Comes with the territory."

Curiosity overcoming her desire to struggle, Dana peered around the darkened house as he carried her through it. The kitchen was spacious and modern, likely a recent addition, with gleaming white appliances and a surprising array of copper pots hanging over a central island.

As they walked into a hallway, Dana glimpsed a painting of a sailing ship rolling against the sunset in the aftermath of a storm. Archer's booted feet clicked against slate-tile flooring, then they headed up a broad, curving stairway. Toward a bedroom, no doubt. She clasped her hands in the handcuffs, feeling intensely vulnerable.

Just as Dana expected, Archer ducked into a huge bedroom at the top of the stairs, where he put her down at the foot of a gleaming mahogany bed, canopied in what looked like navy brocade and spread with a matching comforter.

Nervously she looked around as he stepped away from her and began to rummage in a drawer. The room was flooded with a golden glow from countless white candles that sat on the mahogany dresser and bureau. The floor was polished hardwood, set here and there with thick woven rugs.

"Who lit the candles?"

"Called the caretaker before we left." Returning, Archer reached for her wrists. There was a coil of gleaming rope in his hand that looked like silk. He smiled into her eyes. "I commit my best sins in candlelight."

"Archer!" Dana pulled away, but he was already backing her against the side of the bed and pulling her arms over her head. "What the hell are you doing?"

"What do you think?" Quickly, efficiently, he tied the rope around the handcuff chain and the overhead canopy support, reaching underneath the canopy to lash them together with a few smooth turns.

She watched him, dizzy with a combination of outrage and desire. "I can't believe I'm letting you get away with this."

"Could you stop me?" Feral eyes locking on hers, he grabbed the front of her shirt between his big hands and gave it an easy tug. Buttons popped, bouncing on the polished wooden floor with a salvo of tiny clicks. Dana looked down to see the white flesh of her breasts swelling in the pretty lace cups of her bra.

Archer made a pleased purring sound in his throat and took hold of the fabric that held the cups together between her breasts. He tore it like paper, then snapped the shoulder straps one by one and threw the ripped bra aside.

Dana tried to swallow the moan. Her knees shook.

Archer stepped close, looking into her eyes. She felt his big hands at her waist, heard a snap, the hiss of her zipper. "Actually," he said, pushing the jeans off her hips, "you could stop me. All you have to do..." The fabric slid down her thighs. She could feel his warm hands brushing her legs. "...is say no."

He went to one knee to slip off her running shoes and socks, then tossed them and the jeans aside. His hair brushed her belly in a stroke of cool silk that made her shiver. Then his mouth was there, pressing a soft kiss to her stomach just before his hands came up to grip the thin silk of her panties. He looked up at her, his eyes pale and hypnotic in the candlelight. "Do you want to say no, Dana?"

She licked her lips, swallowed. "Would you really stop?"

"Yes."

She should say it. She knew she should say it. Her parents would have been appalled that she even hesitated.

She didn't say it.

He smiled. Silk ripped.

Chapter Four

Wrists bound over her head, her heart pounding, Dana looked down at Archer as he tossed aside the remnants of her panties. Then, slowly, he leaned forward until his face was barely an inch from her wet, aching sex. His broad chest lifted and fell as he inhaled, scenting her. She quivered.

He brought a hand up, stroked one long finger over the delicate flesh of her outer lips and the blonde fluff that covered them. "Such pale, pretty curls."

Archer leaned forward, extending his tongue. She could see it, pointed and pink in the instant before it slipped between her lips in a single hot, searing stroke.

"Oh, God!" Unable to help herself, she rose on her toes and rolled her hips forward to give him better access.

"You're so wet," he said, his voice a dreamy drawl. "So ready to be fucked."

Slowly, skillfully, Archer licked at her wet folds, stopping occasionally to suckle her clit and set off a detonation of pleasure. Dana writhed in her bonds, tormented by delight, on the verge of climax. But each time she almost went over, he stopped, waiting for her to subside.

Only to begin again, licking and feasting, driving her higher.

"Archer!" she screamed at last, unable to take any more. "God, now! Please!"

He surged to his feet, one hand at the snap of his jeans, the other catching her under the thigh to pull her legs apart as he stepped between them. The expression on his handsome face was feral, blue eyes narrow and hot, his lips pulled back from white fangs. Dana gasped in a combination of fear and arousal.

"Shit!" Archer let her go and spun away, jerking his black T-shirt over his head as he strode across the room.

"Don't stop!" She stared at his magnificent back and pressed her thighs together, burning to feel him between them. "Why are you stopping?"

"I don't want it over this quick," he growled, without turning around. "I want more."

Bewildered, aching in frustration, Dana watched as he stopped at the bureau, where a crystal decanter sat beside a pair of wine glasses on a silver tray. His hands shook with a fine tremor as he picked up the decanter and poured a stream of something dark into one of the glasses.

Archer took a sip as he turned to face her again, then shook his head. "Almost lost control. I never do that." He took another, deeper sip, then grabbed a wingback chair sitting in a corner and carried it across the room, where he put it down directly in front of her. Dropping into it, Archer eyed her broodingly. "How do you make me break all my rules?"

"The same way you make me break mine." She licked her lips. His chest was a tight, curving sculpture of brawn that shifted in the candlelight as he lifted his hand to drink from the cut crystal glass. The snap of his black jeans was undone, and his cock formed a long, thick ridge under the denim. As she watched, the zipper began inching downward on its own, yielding to the strain of that powerful erection. Dana squirmed, imagining how it would feel driving into her.

Any minute now, she was going to start begging.

Archer had played this scene so many times it should have lost its ability to move him. Hell, just yesterday he'd thought he was getting bored with it all—with the women and the dominance games they so often wanted, with the act he'd always thought was light years from his true personality.

But that was before he'd tied Dana Ivory to his bed in nothing but an open shirt that framed her pert centerfold breasts and the tempting moonlit curls of her sex. Below the shirt, her legs looked as long as his life. The way she kept pressing those sweetly muscled thighs together was slowly driving him insane.

Her gray eyes looked huge in her small face, staring at him with a kind of erotic panic as her tongue slipped out to wet her carnal mouth.

Archer drew in a deep breath, trying for control, but the scent of blood and wet woman mingling in the air almost snapped his grip. He burned to jam himself inside her, sink his aching fangs into the delicate column of her throat and ride her without mercy.

But he couldn't give into that lust, no matter how it tormented him. He had to make her so hungry for what he could do to her that she'd agree to anything if he'd only give her more.

Even if it meant becoming a vampire.

A quick, driving fuck wouldn't force her to that level of desperation. He had to keep building her hunger until she was enslaved by it. And him.

If only he could avoid losing control of his own demanding appetite for her...

Dana pulled at the rope that held her handcuffs, less to get free than to express some of the tension she felt under Archer's devouring stare.

Those crystalline eyes kept flicking from her hard nipples to her sex, then up to her face, then back to her nipples again, around and around while he sprawled there in that chair, his cock thick as a truncheon.

"Are you going to do something?" she blurted. "Or just look?"

He took a sip of his wine, lids shuttering over his glowing eyes. "I like to look."

Dana's gaze slid helplessly to his erection. "I can tell."

"Are you feeling... neglected?" Archer bent over and put the wine glass down with a click on the hardwood flood. He stood up in an entrancing display of bare chest and long legs. One corner of his pirate's mouth curled. "Can't have that. A good host keeps his guests satisfied."

She bit her lip, watching in helpless need as he stalked toward her until his broad shoulders were blocking the candlelight. He loomed there, wolf-pale eyes locked on her face, his features sharp with hunger.

Slowly, Archer knelt, first on one knee, then the other. And slowly, so slowly, he lifted his hands to her breasts and put his face to her sex again.

Dana felt the long stroke of his tongue just as his fingers took her tight nipples and began to gently pinch.

She almost screamed. *Not again.*

Oh, yes. *Again.*

Her head fell back, too heavy for her neck, and her eyes slid closed as his skilled tongue savored her, explored her lips, slipped inside, circled delicately over her clit. The sensation was heart-stopping, hot, maddening, like the feeling of his hands squeezing her flesh, rolling and thumbing her nipples until they sent waves of pleasure to her helpless brain.

"God, Archer!" She instinctively ground her hips, pushing against his face as he licked and bit.

One hand abandoned her throbbing breasts, lowered to slip between her legs. A long finger slid into her. "You're tight as a virgin," he whispered, his voice rough velvet. His eyes glinted red as he tilted back his head to look up at her. "It's been a long time for you, hasn't it?"

"College." She shuddered, eyes closing, refusing to think about the callow, greedy young men who hadn't had a tenth of Archer's sorcery. "Once, twice. Too much guilt, not enough pleasure. It was never, never like this... Archer, please...."

A second finger, and she writhed. He was focused on her clit now, circling his tongue until she strained against his mouth.

A third finger, stretching her. Dana imagined what it would feel like when he drove that big, satin-slick cock into her. Her hands fisted in the handcuffs. "Archer!"

He twisted his wrist, pressing his fingers hard up inside her, stuffing her, almost lifting her off the floor as his tongue fluttered over her clit. Pleasure roared over her in a great, burning wave, about to surge into climax...

Archer drew back. The wave began to die.

"No! Please, Archer, how do you want me?" Her voice spiraled into a scream. She had no idea what she was saying, and didn't care. "Whatever you want! *Anything!*"

He stood in a hard rush, his hands jerking down his zipper, then dragging at his jeans just enough to free his cock. She whimpered with need when she saw it jut out at her, an inch longer and twice as thick as anything she'd ever had.

Then Archer's strong hands were under her ass, lifting her, spreading her as he speared forward in one long, relentless thrust.

"God, you're so wet, so tight," he growled in her ear, forcing deeper. "It's like fucking my way into a peach."

Dana clenched her teeth, shuddering, her back arching, as he tightened his grip on her hips and dragged her down on his cock until she was utterly impaled. She felt stuffed with him, surrounded by his hard body, wrapped in his massive arms. Overwhelmed and helpless.

And God, she loved it.

She'd never felt like this—the strength and the heat and the power, the thick, greedy cock driven into her like a spike. She thought she could come just like this, just from having him inside her.

Then Archer began to move. His slow, slick glide out of her body sent curling spirals of heat up her spine. Then in, and in, and in, his muscled belly flexing against her softer one, his organ forcing her walls to spread around him. Dana twisted helplessly in his arms, wishing he'd grind, needing him to show her no mercy. Instinctively, she wrapped her legs around his waist and locked her feet together, squeezing him between her thighs.

"Oh, yeah," he purred. "Like that."

Archer picked up the pace, shortening his strokes, digging into her. Pleasure coiled tighter and tighter in Dana's belly. His powerful torso rolled against hers as he hunched, fucking her faster. His breath gusted hot in her ear. Spasms of delight rippled through her body.

"Look at me," he demanded in a harsh whisper.

Dazed, she opened her eyes. Archer's face was inches from hers, eyes glowing red in the candlelight. His teeth were bared, fangs fully extended.

"Offer me your throat," he growled. "I want to drink from you as you come."

The image seared her—the thought of his teeth piercing her as his cock tunneled deep. "Oh, God. Yes." Dana let her head fall back.

"Yeah, that's right." Archer gathered her closer, pumping even harder between her thighs, his glowing vampire eyes narrow as they focused on the arch of her throat. "Let me have it all!"

His head lowered. The silk of his hair brushed the underside of her jaw. His teeth pierced her skin, then slowly pressed deep, the sensation building to a deep, hot burn. His lips moved against her throat, warm and smooth, suckling in time to the long, driving thrusts of his cock. His torso stretched and rolled as she held him tight between her legs.

Her climax built, hot and cold at once, the contractions in her sex growing into a brutal pounding. Screaming, Dana convulsed as pleasure exploded through her in a long, fiery cascade down her nerves.

Archer's growl rumbled in her ears as he stiffened in climax, his cock jerking deep inside her, his mouth greedy on her throat.

Until finally she lay limp in his arms, exhausted from the power of her orgasm, unable to move, the vampire still buried deep.

Still feasting.

❦❧

Finally Archer carefully released her throat and lowered her feet to the ground. Dana staggered and almost fell, but he caught her close. She could feel the muscles in his arms quivering and jumping. He was still breathing hard.

"Are you all right?" Archer asked, his voice a little hoarse. "I didn't hurt you, did I? I was... rough."

Dana shook her head. It spun, and she stopped. "No. You were ..." She couldn't think of a word incredible enough. "I've never felt like that. Though I realize you've probably..." *Driven thousands of women out of their minds.* She let the sentence trail off, realizing it sounded like a plea for empty reassurance.

Archer lifted her chin with a gentle forefinger. "I've never felt like that either, Dana. You are *not* just the latest in a long line."

She gave him a quavering smile, knowing he had to be lying. A kind lie, but still, a lie. She'd never been the sort of woman that drove a man to that kind of passion. She had no intention of spoiling this lovely moment by saying so, though.

Archer reached up into his back pocket and pulled out the hand-cuff key, then freed her wrists. Leaving the metal bracelets still lashed to the canopy, Dana lowered her stiffened arms with a groan.

"You okay?" He lifted her hands in both of his to examine her wrists anxiously. "They're bruised. I'm sorry, I didn't think I had them that tight."

"You didn't." She felt herself blush. "I seem to remember pulling on them pretty hard, there at the end."

Archer ducked down to bring one arm up under her thighs, sweeping her into his arms.

Dana giggled as he stepped around the bed with her. "What is this thing you've got with carrying me?"

"It's all part of the service." He bent down, caught the navy coverlet with the hand under her knees, and flipped it back out of the way before laying her down on the cool cream sheets. "Masterful Vampires 'R' Us."

Sitting down beside her, he went to work massaging her aching arms. Dana sighed under his strong fingers. "God, I'm tired. You wore me out."

"You've had a busy night—spying on white supremacists, getting busted by a vampire federal agent, then driving him right up the wall with lust. Anybody'd be tired."

She grinned and let her eyes slip closed. Just for a minute.

It was the last thing she knew for hours.

Archer woke curled possessively around Dana's lush little body. He lay there for a moment, allowing himself to savor the sensation of her warm curves nestled against him. From the sound of her breathing and heartbeat, she was still asleep. He lifted his head to look into her profile, at the long fan of her lashes against her cheek, that silly nose, the full, rosy lips slightly parted.

He had a sudden mental image of sliding his cock into that carnal mouth, maybe while she was on her knees with her hands bound between her legs, her fingers stroking her hard little clit...

Jesus, Archer thought as his erection stiffened into a spike, where had *that* come from? He didn't even have bondage fantasies anymore, not after all the times he'd played those scenes in reality.

But only one of them had been with Dana. And he wanted more of her. Much more. Every way he could think of.

Right now.

Archer started to reach for Dana, then hesitated. He'd taken her pretty hard last night. She'd probably be sore. Despite his rapacious hunger, he didn't want to hurt her.

He wondered how long they'd been asleep, and threw a calculating look at the window. The curtains were heavy navy velvet, but there was enough light creeping around the edges to tell him the sun was up. Well up, judging from the clock on the bureau and the "3:45 p.m." glowing on its face.

Archer glanced back at Dana. His gaze caught on her long, slim back as she lay on her side, and followed the curve of her spine down to the tempting mounds of her ass. He thought of another way to take her—draped belly down over a mound of pillows, her wrists tied together at the small of her back...

Breakfast. It was time to fix her breakfast, or she'd *be* breakfast.

Archer flipped the covers aside and rolled to his feet before stalking, naked, in search of a clean pair of jeans. No shirt, she liked him without a shirt. Almost as much as he liked her wearing nothing at all.

⚜

Archer had started work on a batch of crepes when the phone rang. He let go of the whisk to scoop the handset to his ear. "Hello."

"What's this about some new vampire?" Richard Fleming had never been one for pleasantries.

Sandwiching the phone between his head and shoulder, Archer went back to whipping the batter. "Her name is Dana Ivory, Fleming, and she's not a vampire. She's a candidate for the Kiss, that's all. I've put Fitz to doing a background check on her."

Fleming snorted. "Who gives a damn about a fucking background check? I want to know what *you* think. A background check can be fooled, but nobody lies successfully to Gabriel Archer—and God knows, I've tried."

He had, too. Fleming was a dyed in the wool ex-Cold War spook who firmly believed in not telling anybody a damn thing they didn't have good reason to know. It had taken Archer years to break his superior of the habit of automatically lying to him about anything and everything. But the effort had been worth it. Fleming was damn good at covert ops, and after his years in the intelligence community, he was an invaluable resource. Which was why Archer had recruited him away from the CIA to begin with.

"So what do you think of this girl?" Fleming demanded.

I think she's hot as hell and I want to keep her tied to the bed for at least a decade. Instead Archer said, "She's intelligent, and she's got nerve..."

"Huh. Yeah, setting up in that treehouse to spy on those assholes took either nerve or no sense of self-preservation. Which ain't necessarily a bad thing in an agent."

"It's practically a requirement," Archer, agreed, grinning. "But other than that, I don't know enough about her yet to make a decision. I need to find out more."

Fleming cracked out a nasty laugh. "And judging from the photos on my desk, I'll bet research is a ball. God, what tits."

"And which photos are these?" Archer inquired in his best tone of silky menace.

"Jesus, Arch, you're paranoid. No, we didn't put a guy outside your house with a telephoto lens—not that I'm not tempted. It's just a couple of Polaroids Fitz got from one of her old boyfriends. Ivory at the beach in a bikini." He whistled. "Speaking professionally, that's some package of intelligence assets. If you do make her a vampire, tell her she can bite me anywhere, anytime."

Archer was surprised at the flare of jealousy he felt. Fleming was a good-looking bastard, Marlboro-man handsome. It was far too easy to imagine that Dana might find him a tempting meal. "She has better taste."

"And if anybody'd know how she tastes, I'm sure it'd be you," Fleming said, with another annoying laugh. "Whatever you decide, keep me posted."

"It's not just my decision," Archer told him, still frowning at the strength of his own jealousy. "She gets a say in this, too."

"No, she doesn't." His voice went completely flat, with that cold, deadly tone Archer knew well. "If Ivory's a good prospect, recruit her. She can get used to it later."

"Fleming…"

"I mean it, Archer. I've never liked the fact that we have only one of you. Your abilities are too goddamned invaluable to this country. Hell, if not for you, Manhattan would be glowing in the dark and half the eastern seaboard would still be coughing up blood. We need another vampire agent in case somebody puts a stake in your heart."

He snorted. "Nobody's killed me yet. And believe me, it's not for lack of trying."

"We've been lucky," Fleming snapped. "I'll make it a direct order—if you decide she's trustworthy, bite her."

"Betrayal's a hell of a reward for being worthy of trust."

"You're a fucking secret agent, Archer. It's what we do."

Dana awoke to the feeling of soft lips brushing hers, a tongue slipping sweetly between her teeth. "Rise and shine, sleepyhead. There's a nice, hearty breakfast downstairs with your name on it."

She blinked up at Archer's handsome face as he leaned over her. He'd opened the curtains, and sunlight poured into the room, painting his delectable torso with light.

"I gather the whole bursting-into-flames-at-dawn thing is a myth, huh?" Rubbing her eyes, she sat up.

"Mostly, though you won't catch me sunbathing in the nude anytime soon. Second degree burns in half an hour. I'm okay with overcast days, though."

"Hmmm." Dana yawned and stretched, then stopped in mid-gesture, remembering her would-be exclusive. "Have you seen the news? Has the story broken yet?"

Archer raised an arrogant eyebrow. "That story won't break until I'm good and ready for it to break. And I've made sure everybody who knows anything will keep their mouths shut."

"Somebody could check the jail logs, find out that way." It would kill her if another reporter beat her to the punch.

"Isn't the *Trib* the only paper in town?" Archer moved to the mahogany armoire, pulled open the door, and contemplated the contents. "Who checks police records for you?"

Dana gave him a sheepish smile. "Me."

"And right now, the only thing you'll be reporting on is how mouth-watering my crepes are." She was about to launch an indignant protest when he pulled out something long, black and gleaming and brought it to her. It turned out to be a silk robe.

"Here, put this on," Archer said. "All that naked Dana makes my blood supply head south. Hard to have an intelligent conversation when my cock keeps interrupting."

The mention of his cock—and the thought of what he could do with it—deflated her interest in argument. "You do say the nicest things."

He watched with lecherous interest as she rolled out of bed and shrugged into the robe. "The things I do are even nicer. Like letting you eat instead of ravishing you right now."

Dana licked suddenly dry lips. "You could serve me breakfast in bed."

"True, but I thought we could do something really radical—try to hold an actual conversation like people who aren't compelled to couple like crazed mink." Archer caught up her hand and folded it into the crook of his muscular arm. "Come on. I don't know how long this burst of self-control will last."

"But I like coupling like crazed mink," Dana said, trying to make it sound like a joke as he towed her out of the bedroom and down the sweeping staircase.

"Couple later. Talk now."

"I thought it was the woman who always wants conversation instead of sex. Men are supposed to be the insatiable ones."

Archer raised a brow, a humorously dangerous gleam flaring in his eyes. "Are you suggesting I have a weak sex drive?"

"Who me?" Dana squeaked. "Never. I would never do that."

"Good," he purred. "Because my fragile male ego would be compelled to prove you wrong."

"That's not necessary," she assured him. "I like being able to walk."

He laughed. "Beauty and brains. What more could a vampire ask?"

Five minutes later Dana was watching from the breakfast nook as Archer poured crepe batter into an electric skillet with the same graceful skill he'd used in combat.

"How can you cook when you don't eat?" She plucked a ripe strawberry from the bowl of sliced fruit at her elbow.

"I can taste." Archer popped a forefinger into his mouth to suck off the batter. "Besides, I've always thought if a woman feeds me, it's only polite to feed her. Would you like some eggs? Bacon?"

"No, crepes and fruit are fine."

For a moment they were silent as he flipped the crepes, then transferred the finished product to a plate. "I actually enjoy cooking. It's relaxing. Nobody dies, nobody gets screwed. If you mess up, you throw it in the trash." He carried the plate to her, then sat down to watch her eat.

Dana cut off a forkful and popped it in her mouth. Her eyes widened at the burst of delicate flavor as the crepe simply dissolved on her tongue. "God, that's good!" She took another bite and closed her eyes to savor the sensation. "You're an incredible cook."

"Thanks. It's a useful skill," Archer said, smiling slightly as he watched her devour her breakfast. "Chef is one of my favorite covers. You can find out all sorts of interesting things about a household in its kitchen."

"How did you become a spy, anyway?" Dana took a sip of her orange juice. Fresh squeezed, judging from the juicer and pile of orange halves on the cabinet.

"Ah, well. That's a long story."

"I'm not going anywhere." She lifted a brow at him. "Give."

"I'd rather talk about you."

"I'm not nearly as interesting as you are."

"But I know my story, and I don't know yours." Archer's lips curved into the charming smile that had probably been the downfall of many a female spy. "Tell you what, we'll trade. All my evil secrets for yours. How about it?"

It was a tempting proposition. "Okay. But I want to hear about all the spy stuff."

"I'll even show you my secret collection of espionage toys."

She grinned. "I'll just bet you will."

So as they cleaned up the kitchen, Dana told him about herself and her work. She related the challenges of putting out a weekly newspaper: the stories she'd done, the people she'd interviewed, the Byzantine machinations of small town politics—who was sleeping with whom, who was cheating whom, and why.

"You're good at this, aren't you?" Archer asked thoughtfully, as he led the way to the library when they were done with the cleanup. "Sounds like you found out where all the bodies were buried pretty fast."

Dana shrugged. "It's just a matter of listening, getting people to open up to you. You can pick up a lot chatting at the neighborhood diner. Then you hit town hall and start researching the records, and you find out whether there's any truth to the gossip."

"Why bother? Why go to all that effort?" He flung himself into a massive leather wing chair as she settled onto the matching couch. "You work for a weekly. You could be doing stories about the county fair and school kids winning essay contests."

"I have done those stories." She shrugged. "But I have a responsibility to the community. If somebody's using public money to advance his own agenda, people should know it."

He eyed her thoughtfully. "I imagine that goes over real well with the powers that be."

Dana smiled in reluctant amusement at his cynical tone. "Oh, I'm considered a huge pain in the butt. And the public isn't always pleased when I drag things out in the open. At one time or another, the whole town's been furious at me." She tucked her legs beneath her and settled back in a corner of the couch. "But once they calm down, they always wind up doing something about whatever set me off, so I figure I did my job."

"What do your parents think about what you do?"

Dana looked away. "They died just after I got out of college. Car accident."

His eyes darkened in sympathy. "I'm sorry."

"They were strict, but they loved me," she said, staring out the window over the rolling lawn. "They were evangelists. Had a syndicated radio show that was aired around the country in a hundred and twenty markets."

Archer lifted a brow. "Somehow you don't strike me as the daughter of a minister."

Dana laughed. "Oh, I'm the stereotypical P.K." Catching his questioning look, she explained, "Preacher's kid. Rebelling against my upbringing, fighting authority, the whole bit."

"I thought you liked authority." He smiled slowly. "At least the handcuffs."

She glowered at him. "Cheap shot."

"Sorry." He sobered. "Seriously, what was it like for you growing up?"

Dana found herself telling him everything: the frustration, the guilt of never being good enough to meet her parents' high standards, the sense of suffocation under their strictures. And the love she'd felt for the mother and father who always acted out of love and a desire to do what was right.

It was only later that Dana realized how skillfully Archer interrogated her. Before long he had her telling him things she'd never told anyone, seduced by his interest and humor.

She even told him about Mark's collection of erotica.

"I don't know what it is about all that stuff that gets to me," Dana told him, studying her bare toes as a blush heated her face. "I don't believe in women being submissive. God knows I'm don't submit to anybody or anything in my daily life. I'm a dedicated feminist."

"Oh, I know exactly why you like bondage." Archer gave her such a teasing, masculine grin that she lost her discomfort and grinned back.

"Oh? And why is that?"

"You don't have to do any of the work. You can just lie back while the guy licks and nibbles and thrusts in a desperate attempt to please you."

Glad to have the conversation back on a comfortable footing, Dana sat back in her chair and eyed him. "Are you saying I'm lazy?"

He smirked. "If the handcuffs fit."

"For your information, there's a lot a woman can do with both hands tied behind her back."

Archer reached into his back pocket and pulled out his handcuffs, let them dangle by a thumb. "Prove it."

"You're on." Dana stood up and shrugged off the black robe. It landed in a silken pool around her ankles, leaving her wearing nothing but a smile. "Take off those pants, Double-O-Fang, and we'll see who's lazy."

Grinning, he skimmed his jeans and briefs down his hips in one, smooth motion, then stepped out of them. It was the first time she'd seen him totally naked, and for a moment Dana just stopped and stared. His legs were long, roped with muscle, and his cock was a thick, aggressive thrust over the tight, furry pouch of his testicles. He lifted a brow at her. "Well?"

Dana marched over to him and held up both wrists.

"Nope." He gestured for her to turn. "Both hands behind your back, remember?"

She spun around and crossed her wrists at her spine. A moment later she felt the cool caress of metal, heard a double click. Dana turned back around to find him grinning down at her.

"So what are you going to do now, Gloria Steinem?"

Chapter Five

"The possibilities are endless," Dana shot back, grinning. But as she let her eyes play over his face, across his bare, powerful shoulders and down his brawny torso, she felt her amusement fade, replaced by something more urgent. She wanted to touch him, to see how all that male strength felt under her fingers. But her hands were bound behind her.

Inhaling sharply, she caught his scent—dark, spicy. She leaned forward, wanting to draw that tempting Archer smell more deeply into her lungs. The froth of hair covering his chest tickled her nose.

Impulsively, Dana leaned even closer, put out her tongue, licked at a ridge of muscle. He rumbled in approval. She eyed his chest, the swell of a pectoral muscle, the tiny dark bead of his nipple. Testing, she bent her head and flicked her tongue over it. He stiffened, catching his breath.

Encouraged, Dana edged closer until the tips of her breasts brushed his chest, the sensation sending a flare of pleasure through her. She sighed and licked him again, a long pass of her tongue over the hard bulge of his pecs. Intrigued by the sensation, she caught his nipple between her teeth, gave it a slow, gentle bite. His breathing roughened, his chest rising and falling more quickly against her face.

Suddenly there was the breath-stealing sensation of fingers stroking her nipple in a light, velvet flutter. Archer's other hand brushed down her spine to linger on the upper curve of her ass.

Dana shivered at the sensation and lifted her head. Archer looked down at her, his eyes intensely blue, the lids heavy. She stood on her toes and stretched her neck up until she could taste his firm mouth.

A quick brush of the lips, once, then again, then a slow foray with her tongue into the warm cavern of his mouth. He opened for her, letting her explore his lips and trace the edges of his teeth. She touched the point of a fang and drew back, startled. Archer looked down at her, eyes shuttered, subtly challenging.

Quick as an impulse, she leaned forward again and slipped her head up under his jaw to the strong cords of his throat. Taking the smooth skin there between her teeth, she gently bit down. He tasted salty, tempting, male. He moaned.

"I see why you like to bite," she whispered against his skin, and began to nibble.

"It does have its... pleasures," Archer agreed, his voice rasping.

Slowly, Dana worked her way lower, using her tongue and teeth, lapping and raking in turn, exploring his chest, the ridges of his abdominals, the ripples of his ribs. As she moved, the tips of her breasts brushed against him, the pressure sending curls of rosy pleasure through her.

Until she was on her knees, the rigid length of his cock thrusting out beside her face, the hair of his thighs caressing her nipples. She felt languorous, hungry, as bewitched by her own gentle teasing as he was.

And he was bewitched. When Dana tilted a look up at him, she found his azure eyes locked on her, watching her every move with a kind of tortured anticipation. She could almost see him wondering when she was going to take his cock into her mouth, see him aching for the firestorm of sensation her tongue and teeth and lips would bring.

Watching him wait, Dana felt a burst of feminine power. She was doing this to him, just as he'd made her writhe and ache last night.

She turned her eyes to his cock again, studying it, admiring the thick stalk, the big, heart-shaped head that blushed dark with the force of his passion. It quivered and lengthened, taking on a pronounced upward jut.

Dana put out her tongue and licked away a drop of pre-come. He jolted against her mouth. "God, Dana..."

She licked the head again, watching it bob under the stroke, then leaned closer and caught it in her mouth. And began to suck. Gently at first, then harder. She felt him dip, as if his knees had gone weak for an instant. Smiling around his width, Dana pressed her head forward until the thick shaft moved deeper between her lips. Then pulled back, tightening her lips at the same time to create a demanding suction. She closed her eyes as smooth length slid from her mouth, remembering how it had felt when he'd stroked it into her sex.

A strong hand came to rest on top of her head, fingers lacing through her curls. She felt him shudder and reversed her stroke, taking him deeper and deeper, until the big head brushed the back of her throat.

Archer gasped as her mouth drew at him with such power it made his head swim. It felt so good, so hot.

And the sight of her, slim and naked, kneeling between his feet with her wrists bound behind her back and her lips wrapped around his cock. God, he could come just looking at her.

She slid forward again, pleasuring him until he wanted to explode down her throat. Yet it wasn't enough. He needed her sex clamped where her mouth was, hot and tight and wet. He wanted her body pressed to his, flexing against his strength. Surrendering.

And he wanted her blood. He wanted it flooding his mouth in a wave of liquid copper.

Now.

Half-maddened, Archer pulled out of the unbearably seductive suction of her mouth, almost groaning at the loss of her wet heat even as he bent and scooped Dana off the floor.

He turned to the couch and dropped her lush body belly-down over its padded leather arm. The position thrust out her rounded, heart-shaped ass, inviting his possession.

Dana moaned.

Archer grabbed his cock in one hand, aimed for the glistening red folds of her sex. And thrust.

God, she was wet. Sucking him must have aroused her as much as it had him. And she was just as tight, clutching him like a slick fist, her grip so strong he had to bear down to force his way deeper.

The sensation seared its way up his spine to his skull with brutal intensity.

Shivering, Archer settled against her until the full curve of her bottom nestled into his groin. And slowly, he began to thrust.

God, he felt so big in this position. Thick, forcing her to spread. And strong. She couldn't have kept him out even if she'd wanted to.

And she didn't.

Dana hung there over the couch arm, head down, feeling his powerful hands clamping her hips as he tunneled in and out. It felt as if each thrust impaled her to the heart, sending sparks of pleasure spiraling along her nerves. She whimpered in raw delight.

Archer leaned over her, slipping his arms under her torso to gather her close. His fingers found her nipples, plucked and strummed as he fucked her. His thrusts grew even faster, harder, winding the pleasure like a spring. He felt huge inside her, too much, far too much, yet she could only hang there in his hands, bound and helpless. The thought made her close her eyes in wicked delight.

Suddenly Archer crowded hard against her, his thighs trapping hers against the side of the couch as he reamed her in short, hard strokes. One hand gripped her breast as the other dragged her head back by the hair. She stiffened, realizing what he intended.

Just as he sank his fangs into her throat.

Dana convulsed helplessly, the combination of pleasure and pain kicking her over into a long, rolling orgasm that continued to shake her while he drank, still pistoning into her, ruthless, hungry and possessive.

Until he lifted his head from her and roared out his own climax.

꙳꙳(ꙮ)꙳꙳

It took Archer thirty minutes to recover enough to carry her back to bed. Dana protested sleepily that she was perfectly capable of walking under her own steam, but he suspected she was lying. He shouldn't have drunk from her so soon after the last time; he never did that. He had a firm rule against taking from the same partner twice in a six-week period.

But then, he'd never made anyone a vampire before.

Holding her as she sank into a doze, Archer realized that was exactly what he was going to do.

She was everything he'd spent two centuries searching for. A vampire had fantastic power, and he'd always feared giving the Dark Kiss to someone undeserving. But Dana would never misuse those superhuman abilities; she had too keen a sense of idealism and morality. She would be the perfect agent.

More than that, she'd be the perfect wife.

Archer loved her humor and intelligence—not to mention all that shy sensuality. He could easily imagine spending the next three hundred years being fascinated by her, working with her, making love to her.

He almost woke her up right then to blurt out his proposal. But there was no rush.

They had forever.

So he let her sleep, savoring her warm, smooth curves as she nestled into him. Until finally she stirred against him and woke.

Then, heart in his throat, he began telling her everything.

"I met the Countess when I went to her estate in France to negotiate the purchase of a wine shipment," Archer said, his chest vibrating under her chin.

Dana had been staring dreamily into his handsome face. Now she sat up, attention instantly caught. The Countess had been the one who'd made him a vampire. "Shipment?"

"We were merchants," he explained. "My family owned a number of ships, and I'd heard she bottled the best wine in France. We traded letters for a year before she finally invited me to her chateau to finish the negotiations." Archer smiled faintly. "God, that house. I'd never seen anything like it. The furnishings, the art. We were wealthy, but not like her." The amusement drained away. "She realized I could survive the change the moment she met me."

"And seduced you." Dana felt a sting of jealousy, then was instantly ashamed when she remembered he'd said the Countess had been killed by a French mob.

Archer nodded, the look in his eyes distant with memory. "She was lovely—all dark beauty and wicked fascination. It didn't take me long to fall in love. I was willing to do anything for her. Even become a vampire."

She propped her chin on her fist and studied him. "Was she in love with you?"

Archer shrugged. "She said she was. And I know she was lonely. It gets very lonely, after a hundred years or so. You become willing to do damn near anything for company." He hesitated. "But we were very happy in the three years we had together.

"Then my brother wrote to tell me my parents had been murdered."

As Dana listened in horror, he described how his father, James, had thrown his support behind the American fight for independence. During a trip to Boston to meet with leaders of the rebellion, a rival British merchant and a gang of Tories attacked James and Archer's mother at the docks. The men dragged them into a warehouse, where they used clubs to beat James Archer until he was broken and dying. Then they turned their attention to his wife.

The couple was dead by the time they were found two days later.

"Their deaths haunted me," Archer said, his voice distant and terrible. "The thought of my parents dying in that filthy warehouse, each knowing the other was suffering, neither able to help. All because some greedy bastard wanted to get rid of a rival, and some Tories wanted to make a point."

He'd booked passage back on the same ship that had brought his brother's letter. The Countess had cried and begged him to stay, but Archer had turned a deaf ear. She finally told him she'd get her affairs in order and join him.

Archer arrived in Boston like an avenging demon. He used his powers to hunt down the men who'd murdered his mother and father, then systematically killed them all.

"I had no mercy," he said. "They deserved none. My parents weren't the only innocents they'd killed trying to terrorize supporters of the rebellion." Archer paused, his eyes chilling. "And they weren't acting alone. Before he died, one of the Tories told me they'd been carrying out British orders. A particularly brutal Redcoat major out to build a name for himself." His voice flattened. "He told them to make my parents an example."

"What did you do?" Dana swallowed, caught between fascination and horror.

Archer looked away, refusing to meet her gaze. "I slipped into British headquarters when he was working late one night. And I made him an example."

But that wasn't the end of Archer's war. He left the major's bloody body and headed straight for the nearest Continental commander to offer his services. Archer couldn't join the army because he couldn't fight daylight battles, but he could become a spy. It was no job for a gentleman, but in his hate and grief, he didn't care.

Archer spent the rest of the war among the British, assuming various guises to observe their fortifications and troop strength, sometimes even gaining access to commanders and using his psychic influence to discover their plans.

"You could have influenced them into deliberately losing," Dana observed.

He frowned, stroking her slim fingers absently. "There were times I was tempted, but I always drew the line. It didn't seem honorable. Like beating a bound prisoner, there are some things you just don't do."

As Archer went on telling her about his experiences, Dana realized he'd become addicted to the idealism and the danger of his cause. Even after the war was over, he continued using his talents to gather information and undermine the country's enemies.

Yet even in his zeal, he hadn't forgotten his Countess. Archer continued to exchange letters with her, even traveling to France for frequent visits, but he never stayed long. Conditions in the fledgling United States were too uncertain, and he couldn't stand to be away. The Countess swore she'd join him, but busy with her estate and the worsening conditions in France as the country spiraled into revolution, she never did.

Until the day came when Archer got word she had been murdered.

"A mob is the greatest danger to a vampire," he said, his voice soft, bitter. "Once it gets going, you can't stop it. Influence doesn't work on that many people in the grip of bloodlust." He stared broodingly at nothing. "They hacked off her head with a scythe."

Guilt-stricken, Archer returned to France to try to find her killers. This time he had no luck, and he finally returned home to the cause that was now all he had left.

"As the years went on, America became everything to me," Archer said. "Friends and enemies age and die, but she remains. I've watched her grow from a sickly newborn to the queen of the world. I've watched her act from greed and gallantry. I've seen her whore to rich men, then turn and sacrifice her own children for the freedom of others. There is no other nation like her. She's worth every lie I've told, every life I've taken, every morning I've faced with dread."

As Dana listened in spellbound fascination, Archer described the wars he'd fought and the missions he'd carried out. He was brutally frank, describing not only the triumphs but the failures that still made guilt flare in his eyes decades later. His stories were an enthralling glimpse of the past, of the people and events that had molded the country.

And as he spoke, he unwittingly revealed himself—a powerful man moving invisibly among powerful men, using his abilities to play a prominent role in history that he allowed few people to even know about. A ruthless man, yet quietly, intensely honorable.

"Why are you telling me this?" she asked at last, uneasy. It didn't seem in character for a man who'd made secrecy a way of life for two centuries. "You can't make me forget it."

Archer rolled over on his side and braced himself on one elbow. He met her eyes, his expression so serious her unease increased.

"Dana, the Countess knew I could become a vampire because she tried to influence me into giving her a better price on the wine. And it didn't work."

Understanding hit Dana like a punch so brutal she lost her breath. When her heart began beating again, she whispered, "Like me."

"Like you."

Dana licked her lips. "All this... These things you've told me

..." She stopped and almost lost her courage, then forced herself to continue. The words came out in a rush. "Archer, are you saying you want to make me a vampire?"

His blue eyes were steady, staring into hers with a quiet intensity. "If you agree."

A crazy joy bloomed in Dana's chest. He wanted her to stay with him. Forever.

"We could do so much," Archer said, and reached out to cover one of her hands with his own. "Dana, you have no idea how I need you—how the country needs you."

She froze.

"Even with all my abilities, I'm only one man. But working together, we..."

A wave of shock washed over her skin, so cold that for a blessed moment she went completely numb. Humiliated understanding roared in behind it.

Archer had been planning this from the first. He had guessed her secret fantasies, and he'd used them to bring her to heel. He'd played the demon lover, tied her and taken her and made her hotter than she'd ever been in her life. But to him it had been just another mission. It had never touched him at all.

She had never touched him at all. While he had made himself everything to her.

"...Have to undergo training, of course. Weapons and tactics. Languages. You'll need to..."

"No."

Archer blinked. "What?"

Biting off the words, Dana said, "I'm not going to spend the next two hundred years whoring for this country." *I'm not going to spend the next two hundred years in love with you, watching you seduce an endless succession of willing women.*

It was only after she'd thought the word "love" that she realized she meant it.

Jesus, it had only been twenty-four hours. You didn't fall in love in a day. Not with a normal man.

But Archer was not a normal man. He was so damn good, so

damn seductive—not just his body, but his intelligence and idealism and that damn honor. He'd slipped into her heart like the spy he was, and he'd taken it.

"You're not just a spy," she said brutally, wanting to hurt him. "You're a whore."

"No." The word came out as a whisper, sounding somehow wounded. Another of his actor's tricks. "I've... done some things I'm not proud of, but I've also saved a lot of lives." For once his eloquence failed him. Dana could almost see him groping for a way to defend himself. "Just last year there was this terrorist with a nuclear..."

"I need to get dressed." She couldn't take any more of this, or she was going to humiliate herself and start sobbing.

Dana lurched off the bed, then realized she was nude. She couldn't stand to be naked in front of him—he'd stripped her enough as it was. She grabbed the hem of the sheet and tried to drag it off the bed, but it wouldn't come, caught under one of Archer's trim male hips. Dana gave it another ruthless jerk.

Immersing her in a glare that was beginning to sizzle with growing rage, Archer freed it.

"Thank you." Back rigid, Dana wrapped the length of cloth around her body, then turned and made for the bureau where she'd stashed her folded jeans. "Look, do you have a T-shirt? You ripped mine."

"I don't understand you." His voice rumbled with anger, threatening as the thunder before a storm. "I could make you immortal."

In one fluid movement, Archer rolled off the bed and strode naked toward her. She refused to look at that magnificent, deceptive body as he stopped inches away. "You would never grow old. You could take a shotgun blast to the chest and survive. Hell, you could bench press a Toyota, see in the dark..."

"Leap tall buildings in a single bound and turn into a bat. I know." Dana jerked on the jeans with trembling hands.

The corners of his mouth twitched in a bitter fragment of a smile. "The bat thing is a myth."

"Well, if I can't turn into a bat, why bother?" She zipped the jeans.

"Hell, I don't know. Maybe for the men who died at Bunker Hill and Gettysburg and Normandy." Fury emanated from him like his potent body heat. "That old cliché is dead-on, Dana—freedom ain't free. Sometimes people have to step up and pay the bill."

"Oh, that's right—'The tree of Liberty is watered by the blood of Patriots.' Or however the hell that goes." She dragged open a drawer and searched for a shirt. "Well, that tree has all of my blood it's getting." Dana lifted her head to glare back at him. "You drank it already."

For a moment, such rage blazed in his eyes that she instinctively hunched her shoulders.

Seeing her flinch, Archer snarled and spun away. He strode to the door and flung it open, then slammed it shut again behind him.

Dana still couldn't find that damn shirt.

Staggering back to the bed, she collapsed as the tears began.

❧⟨☙☙⟩❧

Damn her! He took the stairs in a rush, pounding down them, still naked and not giving a damn. She was everything he'd always wanted, always needed, and she'd blown him off, left him to the mission that never ended and the women he could never have for more than a single night.

Archer stormed into the kitchen for lack of any other destination. The phone rang just as he passed the counter, and he snatched it up.

"How's the girl working out?" Fleming's rough voice asked.

"Oh, she's just fucking perfect," Archer snarled. "She'd be a great agent. Unfortunately, she just told me she has no interest whatsoever in having anything at all to do with us."

"And that stopped you?" The acid sarcasm in his tone made Archer's lips pull back from his teeth.

"If I did turn her, how the hell would we get her to cooperate? You can't force a vampire to do a damn thing. Believe me, it's been tried on me, and it never worked."

"I know of at least one cell even you couldn't get out of."

"I will not let you lock her up and starve her, Fleming."

"Fine. So convince her. Even after she's a vampire, you'll still be proportionally bigger, stronger and more experienced. Right?"

He frowned. "Yeah. So?"

"So we need this girl, Archer. Quit fucking around and bite her."

Fleming's right.

The words whispered through his skull, chill and tempting. He fought them, knowing it wasn't right to force her.

Until a demonic voice asked, *But what about the lives that could be saved?*

And he couldn't think of an answer.

A wave of burning cold washed over Archer—the same deadly psychic frost he felt when he knew he had to kill.

When he spoke, his voice sounded flat and emotionless in his own ears. "I'll call you when it's done."

⁂

Dana wiped her eyes. He'd be back any moment, and by then she had to have a shirt on and some fragment of self-control.

God, she felt wrecked.

Get hold of yourself, Dana. Concentrate on the practicalities. How was she going to even get home? He'd driven. She'd have to call a car rental company and arrange to have them send over a…

The door opened. Dana whipped around, her arms automatically covering her bare breasts.

Archer filled the doorway like a Roman god brought to life, all beautiful naked strength. But the expression on his handsome face was cold, closed. Flat. She felt a shiver of unease.

Summoning her courage, Dana stood up. "I won't reconsider, Archer, so don't waste your breath."

He didn't even acknowledge her attempt at a preemptive strike, just started toward her in a long, silent stride. Something about the way he moved made her feel stalked, and she took an instinctive step back.

Archer's pale eyes watched her retreat like a cat focused on a canary. "I just got a call from my boss with my next mission." His tone was soft with velvet menace. "You."

One instant he was halfway across the room. The next, she was on her back on the bed, his powerful, naked body pinning her down, a superhuman hand gripping both her wrists. His wolf-pale eyes were merciless. "Dana," he told her, his voice emotionless, "you've been drafted."

Archer fisted his free hand in her hair and pulled her head back to arch her throat. He opened his mouth, revealing the sharp white length of his fangs as he bent to bite.

And she screamed.

Archer hesitated an inch from her flesh and looked up as she bucked under him, terror and rage contorting her face, her hands jerking help-lessly in his. Pity stirred beneath his mental chill. "I'm sorry," he said softly. "This won't be pleasant. I can't even make it quick."

He would have to drink from her several times over the coming days, partially draining her before forcing her to drink his blood. What followed would be worse. Archer could still remember the raw agony he'd suffered two centuries ago as his body was reshaped by the vampire virus. And he, at least, had been willing.

"You have no right to force this on me!" Dana spat, struggling to drag her hands out of his grip.

"No." He contained her desperate jerks carefully. "But I do have a duty. There've been so many times when I have accomplished things no ordinary man could have. Foiled plots, saved lives. If I die, I want to know there's someone to carry on the work. And there's no one else but you."

Realizing she was helpless, Dana subsided to glare up at him bitterly. "I thought you were supposed to be invulnerable."

Archer shrugged. "Not to being crushed, burned, staked or de-capitated. Given my lifestyle, the odds that I'll encounter something I can't walk away from are pretty good."

"I don't give a damn. I will not work for you!" She gritted out the words, her gaze as defiant as a martyr's.

"Yes, you will." Archer smiled sadly. "You're an idealist. No matter how pissed you are at me, when a crisis comes along, you'll have to help."

Recognition and despair flickered in Dana's eyes until she squeezed them closed. She took an angry, hitching breath, half sob, half curse. "Do it then, damn you," she spat, "And get it over with."

Archer started to lower his head—just as something glittered on the side of her face. A lone tear, sliding slowly down the fragile curve of her cheek as she sank her small white teeth into her lower lip.

Something twisted in his chest.

He had done worse things than this, dammit. Betrayed men who believed him a friend, killed gallant enemies and innocents who knew too much. He'd done whatever his country had demanded. Besides, he was giving her a precious gift—immortality. Freedom from the twin mortal curses of old age and disease.

In the end, she would forgive him. He'd see to it, spinning a spell of sex and pleasure around her until she forgot her anger. He already knew he was her weakness.

Another tear beaded on her lashes.

"God *damn* it!"

Suddenly Archer was sitting on the side of the bed, and she was free. Dana blinked at him in bewilderment. His broad shoulders were hunched and knotted as he scrubbed a big hand over his face.

"Goddamn it," he growled again. "I can't do it. I should, and I can't."

Cautiously, Dana sat up, confused. "What's happening? What are you talking about?"

He rose from the bed and strode away from her to brace both arms on the bureau. "I mean you're safe. Now get out before I change my mind."

She stared at the strong muscled V of his back, blinking at a sudden wave of disappointment. *Oh, God*, Dana thought, stunned. *I actually wanted him to do it. Force me to stay with him, even if it meant watching him make love to other women. Never loving me.* "What about all that stuff about duty and country and..."

He whirled on her, fangs bared as he growled, "I said get out!"

She should. She should run like hell, and she knew it. But some perverse demon drove Dana to find out why he'd stopped. "Is this another game? The stories you told me... You never walk away from a job, even when it turns your stomach."

"Which is why you should get the fuck out while you can."

"Not until you tell me why."

He stared at her, bewildered and furious. "You little idiot. Don't you understand what kind of danger you're in? I want to throw you down on that bed, feed from that white throat of yours and *keep* you. And to hell with what you want. So if you don't want to stay with me for the next three hundred years, you'd better get your tight little ass right out that door. Now!"

Hope began to expand through Dana's chest like a slow motion explosion. "Why?"

"Why what?" he roared.

"Why do you want to keep me?" She rolled to her feet and moved toward him, feeling the cool air against her beaded nipples. Deliberately, Dana arched her back and watched his gaze slide hungrily to her breasts. "For duty? For truth, justice and the American way? For sex? What?"

"If that was all it was, I'd already have my fangs in your throat. Get out."

"No." She put a deliberate roll in her hips. "Not until you give me the truth."

He peeled his lips back from his fangs and growled, "Keep it up, Dana, and I'll definitely give you something. But since you've already said you don't *want* it, I strongly advise..."

"Why do you care what I want?" Daringly, she stroked a forefinger over one of her own hard nipples and watched his eyes blaze. "Why aren't we on that bed right now, Archer? I couldn't stop you." His cock was lengthening between his muscled thighs, thickening, tilting slowly upward. "You could tie me down and feast on me, indulge every hunger your keen sense of morality has never allowed you to feed. And you're so good, it wouldn't take you long to make me want it."

He lifted burning eyes to hers and asked in a seductive purr, "Do you want me to rape you, Dana?"

"No." She licked her lips.

Archer watched the movement of her tongue hungrily. "I'm not convinced." He took a long, gliding stride toward her, his cock swaying, fully erect.

Dana stepped back quickly. "I want to know why you didn't take me."

The sensuous mask dropped, and he drew himself up. "Luscious games notwithstanding, I'm not actually a rapist."

"You're whatever your country needs you to be, Archer." She dared to step close enough to look up into his eyes. "Including a rapist. Yet you let me go. For once in your immortal life, you ignored your duty. And I want to know why."

His expression closed, chilled. But his cock was still hard. "Because I've fallen in love with you. And I couldn't stand to doom you to a life you don't want."

Her heart leaped. "We've only known each other twenty-four hours."

"It doesn't seem to matter."

Dana met his gaze with a long, steady stare. "No. It doesn't."

Archer's eyes widened and blazed with incredulous joy, only to cool into caution an instant later. "What we're feeling could be just a product of truly amazing sex."

She grinned. "Got a pretty high opinion of your skills, don't you?"

"I've had a lot of practice."

"I love you."

He moved with that astonishing vampire speed again, and she was in his arms, every inch of his muscled body pressed to hers. She cried out in utter joy, both arms going around his broad back as his mouth met hers greedily.

Dana matched Archer kiss for searing kiss, tongue dancing with his as their demanding hands explored one another, dizzy with love and lust. Until finally she pulled back enough to pant, "Make me a vampire."

Archer stilled. "But you said..."

"I thought you didn't really want me, I thought you were just doing a job," she said in a breathless rush. "And why the hell didn't you know that? You're the bloody telepath."

He gave her a look. "But I can't read *you*. Where you're concerned, I'm just like every other poor bastard, wondering what the hell's going on in his woman's head."

Dana grinned. "If it's any consolation, it sounds like you'll have plenty of time to figure it out."

He smiled slowly, sensually. "Why don't we get started?"

Her grin widened. "Oh, yeah. Let's."

Archer bent down, swept her into his arms, and started toward the bed. "Now where," he purred, "did I put the rope?"

Dana froze in the act of caressing his shoulders. "Rope?"

"What was it you said a minute ago? Oh, yeah. 'You could tie me down and feast on me.' I liked that idea, Dana. I really did."

"I was speaking rhetorically!"

"But I'd love to try it."

She tossed her head, enjoying the game immensely. "Not a chance."

He sighed in mock sympathy. "That's the trouble with being a feast. You don't get much choice."

Archer tossed her on the bed. Dana immediately rolled off it.

And the chase was on.

Just to be polite, he allowed her to elude him for two quick circuits of the bed, slowing down his lunges just enough to let her dart free. Round breasts bouncing as she danced on the balls of her feet on the opposite side of the lake-sized mattress, Dana giggled. "Slowing down in your old age, Archer?"

He grinned and vaulted the width of the bed, enjoying the way her gray eyes widened when he hit the floor beside her and caught her into his arms. "What do you think?"

"Archer!" she squealed, as he swooped in for a hungry kiss of her laughing mouth. He kept her distracted with his tongue while he waltzed her backward to the bedside table, pulled open a drawer with one hand and reached inside. When his fingers found the silken coil of rope, Archer grinned against her lips.

Dana shrieked out a laugh as she felt herself flying through the air to land on the soft surface of the mattress. Before she could even think about rolling off again, Archer was on top of her, jerking her left hand over her head. He tied it to one of the bedposts with a few twists of rope while she playfully pounded at his chest with her free hand.

He ignored her until she sank her teeth into the muscled ribs that were so temptingly close to her face. "Cut that out, you little devil," Archer ordered, stretching out to snap the remaining length of the thick rope so he could tie her other wrist with it.

"Brute!" Dana accused, trying to sound outraged. "Rapist! Pervert!"

"You bet your sweet ass."

As he went about binding her to the bedposts, Dana squirmed, trying to look as tempting as possible as she slowly twisted her half-naked body. The ploy worked; she saw his blue eyes heat as he eyed her struggles. But his hands never hesitated in the task of tying her down. At last she was completely immobilized, arms and legs stretched wide.

Archer straightened to stand over her, scanning her bound body with an expression of lecherous triumph, his cock at full, magnificent erection.

"I hate to mention this, but there's a fatal flaw with your plans," Dana observed, swallowing as she stared at his cock. It looked as thick as her wrist.

"I don't think so." Archer grinned, showing the long points of his fangs. "You're tied up and helpless, ready to serve my every evil appetite."

"Not in these jeans."

"Oh, that." He scanned the tough blue fabric, then focused his attention right between her legs. "That's not going to be a problem."

And it wasn't. Archer reached down, grabbed her waistband in both hands and yanked. The thick fabric tore with a loud rip, splitting right down to her left thigh.

Stunned by the display of raw vampire strength, Dana blinked, then mustered a grumble. "Great. Now I don't have anything to wear at all."

"You don't need anything to wear," he told her, and licked his fangs as he reached for the fabric again. "At all."

Archer shredded the jeans off her body like a greedy boy tearing into a birthday present. In seconds, she was completely nude.

Wide-eyed, Dana watched him toss aside the shreds of her clothing and rock back on his bare heels to give her a long, hungry stare. The air felt cool on her pebbled nipples and spread, wet sex. She tugged at her bound wrists with a blend of excitement and unease.

Archer watched the nervous movement like a starving wolf. "Feeling helpless?" His stare flicked back to her full breasts, then down between her thighs. "You look helpless. And you are. I can do anything I like to you." He looked up into her eyes. "Does that worry you?"

She licked her dry lips. "Should it?"

"Oh, yeah." Slowly he began to stroll around the bed. "I'm remembering all the wickedly creative things I've done to pretty victims over the past two centuries." His eyes glinted. "Sometimes they were a little reluctant to try this or that at first, but I soon had them begging for more." His voice deepened, drawled. "I'd like to make you beg, Dana."

She remembered his tongue, spinning spells of pleasure and frustration around her clit. "You *have* made me beg."

"True." Archer's grin was white and wicked. "But somehow I never get tired of hearing 'Please, Archer!' and 'I'll do anything, Archer!' Gives me a feeling of power." He stopped by the bedside table and pulled open a drawer.

"A feeling of power," Dana repeated, watching him dig around. "Yeah, I can see how that's something alien to you. What are you looking for?"

He pulled out a length of bright red silk. "Ever been blindfolded?"

"Hey, now, wait..." She tried to jerk her head aside as he sat down next to her and covered her eyes with the scarf. "But I like looking at you!" she wailed as he tied it off.

"But I want to keep you in suspense," Archer said, laughter in his voice. "And since I'm not the one who's tied up, guess who gets his wish?"

"Rat," she grumbled, staring into the blackness over her eyes.

Despite the moment's frustration, she felt her anticipation began to rise as she waited for his hands, his mouth, his first, heady touch.

Nothing.

"What are you doing?"

The bedroom door closed with a soft click.

"Archer! Did you just leave? What the hell are you up to?"

Damn. Frowning, Dana blinked against the blindfold. He'd damn well better not be planning to just leave her here like this. She'd kick his vampire butt clear to Washington.

Great, she thought. *Here I am, naked, bound and blindfolded. And my demon lover leaves.*

Hadn't he?

What if he was still in the room? He moved so quietly, he could be standing right beside her and she wouldn't know it. He could be standing over her right now, looking at her hard nipples, thinking about where to touch her first.

Then again, he might be downstairs watching *60 Minutes*. She was definitely going to kick his ass.

Dana stewed behind her blindfold for what seemed an hour but was probably only fifteen minutes before she heard the door open and close again.

"Sorry to leave you hanging, but I had to get a few supplies," Archer said with disgusting cheer.

"When I get lose, I'm going to hurt you," she told him. "How'd you like to have a clove of garlic shoved up your…"

"Oooh, you are pissed." Something rattled. "I hate to disappoint you, but the garlic thing's a myth." A wicked purr entered his voice. "But if you'd like to experiment, I could get some and see how *you* like it."

"That's not what I had in mind at all."

"May I remind you, you're the one who's tied up. It doesn't much matter what you've got in mind."

Dana felt her irritation drain at the note of velvet threat in his tone.

The bed shifted under her, the mattress dipping as though he'd sat down beside her.

Now, she thought. Now he'd touch her.

Something brushed her skin, then retreated. His fingertips?

There it was again, dancing over the tip of her right nipple, faint and delicious. Not a finger. Something thin. Several somethings. Filaments gliding over the sensitive skin of her breasts, swirling circles, tracing the full lower curves. Dana couldn't help squirming as she stared into the darkness of the blindfold and wondered what he was using to inflict those delicately erotic sensations.

"I love to watch a woman writhe," Archer said, his voice silken and deep. "Especially when she's bound."

Now the thing was dancing between her legs, tickling the sensitive skin of her thighs, drawing ghostly patterns of delight. "What is that?" she gasped. "What are you..."

Warm, strong fingers touched her most sensitive flesh, parting the delicate lips of her sex and spreading them, then holding them that way for the filaments' tender dance. Dana gasped at the fairy-like sensations playing over her wet lips, only to zero in on her erect clit, circling and brushing it. Unable to stop herself, she began to roll her hips, not even knowing whether she was trying to elude the sensation or get more.

"No, darlin'," Archer murmured. She felt his warm weight settle across her hips, pinning her down. He must be draped over her on his side, Dana thought, a little dazed.

The filaments continued their play, but now she felt a hot puff of air as well, gusting over her clit. He was blowing on her sex, she realized. The idea of his head so close to her hungry core made her grow even wetter.

His tongue slipped down, flicked over her button. Dana moaned, waiting for more of his delicious mouth.

Instead he rolled off her.

"No!" she whimpered. "Archer, don't stop!"

"Patience, darlin'." There was a rumble of laughter in his voice.

"One of these days I'm going to tie you down and torture you," Dana growled. "We'll see how patient *you* are."

"Promises, promises." Something rattled. She thought she heard his bare feet padding on the floor. Then the mattress shifted, moved. Something rattled again.

He was crawling up between her legs, she thought in growing excitement. Something warm pressed against the inside of both thighs that she recognized as his shoulders.

Rattle.

For a long moment he didn't move as she waited breathlessly for him to begin feasting on her sex. Dana could feel the cream flooding her core in heady anticipation.

Then his mouth was there at last, sucking her clit, hot and wet and setting off a firestorm of burning pleasure. Dana cried out as he drew strongly on the tiny bud, the feelings so intense she could hardly bear them.

Maddened, she rolled her hips. One of his arms clamped across them to pin her down. Another rattle, just before he took his skillful mouth away from her sex. As she was about to groan a protest, she felt the brush of his fingers at her opening.

Cold!

Dana yelled and convulsed as she felt him slide the ice cube up her heated, creamy core, but he held her pinned. Then her clit was in his mouth again, and his free hand was rolling and pinching one nipple. She squirmed and writhed, cursing breathlessly as the ice melted inside her hot sex, the chill warring with the sensation of his wet, clever mouth on her bud, the skilled fingers tormenting her breast.

The orgasm hit her out of nowhere, rolling over her like a train as he suckled her ruthlessly. Dana screamed, unable to bear the raw, brutal pleasure.

Suddenly he was on top of her, his gloriously naked body pressing into hers, touching her everywhere. A hand snatched the blindfold away.

She blinked as Archer reared over her, his fangs bared, taking his big cock in one hand and aiming it for her core. Archer shoved it deep, sucking in a breath as he felt the chill.

"That's what you get for putting ice up my..." she gasped.

"I'll melt it," he growled, and began to drive, fucking her hard and ruthlessly, his thick organ shuttling in and out with such strength she could only twist and moan in her bonds.

The sterling silver ice bucket tilted against her hip, but before it could fall and dump ice on them both, he stopped long enough to grab it up and put it down on the floor. Dana spotted a long ostrich feather curling among the sheets and realized what he'd first used to pleasure her with.

Then he was shafting her again, and she didn't care about anything else except that massive satin cock and the ecstasy it drove into her with each merciless stroke.

Another orgasm swamped her, and she threw her head back in pleasure. She saw his eyes lock on the column of her throat. Deliberately, Dana held the arch, offering herself as he lowered his handsome head. The sting of his fangs pressing deep kicked her climax even higher. He drove to the hilt and stiffened, his cry muffled against her throat.

As the last aftershocks of her climax shuddered through her, she collapsed into the mattress. His big hands stroked her, gentling and soothing as he fed.

Finally Archer drew away.

Dana blinked up at him, a little dizzy, a lot satisfied. "That was... amazing," she sighed.

He stroked tender knuckles over her cheek. "You're pretty amazing yourself. Which must be why I love you."

She felt a goofy smile spread over her face. "I love you too. You want to untie me now?"

Archer's smile took on a wicked cant as his long fingers found her nipple. "I don't think so. I'm nowhere near done yet."

And he started again.

Epilogue

Dana stumbled into the hotel room, staggered to the bed, and fell across it. Archer sauntered in after her, looking, she thought resentfully, disgustingly fresh for a man who'd just spent the last month posing as a terrorist.

"You did good today, darlin'," he told her, pulling his gun out of his shoulder holster. "I was proud of you. Even Fitz thought you handled yourself well."

"It's about time. That man has made my life hell for a solid year." Dana gave him a narrow look. "Come to think of it, so did you."

Archer shrugged as he unloaded the nine millimeter Smith and Wesson. "We had to make sure you were well-trained. And you are. You took down those three mob guys like a pro."

"The look on Galleni's face when I bent that gun barrel..." She laughed, savoring the memory. "I wish I had a picture."

"We probably do. I'll ask." He unbuckled his shoulder holster and shrugged out of it.

Watching the flex of his powerful chest, Dana felt a familiar wash of heat. She rolled to her feet and began to stalk him.

He looked up as she slid nearer and smiled. "Why, Mrs. Archer—whatever do you have in mind?"

Dana grinned, exposing the fangs she'd finally gotten used to. "Just thought we could celebrate the successful closing of my first case." Reaching to the belt of her black combat fatigues, she whipped out a pair of silver bracelets and dangled them from a thumb. "In fact, let's break in my new handcuffs."

With a wicked laugh, Archer reached for them. "I do like the way your mind works, wife."

"Then try this." She grabbed his shoulder and spun him back around. "Up against the wall and spread 'em! I need to practice my strip search."

His rich laughter rolled as he obeyed.

About the author:

Angela Knight is a newspaper reporter who lives in South Carolina with her cop husband and her teenage son. She's written three novellas for **Secrets***, and loved doing every one of them, since, she says, "Nobody else lets me get away with this stuff."*

She welcomes email and letters from readers, and may be contacted through her publisher, Red Sage.

Dear Reader,

We appreciate you taking the time out of your full and busy schedule to answer this questionnaire.

1. Rate the stories in *Secrets Volume 6* (1-10 Scale: 1=Worst, 10=Best)

Rating	Flint's Fuse	Love's Prisoner	Education of Miss Felicity Wells	A Candidate for the Kiss
Story Overall				
Sexual Intensity				
Sensuality				
Characters				
Setting				
Writing Skill				

2. What did you like *best* about *Secrets*? What did you like *least* about *Secrets*?

3. Would you buy other volumes?

4. In future *Secrets*, tell us how you would like your *heroine* and your *hero* to be. One or two words each are okay.

5. What is your idea of the *perfect sensual romantic story*? Use more paper if you wish to add more than this space allows.

Thank you for taking the time to answer this questionnaire. We want to bring you the sensual stories you desire.

Sincerely,
Alexandria Kendall
Publisher

Mail to: Red Sage Publishing, Inc.
P.O. Box 4844
Seminole, FL 33775

If you enjoyed *Secrets Volume 6* but haven't read other volumes, you should see what you're missing!

Secrets Volume 1:

In *A Lady's Quest*, author Bonnie Hamre brings you a London historical where Lady Antonia Blair-Sutworth searches for a lover in a most shocking and pleasing way.

Alice Gaines' *The Spinner's Dream* weaves a seductive fantasy that will leave every woman wishing for her own private love slave, desperate and running for his life.

Ivy Landon takes you for a wild ride. *The Proposal* will taunt you, tease you, even shock you. A contemporary erotica for the adventurous woman's ultimate fantasy.

With *The Gift* by Jeanie LeGendre, you're immersed in the historic tale of exotic seduction and bondage. Read about a concubine's delicious surrender to her Sultan.

Secrets Volume 2:

Surrogate Lover, by Doreen DeSalvo, is a contemporary tale of lust and love in the 90's. A surrogate sex therapist thought he had all the answers until he met Sarah.

Bonnie Hamre's regency tale *Snowbound* delights as the Earl of Howden is teased and tortured by his own desires—finally a woman who equals his overpowering sensuality.

In *Roarke's Prisoner*, by Angela Knight, starship captain Elise remembers the eager animal submission she'd known before at her captor's hands and refuses to be his toy again.

Susan Paul's *Savage Garden* tells the story of Raine's capture by a mysterious revolutionary in Mexico. She quickly finds lush erotic nights in her captor's arms.

Secrets Volume 3:

In Jeanie Cesarini's *The Spy Who Loved Me*, FBI agents Paige Ellison and Christopher Sharp discover excitement and passion in some unusual undercover work.

Warning: This story is only for the most adventurous of readers. Ann Jacobs tells the story of *The Barbarian*. Giles has a sexual arsenal designed to break down proud Lady Brianna's defenses — erotic pleasures learned in a harem.

Wild, sexual hunger is unleashed in this futuristic vampire tale with a twist. In Angela Knight's *Blood and Kisses*, find out just who is seducing whom?

B.J. McCall takes you into the erotic world of strip joints in *Love Undercover*. On assignment, Lt. Amanda Forbes and Det. "Cowboy" Cooper find temptation hard to resist.

Secrets Volume 4:

An Act of Love is Jeanie Cesarini's sequel. Shelby's terrified of sex. Film star Jason Gage must coach her in the ways of love. He wants her to feel true passion in his arms.

The Love Slave, by Emma Holly, is a woman's ultimate fantasy. For one year, Princess Lily will be attended to by three delicious men. She delights in playing with the first two, but it's the reluctant Grae that stirs her desires.

Lady Crystal is in turmoil in *Enslaved*, by Desirée Lindsey. Lord Nicholas' dark passions and irresistible charm have brought her long-hidden desires to the surface.

Betsy Morgan and Susan Paul bring you Kaki York's story in *The Bodyguard*. Watching the wild, erotic romps of her client's sexual conquests on the security cameras is getting to her—and her partner, the ruggedly handsome James Kulick.

Secrets Volume 5:

B.J. McCall is back with *Alias Smith and Jones*. Meredith Collins is stranded overnight at the airport. A handsome stranger named Smith offers her sanctuary for the evening—how can she resist those mesmerizing green-flecked eyes?

Strictly Business, by Shannon Hollis, tells of Elizabeth Forrester's desire to climb the corporate ladder on her merits, not her looks. But the gorgeous Garrett Hill has come along and stirred her wildest fantasies.

Chevon Gael's *Insatiable* is the tale of a man's obsession. After corporate exec Ashlyn Fraser's glamour shot session, photographer Marcus Remington can't get her off his mind. Forget the beautiful models, he must have her —but where did she go?

Sandy Fraser's **Beneath Two Moons** is a futuristic wild ride. Conor is rough and tough like frontiermen of old, and he's on the prowl for a new conquest. Dr. Eva Kelsey got away once before, but this time he'll make sure she begs for more.

Secrets Volume 7:

In **Amelia's Innocence** by Julia Welles, Amelia didn't know her father bet her in a card game with Captain Quentin Hawke, so honor demands a compromise—three days of erotic foreplay, leaving her virginity and future intact.

Jade Lawless brings **The Woman of His Dreams** to life. Artist Gray Avonaco moved in next door to Joanna Morgan and now is plagued by provocative dreams. Is it unrequited lust or Gray's chance to be with the woman he loves?

Surrender by Kathryn Anne Dubois tells of Lady Johanna. She wants no part of the binding strictures of marriage to the powerful Duke. But she doesn't realize he wants sensual adventure, and sexual satisfaction.

Angela Knight's **Kissing the Hunter** finds Navy Seal Logan McLean hunting the vampires who murdered his wife. Virginia Hart is a sexy vampire searching for her lost soul-mate only to find him in a man determined to kill her.

Secrets Volume 8:

In Jeanie Cesarini's latest tale, we meet Kathryn Roman as she inherits a legal brothel. She refuses to trade her Manhattan high-powered career for a life in the wild west. But the town of Love, Nevada has recruited Trey Holliday, one very dominant cowboy, with **Taming Kate**.

In **Jared's Wolf** by MaryJanice Davidson, Jared Rocke will do anything to avenge his sister's death, but he wasn't expecting to fall for Moira Wolfbauer, the she-wolf sworn to protect her werewolf pack. The two enemies must stop a killer while learning that love defies all boundaries.

My Champion, My Love, by Alice Gaines, tells the tale of Celeste Broder, a woman committed for a sexy appetite that is tolerated in men, but not women. Mayor Robert Albright may be her salvation—*if* she can convince him her freedom will mean a chance to indulge their appetites together.

Liz Maverick takes you to a post-apocalyptic world in **Kiss or Kill**. Camille Kazinsky's military career rides on her decision—whether the robo called

Meat should live or die. Meat's future depends on proving he's human enough to live, *man* enough, to make her feel like a woman.

Secrets Volume 9:

Kimberly Dean brings you *Wanted*. FBI Special Agent Jeff Reno wants Danielle Carver. There's her body, brains—and that charge of treason on her head. Unable to clear her name, Dani goes on the run, but the sexy Fed is hot on her trail. What will he do once he catches her? And why is the idea so tempting?

In *Wild for You*. by Kathryn Anne Dubois, college intern Georgie gets lost and captured by a wildman of the Congo. She soon discovers this terrifying specimen of male virility has never seen a woman. The research possibilities are endless! Until he shows her he has research ideas of his own.

Bonnie Hamre is back with *Flights of Fantasy*. Chloe has taught others to see the realities of life but she's never shared the intimate world of her sensual yearnings. Given the chance, will she be woman enough to fulfill her most secret erotic fantasy? Join her as she ventures into her Flights of Fantasy.

Lisa Marie Rice's story, *Secluded*, is a wild one. Nicholas Lee had to claw his way to the top. His wealth and power come with a price—his enemies will kill anyone he loves. When Isabelle Summerby steals his heart, Nicholas secludes her in his underground palace to live a lifetime of desire in only a few days.

Men you've been dreaming about!

Secrets

Satisfy your desire for more.

*F*eel the wild adventure, fierce passion and the power of love in every *Secrets* Collection story. Red Sage Publishing's romance authors create richly crafted, sexy, sensual, novella-length stories. Each one is just the right length for reading after a long and hectic day.

Each volume in the *Secrets* Collection has four diverse, ultra-sexy, romantic novellas brimming with adventure, passion and love. More adventurous tales for the adventurous reader. The *Secrets* Collection are a glorious mix of romance genre; numerous historical settings, contemporary, paranormal, science fiction and suspense. We are always looking for new adventures.

Reader response to the *Secrets* volumes has been great! Here's just a small sample:

> *"I loved the variety of settings. Four completely wonderful time periods, give you four completely wonderful reads."*

> *"Each story was a page-turning tale I hated to put down."*

> *"I love Secrets! When is the next volume coming out? This one was Hot! Loved the heroes!"*

Secrets have won raves and awards. We could go on, but why don't you find out for yourself—order your set of *Secrets* today! See the back for details.

Secrets, Volume 1

Listen to what reviewers say:

"These stories take you beyond romance into the realm of erotica. I found **Secrets** absolutely delicious."

—Virginia Henley,
New York Times Best Selling Author

"**Secrets** is a collection of novellas for the daring, adventurous woman who's not afraid to give her fantasies free reign."

—Kathe Robin, *Romantic Times* Magazine

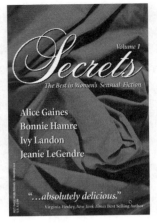

"...In fact, the men featured in all the stories are terrific, they all want to please and pleasure their women. If you like erotic romance you will love **Secrets**."

—*Romantic Readers* Review

In **Secrets, Volume 1** you'll find:

A Lady's Quest by Bonnie Hamre
Widowed Lady Antonia Blair-Sutworth searches for a lover to save her from the handsome Duke of Sutherland. The "auditions" may be shocking but utterly tantalizing.

The Spinner's Dream by Alice Gaines
A seductive fantasy that leaves every woman wishing for her own private love slave, desperate and running for his life.

The Proposal by Ivy Landon
This tale is a walk on the wild side of love. *The Proposal* will taunt you, tease you, and shock you. A contemporary erotica for the adventurous woman.

The Gift by Jeanie LeGendre
Immerse yourself in this historic tale of exotic seduction, bondage and a concubine's surrender to the Sultan's desire. Can Alessandra live the life and give the gift the Sultan demands of her?

Secrets, Volume 2

Listen to what reviewers say:

"*Secrets* offers four novellas of sensual delight; each beautifully written with intense feeling and dedication to character development. For those seeking stories with heightened intimacy, look no further."

—Kathee Card, *Romancing the Web*

"Such a welcome diversity in styles and genres. Rich characterization in sensual tales. An exciting read that's sure to titillate the senses."

—Cheryl Ann Porter

"*Secrets 2* left me breathless. Sensual satisfaction guaranteed...times four!"
—Virginia Henley, *New York Times* Best Selling Author

In *Secrets, Volume 2* you'll find:

Surrogate Lover by Doreen DeSalvo
Adrian Ross is a surrogate sex therapist who has all the answers and control. He thought he'd seen and done it all, but he'd never met Sarah.

Snowbound by Bonnie Hamre
A delicious, sensuous regency tale. The marriage-shy Earl of Howden is teased and tortured by his own desires and finds there is a woman who can equal his overpowering sensuality.

Roarke's Prisoner by Angela Knight
Elise, a starship captain, remembers the eager animal submission she'd known before at her captor's hands and refuses to become his toy again. However, she has no idea of the delights he's planned for her this time.

Savage Garden by Susan Paul
Raine's been captured by a mysterious and dangerous revolutionary leader in Mexico. At first her only concern is survival, but she quickly finds lush erotic nights in her captor's arms.

Winner of the Fallot Literary Award for Fiction!

Secrets, Volume 3

Listen to what reviewers say:

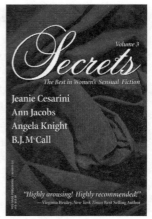

"*Secrets, Volume 3*, leaves the reader breathless. A delicious confection of sensuous treats awaits the reader on each turn of the page!"
— Kathee Card, *Romancing the Web*

"From the FBI to Police Dectective to Vampires to a Medieval Warlord home from the Crusade—*Secrets 3* is simply the best!"
— Susan Paul, award winning author

"An unabashed celebration of sex. Highly arousing! Highly recommended!"
— Virginia Henley, *New York Times* Best Selling Author

In *Secrets, Volume 3* you'll find:

The Spy Who Loved Me by Jeanie Cesarini

Undercover FBI agent Paige Ellison's sexual appetites rise to new levels when she works with leading man Christopher Sharp, the cunning agent who uses all his training to capture her body and heart.

The Barbarian by Ann Jacobs

Lady Brianna vows not to surrender to the barbaric Giles, Earl of Harrow. He must use sexual arts learned in the infidels' harem to conquer his bride. A word of caution—this is not for the faint of heart.

Blood and Kisses by Angela Knight

A vampire assassin is after Beryl St. Cloud. Her only hope lies with Decker, another vampire and ex-mercenary. Broke, she offers herself as payment for his services. Will his seductive powers take her very soul?

Love Undercover by B.J. McCall

Amanda Forbes is the bait in a strip joint sting operation. While she performs, fellow detective "Cowboy" Cooper gets to watch. Though he excites her, she must fight the temptation to surrender to the passion.

Winner of the 1997 Under the Covers Readers Favorite Award

Secrets, Volume 4

Listen to what reviewers say:

"Provocative...seductive...a must read!"
—*Romantic Times* Magazine

"These are the kind of stories that romance readers that 'want a little more' have been looking for all their lives...."
—*Affaire de Coeur* Magazine

"*Secrets, Volume 4*, has something to satisfy every erotic fantasy... simply sexational!"
—Virginia Henley, *New York Times* Best Selling Author

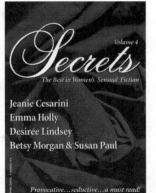

In *Secrets, Volume 4* you'll find:

An Act of Love by Jeanie Cesarini
Shelby Moran's past left her terrified of sex. International film star Jason Gage must gently coach the young starlet in the ways of love. He wants more than an act—he wants Shelby to feel true passion in his arms.

Enslaved by Desirée Lindsey
Lord Nicholas Summer's air of danger, dark passions, and irresistible charm have brought Lady Crystal's long-hidden desires to the surface. Will he be able to give her the one thing she desires before it's too late?

The Bodyguard by Betsy Morgan and Susan Paul
Kaki York is a bodyguard, but watching the wild, erotic romps of her client's sexual conquests on the security cameras is getting to her—and her partner, the ruggedly handsome James Kulick. Can she resist his insistent desire to have her?

The Love Slave by Emma Holly
A woman's ultimate fantasy. For one year, Princess Lily will be attended to by three delicious men of her choice. While she delights in playing with the first two, it's the reluctant Grae, with his powerful chest, black eyes and hair, that stirs her desires.

Secrets, Volume 5

Listen to what reviewers say:

"Hot, hot, hot! Not for the faint-hearted!"
　　　　　　　　　—*Romantic Times* Magazine

"As you make your way through the stories, you will find yourself becoming hotter and hotter. *Secrets* just keeps getting better and better."
　　　　　　　　　—*Affaire de Coeur* Magazine

"*Secrets 5* is a collage of lucious sensuality. Any woman who reads *Secrets* is in for an awakening!"
　　　—Virginia Henley, *New York Times* Best Selling Author

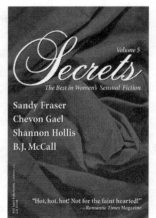

Volume 5

Secrets

The Best in Women's Sensual Fiction

Sandy Fraser
Chevon Gael
Shannon Hollis
B.J. McCall

"Hot, hot, hot! Not for the faint hearted!"
—*Romantic Times* Magazine

In *Secrets, Volume 5* you'll find:

Beneath Two Moons by Sandy Fraser

Ready for a very wild romp? Step into the future and find Conor, rough and masculine like frontiermen of old, on the prowl for a new conquest. In his sights, Dr. Eva Kelsey. She got away once before, but this time Conor makes sure she begs for more.

Insatiable by Chevon Gael

Marcus Remington photographs beautiful models for a living, but it's Ashlyn Fraser, a young corporate exec having some glamour shots done, who has stolen his heart. It's up to Marcus to help her discover her inner sexual self.

Strictly Business by Shannon Hollis

Elizabeth Forrester knows it's tough enough for a woman to make it to the top in the corporate world. Garrett Hill, the most beautiful man in Silicon Valley, has to come along to stir up her wildest fantasies. Dare she give in to both their desires?

Alias Smith and Jones by B.J. McCall

Meredith Collins finds herself stranded overnight at the airport. A handsome stranger by the name of Smith offers her sanctuaty for the evening and she finds those mesmerizing, green-flecked eyes hard to resist. Are they to be just two ships passing in the night?

Secrets, Volume 6

Listen to what reviewers say:

"Red Sage was the first and remains the leader of Women's Erotic Romance Fiction Collections!"

—*Romantic Times* Magazine

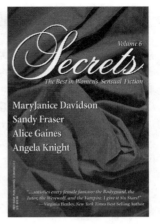

"*Secrets, Volume 6*, is the best of *Secrets* yet. ...four of the most erotic stories in one volume than this reader has yet to see anywhere else. ...These stories are full of erotica at its best and you'll definitely want to keep it handy for lots of re-reading!"

—*Affaire de Coeur* Magazine

"*Secrets 6* satisfies every female fantasy: the Bodyguard, the Tutor, the Werewolf, and the Vampire. I give it Six Stars!"

—Virginia Henley, *New York Times* Best Selling Author

In *Secrets, Volume 6* you'll find:

Flint's Fuse by Sandy Fraser

Dana Madison's father has her "kidnapped" for her own safety. Flint, the tall, dark and dangerous mercenary, is hired for the job. But just which one is the prisoner—Dana will try *anything* to get away.

Love's Prisoner by MaryJanice Davidson

Trapped in an elevator, Jeannie Lawrence experienced unwilling rapture at Michael Windham's hands. She never expected the devilishly handsome man to show back up in her life—or turn out to be a werewolf!

The Education of Miss Felicity Wells by Alice Gaines

Felicity Wells wants to be sure she'll satisfy her soon-to-be husband but she needs a teacher. Dr. Marcus Slade, an experienced lover, agrees to take her on as a student, but can he stop short of taking her completely?

A Candidate for the Kiss by Angela Knight

Working on a story, reporter Dana Ivory stumbles onto a more amazing one—a sexy, secret agent who happens to be a vampire.She wants her story but Gabriel Archer wants more from her than just sex and blood.

Secrets, Volume 7

Listen to what reviewers say:

"Get out your asbestos gloves — *Secrets Volume 7* is…extremely hot, true erotic romance…passionate and titillating. There's nothing quite like baring your secrets!"
— *Romantic Times* Magazine

"…sensual, sexy, steamy fun. A perfect read!"
—Virginia Henley,
New York Times Best Selling Author

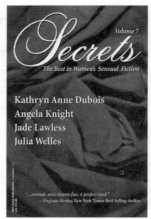

"Intensely provocative and disarmingly romantic, *Secrets, Volume 7*, is a romance reader's paradise that will take you beyond your wildest dreams!"
—Ballston Book House Review

In *Secrets, Volume 7* you'll find:

Amelia's Innocence by Julia Welles

Amelia didn't know her father bet her in a card game with Captain Quentin Hawke, so honor demands a compromise—three days of erotic foreplay, leaving her virginity and future intact.

The Woman of His Dreams by Jade Lawless

From the day artist Gray Avonaco moves in next door, Joanna Morgan is plagued by provocative dreams. But what she believes is unrequited lust, Gray sees as another chance to be with the woman he loves. He must persuade her that even death can't stop true love.

Surrender by Kathryn Anne Dubois

Free-spirited Lady Johanna wants no part of the binding strictures society imposes with her marriage to the powerful Duke. She doesn't know the dark Duke wants sensual adventure, and sexual satisfaction.

Kissing the Hunter by Angela Knight

Navy Seal Logan McLean hunts the vampires who murdered his wife. Virginia Hart is a sexy vampire searching for her lost soul-mate only to find him in a man determined to kill her. She must convince him all vampires aren't created equally.

Winner of the Venus Book Club
Best Book of the Year

Secrets, Volume 8

Listen to what reviewers say:

"*Secrets, Volume 8*, is an amazing compilation of sexy stories covering a wide range of subjects, all designed to titillate the senses. …you'll find something for everybody in this latest version of *Secrets*."

—*Affaire de Coeur* Magazine

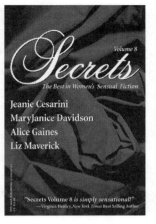

"*Secrets Volume 8*, is simply sensational!"

—Virginia Henley, *New York Times* Best Selling Author

"These delectable stories will have you turning the pages long into the night. Passionate, provocative and perfect for setting the mood…."

—*Escape to Romance* Reviews

In *Secrets, Volume 8* you'll find:

Taming Kate by Jeanie Cesarini

Kathryn Roman inherits a legal brothel. Little does this city girl know the town of Love, Nevada wants her to be their new madam so they've charged Trey Holliday, one very dominant cowboy, with taming her.

Jared's Wolf by MaryJanice Davidson

Jared Rocke will do anything to avenge his sister's death, but ends up attracted to Moira Wolfbauer, the she-wolf sworn to protect her pack. Joining forces to stop a killer, they learn love defies all boundaries.

My Champion, My Lover by Alice Gaines

Celeste Broder is a woman committed for having a sexy appetite. Mayor Robert Albright may be her champion—if she can convince him her freedom will mean a chance to indulge their appetites together.

Kiss or Kill by Liz Maverick

In this post-apocalyptic world, Camille Kazinsky's military career rides on her ability to make a choice—whether the robo called Meat should live or die. Meat's future depends on proving he's human enough to live, man enough…to makes her feel like a woman.

Winner of the Venus Book Club
Best Book of the Year

Secrets, Volume 9

Listen to what reviewers say:

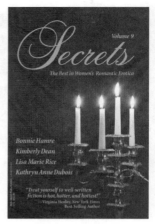

"Everyone should expect only the most erotic stories in a *Secrets* book. ...if you like your stories full of hot sexual scenes, then this is for you!"

　　　　　—Donna Doyle Romance Reviews

"**SECRETS 9**...is sinfully delicious, highly arousing, and hotter than hot as the pages practically burn up as you turn them."

　　　　　—Suzanne Coleburn, Reader To Reader
　　　　　Reviews/Belles & Beaux of Romance

"Treat yourself to well-written fictionthat's hot, hotter, and hottest!"

　　　　　—Virginia Henley, *New York Times* Best Selling Author

In *Secrets, Volume 9* you'll find:

Wild For You by Kathryn Anne Dubois

When college intern, Georgie, gets captured by a Congo wildman, she discovers this specimen of male virility has never seen a woman. The research possibilities are endless!

Wanted by Kimberly Dean

FBI Special Agent Jeff Reno wants Danielle Carver. There's her body, brains—and that charge of treason on her head. Dani goes on the run, but the sexy Fed is hot on her trail.

Secluded by Lisa Marie Rice

Nicholas Lee's wealth and power came with a price—his enemies will kill anyone he loves. When Isabelle steals his heart, Nicholas secludes her in his palace for a lifetime of desire in only a few days.

Flights of Fantasy by Bonnie Hamre

Chloe taught others to see the realities of life but she's never shared the intimate world of her sensual yearnings. Given the chance, will she be woman enough to fulfill her most secret erotic fantasy?

Coming July 2004...

Secrets, Volume 10

Private Eyes by Dominique Sinclair

When a mystery man captivates P.I. Nicolla Black during a stakeout, she discovers her no-seduction rule bending under the pressure of long denied passion. She agrees to the seduction, but he demands her total surrender.

The Ruination of Lady Jane by Bonnie Hamre

To avoid her upcoming marriage, Lady Jane Ponsonby-Maitland flees into the arms of Havyn Attercliffe. She begs him to ruin her rather than turn her over to her odious fiancé.

Code Name: Kiss by Jeanie Cesarini

Agent Lily Justiss is on a mission to defend her country against terrorists that requires giving up her virginity as a sex slave. As her master takes her body, desire for her commanding officer Seth Blackthorn fuels her mind.

The Sacrifice by Kathryn Anne Dubois

Lady Anastasia Bedovier is days from taking her vows as a Nun. Before she denies her sensuality forever, she wants to experience pleasure. Count Maxwell, known for his mastery of dark, sexual secrets, is the perfect man to initiate her into erotic delight.

The Forever Kiss by Angela Knight

For years, Valerie Chase has been haunted by dreams of a Texas Ranger she knows only as "Cowboy." As a child, he rescued her from the nightmare vampires who murdered her parents. As an adult, she still dreams of him—but now he's her seductive lover in nights of erotic pleasure.

Yet "Cowboy" is more than a dream—he's the real Cade McKinnon—and a vampire! For years, he's protected Valerie from Edward Ridgemont, the sadistic vampire who turned him. Now, Ridgmont wants Valerie for his own and Cade is the only one who can protect her.

When Val finds herself abducted by her handsome dream man, she's appalled to discover he's one of the vampires she fears. Now, caught in a web of fear and passion, she and Cade must learn to trust each other, even as an immortal monster stalks their every move.

Their only hope of survival is...***The Forever Kiss***.

It's not just reviewers raving about *Secrets*. See what readers have to say:

"When are you coming out with a new Volume? I want a new one next month!" via email from a reader.

"I loved the hot, wet sex without vulgar words being used to make it exciting." after *Volume 1*

"I loved the blend of sensuality and sexual intensity—HOT!" after *Volume 2*

"The best thing about *Secrets* is they're hot and brief! The least thing is you do not have enough of them!" after *Volume 3*

"I have been extreamly satisfied with *Secrets*, keep up the good writing." after *Volume 4*

"I love the sensuality and sex that is not normally written about or explored in a really romantic context" after *Volume 4*

"Loved it all!!!" after *Volume 5*

"I love the tastful, hot way that *Secrets* pushes the edge. The genre mix is cool, too." after *Volume 5*

"Stories have plot and characters to support the erotica. They would be good strong stories without the heat." after *Volume 5*

"*Secrets* really knows how to push the envelop better than anyone else." after *Volume 6*

"*Secrets*, there is nothing not to like. This is the top banana, so to speak." after *Volume 6*

"'Would you buy *Volume 7*?' YES!!! Inform me ASAP and I am so there!!" after *Volume 6*

"Can I please, please, please pre-order *Volume 7*? I want to be the first to get it of my friends. They don't have email so they can't write you! I can!" after *Volume 6*

Finally, the men you've been dreaming about!

Give the Gift of Spicy Romantic Fiction

Don't want to wait? You can place a retail price ($12.99) order for any of the *Secrets* volumes from the following:

① **Waldenbooks Stores**

② **Amazon.com** or **BarnesandNoble.com**

③ **Book Clearinghouse (800-431-1579)**

④ **Romantic Times Magazine**
Books by Mail (718-237-1097)

⑤ Special order at other bookstores.
Bookstores: Please contact Baker & Taylor Distributors or Red Sage Publishing for bookstore sales.

Order by title or ISBN #:

Vol. 1: 0-9648942-0-3   **Vol. 6:** 0-9648942-6-2

Vol. 2: 0-9648942-1-1   **Vol. 7:** 0-9648942-7-0

Vol. 3: 0-9648942-2-X   **Vol. 8:** 0-9648942-8-9

Vol. 4: 0-9648942-4-6   **Vol. 9:** 0-9648942-9-7

Vol. 5: 0-9648942-5-4   **Vol. 10:** 0-9754516-0-X

The Forever Kiss: 0-9648942-3-8

Red Sage Publishing Mail Order Form:

(Orders shipped in two to three days of receipt.)

	Quantity	Mail Order Price	Total
Secrets **Volume 1** *(Retail $12.99)*	_____	$ 9.99	_____
Secrets **Volume 2** *(Retail $12.99)*	_____	$ 9.99	_____
Secrets **Volume 3** *(Retail $12.99)*	_____	$ 9.99	_____
Secrets **Volume 4** *(Retail $12.99)*	_____	$ 9.99	_____
Secrets **Volume 5** *(Retail $12.99)*	_____	$ 9.99	_____
Secrets **Volume 6** *(Retail $12.99)*	_____	$ 9.99	_____
Secrets **Volume 7** *(Retail $12.99)*	_____	$ 9.99	_____
Secrets **Volume 8** *(Retail $12.99)*	_____	$ 9.99	_____
Secrets **Volume 9** *(Retail $12.99)*	_____	$ 9.99	_____
Secrets **Volume 10** *(Retail $12.99)* [July 2004]	_____	$ 9.99	_____
The Forever Kiss *(Retail $14.00)* [July 2004]	_____	$11.00	_____

Shipping & handling (in the U.S.)

US Priority Mail:
1–2 books .... $ 5.50
3–5 books $11.50
6–9 books $14.50
10–11 books $19.00

UPS insured:
1–4 books $16.00
5–9 books $25.00
10–11 books $29.00

_____

SUBTOTAL _____

Florida 6% sales tax (if delivered in FL) _____

TOTAL AMOUNT ENCLOSED _____

Your personal information is kept private and not shared with anyone.

Name: (please print) _____

Address: (no P.O. Boxes) _____

City/State/Zip: _____

Phone or email: (only regarding order if necessary) _____

Please make check payable to **Red Sage Publishing**. Check must be drawn on a U.S. bank in U.S. dollars. Mail your check and order form to:

Red Sage Publishing, Inc.   Department S6   P.O. Box 4844   Seminole, FL 33775

Or use the order form on our website: **www.redsagepub.com**

Red Sage Publishing Mail Order Form:

(Orders shipped in two to three days of receipt.)

	Quantity	Mail Order Price	Total
Secrets **Volume 1** *(Retail $12.99)*	_____	$ 9.99	_____
Secrets **Volume 2** *(Retail $12.99)*	_____	$ 9.99	_____
Secrets **Volume 3** *(Retail $12.99)*	_____	$ 9.99	_____
Secrets **Volume 4** *(Retail $12.99)*	_____	$ 9.99	_____
Secrets **Volume 5** *(Retail $12.99)*	_____	$ 9.99	_____
Secrets **Volume 6** *(Retail $12.99)*	_____	$ 9.99	_____
Secrets **Volume 7** *(Retail $12.99)*	_____	$ 9.99	_____
Secrets **Volume 8** *(Retail $12.99)*	_____	$ 9.99	_____
Secrets **Volume 9** *(Retail $12.99)*	_____	$ 9.99	_____
Secrets **Volume 10** *(Retail $12.99)* [July 2004]	_____	$ 9.99	_____
The Forever Kiss *(Retail $14.00)* [July 2004]	_____	$11.00	_____

Shipping & handling (in the U.S.)

US Priority Mail:
1–2 books .... $ 5.50
3–5 books $11.50
6–9 books $14.50
10–11 books $19.00

UPS insured:
1–4 books $16.00
5–9 books $25.00
10–11 books $29.00

_____

SUBTOTAL _____

Florida 6% sales tax (if delivered in FL) _____

TOTAL AMOUNT ENCLOSED _____

Your personal information is kept private and not shared with anyone.

Name: (please print) _____

Address: (no P.O. Boxes) _____

City/State/Zip: _____

Phone or email: (only regarding order if necessary) _____

Please make check payable to **Red Sage Publishing**. Check must be drawn on a U.S. bank in U.S. dollars. Mail your check and order form to:

Red Sage Publishing, Inc.   Department S6   P.O. Box 4844   Seminole, FL 33775

Or use the order form on our website: **www.redsagepub.com**